THE MANY CONDITIONS
OF LOVE

D070976S

THE MANY CONDITIONS
OF LOVE

Farahad Zama

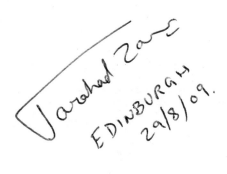

ABACUS

First published in Great Britain as a paperback original in 2009 by Abacus

Copyright © Farahad Zama 2009

The moral right of the author has been asserted.

*All characters and events in this publication, other than those
clearly in the public domain, are fictitious and any resemblance
to real persons, living or dead, is purely coincidental.*

All rights reserved.
No part of this publication may be reproduced, stored in a
retrieval system, or transmitted, in any form or by any means, without
the prior permission in writing of the publisher, nor be otherwise circulated
in any form of binding or cover other than that in which it is published
and without a similar condition including this condition
being imposed on the subsequent purchaser.

A CIP catalogue record for this book
is available from the British Library.

ISBN 978-0-349-12138-3

Typeset in Bembo by M Rules
Printed and bound in Great Britain by
Clays Ltd, St Ives plc

Papers used by Abacus are natural, renewable and
recyclable products sourced from well-managed forests and certified in
accordance with the rules of the Forest Stewardship Council.

Mixed Sources
Product group from well-managed
forests and other controlled sources
www.fsc.org Cert no. SGS-COC-004081
© 1996 Forest Stewardship Council
FSC

Abacus
An imprint of
Little, Brown Book Group
100 Victoria Embankment
London EC4Y 0DY

An Hachette UK Company
www.hachette.co.uk

www.littlebrown.co.uk

To Rehan and Rayvanth

SOME EXTRACTS FROM THE
SPECIAL MARRIAGE ACT, 1954

In India, people of each religion or community are governed by their own personal laws in matters involving marriage, divorce and inheritance. When people of different religions wish to get married, they do so under . . .

An Act to provide a special form of marriage in certain cases . . . enacted by Parliament in the Fifth Year of the Republic of India . . .

Notwithstanding anything contained in any other law for the time being in force relating to the solemnization of marriages, a marriage between any two persons may be solemnized under this Act, if at the time of the marriage the following conditions are fulfilled namely:

(a) neither party has a spouse living:
(b) neither party
    (i) is incapable of giving a valid consent to it in consequence of unsoundness of mind, or
    (ii) though capable of giving a valid consent, has been suffering from mental disorder of such a kind or to such an extent as to be unfit for marriage and the procreation of children; or
    (iii) has been subject to recurrent attacks of insanity or epilepsy;

    (c) the male has completed the age of twenty-one years and the female the age of eighteen years;

    (d) the parties are not within the degrees of prohibited relationship:

Provided that where a custom governing at least one of the parties permits of a marriage between them, such marriage may be solemnized, notwithstanding that they are within the degrees of prohibited relationship.

Explanation I
Relationship includes:

(a) relationship by half or uterine blood as well as by full blood:

(b) illegitimate blood relationship as well as legitimate;

(c) relationship by adoption as well as by blood;

Explanation II
'Full blood' and 'half blood' – two persons are said to be related to each other by full blood when they are descended from a common ancestor by the same wife and by half blood when they are descended from a common ancestor but by different wives.

Explanation III
'Uterine blood' – two persons are said to be related to each other by uterine blood when they are descended from a common ancestress but by different husbands.

Explanation IV
In Explns II and III 'ancestor' includes the father and 'ancestress' the mother.

Notices of intended marriage
When a marriage is intended to be solemnized under this Act, the parties of the marriage shall give notice thereof in

writing in the Form specified in the Second Schedule to the Marriage Officer of the district in which at least one of the parties to the marriage has resided for a period of not less than thirty days immediately preceding the date on which such notice is given.

The Marriage Officer shall cause every such notice to be published by affixing a copy thereof to some conspicuous place in his office.

Objection to marriage

(1) Any person may, before the expiration of thirty days from the date on which any such notice has been published under subsection (2) of Sec. 6, object to the marriage on the ground that it would contravene one or more of the conditions specified in Sec. 4.

(2) After the expiration of thirty days from the date on which notice of an intended marriage has been published under subsection (2) of Sec. 6, the marriage may be solemnized, unless it has been previously objected to under sub-section (1).

Declaration by parties and witnesses

Before the marriage is solemnized the parties and three witnesses shall, in the presence of the Marriage Officer, sign a declaration in the Form specified in the Third Schedule to this Act, and the declaration shall be countersigned by the Marriage Officer.

Place and form of solemnization

(1) The marriage may be solemnized at the office of the Marriage Officer or at such other place within a reasonable distance therefrom as the parties may desire, and upon such conditions and the payments of such additional fees as may be prescribed.

2) The marriage may be solemnized in any form which the

parties may choose to adopt: Provided that it shall not be complete and binding on the parties unless each party says to the other in the presence of the Marriage Officer and the three witnesses and in any language understood by the parties, 'I (A) take thee (B), to be my lawful wife (or husband).'

CHAPTER ONE

The noise level in the café dropped noticeably when the glamorous young woman stepped in. The clientele was exclusively male and mostly rustic. Villagers with dhotis round their waists and white shawls over their bare shoulders were talking loudly at the tightly packed, chipped-Formica tables. The conversations were all about grain prices, crop yields and prospects of rain for the next season. A few salesmen in shirts and trousers, carrying fake leather valises, were sprinkled among the farmers, touting fertilisers, tractors and the benefits of various seed varieties – genetically modified and not. A couple of harried waiters rushed around with plates of steaming idlis and small, half-filled glasses of tea.

The young woman was wearing an elegant, maroon, machine-silk sari that hugged her figure. Her glossy dark mane of hair fell in waves and set off the oval shape of her fair face. Dark sunglasses were pushed up and covered the edge of her hair rather than her eyes. The heels of her shoes went click-clack on the hard cement floor as she ignored everybody and walked to the back of the café, towards an empty table being cleared by a thin boy in a tattered shirt who looked about twelve. He swept the dirty plates and crockery into a red plastic bowl on his hip and wiped the table with a dirty rag. When he finished cleaning the table, the young woman moved past him and said, 'Excuse me.'

The boy was so surprised by the fragrant, well-mannered lady that he gawped silently at her and dropped his rag on the floor. Blushing deeply, he dived to the floor, picked up the dishcloth and ran to another corner of the room.

A young man, sitting at the next table and looking at her with rather more surprise than the others in the café, turned towards her and said, 'We should stop bumping into each other like this, Usha.'

She looked startled at being addressed by name in this place and looked at him sharply for a moment before breaking into a smile. 'Rehman,' she said. 'How come you are here?'

He shrugged his shoulders. 'I was in a neighbouring village for the last few days and I am returning home now.'

'Oh! Am I missing a scoop?' she said and left her table and walked over to his. 'Is the government planning to take over the farmers' lands there?'

'Always the journalist,' said Rehman and Usha laughed. 'No,' he continued. 'That was a different time and a different place. A friend of mine is from the village and I occasionally visit his family.'

Usha was a TV reporter who a few months ago had covered a campaign run by Rehman to prevent a special economic zone being set up on fertile agricultural land that had been compulsorily purchased from farmers who had owned it for generations.

A waiter came over and asked Usha whether she wanted anything. She looked lost and Rehman said to the waiter, 'Mineral water.'

'Normal or cooling?'

'Cooling,' said Rehman and the waiter walked away. Rehman turned to Usha and said, 'What about you? Why are you here?'

'The car had a puncture and the driver decided to get the tyre repaired while we were in town rather than risk going on through the middle of nowhere without a spare. I walked down the street and came in here to get out of the sun.'

The waiter returned with a bottle of water, its outer surface damp in the moist air. He showed them that the seal on the bottle was unbroken and twisted the cap open. He left them with two empty glasses. Rehman stopped Usha when she started pouring water into the glasses. 'You'd better drink straight from the bottle. I wouldn't trust the cleanliness here,' he said, running a finger around the inside of the glass and showing her the resulting greasy smear.

Her face scrunched tight and her shoulders stiffened in a small shudder. 'What about you?' she asked.

'I'll stick to tea,' he said.

Usha smiled at him and took a sip of water; her eyes closed and head raised as the bottle tilted forward. Rehman glanced at her delicate throat for a long moment and looked away before she opened her eyes. He suddenly felt scruffy. His two-week-old beard was at an awkward stage. His usual khadi shirt had been torn at the side and roughly patched by his friend's father. His leather chappals – open-toed slippers – looked the worse for wear after braving the mud of paddy fields for the last ten days.

'How are you getting back to Vizag?' asked Usha.

'By bus,' said Rehman. He looked at his watch. 'The next one is in less than half an hour. I'd better not miss it because there are no more after that until this evening.'

An old man walked into the café with a small boy, and Rehman raised his right hand and waved to them. Usha twisted half round to look. The old man had white whiskers and a beard. His face was dark and the skin stretched over his bones. His open mouth showed gaps in his teeth. The boy was about eight years old and smiling. He skipped ahead of his grandfather and came to their table.

'Rehman Uncle! Look!' he said, his eyes shining, and showed Rehman a book. 'I've got my own maths textbook.'

Rehman ruffled his hair and said, 'Fantastic. Now there's no excuse not to come first in the class.'

'I'm already first in my class. In fact, my teacher has asked me to sit with the older boys.'

'I know. I was just joking,' said Rehman.

'Who is this lady?' asked the boy.

'This is a friend of mine. Her name is Usha Aunty.'

The boy grinned at her. There was a wide gap where two of his upper front teeth had fallen out.

'What's your name?' she asked him.

'Vasu,' said the boy.

Rehman and Usha stood up as the old man reached their table. Rehman pulled a chair over from another table. After they all sat down, Rehman asked the old man, 'How did it go?'

The old man pulled out a bundle of money and showed it to them. 'Very well, thanks to you.'

'Be careful, sir! Don't wave the money about,' said Rehman, looking around the busy café.

'You are right. There are wicked people in this world who will steal a farmer's harvest money without feeling a moment's remorse,' the old man said and put the money away. He turned to Usha. 'This money is not all mine to keep. The previous two harvests were not very good, so most of it will go to repay the loans I took.'

Usha nodded. The waiter came and took their order – tea for the old man and milk for his grandson. Vasu said to his grandfather, 'Thaatha, this lady is Rehman Uncle's Usha Aunty.'

Rehman gave an uncomfortable laugh and said, 'She is not *my* aunty – just a friend.'

Usha's cheeks went red. Vasu's grandfather turned to her and said, 'Namaste.'

Usha joined her hands and inclined her head to him.

He saw her mobile phone on the table and said, 'I never thought these modern things would be useful to a small farmer like me but Rehman's proved me wrong.'

'Oh!' she said. 'How did he do that?'

'This morning, we were not sure whether to come to this mandi or go to another market twenty miles away. So, Rehman called up the grain merchants on his phone and found out that the price here was better. Because I use a bullock cart, once I decide which market to take my harvest to, I cannot change my mind.'

'Rehman Uncle climbed the tree in front of our house to make the call,' said Vasu.

'Really?' asked Usha, looking at him.

Rehman shrugged. 'There was no signal on the ground near the house,' he said.

'He almost fell down,' said Vasu. 'His shirt tore and thaatha had to stitch it, because that was the only clean shirt he had.'

'Shhh!' said Rehman and laughed. For some reason, he felt embarrassed.

'It's time we went. I have to take the cart back to its owner before the evening,' said Vasu's grandfather.

They all stood up. The old man turned to Rehman and said, 'May God keep you well always.'

'With your blessings, Mr Naidu,' said Rehman.

'Thanks for all the help in bringing in the harvest. I don't think even my own son would have done as much,' the old man said, tears brimming in his eyes. He took the boy's hand and left.

Rehman looked at his watch. 'Almost time for my bus. I'd better make my way too.'

'I'll go and see the car as well. It should be fixed by now.'

Rehman picked up his bulging cotton bag and a heavy gunny sack. They walked over to the front of the café where the owner, a podgy man with a round, shiny face, was sitting behind a table. A frayed ten-year-old calendar with the picture of Lakshmi, the goddess of wealth, was hanging behind his head. There were five other people in front of them waiting to pay their bills. The queue moved slowly. Rehman looked at his watch and frowned.

'What is it?' said Usha.

'My bus . . . it's almost time. My mother won't be happy if I don't get home for dinner.'

Usha nodded. She had met Rehman's mother a couple of times and knew that she was not a woman to be crossed lightly. They reached the head of the queue in a few minutes and Rehman smiled at Usha.

'Thank God,' he said.

The owner rang a little bell and their gaunt waiter came rushing over. 'One plate idli, two teas, one milk, one mineral water,' he said.

The owner totalled up their bill and said, 'Ten rupees for food and tea, twelve for the water; total twenty-two, sir.'

Usha tried to take money out from her purse but Rehman waved her down and paid the bill with a twenty-rupee note and a five-rupee coin. The owner returned three rupees and Rehman turned back to give the money to the waiter as a tip but the waiter had already gone back into the café. Rehman shrugged – he didn't have time to hang around. It was silly that he had waited with nothing to do for such a long time and now he was rushed in the last few minutes.

As he turned towards the front of the café, a glint of steel caught his eye from among the assembled customers.

'Rehman, hurry,' said Usha from near the entrance. 'I can see a bus coming.'

But Rehman's attention could not be diverted from the scene unfolding in front of him. He'd noticed what no one else in the café seemed to have seen: a young man in shirt and trousers had cut open the side of a farmer's rough cotton kurta and was extracting a fat, rolled-up bundle of cash from the pocket of the loose shirt.

'Hey!' shouted Rehman, flinging up his hand and pointing towards the youth.

Everybody froze for a moment and then the farmer who was

being pickpocketed reacted. 'How dare you—' he said and grabbed at the thief.

But all he clutched was empty air because the young man moved faster and started running. He pushed a chair at Rehman, sped towards the exit and blundered straight into a bewildered Usha, almost knocking her down. The small delay this caused was enough for Rehman to jump forward and seize the man's shirt just outside the café. A second later the farmer and his friends surrounded Rehman and the pickpocket. The men made the thief turn out his pockets and found two bundles of money. The farmers started shouting and landing blows on the robber. A rage bubbled up inside Rehman, in a way that it hadn't for years. The anger worried him but he suppressed it with an effort and shouted, 'Stop, stop!' He pushed the men away from the snivelling youth. 'Don't beat him. Take him to the police.'

'What will the police do? Garland him with flowers?' said the farmer whose shirt had been cut.

'We cannot take the law into our own hands.'

'Rehman,' said Usha from outside the group of men. 'Your bus has come, you have to leave now.'

Rehman turned to the farmer. 'You caught him because of me and got your money back. Don't beat him up, please. Take him to the thana, the police station. I have to leave now or I'll miss my bus, otherwise I'd come with you.'

Most of the men were still shouting angrily and still trying to hit the man who was now cowering in front of Rehman, trying to keep as much distance from the others as possible.

The farmer nodded. 'I am in your debt – you've saved me today from horrible trouble.' He lifted the bundle of notes that he was clutching in his right hand and said, 'This is not just money. This is the loan that I repay and keep my standing in the community; this is each seed and grain of fertiliser to plant the next crop and remain a farmer and this is every necessity that I provide my family until I harvest that next crop. Because of that debt, I'll do as you say.'

Rehman nodded and the men dragged the pickpocket away. Not all of them resisted giving the young man a smack or a kick every so often. Rehman turned to Usha and they hurried in the opposite direction on the dusty road. The bus was waiting at the stop. It was already full and a mob of people were at its two doors, getting in, women in the front and men at the back. A few boys were doing a brisk business selling tea through the windows to already-seated passengers. Rehman pursed his lips in a silent whistle as he looked at the scene.

'There's no way you'll get on that bus, especially with that sack,' said Usha.

Rehman nodded his head slowly. He looked at his watch and said, 'Well, another four hours to go. I'd better call ammi and tell her that I won't be home for dinner.'

'Don't be ridiculous,' said Usha. 'I'm going back to town too and I can drop you off.'

'Are you sure?' asked Rehman. 'I don't want to be any trouble.'

Usha laughed and said, 'You are so formal. Let's go and find out whether the puncture has been repaired. Do you want me to carry your bag?'

Rehman looked down at the cotton bag holding his soiled clothes and shook his head.

They walked down the road through the busy street, past the cart selling flip-flops, the cart selling coloured ice-water and the shop displaying bright children's clothes and lurid-pink plastic toys. Rehman thought they must make an odd pair – the groomed, perfumed, rich young girl in the classy sari and the rough-looking man with an unkempt beard, carrying a sack of brinjals and red spinach from Mr Naidu's farm on his shoulder, like a coolie. They passed the wide front of a cinema showing posters of a heavy-set man with bloodshot eyes and arrived at a gold-coloured car by the side of the road with one of its wheels on a jack.

'Isn't it ready yet?' said Usha to the short, dark man in his forties standing by the car.

'Sorry, madam,' said the driver. 'Almost done. It will be another five minutes.'

'Make it quick,' said Usha. She pointed to the sack that Rehman was carrying and said, 'Put it in the boot.'

'Right, madam,' the driver said and walked round to the back of the car and opened the boot. He turned to Rehman. 'Be careful. Don't let the sack touch the edge here,' he said, pointing to the sill.

Rehman put the sack into the car. As he turned away, Usha said, 'Why don't you put your bag away too?'

Rehman nodded and said, 'Good idea.'

He swung the bag in and the driver looked at them open-mouthed. 'But . . . madam—' he said.

Usha looked at him severely and said, 'Yes, Narsi? Do you have a problem?'

The driver gulped and closed his mouth. He shook his head and said, 'No, madam. What problem can I have?'

'Good!' said Usha and turned away. Rehman followed her. 'Narsi probably thought you were a porter carrying that sack for me,' she said, smiling at him.

Rehman looked down at himself and shrugged. 'Not surprising, given the way I look. Weren't you a bit severe with him?'

'He's a slime ball. He beats his wife,' she said. 'And I'm sure he's going to carry tales about you to my father.'

'If it's going to be any trouble . . .' began Rehman.

'No, no! I don't mind.' She pointed to a man sitting cross-legged by the roadside on a small mat. He had a tiny wooden cage next to him. 'Look, a parrot astrologer. Let's get our fortunes read.'

Rehman shook his head. 'You can't believe in that, surely?'

Usha smiled and said, 'Maybe I do and maybe I don't. But it'll be a time-pass and we'd be helping keep alive a traditional occupation.'

Rehman met her eyes and smiled, shaking his head. 'You always know what to say, don't you?'

Rehman and Usha sank down to their knees on the mat in front of the astrologer. The man twirled his long moustache and dragged a small stick across the bars of the parrot cages, making a staccato noise. He said, 'Welcome! Are you having family problems, financial or health issues? Is your son not studying well? Is your daughter not getting married? Let my birds read your fortune. Forewarned is forearmed.'

Rehman smiled and asked, 'How long have you been giving that speech?'

Usha frowned at him, but the astrologer did not take offence. 'My family has been in this profession for generations, sir! My grandfather and *his* grandfather before him have all been astrologers.'

Rehman nodded his head, impressed.

Usha asked, 'How much?'

The man said, 'That depends on the birds, madam.'

He lifted the rectangular wooden cage and put it down a couple of feet in front of Usha. Inside were two green parrots, cracking and eating sunflower seeds. He raised the bars in front of the cage like a portcullis. The birds looked at Usha but did not come out of the cage. Usha put a one-rupee coin on the ground in front of them. The parrots pecked at the coin and went back to their seeds. The astrologer continued twirling his moustache. Rehman laughed. Usha stuck out her tongue at him and placed another coin on the ground. The parrots continued eating.

Usha turned to Rehman and said, 'Don't!'

'I didn't say anything,' said Rehman. He covered his mouth with a hand and guffawed. Usha looked at him severely.

'Sorry,' said Rehman, biting a knuckle to stop laughing.

Usha took a deep breath and shook her head, but couldn't

help smiling. She opened her purse and took out a five-rupee coin, placing it on the ground with the other money. One of the parrots left its seeds and walked out of the cage with an awkward gait. The astrologer pocketed the coins and put a deck of cards, face down, on the ground. The parrot picked the top card with its beak and laid it aside. Usha looked at Rehman. He raised his eyebrows and nodded to her.

The parrot continued rejecting the cards. When the pile was about half reduced, it walked over to its master with the next card. The astrologer took the card and gave the parrot a peanut shell. The parrot cracked it open with its red curving beak, quickly ate the two nuts and went back inside the cage.

The man closed the portcullis, twirled his moustache and said, 'Let's see what the bird has picked for you.'

He turned the card and his face blanched. 'Oh dear!'

Usha's hands tightened into fists. 'What?' she said in a low voice.

The astrologer showed them the card's face. It had a picture of two intertwined snakes.

'Snake lovers. This is a really bad sign,' the man said.

'Why?' asked Rehman.

'Did you walk in any fields or past trees recently?' the astrologer said to Usha.

'Yes, there is a neem tree behind my grandmother's house and I've been going for walks there almost every day for the last couple of weeks.'

'Hmm . . .' said the astrologer. 'It cannot be the neem tree because generally nothing bad happens there. Are you sure you haven't been anywhere else?'

'Yes!' said Usha. 'I remember now. The day after I arrived in my grandmother's house, I went with some of the village girls to the communal well. On the way, there is a sprawling banyan tree with many of its branches supported by aerial roots and we stopped in its shade.'

'Just as I thought,' said the man. 'You must have disturbed a pair of cobras making love under the banyan tree. The queen cobra has cast a curse on you. You will encounter serious trouble in your own love life.'

'But I am not married,' said Usha.

'In that case, the curse will create obstacles and stop you from getting married,' said the man.

'How long will it stop me?'

'A cobra's vengeance lasts twelve years,' said the man.

'What can be done?' asked Usha.

'I can offer prayers and food to Naga Devudu – the god of snakes. I cannot break the spell completely but I can mitigate its effects. It will cost a hundred rupees.'

'This is ridiculous!' said Rehman loudly, standing up. Usha looked at him. Rehman continued, 'He is treating you like an illiterate villager, a gullible fool from whom he can extract money. Let's go.'

The astrologer remained impassive. Usha looked from one man to the other, biting her lower lip. She opened her purse and took out a fifty-rupee note. 'Do what you can with this,' she said, getting up and joining Rehman.

They didn't say a word to each other as they went back to the car.

'We are ready to go, madam,' said the driver.

Usha silently nodded and got into the back. Rehman went round the car to the other door. The driver slowly looked him up and down twice before getting in behind the wheel.

They were both silent for a few minutes as the car left the town and sped up. Then, Rehman said, 'I am sorry I shouted earlier at the astrologer's.'

'No, don't apologise. I admit that I was scared for a moment, even though I know I shouldn't have been. I couldn't help it,' said Usha.

She turned to Rehman. Her palm was raised, facing him,

and her middle and index fingers were crossed. 'Friends?' she asked.

This was a childhood gesture – if Rehman separated her fingers, it meant he didn't want to be her friend. He looked at her earnest face for a moment, then raised his palm and touched the tip of her index finger with his own crossed fingers.

He smiled and said, 'Friends.'

Some instinct made him turn his head to the front of the car. He found the driver's eyes looking at him intently in the rear-view mirror.

'Enough, ammi,' said Rehman, pushing his chair back and getting up from the dining table.

'What enough?' said his mother. 'You look so thin. You obviously didn't eat anything in the village. What can you eat in a household without women anyway?'

'Ammi, I am full. Mince, liver, brinjal and peas, radish sambhar, soya beans, curds,' said Rehman, rubbing his stomach. 'And, oh, rice and sweet as well.'

Mrs Ali looked at him doubtfully for a moment and then said, 'All right. Don't sit down straight after dinner like your father. Walk around for a few minutes. I'll clear up the table here.'

Rehman had arrived just over an hour ago. A hot bath, a shave, fresh clothes and his mother's cooking made him feel like a new man. He walked into the living room and saw his father watching the news on TV.

His father turned to him and said, 'So was it a good harvest this year?'

'Yes, abba,' said Rehman. 'Mr Naidu said it was one of the best yields in years. Not just the rice but even the vegetable patch produced a good crop.'

On the television, the newsreader said, 'And now for the weather. The temperature in the four metros . . .'

They both turned to the screen and watched the weather

forecast. His mother came in, wiping her hands on the edge of her sari.

'Sit down, Rehman,' she said. 'Why are you standing there?'

'But—' began Rehman and stopped. He shrugged his shoulders and sat next to his mother on the settee.

She said, 'You need to get married, Rehman. I've been very patient with you but there are limits.'

'Not again, ammi,' said Rehman, groaning.

'It's shameful. Your father is running a successful marriage bureau and our own son is unmarried. Do you know Chote Bhabhi asked me that very question when we went to their house last week? It was on the tip of my tongue to tell her to find a groom for her own daughter before she started talking about other people's children, but I refrained,' said Mrs Ali. She had never got along well with Chote Bhabhi, Mr Ali's younger brother's wife.

Rehman laughed. 'So I have to get married because Chachi, my aunt, made some silly remark?'

'It's not a laughing matter, Rehman,' said his mother severely. 'It's not just her. The whole town is talking. You should get married soon.'

Rehman stayed silent.

After a few moments, she turned to his father. 'Why don't you say something? Don't you want to see your son get married? Or are you only worried about your clients' weddings?'

'What's the point of me saying anything? When did he listen to me?' said his father. 'The English have a saying – you can take a horse to water but you cannot make it drink.'

Mrs Ali turned to Rehman and said, 'If you don't trust our choice, tell us who you like and we'll go and finalise the match. Is there somebody that's caught your eye?'

Rehman, of course, had never brought any girl home. His parents would find it really rude and the very idea of it was quite unthinkable. He supposed he could just about mention the name of a girl and let them take it up family-to-family. He shook his head and said 'Just let it go, ammi. It'll happen when it happens. There's nobody in my mind.'

He closed his eyes to forestall any more argument and was startled when the image of Usha's face looking upwards, eyes closed, her long, fair neck exposed to him as she drank water from a bottle, appeared vividly in front of him.

CHAPTER TWO

Aruna padded on bare feet into the en-suite bathroom for a shower. It was a little past six in the morning and she had already been up for about fifteen minutes. She tucked her hair inside a cap and turned on the tap. Warm water gushed out and she tested the water with an outstretched arm to make sure it was the right temperature before moving into the stream.

Just a few months ago, she had been a poor woman living with her parents and sister in a one-room house with a cramped bathroom. In her parents' house, having a bath meant filling a bucket with cold water and pouring it over herself with a broken-handled mug. She wondered why they had never replaced it – mugs did not cost much, did they? If she wanted a warm bath, she would have had to heat up some water in a vessel and mix it with cold water in the bucket. Except on really severe mornings in midwinter, her mother would not allow water to be heated. Fuel was expensive.

'The water is boiling,' her mother would shout, before it had got little more than lukewarm.

Aruna sighed in pleasure, stretching like a cat under the cascade of hot water as the bathroom fogged up with steam. I could stay here for ever, she thought; but after several minutes she reluctantly got out of the shower, wrapped a towel round herself and walked into the bedroom. Her husband was still sleeping. She opened the wardrobe and looked at the row of silk saris hanging from the long rail, with plastic covers over the tops to keep the dust away. Her entire clothes collection had once fitted into half a shelf of the green metallic cupboard at her parents' house but now she had more saris than she could wear in an entire month. She ignored the expensive hanging saris and took out a simple rose-pink cotton one from a neatly folded pile on the shelf.

Once dressed, Aruna made to leave the room. Just before she opened the door, she took a sideways look at her husband. He had turned and was now lying on his back. He looked so innocent, but she blushed as she thought, He is not a small boy! She walked over, tousled his hair and kissed the fingers that had touched him. She was so happy. Did anybody deserve to be so happy?

Her mother had always told her, 'Don't laugh too much, for then you'll cry.' Aruna was sure her mother was wrong this time.

She left the room, closing the door behind her, and went to the small alcove in the living room that served as a shrine in the house. There was a two-foot-tall brass idol of Venkateswara, Lord of the Seven Hills, and a small silver idol of the elephant-headed Ganesha with a big paunch, sitting beside his mount, a rat. There was a round plate in front of the idols on which stood a lit oil lamp, a small bronze bell, copper coins and a covered, decorated silver pot. An old photograph of her husband's grandfather, surrounded by a garland made of dried, plaited lotus leaves, hung to one side of the alcove. She picked up the bell and rang it for a long minute, saying her morning prayers. After the prayers, she put the bell back in its place, opened the silver pot and dipped the middle finger of her right hand into the sindoor inside. She applied the red powder to her forehead in a round dot and picked up the plate.

Her father-in-law stood up from the sofa as she walked in. He was about to go for a walk and had been waiting for her.

'Namaste,' she said, holding the plate in front of her.

Her father-in-law dipped his open palms towards the fire in the lamp until they were a few inches away, then touched his eyes and forehead with his fingers.

'May you for ever remain a married woman,' he blessed her, in Sanskrit, before adding, 'Ramanujam's mother is in Mani's room.'

She nodded and went there to find her mother-in-law stripping the bed. She stopped her work, dipped her hands towards the fire and touched her eyes. She blessed Aruna and turned back to the bed.

Aruna said, 'Amma, why are you doing it? If you just wait a few moments, I will come and help you.'

'No, that's all right. I know you are busy.'

'At least wait for Shantamma,' Aruna said. Shantamma was the widowed Brahmin woman who ran the kitchen with her never-married brother. At this time in the morning Shantamma was usually busy with breakfast but she would be free for other tasks in an hour or so.

'No, I can't wait. I want to get the room all ready for my daughter. You remember that we are going to her house later today, don't you?' her mother-in-law said to Aruna.

'Yes, amma. I've already told sir that I'm not working this afternoon.'

'It'll be good for Mani to come here. She's been having bad morning sickness all the way.'

'Yes,' said Aruna. 'And it will be good to have her boy here as well. I love children.'

Her mother-in-law smiled at her. 'Yes, dear,' she said. 'Don't let me keep you waiting. Go on, take a cup of tea for your husband.'

Aruna smiled and left the room. She put the plate back in the shrine and went into the kitchen. Shantamma was standing at the hob, mixing something with a spatula. Her brother, Kaka, was sitting on the floor and grating a coconut that had been split into two.

'What's for breakfast?' asked Aruna.

'Upma, chinnamma,' the cook said. All the workers in the house called Aruna chinnamma – younger madam.

'Mmm,' said Aruna. She loved the savoury steamed semolina with onions, chillies and ginger. Unlike at her parents' house, Shantamma sprinkled fried cashew nuts over the upma to make it taste even better. A cup of tea was waiting for her on the granite worktop. Shantamma must have prepared it as soon as she heard the prayer bell. Aruna picked up the tea and left the kitchen.

She walked into her bedroom and closed the door behind her. She put the tea on the bedside cabinet and sat next to her husband's sleeping body.

'Wake up, sleepyhead,' she said, placing her hand on his cheek.

He pulled the sheet over his head and snuggled against her, refusing to get up. Aruna moved her hand to his shoulder and gave him a shake. He started to get up and just as Aruna relaxed, he put his hands round her waist and pulled her down over him.

'Eek!' she screamed.

'Shhh,' he said. 'There are other people in the house.'

After the initial fright, Aruna stopped fighting back and yielded her body against his. After a few minutes, she pushed back and said, 'It's time to get up. I have to help your mother get the house ready for your sister before I leave for the office.'

He rubbed his rough chin against her soft skin for a little bit longer as she squirmed against him and then let her go. He sat up in bed and Aruna handed him the cup of tea. He started sipping it. Aruna straightened her sari and patted her hair back into place. 'I don't know how you can do that. Drink tea as soon as you get up before you've even brushed your teeth,' she said.

He looked up at her and said, 'Try it sometime, dear. Kaka used to get me the morning tea before we got married. I am sure he will bring two cups every morning if we asked him.'

Aruna thought about one of the servants walking in when she was in bed with her husband and blushed. 'No, thank you,' she said. 'Anyway, I am sure it is not healthy to drink tea as soon as you wake up.'

'Who's the doctor in the house?' he asked. 'You or me?'

Aruna laughed and touched her husband on his cheek. 'OK, I am going now. Shantamma's almost finished making breakfast, so come over soon, before it gets cold.'

Just before nine in the morning, Mr Ali came on to the verandah of his house, which served as the office of the marriage bureau that he ran. He opened the wooden wardrobe that was his filing cabinet and took out the previous day's letters. He sat down behind the table and started opening the few that had not yet been dealt with. One contained a filled-in application form and a cheque for five hundred rupees.

He wrote the name of the client in small letters in a corner on the back of the cheque. Last month one of his cheques had been returned by the bank unpaid. He had lost the money because he couldn't figure out whose cheque it was, which had annoyed him a great deal. The door opened just as he finished dealing with all the letters and his assistant walked in.

'Namaste, sir,' said Aruna, bowing her head slightly.

Mr Ali smiled at her and said, 'Good morning, Aruna.'

Once she sat down in her chair, he said, 'I couldn't find the letter from the Christian Madiga from Chennai. He called me very early this morning saying that he hadn't got a reply yet.'

'I dealt with that a couple of days ago, sir. I sent him a new list and I filed it away. Shall I take it out?'

'No, that's fine. If you say you've dealt with it, then there is nothing else to do. He'll probably get your letter in the next day or so. I have to go to the bank today to deposit a cheque and withdraw some money for the ads. When do I have to pay your salary?' he asked.

'Not yet, sir,' she laughed. 'There's still another week to go.'

Mr Ali knew he was absent-minded, so he had told her to remind him a day or two before her salary was due, so he could make arrangements to pay her.

'Don't feel awkward about reminding me,' he had told her. 'I won't take it amiss. In fact, I'll be embarrassed if I don't pay you on time.'

Gopal, the postman, came in for the morning delivery. He had been serving Mr Ali's house for years. He looked thinner than ever and he no longer smiled. Mr Ali took the letters from him and said, 'Gopal, what is this? You have to look after yourself. You are becoming weaker by the day.'

'What is the point any more, sir? I don't know why God has still left me in this world.'

Mr Ali stood up and went closer to the postman. 'No, Gopal. You shouldn't talk like that. Your family depend on you more than ever. You can't let them down like this.'

'Whatever, sir,' said Gopal, lifting the heavy bag of letters on his shoulder.

'Wait a moment. I have something for you,' Mr Ali said and went into the house. He came back with an apple and gave it to the postman.

'Go on; eat this while you go on your rounds.'

'No, no, sir. I am not hungry.'

'Nonsense,' said Mr Ali. 'Take the first bite here in front of me.'

He stood there until Gopal had no choice but to take a chunk of fruit in his mouth. 'Thank you, sir,' said Gopal. 'It has been years since I've eaten an apple.'

Mr Ali nodded. Apples grew only in north India near the Himalayas and they were expensive. When Gopal left, Mr Ali sat back in his chair.

'Poor man,' said Aruna. 'It was good of you to give him the fruit, sir.'

'Yes, poor man,' said Mr Ali, sighing. 'He has not been himself since his daughter was widowed so soon after marriage. I've never understood why Hindu society treats widows so badly. The poor woman cannot even remarry to escape her fate,' said Mr Ali.

Aruna said, 'I know, sir, but what can anyone do? That's just the way it has been for thousands of years. And things have improved a lot since I was a little girl.'

Mr Ali nodded. 'You are right,' he said. 'Widows aren't forced to shave their heads any more and not all of them wear only white now.'

An hour passed. Mr Ali collected the letters he needed to post and the little bag that contained his passbook, chequebook and other bank papers, and stood up to go.

'Sir, do you remember that I'm not coming in this afternoon?' said Aruna.

Mr Ali nodded and said, 'Yes, I remember. I'll see you tomorrow, though, won't I?'

'Yes, sir,' said Aruna. She still had some hours to go in the office before she left, but she wanted to remind her boss about her afternoon off while she remembered.

After Mr Ali left, Aruna moved to the chair behind the table. She opened the cover of the typewriter and took out an old toothbrush from the drawer. Its bristles were half worn out and black with ink. She rubbed the arc of letters vigorously with the brush, dislodging tiny bits of paper that were stuck in the curves of the letters. One minute piece wouldn't come off the centre of the letter 'O' and she blew a puff of air hard on to it. The paper flew straight into her eye, stinging terribly.

'Oww!' she cried, closing her eye and resisting the temptation to rub it. She blinked several times until her tears washed out the foreign object, as her husband might say. She dabbed the edge of her eye with a handkerchief and looked at the typewriter.

'Time to fix you,' she muttered to herself.

She fed a sheet of paper round the roller and started typing a list of Karanam caste brides. She soon got into a rhythm and the typewriter keys rattled away. She finished just before eleven and was relaxing her fingers when Mrs Ali walked into the verandah from the house, carrying a glass of cool water for her.

'Thank you,' said Aruna, taking a sip.

Mrs Ali sat down in the chair near the door and said, 'Are you getting your sister-in-law home today?'

'That's right, madam,' said Aruna. 'She's just entered the seventh month of her confinement.'

'This will be her second child, won't it? I'm sure I saw a small boy with her at your wedding.'

'Yes, madam. Her son has just touched four. Sanjay is his name and he is naughty but very cute,' said Aruna. She finished drinking the water and set the glass aside.

'My niece is just a month or so behind your sister-in-law. In a few weeks, I will be going with my brother Azhar and his wife to get their daughter home. It's her first child so Azhar and his wife are very nervous.'

A skinny, tall man walked out of the house and sat down next to Mrs Ali. It was Rehman. Mrs Ali tousled her son's hair and said, 'Why don't you get your hair cut? You look like a hippie.'

Aruna looked covertly at mother and son. They had clashed so publicly on television when Rehman had ignored his mother's plea not to go back to a protest in which he had been injured and arrested. As she watched him turn to his mother and grin at her while she stroked his hair, it was clear that they loved each other very much.

'Today is Tuesday, ammi,' said Rehman. 'Barber shops will be closed.'

'You always have some excuse or another.'

Rehman stood up and left. Mrs Ali followed him soon after and Aruna returned to her work, answering the morning's post.

An hour later, Mr Ali and another man walked in together. The man was middle-aged and well dressed. The centre of his head was taken up by a bald patch, which he tried, unsuccessfully, to cover with long hair combed over from the side.

Mr Ali said to the gentleman, 'Please tell us how we can help you.'

'My name is Srinivasa Reddy. I am looking for a bridegroom for my daughter. I have a son who is studying in America at Princeton . . .'

'Good university,' said Mr Ali.

'Oh, yes!' said Mr Reddy. 'Einstein was there, you know.'

Aruna and Mr Ali nodded, impressed.

'As I was saying, my son is in America. My daughter Sudha went to college locally and graduated last year.'

'What did Sudha study?' asked Aruna.

'BA in Telugu and psychology,' said Mr Reddy. 'She's just turned twenty-two. Sudha passed with a first-class degree, which is very good because she has also been running the household for the last three years since my wife died.'

Aruna got out an application form and gave it to Mr Ali. He took out a pen from his pocket and began filling in the form. He wrote the name of the bride and her father, then started asking questions.

'What caste are you?'

'Ontari Kapu. Our ancestors were soldiers who served on special missions, which is how our community got its name.'

'I didn't know that,' said Mr Ali, nodding slowly. Ontari Kapu literally meant lone protector. 'Do you want your daughter to marry within your caste?'

'Definitely.'

The questions went on – date of birth, bride's share in family wealth, father's occupation, star sign according to Hindu charts, height and complexion.

Finally, Mr Ali said, 'We charge five hundred rupees. For this, we give you a full list with details of all bridegrooms from your caste. We will also advertise on your behalf in newspapers and forward all responses to you. You can write or call us every six weeks or so for a new list of any members who've joined in the meantime. Do you want to use our services?'

Mr Reddy thought for a moment and then handed over a five-hundred-rupee note. Mr Ali pocketed the money and gave the form to Aruna. She took out the list of Kapu grooms from the cabinet, folded it and put it into an envelope. She handed the envelope to Mr Reddy and said, 'Please bring a photo of Sudha when you come next time. We will keep it in our files and you'll get more responses that way.'

Mr Reddy said, 'Will you give the photo out to people?'

Mr Ali replied, 'No, sir. We don't let anybody take photos out, especially those of girls. They can see the photos only when they come here in person. Any time you want the photo back, just ask us and we'll return it.'

Mr Reddy took his leave.

Later that day, Rehman helped his mother clear up the table after lunch. His father went for a siesta, and he and Mrs Ali sat down on the sofa in the living room.

'When did you say you were starting your new project?' asked his mother.

'Not for a couple of weeks, at least. There's some delay in the municipal office – they aren't clearing any papers at the moment. Apparently, the commissioner's office was censured by the court for signing off planning permissions too easily so orders have

been passed to scrutinise every application much more closely
before clearing it.'

'The staff will probably just use it as an excuse to demand
more bribes,' she said.

Rehman laughed. The planning department was well known
for its corruption. They both sat in companionable silence for
several minutes and then Rehman lay down with his head in his
mother's lap.

'Do you remember how I used to look for nits in your hair
when you were a boy?' she asked, with her hand on his head.

'Yes,' he said. 'You used to be so rough with that fine-toothed
comb.'

'It's a waste of time if you don't do it thoroughly and leave
some behind,' she said. She was silent for a moment and then
continued, 'I still have that comb, but people don't seem to have
nits so much any more.'

'One sign of progress, I suppose,' said Rehman.

'Or a sign that we don't have any school-going children in our
house,' said his mother. He ignored the pointed hint.

Rehman never slept in the afternoon, unlike his father, but
now his eyelids drooped. The fan whirred slowly and the sounds
of traffic outside were muted. A song from an old Telugu movie
played in the background from a flat in the building next door.
It had been a long time since he had spent so much time with his
parents after leaving home for college. Even the arguments with
his father had reduced in intensity and frequency.

His mind drifted to Usha. What was she doing? Interviewing
some politician for television? I should call her, he thought. He
had already met her thrice in the last week. They usually met for
an hour or two by the beach or in one of the cafés in town. He
found that he was thinking more and more of her. It was very
disconcerting to him because girls had never affected him that
much before. Well, apart from just that once. The memory was
so deeply suppressed that this was the first time in years that he

had allowed it to come to the surface without pushing it away immediately.

Lalitha. La–li–tha. He rolled the syllables around in his mind. He had fallen in love with her the moment he saw her that morning on his first day in college. He was eighteen, as was almost everybody in the class. She had been walking with another girl and had laughed aloud at something. He was amazed at his good fortune when he found out that she was in the same department as him. She sat in the front row of the class and he spent so many hours staring at the back of her head. He knew every hairclip that she owned; the dark mole between her shoulder blades that was covered by some of her blouses but not by others, which were cut slightly lower. Every Friday, she probably went to the temple because she always had a dab of sacred ash smeared on her neck and jasmine flowers in her hair.

He had been young and gauche around girls. He certainly did not have the courage to speak to her of his own accord. Almost two years passed in this calf-love. One day, a month or so before their second-year exams, he had been sitting on the stone steps near the library with his best friend and constant companion, Ramu, when she walked over to them.

'Hi,' she said. 'I am Lalitha.'

'I – I know,' he stammered. It must have been a Friday because he still remembered the fragrance of jasmine flowers in her hair.

'I am told that you have the best survey notes. Can I borrow them for a few days?'

'Of c-course. But how do you know about my notes?'

She shrugged. Her slender shoulders were only partly covered by the edge of her sari and the sleeves of her blouse ended high on her arms. He treasured that meeting and the one where she returned the notes. After that she smiled at him when they saw each other and he blushed each time. He never mentioned his infatuation to anybody, not even Ramu, for fear of being teased.

Once the exams were done, the college broke up and Ramu went back to his village. Over the holidays, Rehman spent a lot of time thinking about Lalitha. He decided that when he met up with her again after the break, he would try to make friends with her.

The college reopened and Rehman managed to speak to Lalitha a few times. But he still found it difficult to talk to girls and even harder to speak to *her*. A month later he had a big surprise. He was tightening the screw on a small concrete cube during a Strength of Materials lab when his best friend Ramu told him that he had fallen in love with a girl. Rehman's hands dropped off the handle and he gaped at his friend.

'Who is it? Anybody I know?'

'You'll find out after class. She is coming over to the canteen to meet us.'

As soon as the lab was over, the two of them hurried over to the canteen and found an empty table in a corner. Rehman had his back to the entrance and he couldn't see who was coming in. But he could read the look on Ramu's face and knew the girl had arrived. He refrained from twisting round. A girl came over to them and said, 'Hi.'

Rehman looked up and it was as if a lightning bolt had struck him. 'But . . . but that's . . .'

Ramu slid across the bench to the far side and the girl sat down delicately next to him. 'Yes,' said Ramu. 'Lalitha and I are in love.'

The girl blushed at the bold declaration but held her gaze. Rehman looked away and felt as if his heart was squeezed in a vice. He now knew how the concrete blocks felt in their Strength of Materials labs as they were crushed. He could not speak for a long time but luckily the love-struck couple did not notice. They were too immersed in their own conversation.

After some time, Ramu said loudly, 'Rehman . . .'

Rehman looked up, startled, and found a waiter standing next to the table, waiting to take his order. The smell of food in the canteen suddenly sickened Rehman. His heart thundered in his chest. He wanted to smash his friend's silly, simpering face with his fists. His hands curled and he stood up blindly. He leaned forward, almost reaching across the table.

'Are you all right?' Lalitha's voice broke through the mist in his brain.

He jerked back and stood up straight, his fingers uncurling. 'I am not feeling well. I have to go,' he said.

Ramu and Lalitha looked at him with concern. 'What happened?' asked his friend.

'Nothing. Must be the sun. I have been standing outside too long.'

'But it's been cloudy today,' said Ramu.

'And we had a double period of maths indoors,' said Lalitha.

'I have to go. You stay,' he said and blundered his way out of the canteen. He didn't attend classes for the next three days.

On the fourth day, Rehman joined Ramu as his partner in the lab. 'Where were you? I came to your room so many times but it was locked. What happened?'

Rehman shrugged. 'It doesn't matter. I am feeling better now.'

Thinking back, Rehman felt proud of his younger self. Lalitha spent a lot of time with Ramu and consequently with Rehman too, but he had never, after that day, revealed his feelings. His episodic temper had disappeared too – sublimated in his unrequited love. When Ramu and Lalitha had their inevitable, very occasional, lovers' tiffs, they both came to Rehman and he always played honest broker, doing his best to get them together again as quickly as possible.

Rehman changed in other ways as well. He became much more confident about talking to girls, joking and being friendly with them. And, as is often the way of the world, now that he didn't care much for the girls round him, they showed more interest in him. Lalitha and Ramu got married soon after college

but it didn't last long. They died one after the other, but not
before they had a son, Vasu, who was now living with his grandfather. Now, thought Rehman, was not the time to think about
that tragedy.

He turned his mind to Usha again. How silly she had been to
take the parrot astrologer's words so seriously. The man probably
said the same thing to anybody who looked as if they had money.

A bus went past on the road outside, honking loudly, and
Rehman was jolted out of his reverie. It will be good to catch
up with Usha. Where should he take her? An idea came to him
for just the place – the university canteen. They served good
samosas and there was a continuous supply of tea.

Did he love her? She was certainly in his thoughts far more
than any woman since Lalitha. More importantly, did she love
him? He wasn't sure, but she always answered his calls and agreed
to meet him. That must mean something. I am not making the
same mistake again, thought Rehman. I am not waiting two
years before speaking out this time. Usha was a great catch – her
parents were probably already looking for a bridegroom for her.
He drifted off for a while longer until his mobile phone rang and
he rose slowly to pick it up. He didn't recognise the number of
the caller.

'Hello,' he said.

'Rehman, it's Naidu. How are you?'

'Naidu gaaru, Mr Naidu. Is everything all right on the farm?
I have just been thinking about Vasu's parents.'

'There is not much work on the farm, now that you've helped
me bring in the harvest. Actually I'm calling about Vasu.'

'What about your grandson?' asked Rehman. He sat back on
the sofa, next to his mother.

'Vasu's school has holidays next week and he wants to go over
to the city. I have to be here because the red spinach still needs
watering. I was wondering if you can show Vasu the sights of
Vizag.'

'Of course he can come here,' said Rehman. His mother tapped him on the hand and looked at him quizzically.

'Just a moment, Uncle,' said Rehman and covered the mouthpiece. He asked his mother, 'Can the boy, Vasu, stay with us next week?'

She nodded and he went back on the phone. 'How is he going to come over, Uncle?'

'One of the guys in the village is going back to the city. I will send Vasu with him. Can you pick him up from that man's house?'

'Sure, where does he live?'

'Marripalem, let me tell you the address,' said Mr Naidu.

Rehman hurriedly found a pencil and paper and wrote down the details.

'And one more thing, Rehman. I've decided to sign the contract with Modern Agro.'

'Are you sure, Uncle?'

'Yes, I've thought about it. My ancestors and I have been growing the same rice crop on the same land for ever and all we've ever had is a basic living. If my son was still living . . .' said Mr Naidu and stopped. After a moment, he continued in a hoarse voice, 'If your friend was alive, things would have been different.'

'What exactly is the deal with the company?'

'I have to grow cotton for them. They will provide the seeds and fertiliser, and the herbicide to control weeds. They will also send experts, professors from universities, to advise farmers like me when to water the fields, how much fertiliser and herbicide to apply.'

'I see,' said Rehman. 'Why do you need the contract with the company? Why don't you just grow the cotton yourself?'

'Two things – firstly, they guarantee to purchase the crop from me so I don't have to worry about finding a buyer, and secondly, they explained to me that the seeds the company gives us are different. The man said something about their jeans being changed. I didn't understand exactly – I thought jeans were trousers that men like you wore, but what does an illiterate farmer like me know, eh?'

'Genetically modified, Uncle,' said Rehman.

'Yes, that's what the man said. Cotton is a good cash crop but a pest called the bollworm is almost definite to attack it. Apparently, the plants that grow from these seeds are resistant to this pest, so the yield is better and we don't have to use pesticides.'

'Hmm,' said Rehman.

'Also, the company will come to the village and take the cotton from me. That'll save me having to hire a cart like we did last week and transport it to the market.'

Rehman scratched his head, thinking. It sounded good, but he couldn't help wondering whether there was a catch somewhere. 'Are you sure, Uncle? I don't know . . .'

'We have to move with the times, Rehman. I am an old man with a young grandson. If it was just me, I could have continued the way we've been farming all these years and live from harvest to harvest. But I won't be here for ever and I have to save enough money before my strength goes, so Vasu can go to college and get a job in the city like his father.'

CHAPTER THREE

'Kaka, have you packed the snacks?' The shout came from the hall.

Aruna was pinning the edge of her mustard-yellow silk sari to the blouse on her left shoulder. She smiled at her husband who was almost ready and was putting on his watch.

He said, 'Amma is getting a bit tense.'

'A bit . . .' she laughed.

Ramanujam finished first and sat down on the bed, waiting for Aruna.

'Can you fasten this clasp, please?' She was standing in front of the mirror, holding a necklace. He got off the bed and took a long step towards her. He brought the ends of the gold chains together, lifted some strands of hair out of the way and fastened the clasp. 'Thanks,' she said, centring the pendant over the top of her sari. She tried to move away but was trapped between the dressing table and her husband. 'Thanks,' she said again. He still didn't let her go. 'What is it?' she asked, looking back at him.

'I am looking at my beautiful wife,' he said, gazing into her eyes, and bent down to nibble her ear.

She closed her eyes for a moment and a small shiver went through her body.

'Aruna-a-a, are you ready?' her mother-in-law called from outside the room.

Aruna squirmed in panic, trying to push Ramanujam away. He continued holding her and Aruna looked at him wildly. She whispered fiercely, 'Let me go, your mother's waiting. What if she came in?'

His arms tightened round her slim frame. 'She won't come in. She knows I am in the room with you.'

Aruna fell silent and after a few moments her husband let her go. She was almost opening the door when he said, 'People can see where you've been kissed.'

'What?' she said, shocked, and rushed back to the mirror. 'Where?' she asked, scanning her reflection.

'I'm just joking,' he said and smiled.

'Brute!' she said angrily and then laughed. She hit him lightly on the chest. 'Let's go now. Your mother's waiting.'

The big living room, which they called the hall, was in chaos when they entered it. Her father-in-law was standing by the entrance, wearing a crisply starched dhoti and a long dark Nehru shirt. There were bags of clothes, vegetables and toys everywhere. Her mother-in-law came rushing out of another room with a bunch of bananas and put them in a wicker basket.

'We have only six kinds of snacks,' she said to Aruna. 'What are we going to do?'

'Didn't you say we needed only five varieties?' said Aruna.

'I know. That's what we did last time, but that demoness, Mani's mother-in-law, called up and said we had to bring seven types because this is the second child. I bet she waited until the last minute just to embarrass us.'

Ramanujam went and stood with his father.

Aruna walked over to the basket and said, 'Let's see . . . We have muruku, samosas, boorulu, pakodi, gulab jamun and kaju katri.' She thought for a moment and said, 'Do vadiyalu count?'

Her mother-in-law shook her head. 'No, they are eaten with lunch or dinner. They don't count as snacks.'

Ramanujam said, 'Amma, relax. I'm sure we can find something on the way.'

'You keep quiet,' said his mother. 'Nobody will say anything to you men. It's we women who will be insulted.'

Ramanujam's father said, 'Stand here, son. This is ladies' business. It's better if you don't get involved.'

Aruna said, 'I know. Mirapa kaya bajji – battered green chillies!'

Her mother-in-law's face brightened. 'You are right. We can whip them up in ten minutes.'

Aruna said, 'But there's a problem. We don't have the long mild chillies. The ones we have in the house are quite spicy.'

Aruna's mother-in-law said, 'Even better. I hope the battleaxe bites deep into one and burns her mouth.' She laughed, almost a cackle, and called out, shouting, 'Kaka-a-a!'

'Yes, amma,' he said softly, right behind her.

She jumped, startled, and turned around, looking cross. She said, 'What are you doing, lurking behind me like that? Go, get into the kitchen and mix the senaga pappu flour for the batter. Don't wait.'

Forty-five minutes later, Aruna and her family got out of the car at her sister-in-law's house. Aruna carried a flat cardboard box that contained the silk sari for her sister-in-law's mother-in-law.

Inside the house, Aruna's sister-in-law, Mani, was sitting on the sofa, her big belly showing. Her husband and his parents got up to welcome them. Her son, Sanjay, was watching a big television on one side of the room – Tom was chasing Jerry around a kitchen and pots and pans were crashing to the ground behind them. Aruna handed the sari she was carrying to her mother-in-law. The two older ladies greeted each other effusively. Anybody would think they are old school friends, the way they are greeting each other, thought Aruna. She flicked a glance at her husband and he shook his head, rolling his eyes. She looked down at the floor to hide her smile.

Ramanujam walked over and sat next to his sister. 'Hello, Mani. How are you feeling?'

'Like a whale,' she said. 'I had forgotten what it was like.'

Ramanujam laughed. Mani's husband came over and sat next to them. Aruna looked at the three young people and would have liked to join them, but she didn't move from her mother-in-law's side. A servant maid came out of the kitchen and served them all water and sweets.

Once the maid left and they had all taken a sip, Mani's mother-in-law said, 'What a good daughter-in-law you have.' Her voice was as sweet as sugarcane juice.

'She's not bad,' said Aruna's mother-in-law, in an off-hand manner. 'But she's from a poor family. She didn't bring a single cent of land with her.'

Aruna knew that the two older ladies were playing a game of cat and mouse. They were the cats, their claws sheathed but darting out in quick flashes to try to draw blood. The two daughters-in-law were the mice. By referring to her family's poverty, her mother-in-law was reminding the other lady that they had given a piece of a mango orchard in Sonthyam, on the other side of the temple town of Simhachalam, as part of Mani's dowry. Nevertheless, Aruna felt hurt. She kept a clear face and looked across the room towards her husband. Mani's husband said something, and Ramanujam and Mani laughed. Were they laughing about her? She didn't think so, but she still felt a teensy bit lonely.

'People tell us that because the land is still in Mani's name it doesn't really count.'

'People always talk, how does it matter?' said Aruna's mother-in-law.

Aruna's father-in-law spoke for the first time from the chair where he was sitting. 'You shouldn't go by what people say. Stray dogs may bark but that doesn't stop the wedding guests enjoying their feast.'

Aruna's mother-in-law nodded. 'You are so lucky. You already have a grandson in your family and Mani is expecting again. Aruna here is still not pregnant even though she's been married for six months. We are wondering whether we should take her to see a gynaecologist.'

Aruna jerked her head up and looked at her in-laws, surprised and shocked. This was the first she had heard anything about this. She turned towards Ramanujam and tried to signal him with her eyes, but her husband was busy talking to his sister and brother-in-law and didn't see her.

'I know a good doctor. She is very experienced,' said Mani's mother-in-law. 'Malathi, the corporator's daughter-in-law, didn't conceive for almost three years. They took her to big doctors in Hyderabad and Mumbai but nobody could help. Finally, I told them that they shouldn't waste money going to the big cities when there was such a good doctor right on our doorstep. They took my advice and last month their daughter-in-law gave birth. It was only a daughter, but still . . .'

Aruna's mother-in-law leaned forward. 'Really, who—'

Aruna's heart sank. This was getting worse by the minute. She looked again at her husband and this time he saw her. She signalled with her head and he walked over. Aruna smiled at him in relief.

'What are you all talking about?' he asked, sitting down on the sofa next to Aruna.

'Oh, nothing,' said his mother, relaxing back.

Obviously, they wouldn't dare talk in front of their son.

Ramanujam looked at his watch. 'Let's get going. I have a complicated case tomorrow and I want to study the scans again.'

Ramanujam's father got up and called out to their driver to come in with the basket. The snacks were laid out on plates on the central table.

'One, two, three . . . seven,' counted Aruna's mother-in-law, looking triumphantly at her daughter's mother-in-law, who didn't say anything.

Their driver Peter and the servants of Mani's house carried out a suitcase and two bags. Mani got up from the sofa and arched her back. She asked her son to switch off the television.

'One minute, amma,' said the boy, continuing to watch the cartoon.

Peter came back and picked up a big yellow plastic box overflowing with toys. He grunted and staggered towards the door; one of his legs was weaker than the other so he walked with a limp even when not carrying anything.

'Come on, we are going now. Look, your toys are being put in the car too.'

One of the toys in the box suddenly started beeping loudly. The boy looked at the driver and started crying. 'I don't want to go. Leave my toys here.'

Mani went up to her son. 'Come on, darling. I've already told you. We are going to thaatha's place until the baby is born and big enough to bring back. Daddy will come and visit you every day.'

'No. Don't want to go,' said the boy shaking his head.

His father went and picked him up, laughing as the plump boy struggled. 'I swear this boy is getting heavier by the day.'

'Don't attract the evil eye to him,' Mani said. 'He's just a healthy boy.'

Sanjay started kicking against his father's body.

'That's enough, babu! Stop it now,' he said, as the boy almost slipped out of his grip.

'I'll give you a chocolate when we get to thaatha's place. And, you can go with thaatha tomorrow and buy a toy,' said his mother.

Sanjay stopped crying. 'Can I get the same video game that next-door Om has?'

His mother nodded and they all went outside.

*

That evening, Rehman took his motorbike, which had been lying unused for a while, and drove to Marripalem. He followed the instructions given to him until he reached the right colony but got lost in the warren of narrow, twisting streets lined with small houses. He parked his scooter on the main road and walked into a narrow side street.

Some houses were thatched with palm leaves, others were pukka houses made of brick and cement. Little semi-naked children ran around playing with marbles. A bigger boy was rolling the metal rim of a bicycle wheel along the ground. Some girls sat at the corner of a house, playing with tamarind seeds, flicking them up in the air with the backs of their right hands and then catching them before they fell to the ground. At one end of the street, water poured out of a communal standpipe at which a group of women and older girls were filling a variety of vessels for the next day before it stopped. As he walked past them, a loud fight broke out between two women, each accusing the other of pushing in out of turn.

Rehman shook his head – the flow was never enough to supply all the families with the water they needed and fights were common. When he was a boy, he had lived in a house with one tap for all the families in the building, but there had never been any fights. His mother had ensured that everyone had their turn and nobody went against her because she was scrupulously fair, even for herself. And also because she had a sharp tongue that could strip the bark off a tree, he thought.

Rehman asked a man walking past, 'Do you know where Naidu from Kantakaapalli lives? He works in the steel plant.'

The man scratched his head and said, 'I don't know about him but some people from that village live in the second street down there.'

Rehman followed his directions and turned into another narrow street. The houses here seemed to be better built. They all had more than one light and some were even two storeys high. He stood there, looking a bit lost.

A plump middle-aged woman was walking down the street towards him, carrying two round aluminium pots with narrow necks, one on her head and another on her waist. She stopped and asked him, 'What do you want in our street, babu?'

Rehman smiled at her and said, 'I am looking for Naidu from Kantakaapalli. He works in the steel plant.'

'Is he the one who got married recently?' she asked, the water spilling slightly from the pot on her head and soaking her sari.

'I don't know if he got married recently,' said Rehman. 'But he's just come back from the village and brought a young boy with him.'

'Yes, that's the one. He got married about six months ago. They live in that house,' she said, pointing.

'Thank you,' said Rehman.

'Mention not,' the woman said in English.

Rehman looked at her in surprise as she giggled and went on her way. He walked over to the house she had pointed out. 'Hello, anybody home?' he shouted through the locked grille at the front.

A boy, Vasu, came running out of the house and started jumping up and down on the other side of the grille. 'Rehman Uncle, you are here!' he shouted again and again.

Rehman reached through the grille and tousled Vasu's hair. 'And you are here in the city,' he said laughing.

A young woman came out, tightening the edge of her sari around herself protectively when she saw him. The bottom of her sari was wet – she had probably been carrying water from the communal tap. Around her neck was a double-pendant mangalsootram and, on her forehead, red sindoor – symbols of her status as a married woman. She had a sharp chin and kindly eyes, which she had blackened with mascara. He noticed that she had six fingers on each hand.

She opened the door of the grille and said, 'Please come in, babu.'

'I've just come to take Vasu,' said Rehman standing outside. 'You must be busy. I don't want to be any trouble.'

'This is the first time you've come to our house, babu-gaaru. How can you just walk away like that? You must come in.'

Rehman went on to the verandah. The young woman brought out a metal chair and unfolded it for him. Rehman sat down and pulled Vasu on to his lap. He turned to the woman and said, 'If you have any household work, please go ahead. Don't delay anything for my sake.'

The woman said, 'I've already collected the water, so there's no hurry for anything else.'

Vasu said, 'Her name is Sitakka. She is very good.'

Sitakka blushed. 'He's a cute boy,' she said and went inside.

Vasu said, 'Do you know she has twelve fingers?'

'Really?' said Rehman.

'Yes,' said Vasu. 'She also has twelve toes.'

'Very interesting,' said Rehman. 'But tell me about yourself. What do you think of the city so far?'

'I travelled in an auto-rickshaw,' said Vasu.

'Wow,' said Rehman. 'When?'

'From the bus stop to here. It went so fast. Thaatha tells me that I lived in the city with my parents but I don't remember very much about it.'

Sita came out again, carrying a small plate with two chakram – deep-fried snacks in a spiral shape. There was also a small yellow laddoo.

'I am sorry,' she said. 'My husband had to go off to work as soon as we came back from the village and we don't have any-thing else to offer.'

'This is great. I don't need anything else,' said Rehman, taking the plate from her.

She went back inside and Rehman gave one chakram to Vasu and started eating the other. Sita returned with water – one precious glass from the limited quantity she had carried on her head from the end of the street.

Rehman smiled at her. 'When will your husband return?' he asked.

'He's normally back by this time, but today he is going to the ration shop for sugar. There's always a queue there so I don't know when he'll be back.'

Rehman nodded and went back to eating the snacks. Later, after he had finished eating and drunk the water, he found out that Sita's father-in-law was Mr Naidu's cousin. The cousins' lands shared a border and their houses in the village were next to each other as well.

Vasu said, 'It's the house with the monkey in it.'

Rehman nodded. 'I've met your father-in-law and brother-in-law when I was in the village,' he said. They talked for a while about the village and then Rehman looked at his watch. 'I have to go,' he said.

When Vasu went into the house, Sitakka quickly whispered to Rehman, 'Please look after the boy. He has been very dull for several days now. That's why his grandfather thought it would be a good idea to send him to the city. He only perked up when he saw you.'

Rehman nodded but before he could say anything, Vasu came back with his things. He was carrying an old cotton school bag with books and a bundle of what looked like clothes wrapped in a faded bedsheet. 'Is that it?' asked Rehman, picking up the bundle, which was quite light.

Vasu nodded and put the school bag on his back like a ruck-sack.

Sita said, 'My father-in-law is coming here for a day on

Sunday. If you drop Vasu off any time before then, he can go back with him to the village. You don't have to wait until Sunday – I don't mind looking after him for a few days.'

Rehman said, 'I'm sure he'll be all right. My mother hasn't had any small boys to pamper for a long time.'

Sita hugged Vasu and bent down to kiss him on his forehead. 'Don't be too naughty,' she said. 'And eat whatever they give you. Don't make a fuss.'

'I never do,' said Vasu.

'Of course you don't. You are a good boy,' she said, hugging him again. She turned to Rehman and said, 'You must eat a meal with us when you come to drop Vasu.'

They left the house and reached the main road.

'Wow!' said Vasu. 'Are we really going on a motorbike?'

Rehman unlocked the bike and took it off its stand. He sat down and wedged the bundle of clothes on the petrol tank in front of him. Vasu scrambled up behind.

'Hold my waist,' Rehman said to the boy and started the motorbike.

The traffic was a bit heavy by this time but Rehman weaved in and out, making good time. They stopped at a traffic light and Rehman asked, 'Are you OK there?'

'Oh yes. This is great,' said Vasu.

Rehman looked back and saw Vasu's eyes glittering in the light from the shop fronts by the side of the road. The boy's head did not stay still. He was looking from one side to the other as if he wanted to devour the sights around him.

Vasu pointed out a woman who was driving a scooter and laughed. Pedestrians hurried to their homes. Behind them, pedlars stood by carts or sat on mats by the side of the road selling vegetables. Little shops with bright lights sold clothes, steel vessels and general hardware.

They turned left on to the highway and went past the naval laboratories whose stepped walls kept a constant height above the undulating ground. They passed yellow three-wheeled auto-rickshaws. A white Ambassador car with a little Indian tricolour flag flying on its bonnet overtook them, on some important government business, possibly. They went past a long flat-bed lorry carrying thick, straight tree trunks from some forest.

The lights were coming on now in the houses beyond the road – hundreds of thousands of twinkling lights along their route and halfway up the hills. A thirty-feet tall statue of the monkey-god Hanuman stood on their right, on the roof of an ordinary-looking square house that served as a temple. Rehman felt Vasu touching his right hand to his forehead in prayer.

An elephant was lumbering slowly by the side of the road, a mahout on its neck, occasionally reaching out to a branch with its trunk and stuffing a bunch of leaves into its mouth. Rehman pointed it out and Vasu laughed with delight. To be a boy again, thought Rehman, and see a city for the first time.

CHAPTER FOUR

The next morning the doorbell rang at five minutes to nine and Mr Ali went to answer it. Mr Reddy, long hair combed over from the side to cover the bald centre of his head, was standing there. He had become a client just a few days before and Mr Ali was surprised to see him.

He opened the door and let the man in. 'What can I do for you, sir?' he asked. 'We don't have any more matches other than what we have already given you.'

Mr Reddy sat down and took out the envelope that Aruna had given him when he had joined. He slid the lists out from the cover and turned to Mr Ali.

'I have seen a match that I am very interested in,' he said.

'Oh, good,' said Mr Ali. 'Have you contacted them?'

'No. I was hoping that you could call and talk to them.'

Mr Ali nodded. He wasn't too happy about it because there was nothing really that he could add by being in the middle, but some clients preferred it that way and it was part of the service. He took the list from Mr Reddy and looked at the entry halfway down the paper, circled in red ink. According to the details, the people were Kapus too and well off. The groom was an electrical engineer who worked for a power generation company just outside Chennai.

Mr Ali picked up the phone and dialled. After the introductions, Mr Ali said into the handset, 'I have a match for your son. The girl's father is here with me. He works in the Port Trust as an accountant.'

The man was interested. 'What has the girl studied?' he asked.

'She is a BA,' replied Mr Ali. 'Passed in first class.'

'That's very good. But my son is living far away from all of us and we want a girl who is not just educated but can also run his house. We don't want a career-minded girl.'

'Sudha is very good that way, sir,' said Mr Ali. 'Her mother passed away three years ago and she has been looking after her father's household while also studying.'

'Really? Sounds like a good match, indeed.'

Mr Ali passed the phone to Mr Reddy. Aruna walked in just then and greeted them. Mr Ali smiled at her. She put her handbag under the table and sat down.

Mr Ali showed Aruna the marked-up entry on the list and she nodded. She turned to the wooden wardrobe and looked through the files until she found the photograph and handed it to Mr Ali. The young man was standing in front of the high, wrought-iron gates of the power plant where he worked. There were ganneru trees in bloom by the side of the gates, with gnarled branches and white flowers. He was smiling in the photo and looked smart in jeans and T-shirt. He was tall and a bit dark. His hair had a stylish wave on one side.

Mr Reddy got off the phone and Mr Ali handed him the photograph. He seemed impressed.

'That went very well, sir. They seem like a good family, very similar to ours. And he looks quite handsome in this photo.'

'Fantastic,' said Mr Ali. 'How have you left it?'

'The boy is coming home next month and they will visit us then.'

'That was a quick result,' said Mr Ali.

'Indeed,' said Mr Reddy. 'Thanks very much, sir. We've been

looking for almost six months and we didn't find any matches. You were able to help us find somebody in days. Very good service.'

He left shortly, promising to keep them updated on the progress of the match. Gopal, the postman, came in soon after and delivered the morning post. Aruna started going through the letters and divided them into piles – people asking for information about advertisements they had seen in the papers, letters asking for new lists, two complaints and even one letter containing a completed application form and a cheque. She showed the cheque to Mr Ali who had been creating new advertisements for sending off to the newspapers.

'Good!' he said. 'Please put it in the drawer next to the stationery box.'

This was an old shoebox that Mr Ali had divided into multiple compartments with stiff card, and it contained staples, erasers, ribbons for the typewriter and packets of black and red refills for the ballpoint pens. Aruna put the cheque away and said, 'Sir, the typewriter is getting stiff again.'

'Does it need servicing? I'd better call the maintenance man,' Mr Ali said.

'I've been thinking . . .' she said and paused.

Mr Ali looked up at her and raised his eyebrows quizzically.

'I think it's time to get rid of the typewriter and get ourselves a computer.'

'I don't know anything about those things,' he said, doubtfully. 'And they are expensive, aren't they?'

'They've fallen in price a lot in the last few years and they are not as expensive as you might think. I attended a course for three months in college and they are not difficult to operate.'

Mr Ali was not convinced. 'Maybe . . .'

Aruna added, 'Our lists will be much neater. And we'll probably save money because we can fit more addresses on to each sheet.'

'Do you think so?' said Mr Ali.

Aruna left it at that. She had planted the seed and was happy to let it germinate slowly.

Rehman and a boy came out of the house. Rehman lifted the boy and showed him the wall that Aruna had filled with a collage of letters from clients appreciating their services. There was a photograph in the middle of all the letters and wedding invitations. It showed Rehman with a young couple; the lady was holding a baby in her arms.

'That's amma and naanna,' shouted the boy in his clear voice. 'But who is the baby that my mother is holding?' he continued more softly.

'That's you, Vasu,' said Rehman, laughing.

Aruna looked up with interest. She knew that the couple were dead. Mr Ali had told her the story when she had first started making the collage of letters and wedding cards on the wall. The couple were classmates who had fallen in love with each other. The girl was a rich merchant's daughter and he had been extremely angry when she married Vasu's father. The merchant had disowned her and had not allowed her back in his house even though she had tried to make amends many times. Even the birth of his grandson had not mollified the rich man. After Vasu's father died in a construction accident and his mother committed suicide, Vasu's paternal grandfather had taken him to the village and brought him up there. His maternal grandparents had never asked after him.

The boy touched the photograph and turned to Rehman. 'How did you know amma and naanna?'

'They were classmates of mine in college,' he said. 'They were always smiling and happy people.'

Vasu said, 'I can sometimes smell the fragrance of jasmine flowers in amma's hair, but I don't really remember the way she or naanna looked. Because they look so serious in the photo we have in our house, I think of them like that.'

'I have some more photos of them from before you were born – like when we went on the educational tour in our third year of college. We'll get them out and you can see that your parents were such smiley people.'

Vasu nodded. He suddenly seemed down.

Rehman put him down on the floor and turned to walk back into the house. He said, 'Don't you want to see the photos?'

'It's all my fault, you know.'

Rehman sat down suddenly on the sofa, next to his father. He held Vasu by his shoulders and asked him, 'What's your fault?'

'Everything. Amma and naanna dying. It's all my fault.' Vasu mumbled these last words, looking down at his feet.

Aruna and Mr Ali stopped their work and looked aghast at the little boy.

'How is it your fault, Vasu?' asked Rehman gently. 'Your father's death was an accident. You had nothing to do with it.'

'I asked naanna for a ball.'

'So?'

'I asked him to get a stripy ball. When the police returned naanna's bag, there was a ball in it.'

'I don't understand,' said Rehman.

'If naanna hadn't gone to buy the ball, he wouldn't have been in the building when it collapsed. God was punishing me for being greedy.'

Vasu was looking down at the floor and Rehman lifted his chin with a finger until their eyes met. 'Vasu, it was not your fault. The building collapsed because the contractor who built it did not mix enough cement in the concrete. Your father was not delayed because he bought the ball for you. He had an appointment to inspect the building at that time. Three other workers died when the roof collapsed. It was just bad luck.'

The boy looked confused. 'Are you sure, Rehman Uncle?' he asked.

'Of course, Vasu. I swear on you. It's not your fault. You

should have talked to someone, your thaatha or one of the people in the village, a lot earlier.'

'My grandfather said it was all my fault, too.'

'What?' said Rehman loudly, his hands dropping from the boy's shoulders. 'Did Mr Naidu say it was your fault? I don't believe that. You must have misunderstood.'

'No, not thaatha – the other one. My mother's father. He said it was my fault.'

'When did he say that? I thought you never met him.'

'After my father died, amma took me there. That's when he said it.'

'How do you remember that?' said Rehman. 'You were very young when that happened?'

'Do you think I am lying?' said Vasu, trying to pull out of Rehman's hands.

Rehman held on to the wriggling boy and said, 'Of course not. I am just surprised that you remember it, that's all.'

'I didn't remember for a long time. Then after the harvest, Sitakka and her husband came to the village. One evening, she came to our house with some food. I was already in bed and everybody thought I was sleeping. Sitakka sat on the edge of my cot, put a hand on my head and told thaatha that she could not understand how any mother could leave a young son and go away. I wanted to shout that my mother was in heaven and still looking after me, but I kept my eyes closed.'

Rehman said, 'What did your grandfather say?'

'I remembered some of it as thaatha spoke. The rest, I only found out then.' Vasu's eyes took on a faraway look that was startling in a boy of his age. 'It was a big house. We were stopped at the door in the verandah. Ammamma, mother's mother, sat on a big, heavy swing. Grandfather stood in front of the door as if we would sneak in. Amma told them that she needed help because naanna was dead – that there were a lot of debts outstanding.

'My mother's father said, you broke all ties with this house when you married that lower-caste peasant. You will not get a counterfeit tuppenny from me. I remember a young man coming out of the house and asking my grandfather to forget the past, but both the old people just asked him to shut up and go back inside.'

Rehman nodded. Vasu's uncle had been just a teenager and he had been inconsolable at his sister's funeral – the only one of her family who had turned up. Rehman heard that, shortly after, he left home and went off to America to study. One of Rehman's classmates who was doing his PhD in the same university had told Rehman that the boy was working as a waiter in a fast-food restaurant during weekday evenings and at a garage pumping petrol at weekends so that he did not have to ask for money from his parents.

Vasu continued, 'They asked amma to leave. We don't want you or your inauspicious brat's face darkening our door again, my mother's mother said. At these words, amma got really angry. You can say what you want to me, but don't utter a word against my son, she said. You have no right. My grandfather said, we know why you had to marry that peasant. This bastard was born less than eight months after. You have brought enough ill repute on this house. Get out and don't come back again. My mother hugged me tight and started crying.'

'Your mother was a devi – a goddess, a virtuous woman,' said Rehman in a gruff voice. 'You were born very premature. That taunt must have hurt her a lot.'

'I don't understand how it matters when I was born,' said Vasu.

'You'll know when you are older,' said Rehman, shaking his head. He had to struggle to control himself from showing the rage that he felt towards Lalitha's unknown parents. 'Your grandparents were very cruel.'

'Thaatha said that, as we were leaving, my maternal grandfather shouted, you brat, it's all your fault. By coming into this world, you destroyed my family's good name. And it was to pay for you that your parents took on so much debt that your father worked double duties and killed himself. You are like a crow – a dark, raucous bringer of bad news.' Vasu started crying and Rehman held him close. After a few moments, Vasu pulled back and looked Rehman in the eye. 'Is it true? Was it to pay for me that naanna died?'

Rehman closed his eyes for a moment and opened them again. 'You were born early, very small and weak. You had to stay in hospital for a long time and it cost a lot of money.'

Vasu pulled out of Rehman's grasp and turned away. 'It's true,' he said in a high-pitched voice. 'My father died because of me.'

Rehman caught him and pulled him back. 'That's where you are wrong. Your parents happily took on the loans to save you. They loved you – you were the moon in their lives. Your father could easily have earned double or triple the money by working for a big company or a contractor. Instead, he chose to work on projects that helped poor people. That was his choice. He didn't have to go to the building that collapsed. Nobody was paying him to inspect it. He heard rumours that the construction was shoddy and he went there to gather evidence for the municipality. He died doing what he believed in – what he loved. He was just in the wrong place at the wrong time. It's not your fault. If anybody is at fault, it is the greedy builder who put profits above safety.'

Rehman hugged Vasu and said, 'Your parents were both great friends of mine and wonderful people. I can only say that I am sorry that you knew them for such a short time. Don't blame yourself for their deaths. They loved you and would not want you ever to think like that.'

'If my mother loved me so much, why did she leave me?' said Vasu.

Out of the mouths of babes, thought Aruna. The boy had

asked the one question that had troubled her since she had heard about the incident. How could a mother abandon her young child?

Rehman took a deep breath. 'Your mother was very disturbed and depressed at that time. She didn't think she could provide a good life for you on your own. I had long talks with her in those days but I didn't even imagine what she was planning. If I had, maybe things could have been different . . .' He paused for a long time, staring into the distance. He then looked again at the young boy. 'Your mother genuinely believed that, once she was gone, her family would take you in and bring you up. She thought that you could then have the same kind of childhood that she had when she was growing up – nice toys, good education, big house, no money worries. She wanted a bright future for you. How was she to know how hard-hearted people can be?'

It was an hour past noon and Aruna was waiting for the driver to come and take her home for lunch. She had packed away the files and stacked the letters neatly. She rearranged the pens in the tall, narrow biscuit tin, even though she had just done it once less than five minutes ago. Peter, the driver, was normally very prompt. In fact, he usually came just before twelve-thirty and waited for her. She wondered what was keeping him today.

Mr Ali came out and almost closed the iron-grille gate to the verandah that served as the office before he noticed her.

'What are you still doing here, Aruna?' he asked. 'I thought you had already gone.'

'The driver hasn't come yet, sir.'

'Why don't you call home and find out?' he said.

'Nobody is answering, sir. The phone might be dead.' It was quite common for land phones to go dead during the monsoon season but it was not so common in winter.

Mr Ali said, 'Have lunch with us. We have beans-fry with coconut. Also, tarka dhal – a vegetarian menu today.'

'No, that's all right, sir. I'm sure the driver will be coming soon.'

'All right,' he said. 'Let me know when you are leaving.'

He went back inside. Aruna looked at the dainty watch on her wrist with a tiny diamond just above the six on the dial and frowned. It really was getting late and she was hungry. She didn't feel like starting any task, in case she was interrupted. Her thoughts moved from the morning's conversation between Rehman and the boy to her own famished stomach.

In the tiny garden she saw a butterfly with plain cream-coloured wings flying erratically from an orange kanakaambaram flower on a small plant near the ground to a guava blossom higher up on the tree. A man who owns a house sleeps in only one bedroom, but the homeless man sleeps anywhere he fancies, Mr Ali had told her once, and she remembered the saying now. Before she got married, she didn't have a car to ferry her around and she would have just left and walked down to her parents' house. Now, she had to wait.

Ten minutes later, she saw the car pull up. She picked up her handbag, called out to Mr Ali and rushed out before Peter, the driver, got out with his dicky leg.

'Sorry, chinnamma,' he said, waiting for her to close the door and pulling out into the road. 'Mani madam asked me to pick up a bottle of medicine for her son just as I was leaving to get you.'

'Oh! Is Sanjay all right?' she asked.

'Yes, chinnamma. He was watching TV when I left.'

The car turned on to the highway. There was hardly any traffic at this time of day. They left the highway at the TB Hospital junction. As the car jolted its way slowly past Spencer's super-market, where the road had been dug up months ago and not filled up properly, a wailing siren came from behind them. Peter gave way and an ambulance with a big 108 printed on its side moved past.

'People are driving more carelessly since 108 started,' said Peter.

Government hospitals usually had one or two ambulances but normally they were used to ferry senior hospital officials and their wives around town, and were not generally available for public use. A foundation run by a software company had recently started an ambulance service that anybody could access by dialling the three-digit number.

'Before there were ambulances, people used to drive carefully, but now they are fearless. They have started thinking that if there is an accident, an ambulance will come and take them to a hospital to be patched up.'

Aruna laughed. 'I don't think people think about ambulances when they are driving,' she said. 'Where do they take the patients?'

'If the patient tells them the name of a hospital, they take them there, chinnamma. Otherwise, to the nearest hospital that takes emergency cases. And it is not just for accidents – heart attacks, deliveries, anything urgent.'

'Good,' said Aruna. She wanted to get home and eat lunch. She wished they had a siren on their car, so they could go past all the other traffic. They slowly climbed up the slope towards the university and then went faster downhill towards the sea before they reached home.

Aruna went quickly inside to find Sanjay slumped on a sofa watching television.

'How are you?' she said, patting the boy on the head.

'Fine,' he grunted, not taking his eyes off the screen in front of him.

'Did you take your medicine?' she asked, putting her handbag down on a side cabinet.

'No,' he said.

Aruna washed her hands in the dining-room sink and sat down at the dining table. She lifted the upturned plate that covered a bowl and set it before herself. The bowl contained steamed rice.

She removed smaller side-plates covering three other dishes. Her mouth watered at the sight of the stuffed brinjal curry, sautéed cabbage with mustard seeds and dried chillies, and the drumstick sambhar. Before she had eaten a couple of mouthfuls, Kaka came in with a freshly fried poppadom and vadiyams, sun-dried rice flour and pumpkin crisps. She smiled at him. He went back into the kitchen and returned with a bowl of home-made yoghurt.

'Have amma and naanna eaten?' she asked him.

'Yes, chinnamma. They all ate about half an hour ago. Babu did not come home,' he said.

She nodded. Her husband had told her in the morning that they were taking a retired senior doctor from the hospital to lunch.

She started with rice and the stuffed brinjals and ended the meal with curd rice and spicy mango pickle. As she finished, Kaka came in again to clear the table and she went into the living room. This room had windows on two sides and was lighter than the dining room. Aruna loved looking out of the side window at the dark-green, glossy foliage of ferns, the dusty leaves of a climbing jasmine, pots of sweet marjoram, and a ground-cover plant with little pink flowers that looked like roses and succulent leaves. Sanjay was still watching the television and Aruna sat down beside him on the sofa.

'Do you want to come outside and walk in the garden with me?' she asked.

'No, watching cartoons.'

'You've been watching TV for a long time now. Take a rest.'

Just then Mani and her mother came in. Mani's stomach stuck out in front of her and she walked a little bit like a duck, rolling her hips.

'Namaste,' Aruna greeted her mother-in-law. She smiled and nodded to her sister-in-law.

'Aruna attha doesn't want me to watch cartoons,' said the boy to his mother.

Mani looked at Aruna accusingly. Unaccountably, Aruna felt guilty. 'I didn't . . .' she began.

'You did too,' interrupted Sanjay.

She took a deep breath but before she could say anything, her mother-in-law said, 'What's wrong if your aunt tells you to stop watching television? You've glued your eyelids open, staring at the screen all morning.'

'What's wrong with Sanjay?' asked Aruna. 'Peter told me that he had to get medicine.'

'I thought he had a temperature,' said Mani. 'But I'll wait until the evening before giving him the medicine.'

Then why did you ask Peter to get the medicine just when it was time to pick me up, thought Aruna, her face flushing.

Mani looked at her coolly. 'Yes?'

Aruna couldn't answer her. She felt frustrated at her own inadequacy. Her sister-in-law was the one who was acting mean, so why did she feel petty to ask her about it? Aruna shook her head and went to her room. She would lie down for a couple of hours before going back to the office. An incipient headache was bubbling up.

Aruna's day had gone from bad to worse. It was six in the evening that same day and her temples now throbbed dully. She had made several mistakes in typing a list of Brahmin brides – a twenty-six-year-old had been aged to a sixty-two-year-old; a girl from a village who wanted to marry a boy from a city had been turned into a girl from a city who wanted to marry a village boy; and a career woman on a good salary became a career woman with *no* good salary. Mr Ali had come the closest he ever had to criticising her. She told him she had a headache and he had appeared a bit flustered.

'If you need to, why don't you take tomorrow off as well?' he suggested.

'No need, sir. I will be fine by tomorrow.'

'Are you sure?' he asked.

'Yes, sir. I will be all right.'

He had nodded, looking unconvinced, and she had been puzzled by the conversation. A few minutes later, she realised that he must have thought she was using a euphemism for a period when she said she had a headache. That embarrassed her even more, especially as she couldn't really correct him.

A large group of people came in. Five of them squeezed on to the sofas and chairs and two others remained standing up. Aruna and Mr Ali looked at each other in surprise.

Mr Ali turned to the gentleman sitting nearest to him and asked, 'How can we help you, sir?'

The gentleman, who seemed to be in his late forties or early fifties, had a large, dark spot that ran across his left cheek and into his scalp. The spot looked rather like a map of India, thought Aruna, starting broad at the top and tapering to an inverted triangle at the bottom; Vizag would be about the bottom of his ear.

'My name is Hasan,' said the gentleman. He pointed to the lady sitting next to him. 'This is my missus, Khalida.'

She bobbed her head. The introductions continued. 'Hussein, brother . . . Mr Rizwan, uncle . . . Bilqis, sister . . . Mr Ahmed, wife's uncle . . . Haroun, son.'

Aruna's head whirled, trying to remember so many names.

Mr Ali said to Mr Hasan, 'Who is the bride or groom?'

'My daughter, Sania,' said Mr Hasan.

'Where is she?' asked Mr Ali. 'Didn't you bring her too?'

'We thought about it,' his wife Khalida said. 'But there wasn't room in the car.'

Aruna wondered how even the seven of them had fitted into a car. There were all fairly slim but, even then, it must have been quite cosy.

'Do you wish to become a member and register Sania's details?' Mr Ali asked. He turned to Aruna, who handed him a prospectus and an application form. Mr Ali passed the papers and a pen to Mr Hasan. 'Please read through and fill in the form.'

The whole family crowded round as Mr Hasan started reading the prospectus.

Mr Ali asked, 'By the way, how did you find out about us?'

One of the uncles looked up and said, 'The imam in our mosque told us about you.'

'Which mosque do you go to? I didn't think any mosque leader knew about us enough to recommend us.'

'New Colony mosque,' said the gentleman. 'You helped one of his parishioners who didn't have a father find a very good match. The boy's name was Irshad.'

'Oh, Irshad!' said Mr Ali. 'My wife and I went to his wedding. In fact, I was one of the two official witnesses at the Nikah.'

Aruna smiled and said, 'Yes, that was a difficult case but sir did a very good job. Irshad and his wife still visit us every few months on festivals and holidays.'

Mr Hasan started filling up the form. After some time, his wife said, 'What do you mean, up to thirty-five years? Sania is only twenty-three. We don't want a son-in-law who is twelve years older than our daughter.'

'OK,' said Mr Hasan and scratched out something in the form.

A couple of minutes later, the uncle who had told Mr Ali about Irshad stopped Mr Hasan and said, 'Mention that we are not interested in Muslims from Hyderabad.'

'OK,' said Mr Hasan and continued filling in the form.

His sister, Bilqis, then said, 'We want somebody from a religious family. Make sure that you write about it. The groom must be a man who goes to the mosque at least every Friday, if not more often.'

After Mr Hasan completed the form, his son Haroun took it from him and quickly read through it. 'Abba, we have already talked about this. The groom must be an engineer, preferably in software. You didn't write about this here.'

Mr Ali took the form and the fee, while Aruna put the list of Muslim grooms in an envelope and handed it to Mr Hasan. The family departed.

Aruna clipped the form into the new members' list.

Mr Ali shook his head and said, 'This is not going to be an easy case.'

CHAPTER FIVE

The next morning Rehman got up a bit late and sat down for breakfast. His mother came out of the kitchen with a dosa on a spatula, fresh off the hot tava. She slipped it on to the plate and went back to the stove.

'The onion chutney is in the steel bowl,' she called out over the sizzle of the dosa batter being spread on the griddle.

Rehman served himself the chutney and started eating. 'Has Vasu eaten?' he asked.

'Ages ago. He's having his bath now.'

Rehman was on his third crêpe when Vasu came into the dining room through the back door and the kitchen. He walked with small mincing steps because he had a towel wrapped tightly round his waist. His chest was bare and his hair was wet.

Mrs Ali came up behind the boy with another dosa. She put it on Rehman's plate and turned to Vasu. 'Make sure you dry your hair properly. It is winter and you'll catch a chill.'

Vasu nodded and went into the bedroom, closing the door behind him.

'Are you going out today?' asked Mrs Ali.

Rehman said, 'Yes, ammi. Remember, I'm taking Vasu to the beach today. We won't be back for lunch.'

Mrs Ali went into the kitchen and switched off the stove.

'Don't forget you have to pick up Pari from the railway station. She is coming on the East Coast Express.'

'Is she really leaving Kovvur for ever?' asked Rehman.

'Yes, she wants to live and work here. I've talked to the old woman – the ticket collector's widow – who owns the house opposite and she's agreed to let the room at the top to Pari. She wasn't too keen on letting a room to a single woman but I explained the situation and she agreed. Pari's had a difficult life, poor girl. I hope this change of scenery also marks a change in her fortune.'

Yes, poor girl, Rehman thought, chewing on the dosa. The last time he had seen Pari was just over a year ago. Her husband, Rehman's sportsman cousin, had died when a beam sticking out of a lorry had hit him on the back of his head. When laid out on the bed, his muscled body had been perfect and he had seemed to be sleeping peacefully – even his face was untouched. Pari had been distraught, alternately screaming her grief, wanting to join him, or begging her husband to wake up and show them all that he was not dead. It had been hours before they were able to drag her away from the body so that it could be prepared for burial.

Soon after that, her adopted father had suffered a massive stroke that left him bedridden, incontinent and prone to violent seizures. Pari – her adopted mother having died several years before – had looked after him for almost a year until he too died.

'She's not a pari. She's a farishta – not a fairy but an angel,' said his mother breaking into his thoughts. 'No natural daughter could have looked after her father with more devotion.'

'Where is she going to be working?'

'Don't you listen to anything I say?' said his mother, coming and sitting down at the dining table. 'She's going for an interview at the call centre. You will have to take her.'

'No problem.'

Soon after, Rehman was ready too and he said, 'See you,

ammi. We'll be back by three, so I'll have plenty of time to go to the station.'

Rehman took out his two-wheeler and Vasu scrambled up behind him. They drove down the busy road, especially congested at the choke points where, over the years, two Hindu temples and a Muslim burial ground had prevented the widening of the road. On a traffic island outside the main bus stand, Rehman pointed out the statue of Gurajada Apparao, the first playwright who had written in common spoken Telugu. The great man looked lost among all the vehicles.

'A nation is not its lands; a nation is its hands,' said Vasu.

'He's the author of those words,' said Rehman, turning left.

They went uphill, past the circuit house, before going downhill to the Beach Road. They drove along the coastal road out of town, past the cable car, keeping the long beach on their right and the rolling red clay hills on their left. Fifteen minutes later, they turned into a so-called resort – a hotel with an open-air restaurant. Rehman parked his motorbike and they both sat at a table under a laburnum tree. The place was empty this early in the morning and, apart from the occasional vehicle on the road, the only other sounds were the continuous roar of the sea in the background and the sharper tones of birds – chattering sparrows and singing mynahs mainly. A waiter came over. Vasu ordered a buttermilk and Rehman asked for a fresh-lime soda.

They were sipping their drinks when a car turned in and parked next to their bike. A young lady got out and started walking towards them.

Vasu looked at her and turned to Rehman. 'She is . . . Usha Aunty.'

Rehman smiled at him. 'That's right. I called her yesterday and told her we would be here.'

The pendant that hung on a thin gold chain round her neck flashed in the sun. She passed into the shade of the trees and they both stood up to greet her. She wore open-toed, high-heeled sandals, jeans and a long, dark-blue cotton top, and her glossy black hair was tied in a ponytail. Rehman's throat went dry for a moment. He swallowed and smiled at this glorious vision.

'Hi, Usha. Glad you could make it.'

'I told you I would come, didn't I?' she said, smiling at him. She had not initiated any of their meetings but had never refused to catch up with him whenever he called her.

Rehman nudged Vasu and the boy put his hands together. 'Namaste, Usha Aunty,' he said.

'Lovely to see you again,' she said. 'Are you enjoying the city?'

'Yes, madam.'

They all sat down again and the waiter rushed over. Rehman couldn't help noticing how he fawned over Usha. Was it because she had come in a car or was it just because she was beautiful?

Fifteen minutes later, they had finished their drinks and Vasu had gone round all the chairs on the lawn, twice. He came back and said, 'Come on, Uncle. You said we could go to the beach.'

Rehman looked at Usha and said, 'Shall we?'

She nodded. Rehman called the waiter back and settled the bill. They walked down a path between the thatched cottages that tried to simulate a rural ambience (with air-conditioning and mosquito repellents) and on to the sandy beach. Vasu ran ahead of them as Usha bent down to take off her sandals. She lost her balance as she tried to stand on one leg and unbuckle the other sandal. Rehman put his hand out instinctively and Usha supported herself on his arm. Her hand felt cool. She looked up at him and smiled. Rehman stared unabashedly at her clear face. He noticed that her lipstick had become slightly smudged – probably from the glass – but her lips still looked juicy and well defined. A stray strand of hair had escaped the hairband and cut a dark slash against her fair cheeks.

She held on to his hand for a bit longer, not seeming in any hurry to break contact. She finally let go of his hand and held her sandals by their straps. Rehman, who was wearing flip-flops, didn't bother taking them off. The sharp grains of sand tickled his feet. The sun shone but, because it was still winter, it was nicely warm and not hot. Ahead of them, Vasu had almost reached the water. Rehman shouted out, 'Careful . . .'

The beach was virtually flat up to the high-tide mark and then sloped down quite sharply where the fluffy sand gave way to a smooth, packed surface where the sea had pounded it. There were no other living creatures at that early hour, except a few seagulls wheeling in the air. Vasu was dancing halfway down the slope, shouting challenges to the sea above the continuous noise of the surf. A wave broke several yards in front of him, running out of energy just before it reached him. The boy laughed and went a couple of feet closer to the edge.

The next two waves combined into one and rose danger-ously high before crashing down with a roar. A maelstrom of white water rushed up the shore, overtaking Vasu before he could run away. It reached his knees and he had to stop. The bottom of his shorts got wet before the wave receded. Vasu laughed, his boyish voice clear as birdsong.

A traditional wooden fishing sail boat had been dragged up the beach about a hundred yards away. Rehman pointed towards it and Usha nodded.

'Vasu, we'll be sitting by the boat. Come with us.'

They sat down in the shade of the colourful boat. Vasu fol-lowed, left his rubber flip-flops next to them and went back to the waterline.

Rehman took out a bottle of water from his rucksack and offered it to Usha. She shook her head.

'I should have got a sheet to sit on,' he said.

'I think there is a plastic sheet in the car, but I can't be both-ered to go now,' said Usha.

'Do you want me to get it?' said Rehman.

She shook her head. 'We can dust off the sand when we leave.'

They were both silent for some time, watching Vasu play on

the beach. He was collecting flat shells that looked like a child's slipper and throwing them into the water. A garland of marigolds, probably a fisherman's offering to the sea the previous evening, had washed up. The waves moved it to and fro on the beach. A ship was on the horizon, sailing slowly away from the harbour. Usha and Rehman sat next to each other, their backs against the hard wood of the boat.

'When I was a boy, we lived for a while in a fishermen's colony. In those days, they used to spend all their free time spinning thread. Now they just use nylon,' said Rehman.

'There are so many things like that. Years ago, my mother and the cook in our house used to spend hours every afternoon picking stones out of rice. Nowadays, there are no stones in the rice.'

An eagle flew past them, chased by three crows. It twisted and turned, making abrupt turns to outwit its pursuers. The eagle gave a sharp cry and Usha shivered slightly. 'I feel a premonition – of something,' she said.

Rehman was surprised. He followed her gaze and looked at the eagle's struggle. When it was well over the water the crows gave up and turned back. The eagle soared in the air, gaining altitude, and wheeled in a big arc back towards the coast.

After several moments of silence Rehman laughed and said, 'We are talking like a couple of old people. Tell me about your family – are you scared of your mother or your father?'

Usha answered instantly, 'My father, of course. My mother is almost a doormat. I get so angry with her. I tell her to stand up to naanna, but she just smiles and shrugs. The only time I remember her contradicting my father was when I was offered the television job.'

'Oh! What happened? Didn't she want to you to take it up?'

'On the contrary! I was really surprised. My father came over all traditional and harrumphed about a woman of the family appearing on TV, but amma told him not to be a hen in a coop. He was struck dumb. And so I started working.'

'That must have been a shock to your father.'

Usha smiled. 'Poor man . . . Mind you, if naannamma, my grandmother, had said no, he would have still refused. But she said there was nothing wrong with being a journalist. It's not like acting in movies with heroes, she said. After that my father didn't have a leg to stand on. She can be fierce when necessary and naanna grumbles but he never crosses his mother.'

'You had gone to her house when we met in the café in Kottavalasa, didn't you?'

'That's right. She is always sweet to me. You see, naanna never says no to his mother and naannamma never says no to me, so naanna never says no to me.'

Rehman laughed. 'Transitive logic,' he said.

'What?'

Rehman waved his hand in dismissal. 'Just something I learned in my engineering studies. If A equals B and B equals C, then A equals C.'

'Something like that. What about you? Are your parents happy about what you do? After all, your mother wasn't too keen on you going back to Royyapalem for the protest.'

Rehman shrugged. 'So-so. By the way, she is still embarrassed about what you did.'

Rehman and his friends had been protesting against the setting up of a Special Economic Zone in a village called Royyapalem that would have meant that the villagers would have lost their land. The police had broken up the protest and injured several people, including Rehman, while arresting them. Rehman and his friends had been acquitted on a technicality. When Usha interviewed Rehman outside the court, Rehman had declared that he was going straight back to Royyapalem to continue the protest. Rehman's mother, who had been standing just out of camera shot, disagreed loudly. Usha put her on camera and questioned her. The interview had been telecast repeatedly as 'A Mother's Anguish'.

Usha smiled. 'That and the other interview of your mother I did in Royyapalem itself got the best ratings of any of my work. My producer was really happy.'

'I think my mother was secretly proud of them, too, though she pretends that you jumped on her and she didn't have a choice.'

'I hope so . . .'

The talk moved on to other topics. Would Vizag become the state capital if Telangana split away from Andhra? Did they even want it to happen when it would probably spoil the small-town charm of their city? What kind of events did she like covering? Did he like cricket?

The conversation drifted into a companionable silence. After a couple of minutes, Rehman turned to her and said, 'What—'

At the same time, Usha turned towards him and said, 'I—'

They both laughed and Rehman said, 'You first . . .'

'No, no . . . you first.'

'You.'

'First, you.'

Rehman shook his head, smiling. 'We are acting like the Nawabs of Lucknow who missed the train.'

'I've heard that saying before, but never understood it,' said Usha.

Rehman shrugged. 'By the time railways came to India, Pax Britannica was well established and the noblemen of Lucknow had turned effete and decadent. Unlike their ancestors who fought real wars, they staged pigeon-flying contests or chess competitions among themselves. They spent their spare time listening to poetry, dallying with courtesans and chewing paan. But they were all impeccably well mannered.'

Usha was gazing at him and her wide eyes disturbed him. He looked down at her long fingers trailing in the sand as if sieving it.

'One evening, the story goes, two nawabs reached the first-class compartment of the Lucknow–Delhi Express at the same time. Since neither had arrived before the other, each asked the other to go in first. While they were both saying, you first, their servants made discreet enquiries among themselves and found out that both gentlemen were of the same rank and age. They both had the same amount of land and money. Neither was superior to the other so they both kept saying, you first, until the train left the station and the gents were left standing on the platform.'

Usha laughed – a tinkling, musical sound. 'You have to admire their civilised behaviour. People today just push and shove with no consideration for others. By the way, what made you take up the protest in Royyapalem? I never understood that – you don't have any family or friends there as far as I know.'

'I—'

A shout came from the waterline and Rehman felt his chest tighten as he realised that he had forgotten about Vasu playing in the waves. He should have been more careful; anything could have happened. It was a relief to see the boy running towards them, his dark legs wet up to his thighs.

'Look at what I've caught!'

He slowly opened his cupped hands. A tiny, soft-shelled crab started crawling up his fingers.

'It tickles,' the boy said happily and shook his hand. The crustacean flew in the air and landed on Usha's shoulder.

'Eeek,' screamed Usha, jumping up and trying to brush the crab off. It scuttled on to her back. Usha twisted her arms round but could not get hold of it. She went round in circles but the crab remained safely on her back, out of her reach. After she had made three full revolutions, she stopped and looked at the others.

Rehman was on his feet, bent double, with his hands on his knees, laughing so much that tears were starting. Vasu looked perplexed, staring alternately at Rehman and Usha. After a moment, he too began laughing. Usha moved forward angrily and stomped on Rehman's foot.

'Oww,' said Rehman, hopping on one foot and glaring at her.

'Help me,' said Usha. 'What kind of man are you? Instead of helping a woman, you are laughing at her.'

'Sorry,' said Rehman, wiping the tears away. He couldn't stop grinning, however.

He moved behind Usha and scooped the crab off her. The crab fell to the ground and burrowed into the soft sand, disappearing in a couple of seconds. Her back was warm and exciting under the thin cotton top and his hand lingered. Usha stopped moving and went still under his touch. Rehman's laughter ceased and he jerked his hand away. He stepped back and stared at his palm as if it was branded with a hot iron.

Vasu ran back towards the water and Usha turned towards Rehman, with a smile. She sobered up when she saw his expression. 'Rehman . . .'

He dropped his hand and looked at her seriously. 'Usha, I'm sorry.'

She put a finger vertically across his lips, just touching them. 'Shh. You don't have to apologise.'

He took a deep breath and stepped back. They looked into one another's eyes and Rehman felt himself drowning. It was a while before he said, 'Shall we go for lunch?'

She nodded and Rehman turned to call Vasu back. They left the beach; Rehman talked to the waiter, who said it was OK to leave his motorbike in the restaurant's parking area. They all got into Usha's car and Vasu jumped up and down on the back seat, testing the car's suspension. Rehman turned around and said, 'Vasu, don't do that.'

Vasu just grinned at him. 'This is a fantastic car, Aunty,' he said to Usha.

The air-conditioning came on as they slipped out of the restaurant and on to the road.

'Wow!' said Vasu.

Rehman and Usha looked at each other, smiling.

'Where are we going?' asked Usha.

'This way,' replied Rehman pointing north.

The car ate up the miles. Round each bend, a fresh vista of blue sea, dotted here and there with triangular white sails, was laid before them. They passed little fishing villages. About ten minutes later, Rehman asked Usha to slow down. After a few seconds, he pointed to a row of coconut trees and told her to turn off, down an unmade dirt road. It was bumpy until they came to an open area. Usha parked the car under one of the coconut trees, next to a couple of motorcycles.

An Alsatian dog came over to them, its pink tongue hanging out, as they all got out the car. Vasu hung back behind Rehman but relaxed when he saw that the powerful-looking canine was friendly. A shack made of corrugated tin sheets and palm leaves came into view.

'That's the place,' he said.

'I thought we were going there,' she said, pointing to the other side of the road. About half a mile inland, up a mountain, was a brand new hotel. It was a pukka concrete building, several storeys high with wide glass windows overlooking the sea.

Rehman looked where Usha pointed and said, 'The view from there must be great.'

Usha nodded. 'It is.'

Rehman turned back. 'But the food here is better, I am sure.'

Usha shook her head and followed Rehman and Vasu. A rough sign, painted on an iron sheet that was corroding round the edges, stood outside the shack.

Inn by the Sea
Cool drinks, tea, snacks, lunch
Castrol

'Is this the oil company's canteen?' she asked. 'Look at the rust – how long has this place been here?'

Rehman laughed. 'Don't be snobbish. It's been here for years because the food is good. It's run by a lovely couple. The wife cooks and the man serves the food. You'll love it.'

'If you say so.'

A hole had been dug in the ground next to a standpipe. Usha and Vasu followed Rehman's example and washed their hands at the pipe. Usha stood well back so the water would not spatter over her.

The palm-leaf roof came right down to about chest height and instead of walls there were wooden benches all around the perimeter. They walked through the narrow door and sat on one of the benches. Long black granite slabs – cuddapah stone from the south of the state – served as table tops. On the far side four college students were finishing their meals. A tall, well-built man stepped out from a smoky room and greeted them. He handed Rehman a tin sheet cut from an oil can with the menu written on it.

Rehman looked through the menu and showed it to Usha. 'They do a delicious crab curry here. Do you want to try it?'

Usha pulled a face. 'No, thank you. I've had enough of crabs for one day.'

Vasu laughed. Rehman handed the menu to Usha and turned to the boy. 'Would you like to eat fish?' he asked.

Vasu nodded. Rehman turned to Usha. 'I will have a van-jaram fish curry,' she said.

'Good choice. Let's order three of that.'

The man came back with three glasses and a jug of water. He brought three square stainless-steel plates, each with a number of indentations along one side.

Rehman said, 'Three meals with vanjaram curry.'

The man nodded and went back into the kitchen. He returned and filled the indentations in the plates with different vegetable curries. In the centre, he served them rice. Steam rose from the food.

They started eating. Rehman turned to Usha. 'The fish they use here is really fresh. They buy it in the morning straight off the boats and cook it by midday. They don't serve dinners here, only lunch.'

They were a quarter of the way through their lunch when the fish curry arrived. Red with Guntur chillies, chunks of fish and a mass of spring onions filled the dish. They each got two pieces of fish. Rehman said to Vasu, 'Unlike the river fish you get in the village, there is only one bone in the centre of the vanjaram. You can eat it easily.'

Vasu finished eating well before Rehman and Usha. He sat there looking bored and Rehman was about to tell him that he could leave the table when the college students on the other bench got up. One of them carried a cricket bat and another a ball. One of the students stopped and asked Rehman, 'You are . . . you were in the farmers' protest, weren't you, sir?'

Rehman looked up, surprised, and said, 'Yes, I was. How do you know?'

The student called the others over. 'We were all involved in the protest as well, sir. We marched from the university to the District Collector's office and gave him a signed petition against the farmers' lands being taken away.'

Rehman's face broke into a wide smile. 'Thanks, guys. It was because of all your support that the government backed down on the issue. What are you all studying?'

'Engineering, sir. I am in my third year of a chemical engineering course. My friends are in electronics.' The young man stood in silence for a moment and then said, 'My friends and I are planning to play cricket outside. Our professors didn't turn up today.'

As the students turned to go, Rehman said, 'Can you take Vasu with you? He is getting bored here and would probably enjoy playing cricket. We'll collect him in ten or fifteen minutes.'

They agreed and Vasu jumped out and joined them.

After the boys left, she said, 'You are famous.'

'Thanks to you,' he said and grinned. They went back to their meal.

After a few minutes, Usha said, 'You are right. The food is really good – simple but delicious. By the way, you didn't answer me when I asked you at the beach. Why did the farmers' plight affect you so much? The government was going to pay the farmers for their land, wasn't it?'

Rehman thought for a moment. 'The government would have paid only a fraction of the land's true worth. Then what would the farmers do? Where will they go and buy land and from whom? And that's if they get paid. Even the government admits that more than three quarters of the people displaced by development activities since 1951 are still awaiting rehabilitation. I asked Mr Naidu, Vasu's father, about it some time back and do you know what he said? The land is our mother, he explained. She provides us with everything. How can we sell our mother, for any reason?'

The owner of the restaurant went back into the kitchen, leaving them alone. Rehman felt a cramp in his thigh and moved it slightly. Suddenly it was in contact with Usha's leg from mid-thigh to knee. He was so surprised that he froze and did not immediately move it away. Usha didn't seem to mind their legs touching at all. She casually turned to him and said, 'Do you want some more fish? I can't eat all of it.'

Rehman nodded silently. She delicately broke a small chunk of fish with her fingers and picked it up between her forefinger and thumb. Instead of dropping it in his plate, she raised her hand to his mouth and offered the morsel to him. He bent forward slightly towards her and opened his lips. Her fingers felt soft as he trapped them with his teeth, biting ever so softly. With his clean left hand, he brushed back a lock of her hair that had fallen forward, the pads of his fingers rubbing along her smooth cheeks. He tucked the strand behind her ear and dropped his hand slowly, setting her earring in motion on the way. Her moist lips were slightly parted and they drank in the sight of one another; the dog barked outside and Rehman heard a bat striking a ball; one of the boys shouted and a couple of sparrows chattered, but they all seemed far away. Usha's eyes were smoky and unreadable, but the increased pressure of her leg against his was clear.

CHAPTER SIX

The railway station was busy as usual. The passenger train from Khurda Road had just left and people were streaming out, laden with overstuffed bags, bulging suitcases and bamboo baskets filled with fruit and vegetables, held together precariously with rope. Rehman stood aside as a man, his wife and their seven children, all looking identical and asexual with their clean-shaven heads shining like light bulbs, walked through the gate, probably coming back from the Jagannath temple in Puri.

The East Coast Express was expected on platform two in five minutes, the tannoy announced in three languages. It was on time, for once. Rehman climbed the steps to the overhead bridge and made his way to platform two. Railways fascinated him – the crowds, the shops, the trains themselves, though the steam engines of his childhood were no more. The solid yellow sign, proclaiming the name of the station in English, Hindi and Telugu along with the height of the station above sea level (he'd never figured out why they included that), the rich and poor people mingling together, all united India and made it one country despite all the differences of religion, caste and language.

He bought an *India Today* news magazine from the Higginbothams' stall on the platform and waited for the train. A porter in a red shirt with a big official badge stopped and asked whether he needed help when the train came, but he shook his head. He had been told that Pari wouldn't be carrying much luggage. After another announcement in Hindi, Telugu and English that the East Coast Express was about to arrive on platform two, the train came in, pulled by a diesel engine.

If it was busy before, the platform now burst into activity. Porters ran down the platform, ready to jump into the brick-red, dusty compartments as soon as they slowed down enough, so they could get a head start on touting for business.

The engine gave a long hoot. A drink-seller standing next to Rehman ran a metal bottle opener musically along the bottles.

'Chai, chai,' shouted a boy, carrying glass tumblers and a kettle.

'*Indian Express, Hindu, Business Times, Chandamama*,' shouted a wiry newsvendor in baggy khaki shorts.

'Marie, Britannia biscuits; milk bread, fruit bread,' shouted another.

Passengers with luggage waiting to embark clutched their tickets and anxiously checked their compartment numbers, edged a little closer to the moving train.

Pari had written a postcard to Rehman's mother to say that she would be in the front half, so he stood about two-thirds of the way down the platform. As the train slowed down and the more athletic porters jumped through the open doors up into the carriages, Rehman tried to make out Pari's face among the passengers looking out of the windows. It was several minutes after the train stopped that Rehman finally found Pari, almost at the front.

'No, no, I don't need any help,' she was saying to a porter who tried to grab her suitcase in the narrow aisle between the long sleeper berths and the two seats on the side.

'Are you sure madam doesn't need any help?' Rehman drawled from the door.

Pari's hair was tied back in a tight braid but some strands were windblown in the front. Her face was stark and bare of any jewellery. She had lost weight since he had last seen her and her beaked nose looked too long for her now-angular face. She was wearing a black sari that was supposed to look mournful but was actually very elegant on her fair, slim frame. She looked up at him and a slow smile suffused her face.

'My favourite devar,' she said to her brother-in-law. 'Come to rescue me from grasping coolies.'

Rehman laughed. He had wondered how he would react, seeing her for the first time since that harrowing night of her husband's death, but her smile and words put him at ease.

'Sorry, my shiny armour was a bit rusty and I had to send it off to the dhobi ghat for cleaning,' he said, moving forward. He took her battered suitcase, its grey plastic hidden under a brown cotton cover. She picked up a bulging cloth bag, decorated with lace and an embroidered pink rose, and followed him out of the train.

'I was very proud when I saw you on TV,' she said. 'I wish I could have joined your protest.'

'Really?' he asked, surprised.

He had only ever met her in the presence of her husband, his cousin, and she had always come across as a quiet, demure woman with a shy smile. The intervening year had changed her and not in the way he expected. She had been married young, as her father had not wanted to refuse the match because the bridegroom held a good job in the irrigation department, and was very handsome and athletic too. Even now, after the double tragedy of her husband's sudden death and her father's prolonged illness, she was only twenty-two years old.

They crossed the overbridge, gave her train ticket and his platform ticket to the ticket collector, and made their way into the long queue outside the station for a three-wheeled auto-rickshaw. The line moved slowly.

'Do you know where the bank's call centre is?' she asked.

'Yes, it is in Siripuram junction near the university.'

'I've got an interview there the day after tomorrow at three in the afternoon.'

'How—' began Rehman and fell silent. He was embarrassed. He didn't think she knew any English and was fairly certain that a job in the call centre of a multinational bank would involve speaking English. She had been brought up in a small village by a childless couple who had bought her as a baby from a poor family, who already had six children and hadn't wanted to feed yet another girl, and adopted her. She had been educated in Urdu Medium and, as far as he knew, she hadn't studied past high school.

'The quality of mercy is not strained. What's in a name? That which we call a rose by any other name would smell as sweet. To be or not to be, that is the question.'

Rehman's jaw dropped and Pari laughed. He hurriedly closed his mouth and felt his ears turn pink and hot.

'Double, double toil and trouble, Fire, burn; and cauldron, bubble; Eye of newt, and toe of frog, Wool of bat, and tongue of dog,' she continued, with mischief in her eyes and looking as unlike an old witch as possible. 'Make my devar believe in his sister-in-law.'

Rehman was dumbstruck. Her knowledge of the Bard of Avon went far beyond his. He racked his brains until he remembered a line that had stuck in his mind a little deeper than others. 'Exceedingly well read . . . And as wondrous affable and as bountiful as mines of India,' he said finally.

'*Henry IV, Part 1*,' she said immediately.

'Subhan-Allah! Good God! What did you do? Devour the works of Shakespeare wholesale?'

The people in front of them had moved forward, opening up a gap, so they shuffled ahead dragging the suitcase and bag. Pari turned to him. 'Your cousin encouraged me to study for a degree by correspondence course soon after we got married. I chose English Literature as my major subject.'

'I can throw a stone here and hit ten English Lit. graduates and I bet you that not one of them can quote Shakespeare like you.'

She shrugged. 'I didn't see any point in doing something half-heartedly. But how come an engineer like you knows so much about Shakespeare?'

Rehman laughed. 'There are more things in heaven and earth, Pari-o, than are dreamt of in your philosophy.'

'Touché.'

'You've also got a very good accent – almost like an English mem. You didn't get the enunciation of a proper lady from a correspondence course.'

'BBC World Service. I couldn't leave the house for almost a year while abbu was ill, so I listened to the radio regularly. I knew that once abbu was no more, I didn't want to stay in the village. I decided to work in the city so I finished my degree and practised my English every day.'

Aruna inserted the point of the (new) letter opener into the corner of an envelope and slit it open. She took out the folded sheet from inside and smoothed it flat. A Christian client from Nellore had written thanking them because his daughter had found a match through their efforts. The bridegroom was an accountant from Nuzvid currently working in Kuwait on a good salary.

She gave the letter to Mr Ali, who read it and smiled. 'I remember the girl – she came over with her father a few months ago. They have been looking for a match for years but something or the other was always going wrong. I'm glad we were able to help.'

'I'll stick the letter on the wall there along with the photographs.'

'Aruna, I think we now have enough new Reddy-caste girl members to make a list.'

'Yes, sir. I'll type it up tomorrow. By the way, have you thought some more about buying a computer?'

Mr Ali put down his pen and looked at her. 'I just can't decide. It's a lot of money and I am not sure how useful it will be. I'm afraid that, after a few weeks, it will sit under a plastic cover, unused, like a bridegroom's turban once the wedding is over.'

'But, sir—'

'We bought a washing machine some years back. Madam used it for a month or so and then she gave it up. It was less work to get a washerwoman to do the clothes than to sort them, fill the machine, take the clothes out and hang them out on the line. So, it just occupied a corner under an old bedsheet, used as a shelf for clothes and books. It lay there for years until we got rid of it. I don't trust all this new technology. It always results in more work and is never quite as good as it promises.'

Aruna sighed. It was going to be difficult to convince Mr Ali. She admired him enormously but he could be such a fuddy-duddy sometimes. She noticed that most men became conservative and set in their ways as they got older. Her father, Mr Ali and her father-in-law were all similar – they didn't like change very much. They liked following a routine, meeting the same people, eating the same foods. Of them all, she had to admit that Mr Ali was the most open – probably because of the marriage bureau. Or maybe he had started the marriage bureau because he was the least set in his ways. It was difficult to say.

Just then, Rehman came out with the orphan boy, Vasu.

'Abba, we are going to the supermarket. Do you want anything from there?'

'Nothing,' said Mr Ali. 'Actually, yes. Get some dried fruit. Sanyasi was telling me about the dried figs that he had bought recently.'

'OK, abba,' said Rehman.

Mr Ali then surprised Aruna by saying, 'Rehman, what do

you think about us getting a computer here? Aruna wants it but I am not sure.'

Rehman scratched his head. His eyes met hers and she smiled at him. After a moment he said, 'I think that's a brilliant idea. A PC would help you enormously – you can filter on various conditions and typing the lists will be easier than on that manual clickety-clack.'

'Do you think so?' said Mr Ali.

'Absolutely! I know a man who builds PCs. I will swing by, on the way from the shop, and ask him to come and meet you.'

Rehman nodded to both of them and left with the boy. Aruna went back to her post, but she couldn't stop smiling. That was a lot easier than she had expected.

A few minutes later, Mrs Ali and a young woman came out. 'We are just going to the house opposite,' said Mrs Ali to her husband. 'We'll be about half an hour.'

'And after that, you won't have me under your foot, chaacha,' the young woman said. 'I can then play music loudly.'

'Don't be so sure, Pari,' growled Mr Ali. 'The old hag who will be your landlady will be living next door and she will be a lot stricter than me.'

The young woman laughed loudly – a throaty, open-hearted sound. Madam had told her that the young woman's husband was dead and Aruna had been expecting a serious, unhappy lady. Pari was the merriest widow that Aruna had ever seen in her life.

Soon after the two ladies left, the Hasan clan came in. This was the large family who had become members recently for their daughter. Aruna remembered the dark spot on Mr Hasan's cheek and scalp that looked like a map of India. She had to make sure that she didn't stare at it and be rude. Mr Hasan's wife, his brother, sister and his son had all come as well. Aruna was sure that the last time there had been another gentleman, but instead a fair young girl stepped forward shyly.

'Sania,' said Mr Hasan proudly.

Ha, the bride, thought Aruna.

They all found places to sit and Mr Hasan said, 'We've identified several matches and wanted to know if you have photos or know more about them than what is in the list.'

'All right,' said Mr Ali. 'Show us the matches and we will try to help you.'

Mr Hasan took out the list that Aruna had given him at their last visit. It looked creased, folded and as if it was falling to bits. It must have gone through a lot of hands for it to look so bad in such a short time, thought Aruna.

'We've marked out the ones we are interested in,' said Mr Hasan.

More than twelve names were circled with red ink. Mr Ali read them out. 'Sheikh Hussain, software engineer in Bangalore; Mohammed Rizwan, sales executive in Nestlé; Mirza Beg, central government officer . . . Syed Nizamuddin, assistant professor.'

Aruna went to their filing cabinet to take out the files. Mr Ali looked up at the family and said, 'You have a good choice here. I know that we have the photos of quite a few of them. I am sure that you will find the perfect bridegroom for your daughter from among them.'

'Inshallah, God willing,' said Mr Hasan. 'We've been looking for a while now but nobody seems to be quite right.'

Aruna took out the photos, referring often to the battered sheet of paper in her hand. 'We don't have photos for these two . . .'

Later that evening, after the last of the day's clients had left, Mr Ali closed the verandah gates behind Aruna. He went into the house and found Mrs Ali and Pari having a chat.

'It's interesting how women can talk for hours and still not exhaust their conversation,' he said.

Mrs Ali looked at him and said, 'What do all you retired men do when you meet in the evenings? And we don't stop our work to chat either. Dinner is ready if you want to eat.'

'Yes, I'm hungry. What about the two of you?' he asked, looking at the ladies.

'Hmm,' Mrs Ali said.

'I'll wait for Rehman and Vasu,' said Pari.

Mrs Ali relented. 'No, no. Let's eat now. Rehman said that he and Vasu will have some snacks while they're out and come back late.'

Pari and Mrs Ali set the table while Mr Ali went to wash his hands and less than five minutes later they had sat down for the meal.

'This dried shrimp fry with onion greens is different,' said Mr Ali turning to his wife. 'I don't think you've made this dish before.'

'Pari made it.'

Mr Ali smiled at the young woman. 'It's good.'

'Thanks chaacha. Ammi used to make this dish because we didn't often get fresh prawns in the village.'

They finished the meal, talking about Pari's parents – Mr Ali's cousins.

'Have you got the keys to your room?' asked Mr Ali.

'Yes, chaacha. We gave the old woman the first month's rent and she gave us the key.'

'How are you doing for money?' asked Mr Ali.

'A lot of people think that because I am a widow, I must be poor,' said Pari. 'I don't know what kind of joke Allah is playing on me, but for the first time in my life, money is not a problem. I got a settlement from your nephew's life insurance. I also get a widow's pension from his department. Most of abbu's money and lands went to pay for his treatment, but not as much as you might think, because once he came back home from the hospital, it didn't cost money to look after him – just strength and emotion.'

'It is not a joke, Pari. It is Allah's mercy. You did a great service –
looking after your father with such devotion. He is balancing the
scales of your life,' said Mrs Ali.

'No amount of money or comfort can outweigh the loss of a
loved husband,' said Pari.

'No, of course not,' said Mrs Ali. 'That's not what I meant.
I—'

'Why do you want to work?' interrupted Mr Ali, changing
the topic. 'Why don't you relax for a little while? You've had the
most horrendous year that any woman can have. If money is not
a problem, what's the hurry in looking for a job?'

Pari didn't reply for a moment, chewing slowly on the rice.

'You don't have to answer if you don't want to,' said Mrs Ali,
making eyes at Mr Ali. 'We don't have a right to ask you such
questions. It's your decision whether you want to work or
not.'

'Don't shame me, chaachi,' said Pari. 'Of course you have
the right to question me. After abbu and ammi, you are the
closest relations I have.' She turned to Mr Ali and said, 'You've
raised a valid query, chaacha. I was just thinking about how
to answer it. When my husband was alive, we had a very social
life. He was a popular man, full of joy – the soul of any
party . . .'

She stopped speaking and her eyes closed, her throat gulping.
A tear trickled down her cheek. Mrs Ali put her hand on the
young woman's arm. After a moment, Pari opened her eyes and
smiled at them.

'The pain is always there, waiting silently and ready to strike
me if I let my guard down, like a brown cobra in long, dry grass.
That's one of the reasons I want to start over – get a job and
be among people again. I have to keep busy. I've done my
mourning.'

Mrs Ali said to Pari, 'You've done the right thing – leaving
the small village. As long as you stay there, people will expect

you to dress in white and live an austere life with no fun or entertainment. You are still a young girl and you have much to enjoy.'

'Thank you, chaachi, chaacha.'

Even after dinner was long finished the three of them sat at the table, talking. The bell rang and they looked at each other.

'That must be Rehman,' said Mrs Ali.

'Let me check,' said Mr Ali, getting up from the table.

There was a smart-looking, short man with a trim moustache and a briefcase standing at the gate.

'Hello, sir. I am Venkatesh. Rehman sent me. He said that you were thinking of buying a PC.'

'Yes, yes, please come in.'

Mr Ali slid the bolt of the verandah gate and opened it. They both sat down on the sofa.

'What kind of PC are you looking for, sir?' Venkatesh asked.

Mr Ali shrugged his shoulders. 'Do you want a glass of water?' he asked.

The computer engineer looked surprised. 'Yes, sir. Water would be good.'

Mr Ali went inside, told the ladies who the guest was and came back with a glass.

Venkatesh took a sip and put the glass on the coffee table in front of him. He opened his briefcase and took out some glossy brochures. 'We can make almost any configuration you specify, sir. We are much cheaper than branded PCs. Also, if anything goes wrong, just give us a call and we'll come round on the same day and fix the problem. You won't get that kind of service with the big companies. Let's start with the basics. What kind of processor do you want? Intel Pentium or AMD?'

Mr Ali waved his hand.

'OK, Intel. Good choice, sir. But I forgot to ask you, do want a mini tower or a full tower?'

'What's the difference?' asked Mr Ali.

'There's not that much difference, sir. The full tower is more expandable.'

'That's good, isn't it?'

'Yes, sir. If you have the place to put it.'

'If you have the space, of course,' said Mr Ali, nodding slowly. 'Is it possible to put it away in the bedroom at night or when we go out? We have a bolt on the bedroom door to keep the servants out when necessary so it would be safe there.'

Venkatesh frowned, looking deep in thought. 'That's not really practical unless you get a laptop. But I wouldn't recommend that. They are more expensive and not as powerful.' He looked around and continued, 'You've got a good grille round here and PCs are big. It will be safe here.'

Mr Ali nodded. 'OK,' he said.

'Do you want a seventeen-inch monitor or a nineteen-inch one?'

'What's a monitor?'

'What a joke, sir. I mean the screen.'

'Oh, screen. Two inches can't make that much difference, can it?'

'You will be surprised, sir. Those two inches can make a lot of difference.'

'Right. What else?'

'We haven't even started yet. We still have to finalise the hard disk, memory, graphics card, motherboard.'

'I want a printer,' said Mr Ali. 'That's very important.'

'No problem. Inkjet or bubble jet?'

Mr Ali felt just as he did when he had opened an Arabic novel a long time ago. The alphabets were the same as in his native Urdu, but the words did not make sense. Here he understood almost every word the man was saying, but no sentence was meaningful.

'Look, Venkatesh,' he said. 'I don't understand all this high-technology stuff. I run a marriage bureau. There are lots of members and I want to put all their details into the computer and be able to search for them when a client calls. What is the cheapest computer that can do that?'

The computer builder nodded. 'Even our cheapest computer can do that, sir. But I think you should pay a little bit more and go for a slightly better model.'

'Why is that?'

'You will get more memory, the hard disk will be bigger, the whole computer will be faster.'

'I thought computers were very fast. I saw a programme once on TV and they were saying how computers can carry out millions of operations a second,' said Mr Ali.

Venkatesh laughed. 'They all do, sir. But to do anything meaningful, computers have to do several million instructions.'

'I also want to store photographs on the computer.'

'You need a scanner.'

'Do I?'

'Yes, sir. You do.'

Mr Ali sighed. He shouldn't have listened to Aruna and Rehman. There was no way he was going to make sense of computers or anything complicated like that at his age. It was well known that old dogs could not learn new tricks.

'I don't think—' he began.

Just then, Vasu pushed open the door and skipped in, straight through the verandah and into the house. Rehman came in after him, walking more slowly. He saw Venkatesh and stopped to greet his friend.

Mr Ali turned to Rehman. 'I don't understand all this computer, shumputer nonsense. I am happy with my files and my typewriter. Why do I need all these complicated things?'

'Nonsense, abba. You should move with the times – look at Vasu's grandfather. He is the same age as you and he is trying out new seeds and practices. If an illiterate farmer like him can do it, you can too.'

'All right. Then you talk to your friend and sort it out. I don't want to spend too much. Just make sure that whatever we get is not a waste of money.'

He left the two young men together and went back into the house.

CHAPTER SEVEN

'The house feels empty without the boy,' said Mrs Ali. She was in the living room with Rehman and Pari. Mr Ali had gone for a walk with his friends, leaving Aruna to look after the office. The sun had been hot during the day and the cool of the winter evening was welcome.

Rehman nodded. He had dropped Vasu off at his uncle's house at lunchtime and he was missing the boy too. Vasu had hugged Rehman and cried for several minutes until Rehman promised him that he would come and visit the village soon.

Vasu's aunt, the twelve-fingered young housewife, had said, 'If you come to the village for Sivaratri, the villagers are planning a big function. I am not allowed to tell you what it is, but it promises to be a lot of fun. We are also planning to be there at that time.'

Rehman finished his tea and set his cup aside. He said to his mother, 'I am going to the village in about four weeks, so I will see him then.' He turned to Pari and said, 'What time tomorrow did you say your interview was?'

'Three o'clock,' she said. 'But they asked me to come about fifteen minutes early to fill out some forms.'

'No problem. We'll leave by two-thirty.'

'Don't be too complacent. Give yourselves enough time. You can always go to a teashop if you are early,' said Mrs Ali.

The youngsters nodded in agreement.

'By the way, the planning permission has come through. The housing project can start now,' said Rehman.

Mrs Ali's face lit up. 'You've been unemployed long enough – when will you start the job, then?'

'Anybody would think you didn't like having me around the house,' laughed Rehman.

Mrs Ali waved her hand. 'Of course it's good to have you around. But a man without a job is only half a man.'

Rehman said, 'The contractor is waiting for an auspicious day. He said he'll have the pooja on Saturday and start the work on Monday.'

'What's the job?' asked Pari.

'It's a social housing project for poor people being built by an NGO charity. We'll be building simple houses for about one hundred families. The families have to pay a small amount of money and contribute some labour towards building the houses.'

The curtains parted and a man in his mid-fifties, sporting a neatly trimmed beard, walked in briskly. Rehman and Pari stood up and a chorus of salaam wa'laikums followed.

'Sit down, Azhar. Do you want tea?' said Mrs Ali to her brother.

'No, I'm fine. I wouldn't mind water, though.'

Pari jumped up and went into the kitchen. She came back with a silver glass of water. 'Here it is, maama. Old people like you need to take it easy,' she said, smiling to take the sting out of her words.

'Let it be known, young lady, that I took VRS – voluntary retirement from service because the department offered such a good deal. I am not old.'

'Oooh!' said Pari, stepping back. 'Did I touch a sensitive spot?'

Rehman laughed and Mrs Ali shushed them both. 'Show some respect for a man with silver hair,' she said, then clapped her hands to her mouth. 'Oops, sorry.'

'Did I come here to be insulted?' said Azhar, trying to look angry. He made as if to stand up.

Pari rushed over to him and pushed him gently back into the chair. She went behind him, massaged his shoulders and said, 'I was just joking, maama, and you became serious. Don't I even have the right to make fun of you any more?'

Azhar reached back to pat Pari's hand. 'OK, OK,' he said gruffly. 'Go and sit down. You cannot drive me away from my own sister's house.'

Pari went back to sit next to Mrs Ali and Azhar finished drinking the water. He put the glass down on the floor next to his chair and said, 'We are planning to go on Sunday to bring Nafisa home.'

'Finally!' said Mrs Ali. 'What time?'

'We'll leave straight after lunch so we can be back by four or so.'

'Is Nafisa all right now? What do the doctors say?'

Nafisa, Azhar's daughter, was just over five months pregnant. She had been married for almost six years and suffered two previous miscarriages. There had been panic when she had reported some bleeding a few weeks ago.

Azhar pointed a finger towards the sky and said, 'By the mercy of Allah, everything is fine. The doctor recommended bed rest for a week but she's given the all-clear now.'

'Alhamdulillah, thanks be to God,' said Mrs Ali.

'What's the plan? Will you come and pick us up or do you want us to come to your house?' asked Mrs Ali.

Azhar squirmed in his chair and looked uncomfortable. 'I'm sorry but the invitation is only for you, aapa,' he said to his sister, mumbling a little.

'That's OK. This kind of function is just for ladies anyway,' replied Mrs Ali.

Rehman noticed that Pari's face fell. Her fingers twisted the knotted fringes on the edge of her sari as if to tear them out. He realised with a rush what his uncle was saying and he looked up. 'You mean that Pari is not invited.'

His uncle took a deep breath and shrugged his shoulders slightly. His mother's face went stiff and stony.

Rehman stood up, his eyes glaring and pointing his right index finger accusingly at his uncle. 'Why is that, maama? Are you saying that Pari is not welcome because she is a widow?' he shouted.

Azhar did not say anything, but Mrs Ali jumped up. 'Rehman, how dare you stare angrily at your uncle and point a finger towards him? Have you no manners? Is that what you've learned from me – to disrespect your elders?'

Rehman looked at her furiously, but lowered his finger. 'Respect burn to ash,' he said.

'This function is only for married women,' said Azhar. 'It will be considered unlucky for a widow to be present.'

'Maama, what kind of ignorant talk is that? We are in the twenty-first century now. Surely you cannot believe something so ridiculous.'

Mrs Ali said, 'Rehman, I won't have you talk like that to your uncle. Go out of the room now before somebody says something they cannot take back.'

'But ammi,' said Rehman, gnashing his teeth in frustration.

Mrs Ali was still standing and she poked him in the chest. 'Now, Rehman.'

Pari stood up and touched Rehman slightly on the shoulder. He turned his head to look at the young widow. Her face was a mask. 'You heard your mother, Rehman. I don't want to go to the function anyway. I don't know Nafisa's in-laws.'

'That's not the point . . .' said Rehman, but let himself be guided out of the room.

As they went into the kitchen, Rehman heard Azhar say, 'I am

sorry, aapa. But what can I do? Praying for this day for so long
. . . Sentiment . . . Bad luck . . . Afraid . . .'

   Pari closed the door to the kitchen, shutting out the voice.

Aruna sat in the car with her eyes closed and her head stretched
back while the driver accelerated and braked alternately, honking
almost continuously in the heavy evening traffic. She wondered
what the shouting in Madam's house earlier had been about.
Both Rehman and his mother had sounded upset and it seemed
as if the new girl had been trying to pacify them. But they had
been talking in Urdu and she still couldn't follow the language
well. From what she could gather, it had been something about
an invitation by Madam's brother. But how can an invitation
cause such a ruckus? Aruna shrugged her shoulders. She had her
own life to think about.

   She got down from the car, smiling her thanks to Peter, the
driver, and went into the house. Her mother-in-law and the
obviously pregnant Mani were sitting on the sofa, watching a
cookery programme on the television. She greeted them and
went to her room to change. There was a neat pile of ironed
saris on the edge of the bed and she put them away in her
wardrobe. She opened Ramanujam's wardrobe to make sure
that his clothes had been done too. They were and she closed
the door, smiling – she was still not totally blasé about clothes
that somehow ironed themselves while she was out. It was
probably the best thing about being rich, she thought.
Except . . .

   The long, hot shower – the second of the day – felt wonderful. Aruna felt a little remorseful that she had spent so much time
in the shower. She should have gone into the kitchen to make
sure that the dinner was all prepared and ready to be served. She
hurriedly put on a comfortable mauve cotton sari, brushed her
hair and left the room.

   'Were you feeling dirty after working outside?' asked Mani,

smiling sweetly at her from the dining table where she was eating a yellow bundi-laddu.

Aruna flushed guiltily and went into the kitchen without answering. Shantamma was scooping the mixed vegetable curry from the pan into a serving dish.

'This is the last one, chinnamma,' she said, pointing to the other serving dishes on the worktop.

'Let me ask if anybody wants to eat right now. I'll wait for babu,' Aruna said, referring to her husband, Ramanujam.

Nobody except Mani wanted to eat so Aruna filled one plate and brought it out for her sister-in-law. Mani's son, Sanjay, came in and wanted to eat too. Aruna got another plate of food and asked her sister-in-law, 'Shall I feed him?'

Mani nodded, her mouth too full to speak. For once, Sanjay did not kick up any fuss and ate his food quickly before bolting from the room.

'Don't just let him go,' said Mani. 'He has to drink water.'

Aruna nodded and followed him with a glass of water. She caught up with him in the corridor and made him drink after a little struggle.

Mani was on the third course – yoghurt rice with lemon pickle – when Ramanujam came in, had a quick wash and sat down at the dining table. His parents joined them, and Shantamma and Kaka brought out the serving dishes. Aruna stood up, serving them all before sitting down next to her husband.

Mani said to her brother, 'I was so controlled when I was pregnant with Sanjay but now I am a glutton. I feel ravenous all the time. Is that normal?'

Ramanujam said, 'Every pregnancy is different – feeling hungry is quite normal. Maybe the baby will be a strong boy like Bhima from the epics.'

Ramanujam's mother said, 'I am sure it's not a boy. Look at how her skin is glowing and her complexion has really opened up. It's definitely a girl.'

Mani turned to Ramanujam. 'Do you think that's true or is it just an old midwives' tale?'

Ramanujam said, 'Where pregnancy is concerned, I wouldn't argue against old Indian midwives. They have a lot of experience, after all.'

They all laughed. Shantamma came out of the kitchen. Aruna pointed to her vegetable curry and signalled to Shantamma to check her father-in-law's plate. The maid nodded and ladled out a large spoonful of the curry for the old man.

Aruna turned to Ramanujam and asked, 'My mother said the same thing when my cousin was pregnant and she was correct. My cousin gave birth to a girl. Do you think it could be true or is it just coincidence?'

Ramanujam scratched his chin with his left hand and frowned in thought. 'It could be true. There must be more oestrogen or at least less testosterone in the body when the foetus is female.' He turned to Aruna and smiled. 'It's possible. By the way, I showed the head of the department the statistics I've been collecting about post-operative recovery periods after removing tumours that involve both mass and infiltration effect.'

Ramanujam had previously explained to her how some tumours caused problems simply because of the pressure they exerted by taking up space in the skull, while other tumours actually interfered with the brain structures, so she nodded in understanding.

'He was very interested and he thinks I should collect more information and present it as a paper at the Indo-German Neurosurgical conference in AIIMS later this year.'

'Your alma mater – the All India Institute of Medical Sciences? That's fantastic,' said Aruna. She looked at her husband proudly.

'The paper has to be accepted first. I'd better contact my old professor there. He is one of the organisers of the conference.'

'I'm sure it will be accepted,' said Aruna. 'If I can help in any way, just let me know – I can type the paper or something . . .'

Husband and wife smiled at each other, oblivious to the rest of the family.

'You look beautiful,' Mrs Ali said, looking at Pari on the following afternoon.

The young woman had just come over from her room across the road, ready to go for the interview. She was dressed in a dark maroon, almost black, salwar kameez. As usual, she was wearing no jewellery and her neck and ears were bare.

Pari shrugged. 'Thanks, chaachi, but what's the point? He's not here to see my beauty.'

Mrs Ali smiled sadly. To be a widow at such a tender age must be so horrible. 'I know, dear. But you can still look beautiful for yourself. Wait a moment; I have just the thing for you.' She went out and came back with a small plastic box. Opening it, she took out a chain with long, curved, interlocking links and matching earrings, made of oxidised silver. 'Here, put these on,' she said, handing them over.

Pari held them in her open palm and a look of wonder came over her. 'But these are ammi's. My mother had them for years. How did you get them?'

'When she died, I asked your father for a memento and he gave me these. Put them on. I think they've now come back to their rightful owner.'

Pari's eyes filled and she shook her head. 'I can't . . . I am not supposed to . . .'

Mrs Ali took one of the earrings and moved to Pari's side. She removed the screw from the top of the earring and brushed the hair behind Pari's ear.

'Silly girl,' she said. 'People would rather that you quietly crawled into a corner and disappeared. But you've already taken the big steps. You've moved out of the village and you are looking for a job when you don't actually need the money. What's a little silver jewellery? It's not even gold.'

Pari hugged Mrs Ali and held her close for a moment. Mrs Ali led her to a sofa and they sat side by side.

'It's OK, Pari. Don't worry about what people say. You are in a very unique situation. A woman is always being defined by her relationships – she is a daughter or a wife or a daughter-in-law. For good or bad, you are free – free to make what you want of life. Trust yourself, trust the values your parents have given you and trust the memory of your husband that you still hold dear, and you won't go far wrong.'

Mrs Ali tightened the screw of the earring through Pari's earlobe and said, 'The holes are closing up. Don't take these off for a few days and they'll open again.' She looked critically at the young woman. 'And stop crying now. You don't want to go red-eyed for your interview.'

Pari finished putting on the chain round her neck and Mrs Ali continued, 'You'll fit right in with the girls who work in those offices. They think it is some sort of fashion not to wear gold – as if they were poor girls whose parents can't afford the yellow metal.' She got up and said, 'Let me find out what Rehman is doing. Silly boy – he should have been ready about ten minutes ago.'

'That's the building,' said Rehman, pointing at the blue-glass-fronted building across the road.

'That looks so modern – like buildings you see on television in foreign countries,' said Pari. 'Do you really think somebody like me can get a job there?'

Rehman glanced at her and noticed that she looked nervous. She had been so confident until now, but the neat building with the clean lines in the posh Waltair Uplands area on the edge of the university had unnerved her. He looked at his watch.

'Come on; let's go for a coffee in Dutt Bungalow. There's a

lovely shop in the basement there and it's only twenty minutes past two. We've got plenty of time.'

They crossed the road near the roundabout. Pari looked at the multi-storeyed building filled with car showrooms, restaurants and shops. 'That's not a bungalow,' she said.

Rehman laughed. 'When I was a boy, this was a small house with a garden all round it.'

They walked down the stairs.

'Coffee, Pastries and Conversation,' said Pari, reading the sign above the café. She looked at him and pursed her lips. 'Nice!' she said. 'One wouldn't think it, looking at your jholi, but you know how to treat a girl.'

'What's wrong with my bag?' said Rehman, lifting the rough cotton sling bag that was hanging over his shoulder.

'Nothing,' said Pari solemnly and then spoiled the effect by giggling.

Rehman shook his head as he pushed the door open. At least she seemed to be forgetting her nervousness. Once they had ordered, Pari said, 'Let's sit outside. It's still winter.'

They took a small table outside the shop door and watched the traffic go past on the road high above them. Songs from Hindi films could be heard from speakers in the kebabri round the corner.

A young couple, probably university students, walked past on the road, talking closely, almost touching, engrossed in each other. Even a lorry honking loudly as it came to the roundabout did not disturb their concentration.

'Do you think their parents know that their children are in love?' asked Pari.

Rehman laughed. 'I doubt it. They'd probably be shocked.'

'Young people these days . . .' said Pari, shaking her head. Her earrings swayed gently with her.

'My dear naani,' said Rehman, 'stop talking like a grandmother. I doubt if you are more than a couple of years older than them.'

Pari turned towards him and gave him a look. Rehman felt a tingle up his spine; he had the feeling that this was how the Rani of Jhansi must have looked as she strapped her infant son on her back and got on to her horse to lead her soldiers against the British in the Sepoy Mutiny.

'Age has nothing to do with how many birthdays you've had, Rehman,' she said.

Rehman looked into the deep pools of her brown eyes for a long moment. 'You are right,' he said finally.

Pari nodded seriously and went back to her coffee.

Rehman chuckled. 'Some people are born old, others are old before their time . . .'

Pari smiled gently at him and Rehman's mirth vanished. 'Yet others have age thrust upon them.'

A few minutes passed in silence.

'Is somebody like me from a small village really eligible to work in a modern place like that?'

Rehman put down his cup and glanced at her. She seemed nervous again. 'Your qualifications are second to none. It doesn't matter that you come from Kovvur and not from Bangalore. You've worked hard and got yourself a degree in English and even learned how to speak it properly. What more do you need to work in a call centre?'

Pari looked away, staring into the distance.

'The dark silver goes well with your dress,' said Rehman.

Pari turned quickly towards him. Her right hand went to her neck and she rubbed the chain with her fingers. A blush stole over her cheek and she didn't say anything.

'What made you change your mind about wearing jewellery?' he said.

'Don't you think widows should wear ornaments?' she asked.

Rehman stiffened. 'I thought you knew me better than that,' he said.

Pari laughed and touched his hand. 'You are so easy to tease.'

After a moment's silence, she added, 'Chaachi, your mother, gave them to me just before we left. They actually belonged to my mother.'

They were silent, wrapped in their own thoughts for a while. The song in the background, coming from the kebab shop, changed:

There is a girl; beauty of the town,
She smiles and raindrops come tinkling down.
There is a boy; the city's most brave,
He laughs and the monsoon rolls in on a wave.

Pari stared at her coffee cup and her face took on a pensive cast. 'You know, not everything Shakespeare wrote makes sense. I agree with that song more than . . . Shall I compare thee to a summer's day, indeed. I wouldn't want to be likened to a hot, uncomfortable day instead of to a nice gentle shower!'

Rehman laughed. 'England is a cold country,' he said. 'A summer's day is probably quite good over there and girls might want to be thought of like that.'

'Whatever . . . There's another line from *A Midsummer Night's Dream* which I disagree with: O hell! To choose love with another's eye.' She looked up at him and said, 'Your cousin was chosen for me by abbu. I didn't even see him until after our wedding. He was the love of my life – always smiling, tall, handsome, kind. He brought me so much laughter, though in the end he made me cry.'

Rehman didn't know what to say and he stayed silent.

Pari continued, 'He used to add dollops of ghee to hot rice – he loved the smell and taste of it. I read in a magazine that eating fatty food can cause heart attacks, so I made him stop. We had so many arguments over it. He said that the food just wasn't as flavoursome but I didn't back down. That's what I regret the most. If only I'd known . . .'

They finished their coffees slowly. Finally, Rehman looked at his watch and said, 'Let's go.'

They climbed back up the stairs on to the road. A deformed man with a twisted spine dragged himself to them on a small-wheeled wooden cart and stretched out a hand, begging. 'Amma . . . Babu . . .'

The man's outstretched hand was swathed in bandages, the fingers gnawed to little stubs by leprosy. Pari took out a one-rupee coin from her purse and put it in his palm. The man transferred the coin to a small aluminium tumbler and saluted her.

'May God bless you, my lady, and grant you success,' said the crippled man, dragging his cart back into the shade of a low wall.

They crossed the road and went to the call centre. 'I'll walk down to the university library and work on my plans there,' said Rehman. 'Give me a call from your mobile when you come out and I'll be here in less than ten minutes.'

Pari nodded and walked towards the entrance. Just as she reached the door, Rehman called out, 'Best of luck.'

Pari turned, waved and went inside.

Rehman worked for over an hour in the quiet, slightly dusty reference section of the library, drawing up page after page of building plans. He had put his mobile phone on vibrate because he didn't want it to ring loudly in this sanctuary of books. He took it out to make sure it wasn't on silent by mistake and he had missed Pari's call. Finally, after another ten minutes, he put all his papers back into his cotton bag and got up from the comfortable chair.

The sun was bright when he came out from under the trees that surrounded the library. He walked up the road towards the call centre. His mother had prudishly told him to take an auto-rickshaw rather than his bike. She didn't think it would look good for Pari to be seen riding pillion behind a young man.

He sat down on a low wall by the roadside from where he could keep an eye on the call centre and watched youngsters on motorcycles, girls and older men on scooters, noisy three-wheeled auto-rickshaws, cars and buses go past. Fifteen minutes crawled slowly by. He had been growing steadily anxious when his phone vibrated in his shirt pocket. He took it out quickly but it wasn't Pari. It was his mother.

'She hasn't come out yet,' he said, when she asked him what was going on.

He put the phone away and wondered whether to take out his work. Before he could do so, Pari emerged from the building and he stood up. She walked slowly and elegantly towards him. When she was just a couple of feet away, she threw her arms in the air and whooped.

'I got it!' she shouted.

An older man in a khaki shirt and shorts, cycling past on the road was startled by her shout, wobbled alarmingly and fell off.

'Are you all right?' said Rehman to the man, going forward to help him. The cyclist got up, dusted himself down and glared at them angrily before cycling away. Rehman gazed after him in amazement at his rudeness.

He shrugged and turned towards Pari. He laughed aloud at the wide smile on her face and said, 'I knew you would get the job.'

They gave one another a high five.

Rehman and Pari got off the auto-rickshaw on her side of the road. 'Tell chaachi that I will come round later in the evening,' said Pari.

Rehman nodded and crossed the road to his own house. At the gate he saw a red car that looked familiar. He stared at it for a moment in puzzlement and then his heart raced in his chest. He pushed open the gate and rushed in. Nobody was on the verandah so he went into the living room.

'Hello, Rehman,' said Usha, smiling sweetly at him.

'What are you doing here?' he asked.

'*Rehman*,' said his mother. 'Is that the way you talk to a guest? Where are your manners?'

'Sorry,' said Rehman and gulped. 'I was just taken by surprise.'

Usha said, 'I wanted to meet your mother and ask her if she would like to do a follow-up interview.'

'I see,' said Rehman and looked at his mother.

She shook her head. 'I was telling Usha just before you came in that I didn't want to go in front of a camera again.'

'But, madam, you were so good. Your interviews gave me the best ratings I ever had.'

'The interviews were not popular because of me,' said Rehman's mother. 'It was because at that time I was a mother who was worried about her son. If you put me on camera now, I will be just another old woman and nobody will watch it.' She stood up. 'Do you want tea or coffee?'

'No, thank you, Madam. I am all right,' said Usha.

'Nonsense,' said Mrs Ali. 'Of course you will have a drink in our house. This is the first time you've visited us. Tea or coffee?'

'She usually drinks tea,' said Rehman.

His mother looked at him with a frown on her face. 'How do you know?' she said.

Usha said, 'In the village . . .'

Rehman said 'In the city . . .'

They stopped in confusion and looked at each other. Usha gave a small laugh and Rehman's face burned.

'Hmmm,' said Mrs Ali and walked out to the kitchen.

'Why did you come here?' said Rehman in an urgent whisper, sitting down in a chair opposite Usha and leaning close to her, as soon as his mother was out of earshot.

Usha shrugged. 'I just wanted to see your house and meet your parents.'

'You shouldn't—' he began, but before he could say anything

more, his father came in with a thin polythene bag of oranges and chikus. Rehman jerked back and continued in a more normal voice, '. . . have troubled yourself.'

Mr Ali did not recognise the guest. He just nodded and walked through towards the kitchen.

Usha giggled and Rehman frowned.

'You should have told me you were coming over,' whispered Rehman, again leaning closer to Usha. 'Have you told them that we've been meeting in the city?'

Usha frowned. She bent her head, almost touching his. 'Don't you want them to know?'

He flushed. The conversation was going into dangerous waters. He whispered back, 'It's not like—'

They heard steps and sat up straight.

Rehman said in a louder voice, '. . . she's a celebrity. Why do you want to put her on camera?'

His father walked back through the living room and on to the verandah.

'Why? I think it's a great idea if I can convince your mum to talk on camera. I am sure I can come up with a topic where the public wants to listen to an ordinary housewife's opinion rather than some politician with an axe to grind.' She reached out and touched his knee. 'Don't panic,' she said.

But Rehman could not relax. He brushed away her hand. 'Don't touch.'

Rehman wanted to say more but the front of her kameez had fallen forward as she leaned towards him and the sight of her creamy cleavage made his mouth dry and silenced him. He heard steps and leaned back swiftly, then glared at her. His mother came into the room with a tray. Rehman gave her a quick look and turned back to Usha.

She was sitting up straight in the chair again. Her smile convinced him that she was not unaware of the effect of her display on him. He could have strangled her.

'Did Pari get the job?' his mother asked him.

'Yes, ammi. She got it.'

'Who is Pari?' Usha asked.

'My nephew's widow,' Mrs Ali said. 'Rehman took her to an interview at the call centre.'

Pari nodded slowly.

'She is a remarkable girl,' Mrs Ali continued. 'If you look at the way she acts most of the time, you would not think that she had lost her husband. And Rehman's really helping by being very friendly with her, taking her round the town and everything.'

Usha raised her elegantly arched eyebrows. Rehman quickly said, 'Her nose is too long.'

'*Rehman,*' said his mother, using that tone of voice again. 'What a silly thing to say. Pari is an attractive girl, and when did you start commenting on a girl's appearance anyway, like some roadside Romeo?'

Usha left after half an hour, unable to convince Mrs Ali to appear on television. Mrs Ali was impressed. 'What an amazing woman,' she said. 'She has a wonderful career and drives her own car.'

Mr Ali, who had joined them, said, 'Modern, though.'

Rehman said, 'What's wrong with a girl driving a car? Nafisa drives a car too.'

'Nafisa drives only when her husband is sitting next to her,' said Mrs Ali. 'I didn't say there was anything wrong with it. But that dress! So tight around her body and she wasn't wearing a dupatta to veil her chest either. And those heels . . . Clack clack, they went outside. She must need a lot of practice to walk like that. I am sure I would fall down if I tried walking on high heels. They make her look tall but I wonder if they cause any back problems.'

'They were not particularly high heels, ammi,' said Rehman.

'I don't understand what's got into you today,' said his mother. 'You make that silly remark about Pari and now you are so defensive about Usha. Anybody would think there was some chakkar, relationship, between you two.'

Rehman gave an exaggerated sigh and walked out of the room.

'Very modern . . .' he heard his father say behind him.

CHAPTER EIGHT

On Friday, at four in the afternoon, Mr Ali was eating peanuts, steamed in their shells, while sitting on the verandah. Aruna, who had declined the snack, was looking through an album to identify the photograph of a man who had written to tell them that his marriage had been fixed elsewhere.

'What shall I do with this photo, sir?' she asked, once she had found the picture of a thick-haired man with a bushy moustache, and removed it from its plastic sleeve. The photo was clearly taken in a studio – the painting of the snow-covered mountain range in the background was a dead giveaway.

'Keep it under the pen box,' said Mr Ali. 'If he doesn't ask for the photo in a couple of months, we'll get rid of it.'

Aruna nodded and slid the photograph under the shoebox that held the pens, staplers, clips and other small items. She scrunched up the letter and threw it in the bin.

The front gate of the house opened and Mr Ali went into the living room, taking the bowl of peanuts with him. The clients came in before Mr Ali, sans food, returned to the office.

Aruna recognised Mr Hasan from the large map of India spot on his face. She thought of him now as Mr India, the hero from the eponymous Bollywood movie who fought against terrorists and idol-snatchers with the help of an invisibility bracelet invented by his late father.

'Hello, Mr In— Hasan,' she said, catching herself before she committed a serious faux pas.

'Good afternoon, beti,' he said heartily. 'I hope you don't mind if I refer to you as a daughter.'

Aruna shook her head and smiled. He turned and exchanged greetings with Mr Ali.

His clan – wife, brother, uncle, sister, wife's uncle and son – took up all the available room. Aruna noticed that the bride, Sania, had not come with them.

Aruna took out their file and gave it to Mr Ali. He turned to Mr Hasan and said, 'The last time you came, you said you liked several matches and were looking for their photographs.'

'That's right,' said Mr Hasan. 'But unfortunately, we didn't like any of them.'

'What?' said Mr Ali. He opened the file and took out a piece of paper. 'Sheikh Hussain, software engineer. He earns a very good salary.'

'I said no to that,' said Khalida, Mr Hasan's wife. 'I've heard that computer people go off to foreign countries and I don't want my daughter to leave us and go away to a far-off land.'

'Fair enough,' said Mr Ali. 'What's wrong with Mohammed Rizwan, sales executive in Nestlé?'

Mr Hasan's brother spoke up. 'What does sales executive mean? He's probably just going around selling coffee and milk-powder up and down the country. It'll be no fun for our Sania if her husband is going on tours all the time.'

Mr Ali shot a glance at Aruna. She shook her head impercepti-bly. 'What about Mirza Beg, the officer in central government?'

'We were very interested in that match,' said Mr Hasan. 'However, when we checked, I found out that even though he is well educated and has a good job, his father was just a peon in a private office. So I said no.'

'Surely it is even more to the young man's credit that he was able to overcome the limitations of his family circumstances and do well in life. I think you should reconsider.'

'No, no,' said Mr Hasan. 'It is very important what kind of background my son-in-law comes from. Who knows what kind of culture a poor family like that has? And my daughter? She will have to be family members with all these people. It is unthinkable.'

Aruna's eyes flashed. Even though she was now married into a rich family, she came from a poor one. Her parents and sister still lived in a small, one-room house with few comforts. 'Sir,' she said, 'You should not automatically assume that just because somebody is poor, they are boorish and uncultured.'

'Beti, you look as if you are from a wealthy family. You don't know how poor people live. They might be drunkards or beat their women or—'

A hot response came to Aruna's lips, but before she could say anything, Mr Ali held up a hand. Aruna subsided and dropped her gaze to her feet. She knew she looked sulky but she couldn't help it. The man's prejudice was just unbelievable.

'I think you are wrong, sir,' said Mr Ali. 'But I can appreciate your feelings. Let's move on. What about the assistant professor, Nizam? He lives locally and I've met him. He's a super boy. A total gentleman – and they are Syeds, very cultured.'

'Sania didn't like the idea of marrying a professor. She thinks he will be too serious.'

'What about the others? There were at least six others,' said Mr Ali.

'None of them was suitable. My brother thought two of them were not very good,' Mr Hasan said. He pointed to the lady sitting opposite and said, 'My sister here thought that three of the families were asking for too much dowry. We need to see more matches.'

Mr Ali thought for a moment, his eyes on the table. He then

looked up and said to all of them, 'I am glad that Sania is not here because what I am about to say might have hurt her. The way you are going about this whole exercise seems guaranteed to leave your girl unmarried.'

The entire family stirred like a muster of crows that had seen a seagull come into their feeding grounds.

Before they could say anything, Mr Ali raised his voice. 'I have gained some experience in this matter while running the marriage bureau, so listen to me.'

He stared at each of them until they lowered their eyes.

'You were very lucky that you saw so many matches. It is unfortunate but true that, in this country, Muslims generally are not as educated as people of other communities. Most Muslims are self-employed – they run shops or other small businesses. This is not surprising – most Muslims in good positions went over to Pakistan when the country was partitioned. Here you saw so many educated boys in good jobs and not one of them was suitable. Why do you think that is?'

Nobody said a word.

Mr Ali continued, 'If you saw another hundred matches, I can tell you that none of them will become your son-in-law. That's because there are too many people involved in the selection. They say that a camel is a horse designed by a committee and that's how you are trying to find a bridegroom for Sania. One of you doesn't like a boy's family, another doesn't like his job and a third vetoes yet another boy because he might move far away. You cannot do this. Each of you can have an opinion – after all, this is an important matter and you are all interested in Sania's welfare – but at the end of the day, it has to be one person's decision. Or, at the most, one person plus Sania.'

Mr Ali looked at Mr Hasan.

'Why don't *you* decide, sir? You can look for another year and not find a better match. So choose – of all the people you've seen in the past few weeks, who do you think is the best?'

'I don't know . . .' demurred Mr Hasan, wilting under Mr Ali's eyes.

'Choose,' said Mr Ali remorselessly.

'Umm . . . Rizwan, the sales executive in the multinational. He has a good job with excellent prospects. He is a very outgoing chap; easy to talk to and always cheerful. I've been to his parents' house and they are good people – devout but not fanatical. He is also an only son, so Sania won't have problems with sisters-in-law or other daughters-in-law.'

'What does your daughter think of him?'

'She hasn't met him but she liked the look of him from the photo. I know that she will get along well with him.'

'All right, then, why not Rizwan? If he and his family are agreeable, why not settle the matter?'

'But my brother . . .' said Mr Hasan, pointing to the man sitting in the other chair. 'He thinks Rizwan's job involves too much travel and that he is only a glorified salesman.'

Mr Ali turned to Aruna and said, 'Please take out Rizwan's file.'

Aruna found it and handed it to Mr Ali. He opened it and revealed the form that the young man had filled in when he joined. 'Rizwan earns thirty-five thousand rupees a month. Do you think he's just a salesman? And even if he is, how does it matter? We are all salespeople of one sort or another, anyway. If he earns well and can keep Sania in comfort . . .'

Mr Ali shrugged.

'I am not saying that you should make the decision right here and now. It is an important matter and you should give it due thought. But one of you has to stand up and take a decision after listening to all the available information.'

'How can I be sure that I am making the right choice?' said Mr Hasan.

'Whatever you do, there are no guarantees in life. What did our Prophet, peace be upon him, tell us to do when faced with a difficult problem?' said Mr Ali.

They all looked blankly at him.

'He told us to seek Istikharah – guidance – from Allah. The Prophet said that we should consult our friends and, if there is still no resolution, say a special prayer: Allahumma innee astakheeruka ... O Allah! I ask you for guidance through your knowledge ... For surely you have power and I have none. You know all and I know not. O Allah! If in your knowledge this matter be good for me, then ordain it for me, and make it easy for me, and bless me therein. But if in your knowledge, this matter be bad for me, then turn it away from me ...'

Mr Ali stood up and went round the table.

'It is simple, my friend. Think through what you can. Ask your friends and well-wishers for their thoughts; beyond that, put your trust in God. After all, what else can we mere mortals do?'

Mr Hasan stood up and hugged Mr Ali thrice as if he had just come back from a mosque. 'You are a wise man and you have opened my eyes.'

Aruna was clearing up the table that evening, ready to go home, when the gate opened. She looked out, wondering whether it was another client. After the Hasan family had left, five people had come in, four completely new and one existing member wanting to look at a new list. Three of the four had become members, which was something of a record, and Mr Ali had given her a hundred-rupee note as commission for four people, including one person who had become a member in the morning. She didn't want to deal with any more clients.

Her face broke into a smile when she recognised the visitor – her younger sister, Vani. She was probably coming straight from college because she was carrying books in the crook of her right arm.

'Hello, akka!' she said lightly and sat down on one of the chairs, unselfconsciously extending her legs, clad in a sky-blue, cotton salwar.

When Mr Ali poked his head out of the door to see who the visitor was, Vani pulled her legs in closer to the chair.

'Namaste, Uncle,' she said.

Mr Ali smiled at her and said, 'Have you decided to become a member, then?'

Vani smiled back, 'Not yet, Uncle. Not yet.'

Mr Ali laughed and withdrew, leaving the sisters on the verandah.

'What have you done to your hair?' asked Aruna.

'You noticed?' said Vani, pulling it forward over her shoulder. 'I got a perm and a cut. It's lovely, isn't it?'

'The wavy hair really suits you, but isn't a perm supposed to damage hair?' asked Aruna.

'It should be all right to do it once in a while,' said Vani. 'Do you remember Srishti, the girl from two doors down?'

'Yes, of course I remember her,' said Aruna, puzzled.

'She is doing a beautician's course and for practice she had to find five of her own people to be models. She asked me and I agreed. It was free.'

'Oooh!' said Aruna, wincing. 'A trainee beautician? I am not sure that's such a good idea.'

Vani waved her hand dismissively. 'She was supervised, so it was no problem. Besides, not all of us have Mr Money Bags for a husband.'

Aruna laughed. 'What can I do for you?' she asked.

'Do?' said Vani. 'Can't I just visit my elder sister at her work-place?'

Aruna bent her head and looked unblinkingly at Vani. After a moment, her sister laughed.

'You are right. I've come to ask for a hundred rupees.'

'Why?' asked Aruna.

'All my classmates are going for a picnic at Yarada Park on Thursday. I want to go too and I need the money for travel and food.'

'What about your classes?' asked Aruna.

'It's Republic Day, in case you had forgotten.'

'I did forget. I'll have to tell sir and not come in. Your brother-in-law will have the day off as well.'

'Doing anything romantic?' asked Vani.

'Shut up, silly girl,' laughed Aruna, blushing. 'Have you told amma and naanna about the picnic?'

'Not yet. I thought I'd ask you first.'

Aruna nodded and reached into her bag. She took out the crisp one-hundred-rupee note that Mr Ali had given her earlier and handed it to Vani. 'Will there be other girls at the picnic?' she asked casually.

'Of course,' said Vani. 'The whole class is going.'

'Tell amma that we might drop in on Thursday.' Aruna put the last file in the wardrobe and closed it. 'Do you want me to drop you off?'

Vani nodded. 'Just on the main road will do. You don't need to come down the lane.'

They said goodbye to Mr and Mrs Ali and got into the car. When she saw Vani's reaction, Aruna realised how much of a luxury having a car was. I must never become off-hand about my wonderful life and must always remember that these cars, servants, expensive clothes and multiple pairs of shoes are extravagances and not necessities, she thought.

A few days later, she came home from the office and sensed that something was wrong as soon as she entered the house – her mother-in-law didn't return her greeting and her sister-in-law, Mani, just made a sneering moue and turned away from her. Aruna sighed and walked through the hall to her room. She was sure that, whatever it was, the issue would blow over.

She opened the door to her room and went in. Strangely, the curtains were drawn and it was dark inside. When her eyes adjusted to the gloom, she saw a tall figure stretched out on the bed, covered by a sheet. Her heart gave a lurch as she pulled off the sheet to reveal her sleeping husband.

'What—' she began, touching his cheek. She jerked her hand back – his body was burning with fever.

Ramanujam opened his eyes and smiled wanly.

'When did this happen?' she asked. 'Why didn't you call me?'

Ramanujam waved his hand, but the effort left him weak and he closed his eyes again.

'Oh,' said Aruna, when she realised just how frail he was. 'What is wrong?'

'I think it is malaria,' he said, with his eyes still closed.

'Malaria!' she squeaked.

'I think so. I am feeling hot sometimes and then shivering with cold other times.'

Memories of her father falling ill rushed upon her. That had been a long and debilitating illness. Ramanujam was always so vital and healthy – she was appalled to see him laid low like this.

'Have you seen a doctor?' she asked.

'I am a doctor.'

The usual joke left her unmoved this time. 'No, you cannot diagnose yourself. Which of your friends would be best for this?'

'No need. I've already written a prescription and naanna has taken Kaka to get the medicines.'

'I think you should see another doctor. Shall I call Ravi?'

'He is an optical doctor. Good for cataracts but not for malaria.'

'Who else? What about Bhushan?'

'He is an ENT surgeon. Just leave it, Aruna, let me rest.'

'No, I cannot let you rest . . .' said Aruna.

The door opened and her mother-in-law walked in. 'What's going on? Why can't you let him rest?' she asked.

Aruna cringed – the sentence sounded very wrong when she heard it back from the older woman.

'It's not like that,' she said. 'I want another doctor to see him.'

'I don't need another doctor. I can tell what's wrong with me,' said Ramanujam.

'Of course you do, son. Take a rest.' Her mother-in-law crooked a finger and signalled to her to come out.

Aruna gave a last look at Ramanujam, pulled the sheet up to his shoulders and made her way slowly out of the room.

'I think he should see another doctor,' said Aruna as soon as they were in the corridor.

'Shhh!' said her mother-in-law and walked back into the hall. Aruna trailed behind her.

Mani was standing in the living room, hands on hips, and arching her back, pushing her already big stomach further out. Her face was strained and her eyes were screwed shut. She straightened up, opened her eyes and looked at them. 'Oof! My back feels like an elephant has been trampling all over it,' she said. 'Aruna, thanks for taking the time off from your high-flying career to look in on your sick husband.'

Aruna flushed, but didn't say anything. Even though Mani's comment wasn't reasonable, she couldn't help feeling guilty. After a moment she said, 'Somebody should have called me. I would have come straight away.'

'We were all too worried about my brother to call you,' said Mani.

Aruna's mother-in-law waved a hand at her daughter, but didn't admonish her.

Aruna said to her mother-in-law, 'Let's call another doctor to see him.'

'What, you don't trust my brother's medical knowledge now?' said Mani, looking outraged.

The older woman sighed and said, 'Stop it, Mani. I think Aruna is saying something sensible. I am sure it's difficult to treat yourself – like a cook checking the spices in a curry she's cooked herself.'

Mani turned away with a small flounce.

Aruna's mother-in-law continued, 'However, Aruna, it was not a good idea to go on and on about it with Ramanujam in the room. Men become babies when they are even a little unwell. They are not strong like us in that respect. And my poor son, he really is unwell.'

Aruna said softly, 'Yes, amma. I will call Ravi. I know he is an eye doctor but I am sure he'll refer me to somebody more suitable.'

Aruna went back into the room on tiptoe and peeped in. Ramanujam was sleeping, so she stole noiselessly in and came out with Ramanujam's mobile phone. She looked up Ravi's number and dialled it.

A hearty voice answered. 'Hi, Ramanujam! What's going on? Any more old widows going blind?'

Before they were married, Aruna and Ramanujam had come across an old villager whose eyes had been clouded over with cataracts and Ramanujam had sent her to Ravi to be treated.

'Hello, it's me, Aruna, his wife,' she said.

'Hi, Aruna. This is a surprise. What can I do for you?' he said, after a brief but noticeable pause.

'He is not well. He has a very high temperature and feels alternately cold and hot. He says it is malaria and doesn't want to see another doctor. Can you refer me to somebody who can see him?'

'Oh, I am sorry to hear that. How high is his temperature?'

'I don't know for sure but at least a hundred and two, I think, if not more.'

'How long has he had the fever?'

'He was fine this morning and even went to the hospital. He came back in the afternoon.'

'OK, no problem. Don't worry. I will talk to somebody and send them over straight away.'

'Thank you,' she said.

'No need for thanks. We'll have him up and running again in no time.'

She closed the phone and went in search of her mother-in-law and Mani. 'Ravi said he will send a doctor round soon.'

'Amma!' shouted Mani's son as he ran towards her.

'Don't jump on me, baby. My back's really hurting,' said Mani hurriedly.

'I got an aeroplane!' he said loudly, as his grandfather walked sedately in.

'Shh,' said Aruna, looking down at the young boy. 'Your uncle is not well and sleeping.'

'I know,' he said, just a little less loudly as Aruna winced. 'We've got medicines too.'

'Namaste,' said Aruna, turning to the old man.

He nodded in reply and handed her a small brown packet of tablets.

'I've arranged for another doctor to come. We'll show him the medicines before giving them to him,' said Aruna.

The adults sat around on the sofa while the boy held his plane above his head and ran round the room with it. Aruna wanted to change but didn't want to go back into her room in case she disturbed Ramanujam. This waiting was hard – she was getting more and more tense as the minutes ticked by.

Mani turned to her and said, 'Didn't you and anna go to your parents' house on Thursday?'

Aruna nodded in reply.

'He must have been bitten by mosquitoes there. I was wondering just how a healthy young man like him can get malaria.'

Aruna looked at her sister-in-law, shocked. Suddenly she got up and ran to the shrine in the corner. Behind her, she heard her father-in-law say, 'Mosquitoes are everywhere, Mani. Who can say where he got it from?'

Aruna stood in front of the idol of Venkatesha and bowed her head. She closed her eyes and folded her hands in supplication. The lamp by the idol, which was kept always lit, cast a warm, golden, flickering glow on her face. 'O Lord of the Seven Hills, Lord of the three worlds, please make my husband better.'

I was so silly, thinking that nothing could touch my happiness now. I, of all people, should have known better, she thought. When my father fell ill, there was no warning. He was ill for so long and wiped out our savings. But ultimately that led to a good end, she reminded herself. I was forced to give up my studies and take up a job. Otherwise I wouldn't have started working with Sir and Madam, and I would never have met Ramanujam. I would not have known his love or the luxury of this wealth. This, however, was different. No good can come of Ram falling ill, she thought.

She started reciting her favourite hymn that she always turned to in times of trouble – the Gayatri Mantram. 'Om Bhoor Bhuvasvaha . . .'

She could not complete the recitation – her mind was in too much turmoil.

'Lord, if my husband is cured, I will feed one hundred and sixteen Brahmins and poor people.'

Now that she had resolved on an action, her mind quietened and she completed the prayer. When she opened her eyes and turned back to the others, she was surprised to see that her mother-in-law had been praying too.

'He will be all right,' said her mother-in-law.

Aruna nodded. Their servant, Kaka, came in carrying a leather valise, ahead of a very dignified-looking man with thinning, grey hair and metal-framed glasses.

'Namaste,' said the man. 'I am Doctor Someswar. Ravi called and told me about Ramanujam.'

Aruna's father-in-law stepped forward. 'Thank you for coming so soon, sir. We are very worried. He is normally such a healthy boy . . .'

'No problem at all,' said the doctor. 'I retired last year but Ravi and Ramanujam are both old students of mine. Where is he?'

'In the bedroom,' said Aruna's father-in-law and began to move towards it. The ladies fell in behind the men.

'No, all of you stay here,' said the doctor. He turned to Kaka. 'You show me the way.'

They went in and closed the door. All the family members waited nervously in the hall. After some time, Kaka came out and Aruna asked him, 'What's happening?'

Kaka said, 'I don't know, chinnamma. The doctor asked me to get a flask with ice in it.'

He hurried away into the kitchen and Aruna exchanged a glance with her in-laws. They were all as puzzled as she was. A few minutes later, Kaka went back into the room with a stainless-steel thermos flask.

It was another five minutes before the doctor came out.

'What's wrong with him, doctor uncle?' asked Aruna.

'I am not sure,' the old doctor said, frowning. 'He is presenting many of the symptoms of malaria but he is not perspiring and his cold phases are not as long lasting as I would expect.'

'Do you think we should give him these medicines, doctor?' asked Aruna, showing him the anti-malarial drugs that had just been bought.

The doctor looked at them and shook his head. 'These medicines can have nasty side-effects, so I wouldn't use them just now. First, I want to find out what's wrong with him – I've taken a blood sample.'

The doctor tore a sheet from his prescription pad and gave it to Ramanujam's father.

'The sample is in the flask. Take it to a diagnostic laboratory and give them this paper. I've written the tests that I want carried out.'

Ramanujam's father nodded and took the prescription. 'What – fees . . .' he said hesitantly.

Doctor Someswar waved him away. 'Your son is an old student of mine. How can I charge him anything?'

Aruna came forward and, bowing to him, said, 'Thank you, Uncle.'

The older man patted her head. 'God bless you, my daughter. Be brave.'

CHAPTER NINE

Five evenings later, Rehman came back from work before six and his clothes were red with dust.

His mother was in the kitchen, scraping the small, light-green spines off bite-sized aaakaakarakai. With their tough skin and big, semi-hard seeds, they were not Rehman's favourite vegetable. His mother noticed the look on his face and pointed to a roughly tied, green-leaf packet sitting on an out-of-shape aluminium lid. 'Your father got meat from the butcher.'

Rehman smiled. The spiny vegetable mixed with mutton made a good curry. 'I am quite dusty. I'll take a bath and then go out, ammi,' he said.

'You will come back for dinner, won't you? Pari will be here and so will Nafisa and her family,' said his mother.

Rehman nodded. 'I should be back by eight or so.'

When he came out of the bath, Pari and Mrs Ali were talking in the living room.

'Hi, Pari,' he said.

Pari looked him up and down and said, 'Are you really going to wear that orange-brown checked kurta with the jeans?'

Rehman looked down at his long, ethnic shirt. 'What's wrong with it?' he asked.

'Everything,' she said.

'Leave it, Pari. I've tried to tell him many times but he just doesn't care. His father is the same, but at least *he* listens to me,' said Mrs Ali.

'How's your job going?' he asked Pari, to change the subject.

'I am still in training. There are so many products,' she said.

'What do you mean by products?' asked Mrs Ali. 'I don't really understand what you people do in a call centre.'

'When customers need help with their banking, they call us,' said Pari.

Mrs Ali thought about it for a moment and then said, 'But why don't they just go to their branch and ask somebody who knows about their account?'

Pari laughed. 'I guess it is more convenient to pick up a phone than go to a branch. And we handle all sorts of queries, not just bank accounts. Do you know how many different kinds of insurance there are?'

Mrs Ali shook her head.

'There is life insurance, of course. But there's also buildings insurance in case your house burns down, contents insurance in case you get burgled, health insurance in case you fall ill, pet insurance in case your dog or cat becomes sick, even insurance to pay off your loan if you lose your job or fall ill.'

Mrs Ali shook her head. 'Life must be so complicated and expensive if people have to take out loans and then insurance on top to pay it off if they cannot.'

'That's the modern world, ammi,' said Rehman. 'Not many people are as lucky as you that they can buy land and build their house without taking out a loan of a single rupee.'

Pari said, 'The other day I was listening in to some customer calls and a woman from London rang in. Young – twenty-six years. She asked us to remove her boyfriend from her car insurance.'

'Boyfriend?' said Mrs Ali.

'Yes,' said Pari. 'She said she had broken off with him and he wouldn't be driving her car any more.'

'Did she sound ashamed at all when talking of boyfriends and breaking up with them?'

'No,' said Pari. 'She was very matter-of-fact.'

'Tauba,' said Mrs Ali, 'God forbid.' She crossed her hands and touched her right cheek with the fingers of her left hand and left cheek with her right hand. 'Not just in money – but their lives must be so complicated in personal matters too. Find a boyfriend, break off, find another one. It must be so stressful. Thank God we don't have to go through that repeated struggle.'

Rehman laughed, feeling a bit guilty. 'Right,' he said. 'I am off. See you in a couple of hours.'

Ten minutes later, Rehman managed to find an empty spot to park in a row of two-wheelers and went into a café. He barely had time to order a cup of tea before Usha walked in.

'Sorry, I am late,' she said. 'It is getting more and more difficult to park a car nowadays in the city.'

'I've just arrived myself.'

Rehman called over the waiter and ordered another cup of tea. 'How's your job going?' he asked.

'So-so. I need another scoop or human-interest story. When are you starting another campaign?' she asked.

He laughed. 'No campaigns for me. I've just started working on a housing project.'

'How is it going?' she asked.

Rehman was distracted by her smile. For some reason, the image of serried white cirrus clouds against a deep blue sky came to his mind.

'What is it? Have I got something on my lip?' She touched her upper lip with her finger.

'No, no. I was just thinking of clouds.'

'Clouds?' The doubt in her voice was clear. She shook her head and said, 'Anyway, that shirt looks horrible. Let's go to a shop – I'll choose something better for you.'

Rehman waved his hand. 'Don't worry about it. It's not important. What—'

Usha cut in, interrupting him. 'Not important? Don't be silly. Nobody will take you seriously if you don't look the part. Come on, let's go.'

'Where?' he asked, not rising from his chair, even though she had.

'Khan's is just opposite. Let's go there.'

They came out of the café and strolled down the road before crossing it hurriedly, dodging three-wheeled auto-rickshaws, two-wheelers and an overloaded bus leaning to one side from the weight of the passengers hanging off the exits. The doorman opened the glass door to the shop as they reached it.

Neither of them noticed a pair of eyes across the road, following their progress with interest. As soon as they entered the shop, the man took out a mobile phone.

'Sir, there's no doubt . . .'

'What do you want, sir?' asked a young salesman as soon as Rehman and Usha walked up to him.

There were no other customers and the salespeople were huddled in a couple of groups, chatting.

'Shirts for the gentleman,' said Usha, before Rehman could reply.

'This way, sir, madam . . .'

He took them to another room towards the back and turned to Usha. 'For office use, madam, or casual?'

'Show us both,' she said.

'What size, sir?' asked the salesman.

Rehman shrugged. 'I don't know,' he said.

The salesman took out a tape and measured Rehman's shoulders, nodding to himself. The room was large with counters along three walls. Though there were air-conditioning ducts along the ceiling, they were silent; the shop was very warm and smelled of fabric and new textiles. The salesman switched on a pedestal fan standing in one corner and its blades started revolving loudly.

'That feels good,' said Usha, standing in the breeze of the fan.

The salesman pulled out a number of shirts from a shelf along the wall and spread them out on the counter. Usha felt one of the shirts between her fingers and said, 'Pure cotton only.'

'No problem, madam. Come behind this counter,' said the salesman, pointing to the far wall.

He pulled out some more shirts and Rehman looked at one of the price tags. 'Fifteen hundred rupees? You must be joking. I never pay more than three or four hundred rupees for a shirt.'

'Yes, I can see that,' said Usha. 'My treat – let me pay for it.'

'That's not the point,' said Rehman.

'The point is that clothes make a difference,' said Usha. 'People take you more seriously if you dress well.'

'They shouldn't—' said Rehman.

'But they do, Rehman,' said Usha. 'You cannot always see the world as it ought to be. Some things just are and you have to take them as you find them.'

Rehman shook his head, but couldn't think of an answer.

She turned to the salesman. 'Do you have any T-shirts?'

'T-shirts? I've never worn a T-shirt,' said Rehman.

'I know. That's why I want to buy you one. I think you'll look good in a T-shirt.'

The salesman pulled out several from an open cupboard and spread them out on the counter – bright blue and pale yellow, plain and stripy, with and without collars.

Rehman looked unhappy.

'This looks good,' Usha said, picking out a pale T-shirt with dark stripes.

'No way!' said Rehman. 'I am not wearing that.'

'Why not?' Usha said.

'Madam is right, sir. It is very good. This is the latest fashion. All college students are now wearing T-shirts like this,' said the salesman.

'Fashion, pah!' Rehman said.

Usha waved to the salesman, asking him to leave. He looked at her and she stared back at him until he dropped his gaze. 'I will be in the front. Please call me when you want to see more clothes.'

When they were alone in the room Usha turned to Rehman. 'Right, why is this not suitable?'

'I don't know. It's just not me.'

'I do understand, Rehman. It's different from what you normally wear. But you are a young man – be adventurous.'

Rehman shook his head. 'No thanks,' he said. 'I am happy with my clothes and don't see any need to change. If you want to buy me a shirt, let's go to Khadi Bhandar and we can get one made from hand-loom cloth. That way, we'll be helping an artisan too.'

'You already have shirts like that – you are wearing one. I want something different . . .' Usha said and trailed off in mid-sentence.

'Yes?' said Rehman.

'That's the problem, isn't it?'

'What problem?'

'That's it. You think that a hand-loom shirt in rough cotton is Indian but a fine T-shirt is not.'

'Well . . . It's true, isn't it?' said Rehman.

'That kind of thinking is so old-fashioned, Rehman. Gandhi asked people to avoid machine-loom cloth during the Independence struggle because it was being imported from Manchester but that was before you and I were born. Look at this,' she said and showed him the label on the collar of the T-shirt.

The manufacturer's name, Saffron Colours, was printed in big letters. Below it, in smaller letters, it said, Made in India.

'Our country is one of the biggest cotton growers in the world, and as far as I know, we import only a small fraction of our total use. So, the black soil, the monsoon rain, the farmer who planted the seeds and toiled in the hot sun, the bulls that pulled the plough, the croppers who picked the cotton, the workers who ran the mill, the tailors who stitched the shirt, the driver who got it from the factory to here, this shop's owner, the salesman . . .'

Usha stopped speaking for a moment. Her cheeks were rosy and, despite the fan's breeze, her forehead glistened with perspiration.

She continued, 'Every single element in the chain is of this land, so how is it any less Indian than the rough kurta you are wearing?'

Rehman stared at her.

'Well?' she said, impatiently after a moment.

'I love you,' he said finally.

'Just because Gandhi . . .' she began and stopped suddenly. 'What did you say?' she asked, her voice a high-pitched squeak like the thinnest string of a sitar.

'I love you,' he repeated.

'What are you talking about?'

'You . . . and me,' said Rehman. 'Will you marry me?'

Usha looked around wildly but there was nobody else in the big room. She faced Rehman again.

'Don't be silly,' she said.

'I am not being silly. I am proposing,' said Rehman. 'I want to marry you and live with you for ever.'

Usha looked suspiciously at him for a moment and then smiled. 'Yes,' she said. 'Yes, yes, yes!'

He took her hand in his hand and marvelled at the soft, smooth feel of her skin. Her face was as bright as the full moon and she was laughing. She caught his eye and blushed.

'Let's go,' she said.

He nodded and released her hand. They walked out of the shop. When they were out on the side of the busy road, she said, 'I promised my mother that I'd be back for dinner. I have to go.'

Rehman nodded. 'Me too. Let's meet at the beach tomorrow evening.'

She nodded. 'That would be lovely,' she said and then laughed. 'You got your way after all.'

'What?'

'You didn't buy the T-shirt.'

He laughed with her as they crossed the road side by side, dodging the traffic, happy as only a pair of young lovers together can be.

Usha waved to Rehman from inside the car and drove away. She couldn't stop smiling. It was probably the happiest day of her life – even happier than the day when she had been eight years old and her father had agreed to her request and brought home a puppy.

She negotiated the busy traffic at the main bus station complex and sped up on the Rama Talkies Road beyond. She wondered how to tell her parents – not just that she was opting for a 'love' match but also that Rehman was not from their own caste – in fact, he was not even a Hindu. She would have to make sure her father was in a good mood before she broke the news.

Still, it was exciting. Rehman was a fantastic guy – sure, his clothes sense was horrible, but she could sort that out. The proposal had come a bit out of the blue – they had been meeting each other regularly for only a short time. She had been aware that her feelings for him were deepening but she knew that there would be opposition to the match from both families so she was being cautious about letting the relationship develop. But the moment Rehman had declared his love, all her own doubts had disappeared in a flash. She was surprised that Rehman had moved so quickly but, hey, that's what I love about him, she thought. His heart leads him and he doesn't stop to think with his head.

Usha parked the car and walked towards the house, trailing her hand over a basil plant and skipping up the steps. The 'Night Queen' in the corner of the front garden was just starting to fill the air with its powerful, sweet, perfume. Later on, the fragrance would be sickly strong, reminding her of the time when she ate too many mangoes in one sitting, but Usha loved the way it smelled now. Her senses were heightened tonight. She could hear the low talk and the jingle of the pots used by the worker family who lived in a shack under the banyan tree on the foot-path outside. They pressed clothes on a cart with a heavy coal-fired iron for a living.

She looked over the fence at the forlorn house next door. Normally, the sight of it sucked away some of her happiness, but this evening it had lost its power to reduce her joy. The mad-eyed man who lived there was standing on the verandah, gazing straight ahead like a granite statue. He and his dotty wife were the only occupants of the large bungalow. They had no servants and their garden was overgrown with weeds, luxuriant creepers and out-of-control fruit trees.

The moon was a couple of days past full and high up in the sky, flooding the gardens with a silvery light. She walked into the house through the open doors and saw her parents sitting on the sofa facing her. Lightly she called out, 'Hi, Mum. Hi, Dad. Ready for dinner? I am starving.'

Her mother would not meet her eyes while her father was glowering at her.

'Where have you been?' he asked.

'Just out meeting a friend,' she said, shrugging. She wondered what her father was upset about. This was obviously not the time to tell them about Rehman's proposal and her acceptance.

'Which friend?'

A tiny warning bell started ringing in her head, but she didn't want to lie to her parents. 'Somebody you don't know,' she said, moving to her bedroom. 'Let me change into something more comfortable for dinner.'

'Stop right there, young lady,' said her father, standing up. 'Don't think that we are blind already. We know where you've been and who you are seeing.'

Usha turned back. This was not the way she would have chosen to bring up the topic but there was no help for it. 'Yes, naanna,' she said. 'I've been to meet Rehman. He's a fantastic man and I want to marry him.'

'Ohhh!' moaned her mother.

'Shameless hussy,' roared her father. 'How dare you talk like that in front of your parents? Is this what your education has taught you?'

'What is there to be ashamed about?' said Usha. 'Rehman loves me and I love him. He has asked me to marry him and I've said yes.'

'This family has a reputation. When I walk on the street, nobody dares raise their eyes to my level. People come to me, asking for advice. I will not let you ruin the name that we have in this town with your brazen activities.'

'Naanna, don't be so feudal. What you think of as respect is just fear – fear of your money, fear of your connections and fear of your temper. Well, I am not afraid of you,' she said, jerking her head back to dislodge a lock of hair from her face.

'No fear? I'll show you something to be scared about,' said her father in a strangled voice. His face was mottled with strain and his Adam's apple convulsed up and down. Usha shrank back before his anger and wondered whether she had pushed him too far.

He rushed towards her and grabbed her arm above the elbow in his right hand. Time seemed to still as she looked at her father in horror while he slowly raised his left hand to strike her. Her mouth opened in an O, but no sound came out. Even when she was a child, he had never hit her – leaving corporal punishment to her mother – and she could not believe what was happening.

'Husband . . .' Her mother's voice rang out.

Her father seemed to come to his senses – the wild look left his eyes – but he did not let go of her arm. He turned to Usha's mother and said, 'You shut up. It's entirely your fault. If I had not listened to you and let her go to work for that television channel, we wouldn't be having this tamasha today.'

Yes, thought Usha. The whole scene was rather like a drama. Her mother looked as if she was trying to meld into the sofa, cowed by his anger. Her father turned back to Usha and wagged his finger in her face, dragging her deeper into the house.

'Where are you taking me?' she said, trying but failing to dig her heels into the hard marble floor. Her mother followed them, making futile, useless gestures with her hands. Usha noticed the way her mother's greying hair hung lifelessly. Amma looks like a scared bird, she thought, surprised to be thinking about her mother when she should be concerned about her own fate. Strangely, she did not feel personally involved. It was almost as if this could not be real. It might be happening to a character in a movie.

The procession came to a stop outside Usha's bedroom and her father kicked the door open. He pushed her with surprising strength into the room and shut her in. By the time Usha recovered her balance and went to the solid teak door, she heard the squeaking noise of the iron bolt being drawn across it. Normally used to keep servants out, it would now be used to lock the daughter of the house in.

Usha heard a final clang as the bolt banged home against the wood. She pushed the door but her puny, human strength was no match for its inanimate solidity. She banged her fists on the door, to no effect.

She heard her mother say, 'What are you doing? She hasn't had dinner, the poor girl.'

She could hear the fury in her father's voice as he said to her mother, 'Let her go hungry – her lard might dissolve and lower her passions a bit.'

Usha cried out, 'Let me out, naanna. Don't do this.'

'You stay in that room and think about your family too instead of just about yourself.'

'How long?' she said in a softer voice.

'Until you come to your senses – as long as it takes.'

She heard footsteps moving away. Her father was saying, 'You stay away from that room. Nobody'll be worse than me if she leaves there, understand?'

'Food,' she heard her mother say.

'Only when I am here and only when I say so.'

Usha went to sit on the bed. She looked out through the iron bars of the window – it was dark outside but she could hear the noise of traffic. The sound of a cricket came from somewhere in the garden, calling out to its mate. That insect will probably have better luck than me, she thought, realising that her mobile phone was in her handbag. She could remember the exact spot where she had put her bag down on entering the house – on the small sofa in the living room, on the other side of the door.

A thought came to her. She suddenly jumped up, ran over to her table, pushing off papers and books until she dug out the black telephone extension from underneath the mess. She started dialling even before the handset reached her ear. She waited almost a minute without breathing before it hit her that the silence was final. The phone was dead. She traced the wire and found it plugged into its socket in the wall. What had her father done to kill the phone?

'Aargh!' Usha lifted the phone in both hands and threw it against the wall where it bounced with a crash. She had taken this incarceration lightly, almost like a joke, thinking that she could escape any time she wanted, but now a cold horror gripped her heart and she felt breathless. What if this was serious? What if she couldn't leave?

It was almost half an hour before she recovered enough to look around the large room that had been hers since they had moved into this house four years ago. It was now her prison: a fairly luxurious one, she acknowledged – with its table and chair, air-conditioner, fan, a queen-sized bed, wardrobe full of clothes, en-suite bathroom and shower. The servant maid had left a carafe of water as usual by the bedside cabinet earlier in the evening, so she wouldn't go thirsty, at least.

Usha changed into a loose cotton kaftan and lay down on the bed. She tried to recapture some of the early-evening mood. Only Rehman would propose to a girl when she was haranguing him about nationalism, she thought. She smiled at the memory. She wondered when she would see him again. She suddenly remembered that she was supposed to interview the mayor tomorrow about the beach festival that the municipal council was organising later in the month. She had to get word to her controller – he was an MCP, keeping up a low-level murmur of complaint about the unreliability of female staff. If she didn't call, her working life would be miserable for months afterwards.

She heard a scratching on the door a couple of times before she realised what it was. She jumped up from the bed and padded over to it. 'Who is it?' she asked.

'Shhh! Not so loud,' whispered her mother, from the other side.

'Where is naanna?' she asked.

'Your father is sleeping. How are you?'

'I'll feel even better if you open the door,' Usha said.

'I can't do that,' said her mother. 'How could you do this, Usha? A Muslim, of all people. If he had been a Hindu, even of a different caste, I could have talked your father round, but now—'

'How long will you keep me in this room? I am an adult and I can make my own choices. I am going to marry Rehman and that's it. This is the twenty-first century and you cannot stop me.'

She could hear her mother sigh. 'You take after your dad – both of you are as stubborn as a pair of a washerman's mules.'

'Amma, before I forget – do me a favour. Call my colleague, Bhavani, and tell her that I can't come in tomorrow. It's important.'

'I can't,' said her mother. 'Your father has pulled the phone line out of the wall.'

'Use my mobile.'

'Number?'

'In my phone, look up Bhavani's name.'

'OK. I'll tell her that you are not well.'

They were both silent for a moment.

'How did you all find out anyway?' asked Usha. 'I was going to tell you at the proper time, not like this.'

'Narsi told your father. He dressed it up in high-sounding words – said that he had eaten our salt and it would be disloyal if he allowed shame to come on our family by being silent – but he was just sucking up.'

Narsi, the wife-beating slime ball! She would sort out their driver if it was the last thing she did. With that thought to fill her belly, she went to bed.

CHAPTER TEN

The previous five days had been a sore trial for Aruna. She had informed Mr Ali that her husband was ill and she needed to stay at home. The first couple of days, Ramanujam had been confined to bed and had needed her support even to go to the bathroom. It had been a relief when his doctor, the old professor, had looked at the test results and told them that Ramanujam did not have malaria; he had a viral infection that needed to run its course.

After that, Ramanujam had been able to come into the living room and sit on the sofa, but was too weak to do anything but watch the family continue their activities round him.

'Drink this fresh-lime juice,' Aruna said, sitting down next to Ramanujam with a tall, frosted glass.

'Not thirsty,' he said.

'Please drink it,' she said. 'It's got both sugar and salt and is good for you.'

'I said no, didn't I?' he snapped at her.

'Sorry,' she said in a small voice, involuntarily withdrawing from his unaccustomed anger. 'I'll leave the glass here in case you want it later.'

He sat glowering on the sofa, saying nothing.

I hope he gets better soon, she thought. He is as irritable as a bear plagued by buzzing honey bees.

Aruna went into their bedroom, where she saw Sanjay, Ramanujam's sister's son, sitting at the table.

'Hello! What are you doing in here?' she asked.

'Nothing,' said the boy, quickly jumping away from the table.

Aruna frowned and went to where he had been sitting. She couldn't see anything obviously wrong and she turned back to Sanjay. His hands were behind his back and she said, 'What have you got in your hands?'

'Nothing,' he said, quickly.

'Sanjay, show me your hands.'

'I didn't do anything,' he said.

'Show me your hands,' she said, her voice rising a little.

The boy slowly brought his hands into view. He was holding Ramanujam's fountain pen. She took it away from him and said, 'Your uncle keeps important papers and other things on that table. You are not to come in here and disturb anything. Do you understand?'

Sanjay nodded stiffly and went out of the room. She sighed and put the pen away. She had forgotten what she had come into the room for and she looked around, hoping that the sight of something would remind her. Suddenly, she heard a wailing noise from outside. Aruna rushed out and was shocked to see Sanjay crying.

'What happened?' she asked. 'Did you fall down?'

He ignored her and continued weeping. Ramanujam and his parents came running over. Even Sanjay's pregnant mother came over, walking as quickly as she could.

'What is it, babu?' she said and the boy hurled himself into his mother's arms, sobbing.

Ramanujam looked at Aruna quizzically. She shrugged and mimed, 'I don't know.'

He nodded and turned to Mani. Sanjay's crying reduced to

the occasional sniffle when his mother promised him a chocolate.

'What is the problem, babu? Why did you cry?' she asked again, smoothing his hair with her hand.

'She!' he said rudely and dramatically pointed a chubby finger at Aruna. 'She shouted at me and told me not to go into her room.'

Everybody looked at her as if she was an evil hag and Aruna clamped a hand over her mouth, shocked.

'Did you say that, Aruna?' asked Ramanujam.

'Yes, but . . .'

Ramanujam shook his head and turned back. She looked at his parents but they wouldn't meet her eyes. Mani's eyes blazed like Lord Shiva's angry third eye that was reputed to reduce anything it looked at to ashes.

'*Your* room?' she hissed. 'How dare you?' She turned to her brother like an angry cat. 'Why are you just standing there like a stone idol? Your wife insults me and my son in my own parents' house and you have no words. It is true what they say – a woman is a guest in her father's house. Is this what all our shared childhood has come down to? This . . . this . . .' Mani's bosom heaved and tears came into her eyes. 'This two-bit woman who has come here less than a year ago dares to speak like this.'

'Mani—' said Ramanujam.

Mani turned away and led Sanjay out. Aruna stood still for several moments. 'I—' she then began.

'Leave it, Aruna. Don't say anything,' he said. His bleak voice cut through her, like a thorn through a banana leaf. He got up and went back into their room, closing the door behind him, leaving Aruna alone and miserable in the rich surroundings. The only sound was the whirr of the ceiling fan, going round and round, just like her thoughts.

The next morning Usha woke later than usual, after the curtains had given up their fight to hold back the bright sun. She looked at the clock and jumped up into a sitting position on the bed, annoyed that the servant maid had not come in to wake her up. Her feet touched the cool marble floor before she remembered the events of last night.

Had Rehman really proposed to her? Was she truly imprisoned in her own room? She quietly walked over to the door and tried it. It did not budge. Annoyed, she pulled the handle more violently. It made a noise but did not open. She banged on the wood and shouted, 'Let me out.'

Her stomach rumbled and she realised that she had not had dinner the previous night. She heard footsteps on the other side of the door and shouted even louder, 'I am starving.'

The door opened and her father stood there with his arms folded on his chest. She started to sidle out around him but he shook his head. 'Stay where you are,' he said. 'We need to talk.'

She calculated the odds of pushing past her father, but then what would she do? She was still in her nightclothes. And where would she go? 'I am not talking until I have had breakfast,' she said, turning back.

'Your mother is bringing it in a few minutes. Let's have a chat until then.'

She sat down on the bed, hugging her knees. 'Right, when are you going to let me out?'

'You can leave the room as soon as you give up the ridiculous notion of marrying such an unsuitable boy.'

'Never.'

'Then you'll be here a long time. It doesn't give me any pleasure to play the heavy-handed father, but if that's what I have to do, that's exactly what I will do. I shouldn't blame you, though I thought I raised you better. It's our own fault for spoiling you by giving you too much freedom.'

Her mother came in with a pile of hot puffy puris and steaming, yellow potato and onion curry – Usha's favourite. She cleared the study table and set the breakfast down without meeting Usha's eyes. Even though Usha hadn't brushed her teeth, she sat down at the table and polished off the food. Her mother got her a fresh jug of water.

'Think about what I told you,' said her father.

Her parents left the room and she heard the bolt slamming home loudly on the other side of the door. Even though she hadn't expected anything else, it was still a shock to find herself alone again. With nothing better to do, she completed her ablutions, took a bath and changed into fresh clothes. She tried to read a book but threw it petulantly down.

This is getting tiresome, she thought. She prowled round her room like a restless tigress in a cage, looking for a way to escape. It faced the side and back of the house with windows on two walls. Behind the glass panes, the windows were barred with iron rods, solidly fastened to the wooden frames to keep out burglars. High on the walls, just below the ceiling, there were ventilator holes, but as they were too small to let a sparrow in, she didn't think they were any use to her.

The window on the side of the house just looked out on to their own garden, but the other one was different. Because of the way the land fell away behind their house, from her window she could see through the iron bars over the compound wall and into a narrow lane. The boundary wall was built of stone, its top rounded and studded with broken glass to keep out thieves. She had never noticed it before, but the view from her room made it look like a prison.

She was annoyed, both at her plight and with her father. She was an educated woman with a good job, earning a decent salary, and here she was, trapped like an illiterate, lower-class woman. She was a journalist, for heaven's sake. She should be reporting stories like this, not caught up in one herself. Why blame her father entirely? Her mother could let her out easily, but she hadn't. Sure, she said that she was scared of her father, but was that the entire truth? Her mother obviously thought that Usha was acting wrongly by marrying somebody for love outside their caste and religion. Argh! She could strangle them both.

She thought about Rehman for a while – remembering some of the jokes he cracked. For such a serious guy, he could be funny when he wanted to be. He must be trying to get in touch with her, she thought. If only she could contact him somehow. What would he do if he found out about her situation? He would march straight into the house and confront her father. While she loved Rehman, he was not the type of man her father wanted for a son-in-law, even ignoring Rehman's religion. Her father wanted someone suave, well-dressed and rich, who drove an expensive car. Rehman, with his ethnic, hand-made cotton tunics, open leather slippers and cotton sling bag, would not impress her father.

At the rattle of a key she sat up. The door opened and her mother walked in with a glass of buttermilk. Her father stood in the doorway. For some reason, a smile had replaced his usual frown and that worried her. What was going on? She finished the drink and wiped her lips with the back of her hand.

'What's happening?' she asked.

Her mother took the glass from her with a nervous, quick movement and glanced over at her father. She said, 'Your father's contacted a marriage broker.'

Usha looked at her father and shook her head. 'Oh no, you haven't,' she said loudly.

'Yes, I have,' said her father. 'He's a shifty character, goes round from one house to another with a bunch of photographs and horoscopes; all he cares about is his commission on the dowry. I told him we were in a hurry and he had the gall to increase his rate. He backed down when I told him that there were others who could find me a match and that I was going to see one of them this evening. Stupid fool – thinks he can negotiate with *me*.' Her father smiled to himself and then continued, 'But he had one particular match immediately available. A young man called Sankar. I asked the broker to send him over to see us tomorrow. He's not everything I wanted in a son-in-law but it's your own fault for putting me in such a rush.'

Usha frowned. 'Where is this Sankar coming over from?'

'A village near Alamanda. His father is a big landlord there.'

'You are joking,' said Usha. 'You want me to marry a villager? No way.'

'He is dark but still looks quite good in the photo,' said her mother.

'Looks good in the photo?' exploded Usha. 'Have you been listening to anything I've been saying for the last couple of days? I am engaged to marry Rehman. You can forget anything else, especially some country bumpkin you people have found who can probably only talk about how many buffaloes his father owns.'

'It's not so bad,' said her mother. 'He is a younger son and he has agreed to leave his father's house and stay here. You can continue to live here after marriage. He has agreed to let you continue working too.'

'A house son-in-law! What kind of man with even an ounce of self-respect would agree to stay in his wife's house after marriage?' said Usha. She half-closed her eyes and said in a high-pitched, sing-song voice, 'He has agreed to let me continue working.' She opened her eyes and her voice took on a note of steel. 'Listen to me, both of you. I am not marrying this worm that you've conjured up under any circumstances. I am not some helpless girl who does not know her rights or cannot stand up for herself. I have a successful career with a good salary and can easily look after myself. If I haven't walked away from this house, it's because I am still giving you a little respect. Don't force me to do anything drastic.'

'What career?' said her father. 'I called Binoy, your um . . .

controller, and told him that your marriage has been fixed and you didn't want to work from now on. You don't have a job any more. And I told him that a rowdy, a bad character, was trying to break up the engagement and he was not to give out our address to anybody who came asking. Your controller said that he would pass on the message to all your colleagues as well.'

Usha struck her forehead with the palm of her right hand. Binoy was male chauvinist enough to take her father's word without insisting on speaking to her. None of her colleagues knew where she lived, anyway – only the office. She hadn't wanted them to know how rich her family was.

'How dare you go behind my back to my employer? You can drag me to the altar but I have to walk around the fire seven times on my own legs to get married and I am not doing that. Now both of you get out and leave me alone.' She sat down on the edge of the bed.

Her mother scurried away quickly. Just as her father was closing the door, Usha said, 'Cancel that viewing tomorrow if you don't want to be insulted in your own house.'

Her father bolted the door and said from the other side, 'You will marry this man. After that we'll see what happens.'

Usha lay back and closed her eyes. Her thoughts drifted. She must have nodded off but suddenly her eyes snapped wide open. She had to get a message out urgently. She had been prepared to sit it out and rely on her father coming to his senses but this was getting out of hand.

She jumped up, went to the table and took out a piece of paper. She scribbled a letter and found an envelope. But she had no stamps. That would complicate matters. It wasn't just a question of asking somebody to drop an envelope in the nearest postbox. They would have to go to the post office, buy a stamp and then post the letter. Not many people would want to go to so much trouble. But she knew one person who would – their servant maid. She was a thin young woman who wore pink saris and liked to watch romantic movies. She could be easily convinced to carry a letter for her.

A knock came at the door and she hastily hid the envelope before shouting, 'Come in.' She looked at the clock on the wall and was surprised to see that over an hour had passed since her parents had brought her the drink.

Her father stood by the door while her mother brought in lunch.

'Where is Subbi?' asked Usha, referring to the maid.

'I asked her to take a few days off – paid.'

'Did she rush out without asking any questions in case you changed your mind?' asked Usha.

'Something like that,' said her mother glumly.

Usha laughed. She knew how much her mother hated it when servant maids took time off. But it was a blow. Now what would she do? To Usha's surprise, her mother sat down with her and they had the meal together. Her father continued standing by the door. Once they had finished the meal, her mother collected the dishes and soon Usha was left alone again.

She walked to the window and looked out. It wasn't a busy street but someone went past every so often. She would send a message through a stranger, she decided. But she would have to be careful. She didn't want to hail someone, only to have them go round and knock on the front door. Or ignore her message.

An old man hobbled slowly past her window. His back was stooped and his head was bald. She stared at him for a few minutes and then shook her head. He would definitely go to her father.

Several minutes later, another man shuffled past. He was younger and had once been fatter, but now the skin hung loosely on him. The side of the face towards her was slack and his hand was twisted in the characteristic shape of a stroke victim. Slap, shuffle, slap – she watched silently as he dragged himself on one good leg. The man had enough troubles of his own and she doubted that he had the dexterity to go to a post office with her letter.

After that several people went past on motorcycles and scooters but it was almost half an hour before another pedestrian came into view. A young man strolled past, carrying books in one hand and holding a mobile phone against his ear in the other. She waved to him and even shouted, softly, but he walked on, engrossed in his conversation and oblivious to her. She stamped her foot in frustration after he had disappeared.

A small skinny boy, about ten years old, skipped past, wearing ancient shorts that looked too big for him and a shirt that flapped loose because it was missing a few buttons. He threw one marble ahead of him and then tried to hit it with another. He then collected both the marbles and started again. Too young, she thought.

The pedestrians after that walked so close to the boundary wall of their house that she could see only the tops of their heads. She was puzzled for a moment before she realised that the sun had climbed in the sky and the people were walking in the shadow of the wall to escape it. It's winter, you fools, she screamed in her head. Walk in the sun! The meal, the enforced idleness and the half-completed nap of the morning made her drowsy, so she had a siesta.

She woke up at about three-thirty in the afternoon and went to the window immediately. At this time, the scene outside had taken on a sleepy atmosphere. Even the fresh winter-green leaves on the trees did not stand at attention and seemed to wilt a little. She saw again the boy from the morning, carrying a bamboo basket on head and walking slowly. He held the basket up with his left hand and continued playing marbles with his right. His thin legs stuck out like black sticks from the bottom of his outsized shorts. She remembered where she had seen him before. He belonged to the street-family outside who ironed clothes. He disappeared round the bend of the lane. She wondered where he was taking whatever was inside the basket.

About ten minutes later, the same boy returned along the path. No other pedestrians had used the lane in the meantime. He was free of his burden now and more enthusiastic. The target marble came to rest just opposite her window. The boy concentrated, his face pinched with the effort and his tongue protruding slightly, as he threw the second overhand. It hit a small stone near the first marble and ricocheted away into the storm drain that went along the base of the wall. The boy ran quickly and vanished from her view as he jumped into the gutter. It was almost five minutes before he reappeared and picked up his first marble.

His face was miserable and tears streaked down his dusty cheeks in wet channels.

'Boy,' Usha called out. 'Have you lost a marble?'

The boy looked around in surprise and didn't notice her at first. She called out again before he saw her at the window.

'Yes,' he said. 'It fell into the gutter and I can't find it. I've only got one marble now. I'll have to play with a pebble but it won't be as good and the other boys will make fun of me.'

His eyes welled up again, though he swallowed and manfully tried to hold back the tears.

'Don't worry,' she said. 'You can buy one more.'

'No,' he said. 'I'll have to wait until Granny comes back from the village before I get any more money. She won't be back for at least two months.'

He rubbed his eyes with the back of his hand, smearing more dust on his wet face.

'Would you like to earn enough money to buy ten marbles?' she asked.

'Ten! That's more than even Siva's got.'

'You'll have to do something for me first.'

'What?' he said.

'Not a lot. I'll give you a letter and some money. You need to buy a stamp at the post office, stick it on the letter and post it in the postbox. You will have enough money left over to buy more than ten marbles.'

'Really?'

'Yes. So, will you do it?'

The boy thought for a moment. 'Why can't you do it yourself?'

'Never you mind that. You are the boy who lives opposite, aren't you? What's your name?' she asked.

'My name is Balu and yes, we live on the footpath under the tree,' he said. 'I know you. You are the lady who drives the red car.'

She nodded and suddenly had an inspiration to make sure that he carried out her instructions. 'I will know in a few days whether you posted the letter or not. If you do as I say and post the letter properly, I will give you a ride in my car.'

'All the way to the end of the road?' Balu asked.

'Even further. I will take you all the way round the block.'

'Can I sit in the front?' the boy asked.

'Yes. Hang on a moment.'

She wedged the envelope and a ten-rupee note tightly in the spine of a book. She put her arm carefully past the elbow through the bars on the window. She bent her hand and straightened it forcefully. The book sailed through the air but her throw had not been powerful enough. Her heart almost stopped as the book reached its zenith far too early and swooped down.

'Oh!' she cried in disappointment as it hit the wall and seemingly stayed there, poised on the top.

But luckily, it had hit a piece of thick blue soda-bottle glass on the far edge and, after a split second, it slowly slid down the other side. Balu disappeared from view as he dived towards it. Moments later, he came back into view, jumping like a monkey, waving the book in one hand and the envelope and money in the other. Usha sagged against the window in relief.

'Don't show the money to anyone, including your mother. They might take it away and you won't get the marbles and the car ride,' she said, feeling guilty at manipulating the boy so shamelessly.

Balu just nodded and ran off down the lane. Usha went back to her bed. Now, she would just have to wait for the letter to do what she hoped it would.

Rehman was waiting for Pari outside her office with his bike that afternoon to take her to the beach. He nodded to her and she rode the pillion side-saddle all the way.

Rehman bought them two corn on the cobs from an old woman sitting on the pavement outside the beach with a small charcoal brazier. They moved to the low wall overlooking the sand and Pari turned to Rehman.

'What did you want to talk about?' she asked. 'Why couldn't you tell me on the phone?'

Rehman sighed and said, 'I need your advice. Do you remember that yesterday I came home late for dinner?'

'Yes, so?'

He looked straight ahead, concentrating on the far horizon where the dark blue of the sea met the lighter blue of the sky. 'I had gone out to meet a girl. I proposed to her and she accepted.'

Pari's face lit up with surprise. 'Wow! You've turned out to be a chuppa Rustom, a hidden hero. Who is it? Do I know her? How long have you been meeting up? What—'

'Whoa . . . Hold your horses. Her name is Usha and you don't know her.'

'Usha?' said Pari.

Rehman turned to Pari and found her staring at him – her eyes wide. A small, yellow piece of corn kernel was on a corner of her upper lip.

'Usha?' repeated Pari. 'She's not . . . Muslim . . .'

'No, she's not. Is that an issue?' asked Rehman. His voice was loud and his jaw jutted forward.

'No, not for me. But what about your parents? What will they say if you tell them you want to marry a Hindu girl?' said Pari.

When he didn't say anything for a moment, she shook her head. 'Oh, no. I am not getting into the firing line with chaacha and chaachi. I'm not telling them about you and Usha. They have been very good to me and I am not going to repay them by giving them bad news.'

Rehman waved the corn in his hand dismissively. 'I don't expect you to do that. I will tell them myself. Ammi and abba will be unhappy but that's my burden. I won't push it on to anybody else.'

'Right,' said Pari. 'So what's the problem?' She looked at him and covered her mouth with her hand. 'Have you changed your mind after sleeping on it overnight?'

'No!' said Rehman. 'Stop jumping to conclusions and let me finish talking.'

'Sorry,' said Pari. 'Carry on.'

Rehman took a deep breath. 'Last night, I came home all ready to tell ammi and abba the news. But Nafisa and her loud-mouthed husband were there, so I didn't say anything. Then this morning, I called Usha and she cut the phone on me as soon as I started to talk. I've been ringing every few minutes after that but the phone is switched off. I don't know what to think. Does she regret what she agreed to yesterday? Does Usha not want to marry me any more?'

Pari looked at him for a moment and then took his hand in hers. 'Oh, Rehman,' she said. 'I am sure there's a simple explanation for it. She said yes last night, didn't she?'

Rehman nodded.

Pari continued, 'Go to her house and ask her in person. She cannot have changed her mind so quickly.'

'I've thought about it,' said Rehman. 'But I don't know where she lives.'

'What?'

'I've never met her at home. We just talk on our mobile phones and meet up somewhere in town or at the beach. She lives in MVP colony but I am not sure exactly where. I didn't want to tell ammi and abba without being sure, but I needed to talk to somebody, so I called you.'

She pressed his hand and said, 'Thank you, Rehman. It means a lot that you've decided to confide in me.'

Rehman said, 'What do I do?'

Pari thought for a moment. Then she said, 'Where does she work?'

Rehman's face broke into a smile. 'You are a genius! She's a journalist with a TV channel.' He looked at his watch. 'It's too late now. I'll go over there first thing tomorrow and find out where she lives from them.'

'Love may be blind, but it also seems to turn one into a simpleton,' said Pari. 'I cannot believe you didn't think of such a simple thing yourself.'

Rehman shrugged, too happy to take offence. They were silent for a little while and then Pari said, 'What kind of wedding will you have? Will you ask Usha to convert and become a Muslim?'

'I haven't thought about it,' said Rehman. 'But I don't think so.'

'It will be quite important for your mother that you have a religious wedding.'

'No,' said Rehman. 'We'll probably have a civil ceremony.'

'Civil? Oh, you mean a registered wedding,' said Pari.

'That's right.'

Pari shook her head and looked away. Rehman sighed, some of his happiness dissipating. It looked as if life was going to be a lot more complicated than he thought.

CHAPTER ELEVEN

'You are fine. You can go back to work tomorrow,' said the older doctor, closing his bag.

'Thank you, sir,' said Ramanujam and looked at Aruna with a frown on his face. 'And sorry to have troubled you.'

Aruna refused to be intimidated and looked steadily back at her husband.

'No problem, my boy. It's always good to see old students,' said the older man. 'Ravi tells me that you are presenting a paper at a neurology conference in AIIMS.'

'Yes, sir,' said Ramanujam. 'At the Indo-German Neurosurgical conference – about post-operative recovery after removing brain tumours.'

'Oh,' said his old professor. 'Are these tumours involving intrinsic effects?'

'Both intrinsic and mass effect, sir. The study is about tumours bigger than . . .'

The men looked as if they could talk about the topic a lot longer than Aruna could listen to it, so she left them and went into the living room. Her sister-in-law's son Sanjay was sitting on his own, watching television. Aruna sat next to him and watched the children's programme along with him. The characters in the cartoon looked oriental and were drawn in a particular way that she could not quite define – they had spiky hair and the girls wore very short skirts. There seemed to be a lot of fantastic beasts and violence as well. She couldn't follow head nor tail of the story but when she looked at Sanjay's face, he was engrossed. Finally, one character beat up another on the screen and Sanjay jumped up on the sofa, his arm raised. 'Yay!' he shouted.

'Do you want to play outside with me?' she asked the boy, wanting a truce after the previous day's trouble.

'OK,' he said. 'The next programme is for girls anyway – it's stupid.'

They went out into the garden and found an old tennis ball.

'Let's play catch,' she suggested.

They took their places and started throwing the ball to each other. 'What outdoor games do you play with your friends?' she asked.

'We play cricket and sometimes football,' he said.

'Don't you play seven-stones tag or kabbadi?'

'Those are boring native games. Anyway, we don't know how to play them. What is seven-stones tag?' he asked.

Aruna felt sad, but not surprised, that Sanjay and his friends didn't play traditional games.

'You need more kids to play the game,' she said. 'Seven flat stones are placed on each other in a pile in the centre. The children are divided into two teams and each side takes turns to hit the pile from a distance with a ball. As soon as the stones come tumbling down, all the members of the team that hit the stones scatter. The other team tries to hit any one of the first team with the ball while they try to pile the stones back. If the pile of stones is made, the first team wins; if a team member is hit with the ball before that, the second team wins.'

Sanjay threw the ball towards her but the aim was wrong and it went into the bushes. Aruna found the ball and pulled it out of the bushes with a stick.

'Of course, we didn't always have a ball with us. So we played with marbles.'

'I played a couple of times with marbles,' said Sanjay. 'Thaatha bought a bag of one hundred marbles for me.'

'Oh,' said Aruna.

She never had more than three or four marbles. She remembered the time when she had been thirteen years old. They had been living in a village and her mother had forbidden her going to the river with the boys because she had reached puberty and her body was developing. One day she had ignored her mother and was discovered on the way back by her sister Vani, who had threatened to inform on her. After pleading for several minutes, Aruna had finally bribed her – she offered to give Vani all her marbles. Aruna had been pleased with the deal because she was no longer interested in playing with marbles while Vani still liked them. Those few marbles had been the price of her sister's silence, but what possible value could they have when they were available by the bagful?

'Come on,' said Sanjay. Dismissing her memories, she threw the ball to him.

'We also played tag,' she said.

'We play tag and hide-and-seek too,' he said, running after the ball as it rolled away.

'I bet you don't play monkey tag,' she said.

'What's monkey tag?' he asked.

'It's just like tag,' she said, 'but it's played in the trees. We used to chase each other in the branches of trees like monkeys.'

'I don't believe that you actually climbed trees,' he said.

'When I was a girl, I could climb trees as well as any boy. It was great fun,' she said. She laughed at the expression on his face – he was obviously trying to imagine his staid aunty as a young girl, swinging from branch to branch like a langur monkey. She threw the ball up in the air and a hand caught it before it came down to Sanjay's height.

He turned to see Ramanujam and the old doctor behind him. 'Aww, maava. I was about to catch it.'

Ramanujam handed the ball to the boy. Aruna said, 'Let's take a break.'

She walked with the two men to the gate. They bade farewell to the doctor with many thanks and asked their driver to drop the doctor off.

'No problem,' the older man said. 'I'll walk.'

'Please allow us to do this much for you at least,' said Ramanujam and the doctor acquiesced.

They stood by the gate after the car drove off. 'Are you going back to work tomorrow?' she asked.

'Yes, I will. I wonder what's happening with the patients. There was one tricky case before I fell ill.'

'In that case, I'll go back to work too. Sir was going to get a computer and he must be struggling with it.'

They heard a thud behind them and a scream. They turned back and saw Sanjay on the ground, holding his hand and crying loudly. They ran over to him and everybody in the house came out as well. Ramanujam reached the boy first.

'What happened? Are you all right?' he asked.

Sanjay held out his left hand. 'It hurts here,' he said, pointing to his wrist.

Ramanujam felt it gently with his fingers. When he poked one particular spot on his wrist Sanjay cried out, 'Aww.'

By this time, Ramanujam's parents and his sister, Mani, had come over.

'I don't think it's a fracture,' said Ramanujam. Aruna exhaled in relief.

'Fracture?' screamed Mani. 'What did you do, son?'

'I was climbing the mango tree and I slipped and fell,' he said.

'Climbing a tree? Whatever made you do such a silly thing?' said his mother.

'Aruna-atta said it is fun to climb trees.'

Mani turned to Aruna, her face red and chest heaving above her big belly. 'You,' she said. She then turned to Sanjay and smacked him on the back of his head, sending him into a fresh paroxysm of wailing. She twisted his ear and dragged him back into the house. 'I don't want you ever talking to her, you fool.'

Ramanujam's parents went after their daughter. 'Leave him be. Boys will be boys, after all. It's just a simple fall,' said her father. They disappeared into the house.

Aruna turned to Ramanujam. 'I—' she began.

'Why do you provoke the boy? Stay away from him. It's obvious that you don't know how to look after children,' he said and followed his parents into the house.

Not know how to care for children? She had been a teenager when her sister Vani was just seven years old. She had nephews and nieces who adored her. The unfairness of her husband's comments brought tears to her eyes. She just stood there and it was a long time before she noticed that it had grown dark, the birds had gone to their roosts and thirsty mosquitoes had come out for their nightly feast.

The next day Aruna reached Mr Ali's house by nine in the morning. She was surprised to see the typewriter still taking pride of place on the table.

'It won't be staying here for long now that you are here,' said Mr Ali, picking up the phone to ring the computer dealer. 'Venkatesh? Mr Ali here. When can you deliver the computer?' They talked for a few moments and Mr Ali hung up. He turned to Aruna. 'They are bringing the computer now. I think he is in a hurry for his money. He's already had to wait a week.'

Gopal, the postman, came over with the morning delivery. 'Sir told me that your husband was not well. Is he all right now?' he said, handing over a bundle of letters.

'He had a viral fever, but he's recovered, thank you,' she

said, smiling at him, touched that he was enquiring after her family when he must be worried sick about his widowed daughter and the uncleared debts that he had run up to get her married off.

Gopal nodded to both of them, hefted his heavy bag and left. The ad agent came next and Mr Ali handed over the weekend's advertisements to him. Aruna started going through the post, sorting the letters into different piles depending on what action needed to be taken. The corner shopkeeper's son came over with copies of a reminder letter that Mr Ali had drafted. Aruna got into the rhythm of the office day and soon felt as if she had never been away. Mrs Ali came out from inside the house with a pan of freshly rolled poppadums and spread them out to dry in the sun in the front yard. She came back onto the verandah and sat in her usual chair by the door.

'How is Ramanujam? Has he fully recovered?' she said.

'Yes, madam,' said Aruna. 'He has even gone to the hospital today.'

'Thank goodness,' said Mrs Ali. 'So it wasn't malaria. I told you not to worry, didn't I? After all, he is a young, healthy man.'

'I know, madam,' said Aruna. 'But I couldn't help worrying though.'

'That's true,' said Mrs Ali. 'We women can no more stop getting distressed than we can close our ears and stop hearing.'

They sat in companionable silence for a bit before the washerwoman came with ironed clothes. Mrs Ali counted them and took them inside. Aruna worked on.

Less than an hour later, she heard the door open and looked up to see three young men dressed in dark trousers, pale shirts and thin, stringy ties walking onto the verandah, each carrying one or more cardboard boxes. Aruna hurriedly cleared all the papers from the table and Mr Ali lifted the typewriter and put it on the sofa. Aruna noticed that, while she was away, Mr Ali had put in extra sockets on the wall behind the table.

The young men opened the boxes and lifted out the computer, keyboard and mouse, monitor and printer. They then opened smaller boxes and took out masses of cables that were all an identical grey colour but seemed to have slightly different ends on them. The men started connecting the various units together and plugging them in. She wondered how the boys (as she was now thinking of them, even though she was not much older than them) knew which cable went where.

Mrs Ali called to Aruna from the door and handed her a tray with three glasses of water. She asked the boys whether they wanted to drink. One of them took a glass with shy thanks but the other two declined.

'It's ready, sir,' said Venkatesh, the oldest of the three, soon after. 'If you come and sit here, we can take you through the system and show you all the packages.'

'Aruna, you do it,' said Mr Ali.

Aruna sat on the chair behind the table and pulled the keyboard closer to her. She had learned basic computer operations one summer a few years back. Last year, when she had seriously decided to learn new skills so she could take up a job, she had had to say no to computer lessons because they were too expensive. She had taken up typing instead. It was strange how such a simple but difficult-at-the-time decision had led to her being noticed by Mrs Ali, being offered a job at the marriage bureau and then Ram, her dear Ram, stepping into her life. She remembered the first time she had seen him as he walked in through that very front door, looking so handsome and rich and unattainable. She wondered if his irritability would fade now that he was well again and back at work.

Venkatesh coughed and Aruna almost jumped, startled. She looked around at all the men staring at her and said, 'Sorry, I was miles away. I've used a computer before but you'd better start again from the basics.'

'You switch the computer on by pressing this big button here,' said Venkatesh.

'Oh! Is that the computer? I thought that was the computer,' said Mr Ali, pointing to the screen.

'No, sir. That's just the monitor. It shows you what is going on in the computer but this big box down here is where the real action is.'

'Why does it make so much noise?' asked Mr Ali.

'Those are the fans, sir. Most of that box is actually just air. Computing is hard work and generates a lot of heat. Did you know that we lose almost a third of our body heat through the head?'

Mr Ali raised his eyebrows and shook his head.

Venkatesh pointed to the tiny pictures on the screen and said, 'Those are icons. Each one of those is a program. You move the mouse until the arrow is on the icon you want and double-click to start it.'

Aruna nodded but Mr Ali said, 'Double-click?'

'Click twice, very quickly.'

Venkatesh took them through how to use a word processor, explaining about cut and paste, search and replace, fonts and styles, files, folders and forty-five other things.

'If you need help at any time, please call me, sir.' He handed Mr Ali a business card. Mr Ali gave him a cheque and the three men left.

'Did you understand all that?' asked Mr Ali.

Aruna nodded. 'Yes, sir.'

'I am glad that one of us has understood it. I only got every other word.'

'It's not that difficult, sir,' laughed Aruna. 'You will be an expert after a few days.'

'I hope so. Otherwise it will be an expensive paperweight. Let me type a letter,' he said.

Aruna got up from the chair and he sat down in front of the keyboard. He placed his fingers on the middle row. Suddenly a string of 'A's interspersed with strings of 'F's ran across the screen like little ants towards a bowl of sugar. Mr Ali hurriedly lifted his hands off the keyboard and said, 'Oh dear! The keys are so much lighter than on the typewriter.' He looked for the backspace key.

Aruna quickly reached out from behind him and hit a couple of keys. The row of letters vanished. He looked up at her in surprise and said, 'How did you do that?'

'I just typed the undo key,' she said. 'It reverses what you've just done as if you've never done it.'

'Wow!' said Mr Ali. 'Imagine if we had an undo key in real life. So many problems in this world could be solved.'

Aruna smiled at him, thinking what she would undo in her life if she had a mantra to do it. Would she have taken back her words to Sanjay about playing in trees? She didn't think so – the boy had woken up with no ill effects from the evening's adventures, his wrist was fine. What was wrong with kids climbing trees, anyway? She understood Mani's reaction; she was a mother and a heavily pregnant woman. It was her husband's response that hurt her. He should have been supporting her and not telling her off.

About ten-thirty the next morning there was a knock and the door to Usha's room opened. Her mother was wearing a stiff silk sari; her father had been to the barber and was wearing a formal shirt and dhoti. Usha had already had her bath and changed. Her mother looked at her critically and said, 'Not bad, it will do, I suppose.'

'Do for what?' said Usha.

'Sankar, the young man the marriage broker introduced, is coming here at any moment now,' said her father.

'So you are going ahead with this charade,' said Usha. 'Don't say I didn't warn you. I am not going to play the simpering bride-to-be. By the time we are finished here, you will be wishing that you hadn't started down this path.'

Her father just moved his hand desultorily as if he was brushing away a fly. Why was he so confident?

'Does it mean I can go into the living room now?' asked Usha.

'No,' said her father. 'We'll do the bride-viewing right here.'

Usha was outraged. 'This is my bedroom. How dare you bring strangers into it?'

'You've brought this on yourself,' said her father.

'There won't be anybody else,' said her mother. 'He said he was coming here on his own.'

Usha rolled her eyes. They waited stiffly like three mannequins in a shop window until the bell rang. Usha's father went out, locking Usha and her mother in the room. He soon came back with a young man. Despite herself, Usha looked at him curiously. He was of medium height, a couple of inches taller than her. As her mother had already mentioned, he had dark skin. He had fat lips, a thick moustache, a wide nose and his face was broad. He wore a horrible stripy shirt that looked like polyester, with damp rings of sweat under his armpits. His hair was slicked back with litres of coconut oil. His shirt pocket was overflowing with papers and a pen.

He bowed to the two women with joined hands and said, 'Good morning, ladies.'

Usha ignored him while her mother smiled and greeted him back.

He took out a business card and handed it to Usha's father. 'I got these cards specially made for this visit,' he said. 'The printer owes me a favour and he printed them for me as a special rush job.'

Her father nodded and took the card from him. He read it with raised eyebrows and pushed it in front of Usha. Usha folded her hands in front of her, ignoring it.

'My name Sankar,' he said. 'I—'

His mobile phone rang with an extremely loud, popular song

as the ringtone and he fished through his large trouser pockets, taking out coins, scraps of paper and two sets of keys. The merry song went on and on in an irritating, tinny tune. He finally found the phone.

'Sorry, everybody,' he said to all three of them and answered the call. 'Hello.'

He listened for several seconds while a voice squawked at the other end.

Usha sneaked a glance at the visiting card – Mr Jhampala Sankar, MA, BF, IAS. Usha raised her eyebrows in surprise. The man in front of her was a postgraduate? And a member of the Indian Administrative Service? The central government ran an extremely competitive annual exam for recruiting civil servants. The test was tough and the very top rankers were chosen for the administrative service – the steel frame of the Indian civil service. These senior bureaucrats were well educated and generally quite smart. Usha looked at Sankar through narrowed eyes. He didn't fit her image of a high-ranking government officer.

'Shut up and listen to me,' said Sankar into the phone. The other person said something. 'I said, shut up and listen, you fool.' Sankar's voice rose and he seemed to have forgotten Usha and her family. He waved his hand in a chopping motion. The other man fell silent. 'Good,' continued Sankar. 'Just pay that son of a whore some money and get the consignment released. Is your head full of dung that I have to tell you simple things? And don't call me for the next hour. I am in the middle of an important transaction.'

He put the phone back in his pocket and turned to them. He was smiling again, his manner oily in some way that Usha could not describe.

'Drivers and government officials – they are like leeches that will suck your body dry if you just give them a chance.'

Usha's father bared his teeth in a smile that quickly disappeared. 'I am really impressed that you are an MA,' he said.

'And IAS too, of course. But what does BF mean?'

'Of course it is true,' Sankar said. 'But it's not what you think. The letters stand for Matriculation Appeared, But Failed, In All Subjects.' He laughed, clapping his hands on his thighs. Matriculation was the exam taken at the end of school, after ten years of study.

'If you are so open about it, why do you put those letters on your business cards?' said Usha's father.

'It's the first impression, you see,' Sankar said. 'You might find out about it later that I have not passed high school but because you first thought I could be an important official, you will continue to treat me with more deference than you would do otherwise. It is called psychology.' He pronounced the word with a hard 'P' at the beginning.

Usha and her mother exchanged glances. Her mother quickly turned away and looked out of the window as if she could not meet Usha's eyes. 'I am not—' began Usha.

Sankar raised his hand. 'In my family, women don't talk when their menfolk are discussing matters.' He turned to Usha's father. 'I understand that in cities men have become weak and let their women become disrespectful. I am still old-fashioned in these matters. If I marry your daughter, I will impose strict discipline.'

Before her father could say anything, Usha jumped up. 'Hey, mister,' she said. 'I am not marrying you. Now get out and stop wasting everybody's time.'

Sankar said, 'Jump up while you still can. Once we are married I will know how to make you understand my authority.'

Usha turned to her parents. 'What are you people still sitting there for? Throw this uncouth man out.'

Sankar spoke before her father. 'Just because I come from a village and did not go to college, don't think I am a fool. With one look I can tell when a driver is short-changing me. I started my trucking business before I was twenty and in ten years I now run more than twenty-five trucks. Big, big leaders, politicians, come to me when they need help during elections. When your father first called, I thought that you might be fat or squint-eyed or both. Looking at you, I can see that you are pretty so you must obviously be having an affair. But I am a broad-minded man. I don't care what you have done so far. But remember, once we are married, all this ends. Khallas – finish.' His right hand chopped down into his left palm with a loud snap. He turned to Usha's father. 'Let's talk business. You have a big problem – your daughter is obviously out of control. What are you offering me to take her off your hands?'

Usha expected her father to blow the rude young man away but she was surprised when he answered Sankar politely. She was more and more astounded as the discussion went on. She started calculating the odds of making a run for it.

'One kilo gold . . .'

'Land?'

'Farmhouse . . . forty cents of land on the national high-way . . . daughter's car . . .'

'Don't need a car! I always ride next to the drivers on my trucks and she won't be driving anywhere.'

'Cash . . .'

Half an hour later, Sankar and her parents stood up. Usha saw the opportunity, sidled towards the door and broke into a run. She reached the end of the corridor outside her room before Sankar grabbed her arm. 'Oww . . . Let me go . . .'

He dragged her back towards her room. Just before they reached it, he spoke quietly to her out of the corner of his mouth. 'I like a bit of fire in a girl myself, it's more fun, but it needs to be in its place. Once we are married, these kinds of games won't work with me. I will break your legs if you try to run away from me, wench.'

Once in the room, he pushed her heavily towards the bed and she went sprawling on the mattress. He turned to her father and bowed slightly, a smile on his face. With a mild voice and bobbing head, he said, 'The girl is feeling shy, as a proper bride should. Once she gets to know me, she won't run away at all. Keep her safe until the wedding and after that she will be my responsibility.'

Usha looked back towards her parents and shouted, 'You don't know what this fiend said—' But before she could complete the sentence or get up from the bed, the door was locked behind her.

The third day of Usha's captivity dawned and soon she was at the window, looking out. Sankar's visit on the previous day had unnerved her. She hoped that Rehman was trying to find her. But her father had been quite thorough. Going to her employers was the obvious way to find her but now they wouldn't reveal where she lived. She had a sickening thought: could Rehman get into difficulty by trying to locate her? After all, her father had let everybody know that a troublemaker was trying to break off her engagement. After a few second's reflection, she felt sure that Rehman could look after himself.

She was the one who needed help right now and she wished that he would somehow find her and rescue her. She continued to look out of the window. She had spent hours on both the previous days in the same spot, searching for her young messenger. He had completely disappeared and she wondered whether he had been a figment of her imagination.

Usha remembered the Sanskrit classic she had studied at university – *Meghdoot*, or *The Cloud Messenger*, written by the great Kalidasa about two thousand years ago. In that lyrical poem, a prisoner on a mountain in central India sees the monsoon clouds gathering in the sky above him and asks one of them to take a message to his beloved wife in a city in the Himalayas. The prisoner describes all the landmarks of India that the cloud will see on its journey along the length of the country, so that it knows when it reaches his home. The prisoner extols his wife's beauty so she can be recognised and finally he tells the cloud his message of love and longing.

Usha shook her head – she had to keep her spirits up. Her

position wasn't as bad as that. She had sent a message out that was more concrete than words shouted out to a passing cloud.

Usha's mood swung like a bipolar pendulum. Her mind was in turmoil. She had been willing to play a game of chicken with her father, waiting for him to blink and release her, but the stakes had gone up. It looked as if Sankar didn't care what she said or did – he was willing to take the bribes her father offered and marry her, regardless. She shuddered when she thought of what would happen to her after – if, *if*, she told herself – she got married to that monster.

Had her letter reached its destination? She couldn't just wait for that now. She went to her desk and wrote another letter – to the police. She informed them that she was an adult, held against her will by her parents and being forced to marry somebody she did not like. She gave her address and asked them to come and rescue her right away. This time she did not bother putting it in an envelope. She looked around on her table and found a heavy paperweight with a colourful red pattern inside clear glass. She wrapped the letter round it and held it in place with a couple of rubber bands. She hoped that when she found somebody will-ing to deliver the letter to the local police station, she would not hit them on the head with the paperweight. She couldn't afford for anything to go wrong now. Her parents would get into trou-ble when the letter reached the police, but she didn't have a choice. It will serve naanna right if he gets into difficulties, she thought.

She looked outside. For a few minutes there was nobody around and then Balu, the boy she had talked to on the first day, came skipping down. He came to a stop opposite her window and waved his arms.

'Did you post my letter?' asked Usha.

'Yes, madam. I sent it off that very day.' He took a small cloth bag from his packet and shook it. She heard a tinkling noise. 'With the rest of the money, I got marbles and a rattle for the baby.'

'Why didn't you come here the last two days? I've been look-ing for you,' said Usha.

'Amma was very angry with me when she found out that I had some money and I used it to buy marbles. She hit me and I had to help her with the chores all day. She did not let me leave her side even for a moment. She said she could have used the money to buy medicine to make the baby burp after drinking milk. Luckily, the baby liked the rattle I got for her and she stopped crying so amma's anger did not last long.'

'Oh!' said Usha, a bit subdued. 'I'm sorry I got you into trouble.'

'I don't mind. It was a small price to pay. Now I have more marbles than any of my friends and cousins. But that was the day before. I came here twice yesterday and I didn't see you.'

'I was busy yesterday. Now I need you to do me one more favour. I'll throw a letter wrapped around a weight. Take it to the police station.'

Balu shook his head vigorously. 'I am not going there. The police smashed my uncle's cart when he was ironing clothes in the Doctor's Colony and took him away. He came home after two days and he said the police station was a bad place where people are beaten every day.'

Usha sighed. It would be terrible if he refused to carry the letter to the police.

'Nothing is going to happen to you. Just give the note to the first policeman you see and tell him it is an important message from a lady. Stand back,' she said and threw the paperweight with all her strength. It landed on the other side of the wall in the dusty verge of the lane.

Balu picked it up and took off the rubber bands. He dropped the missive on the ground and stood up with the paperweight in his outstretched hands.

'The letter . . .' said Usha, stretching her arms out.

'Wow, a huge marble,' he said. 'Who plays with it?'

'What?' said Usha, confused. 'Marble?'

'This,' said Balu, pointing with his head at the big glass sphere in his hands.

'That is a paperweight. It is used to stop paper from flying away when the fan is on.'

'Oh!' said Balu, his hands dropping to his side. 'I didn't know. We don't have paper in our house, or a fan either.'

Usha was speechless for just a moment and then she said, 'Forget the weight. Pick up the paper and take it to the police.'

Balu picked up the letter without letting go of the paper-weight, waved it in the air and ran off. Usha stared after the boy until he disappeared from view and then moved slowly to her bed to think.

The police should be here soon. To keep her mind off Sankar, she thought about the boy who was helping her. It shamed her to think that she knew nothing about the family that had lived just outside their house for so many years. How many members did it have? He probably didn't attend school because she had seen him both before noon and afterwards. Did he want to study but could not go to school because his parents could not afford the fees and the books? How did he sleep at the height of summer without a fan and mosquitoes buzzing for blood?

The truth was that she had never paid any attention to Balu and his family before this. It was as if they were less than human by not living in a pukka house. She felt ashamed of herself. She was sure that if Rehman had been living in her house, he would have known all about the family living opposite. They would have probably come to him for help when Balu's uncle was arrested and he would have fought the police on their behalf – she had no doubt. She was so proud of Rehman and yet her parents wanted to choose a brutish man like Sankar. Why were her parents so foolish? Was it just because Rehman followed a different religion? Or was it because *she* had made the choice and not her parents?

CHAPTER TWELVE

Rehman had been waiting in the corridor for almost half an hour. A young woman came out of the room at the far end and started to walk past him.

'Excuse me,' he said, half raising his hand.

The young woman stopped and looked at him with the expression of someone who has just popped the last peanut from a packet into her mouth and found it to be bitter. Then, without a word, she walked away. It wasn't just her – all the people in the office were behaving like this. Rehman was really surprised. He wasn't used to be treated like something dragged in off the road and he found it demeaning. He had come to Usha's office with high hopes of getting her address but it was turning into a nightmare. He hoped that her boss would be more amenable to his request.

It was another fifteen minutes before he was allowed into the office at the far end of the corridor. He pushed through the bat-wing doors. A fat, almost obese, middle-aged man with gold rings on all of his fingers, who looked as if he loved sweets, was sitting behind the desk.

'Mr Binoy?' asked Rehman.

The man waved a podgy hand languidly towards a chair.

Rehman sat down but still the man did not speak. The silence stretched for almost a minute before Rehman, uncomfortable with the lack of conversation, said, 'I want to find out where Usha lives.'

'Why do you want to know that?'

'It's a personal reason,' said Rehman. 'It's really important that I meet her.'

'Really important, is it?' said Binoy, stroking his three chins and looking thoughtful.

Rehman's hopes rose. At least the man was talking. 'Yes, sir. Usha is a very good friend of mine and I need some information from her urgently. I have been trying to call her but her mobile phone is switched off.'

Binoy stroked his chin for a few seconds longer. The air-conditioner in the window of the room kicked in with a loud sound and Rehman was startled, involuntarily flicking his glance towards it. When his eyes came back to Binoy, the large man half stood up from his chair and half leaned over the table between them.

'How dare you chase after an unmarried girl?'

Rehman flinched as spittle flew from Binoy's mouth towards him. 'I simply—'

But Binoy had only begun. 'Just because you see a woman a few times on television, sickos like you imagine that she is somehow your friend. Do you think we are just sitting here, waiting for people like you to come so we can give you our presenters' addresses?'

'But I—'

'The Commissioner of Police was sitting in the same chair that you are sitting in now less than two days ago. I can make one phone call and have you arrested.'

'All—'

'Usha is a respectable girl from a good family. Her family has found a match for her and she is getting married soon. She doesn't need lafangas, loafers, like you sniffing round her.'

'You—'

'Get out before I have you thrown out,' said Binoy.

Rehman flinched again and with his sleeve wiped a spot of spittle off his cheek.

'Sir, I am not some random viewer who is trying to stalk a presenter. I know Usha personally.'

Binoy clicked his fingers and waved him away rudely.

Rehman waited for a few seconds but Binoy went back to work, completely ignoring him. Finally Rehman shook his head and left the office. Outside, all the staff in their cubicles stared at him as he walked down the long corridor, keeping his head up and avoiding every eye.

What a nuisance, Rehman thought to himself as he came back home and stepped onto the verandah. He didn't understand why everybody in Usha's office had been so frosty and unfriendly. And what did Binoy mean by saying that Usha's family was arranging a wedding for her? He really had to get in touch with Usha and talk to her. But how?

His father was nowhere to be seen and only the assistant, Aruna, was at the table, filing some photographs. He gave her a quick, thin smile with tight lips and looked away, making for the inner door.

'Excuse me,' Aruna said.

Rehman looked up at her in surprise. 'Yes?' They usually didn't exchange more than the occasional word.

'You know this girl, don't you?' She was waving a photograph.

Rehman went over to the table and took the photograph. It was Usha. 'How did you get this?' he said.

Aruna took out a form from underneath some papers. 'Her father came yesterday and became a member. He said he wanted his daughter to be wedded as soon as possible.' She gave him the form.

As Rehman read it, a slow smile spread over his face. Usha's date of birth, her horoscope, caste, family wealth, native village and address were all filled in. 'Thank you,' he said, leaning forward and taking her hand. '*Thank you.* You are a star.'

Aruna looked shocked and withdrew her hand from his. Rehman said, 'Sorry about that. You are a godsend. I could kiss you.'

Aruna shrank back in horror.

Rehman laughed. 'Don't worry, I won't! But you've just saved a life – maybe two.'

About an hour later, Usha heard voices outside. She went to the door and listened.

'Open the room now,' said a woman's voice and Usha smiled. Her letter had reached its destination after all. She was suddenly glad that Rehman had not come over after all. Her fiancé would have just put her father's back up and made the whole situation more difficult. Her grandmother was a much more powerful rescuer, anyway. She could imagine her standing there, bamboo-thin and arrow-straight but for a slight stoop to her shoulders.

'He is not here at the moment. He will be back in less than an hour. Let us wait,' said her mother, on the other side of the door.

'No, I don't want to wait. Open it now,' said her grandmother.

'My husband told me not to open it.'

'And I am your mother-in-law. Are you going against my wishes?'

'No, but . . .' said her mother. Her voice trailed away and Usha could imagine her mother twisting uncomfortably. She had always been intimidated by Usha's grandmother.

'Now, Devaki,' said her grandmother. 'I am running out of patience. What was wrong with you anyway that you allowed such a silly thing to happen in the first place?'

'Your son—'

'Tchah!' said her grandmother, clicking her tongue. 'Men are like that. Their judgement is easily clouded by aggression. You should have controlled him and made sure that things didn't get this far. Anyway, it is not too late even now – just open the door.'

'I cannot do it,' said her mother, surprising Usha with her stubbornness.

Usha could sense the old lady sighing in irritation. She wasn't used to having her wishes thwarted. 'All right, I can understand that you don't want to go against your husband's direct orders,' she heard her grandmother say. 'Just give me the keys. I'll unlock it myself.'

Soon the key rattled and the door was thrown open. Usha rushed out and hugged her grandmother.

'I am so glad to see you, naannamma,' she said. Unexpectedly, tears came to her eyes and she started sobbing.

'There, there. It's all right,' said her grandmother and led her into the living room. They sat down on the sofa, while her mother got them buttermilk and took a seat on the settee opposite.

'How did you find out about Usha?' her mother asked the older lady.

Usha's grandmother tapped her nose twice with her index finger and said, 'I have my sources. Right, tell me everything.'

Usha and her mother both started talking at the same time. After a minute her grandmother raised her hands. 'One by one,' she said. She pointed to Usha and said, 'You go first.'

Usha told her story and her grandmother looked pensive. She turned to Usha's mother and said, 'Who is this guy, Sankar, from Alamanda that you've found? What do you know about him?'

'The marriage broker brought us the details. His father is a big landlord with seventy acres of land. They plant rice, peanuts and vegetables. He has two older brothers and a younger sister who are already married,' said her mother. She turned to Usha and said, 'They don't have any buffaloes, except one they keep for their family's milk and butter. He runs a successful transport business.'

'What did he study?' said her grandmother.

'He didn't pass high school,' interrupted Usha.

'You and my son have both been idiots,' the old woman said to Usha's mother. 'You have borne and raised a daughter, unlike me who had only sons, but you don't know anything about girls.'

'The water is hot,' said her mother. 'Why don't you take a shower and wash off the dust from your journey?'

Usha tightened her grip on her grandmother's hand. Her grandmother patted her arm and got up. 'Don't worry,' she said. 'Nobody is going to lock you up again now that I'm here.' She turned to Usha's mother and said, 'That's the first sensible thing you've said since I came here. Bring my bag into my room.'

The old lady walked regally out of the hall, followed by her daughter-in-law carrying her suitcase.

Usha sat alone, sipping her buttermilk, after they departed. She was really glad to be out of her room – there was no way Sankar was getting her now. The noise of the mynah chirping in the garden outside, the roar of a motorcycle, the honk of a car on the road and the tick-tock of the big pendulum clock in the hall had never sounded more vivid. She would sleep with her grandmother for the next few days, she decided. Just in case . . .

Ten minutes later, her father appeared and stopped abruptly when he saw her sitting there.

'How?' he said. He turned to the interior of the house and shouted, 'Devaki . . .'

Her mother came running and stood by the sofa wringing her hands.

Her father shouted, only a little less loudly, 'How dare you let her out? Didn't I tell you not to open her door when I am not in the house?'

Usha's mother said nothing. Her father's eyes bulged and looked as big as an owl's. He moved forward with a raised hand as if he would strike her mother. Usha stood up and said, 'Stop it, naanna. Amma didn't let me out.'

Her father's hand fell to his side and he turned to her. 'Then who?'

'I let her out,' said a voice from the other side of the room and her father turned towards it. Her grandmother was in a fresh mustard-coloured sari. Her thin, grey hair was tied in a rough knot, the skin on her cheeks baggy on the bones. Her collarbones stood out above her loose blouse. She looks aged, thought Usha suddenly. Her journey must have taken its toll on her. She normally came in the car with Usha or her father so how had she come to the city now? But there was no weakness in the way she stood straight as a lathi and faced her son. 'I unlocked the door and let your daughter out.'

'Why?' said Usha's father. 'I locked her in to bring her to her senses. She is bent on bringing dishonour to our family name. Her wedding is arranged in just a few more days.'

'You should have locked yourself up before your sense abandoned you and climbed up a palm tree,' said her grandmother to Usha's father. 'Did you think that forcibly marrying her off to the first man you find on the street is the answer? That marriage would have broken down within a year and then where would your precious family honour be?'

'Don't interfere, old woman. You don't understand these matters. Go back to the village and I will call you for your granddaughter's wedding.'

'Wah Wah!' said her grandmother, clapping her hands. 'This

was all that was left for me in life – to hear my son insult me. My husband never spoke to me like that, so why should I hear such words from you?' She came closer to her son, raised a finger and wagged it in front of his nose. 'Listen to me and listen carefully. Locking up your daughter was wrong and trying to marry her off against her will to somebody you don't know anything about is even worse.'

'So, am I a eunuch that you expect me to just stand and watch while our daughter washes our honour out on the street?'

'Don't be crude,' said Usha's grandmother. She and her son stood eye to eye, glaring at each other. 'Do as—'

The bell rang, its loud clang making them all jump. Usha went past her unmoving father and opened the door. She was surprised to see a police officer and some constables standing outside.

'May we come in?'

'Oh!' said Usha, smacking her forehead with her hand. She had forgotten all about the message she had sent with the boy, Balu, earlier in the day. 'It's all right, inspector. There is no need to come in. See, I am not locked up any more.'

The police inspector said, 'We need to carry out our checks, madam. We would like to come in.'

Usha nodded and turned back. They all went into the living room.

'What's going on?' said her father. 'Why are the police here?'

'I am Inspector Verma from the Five Town police station,' said the police officer, adjusting the cap on his head. Two men constables and a woman constable stood silently behind him. 'We received a report that a woman is being held against her will in this house. We need to investigate. Do we have permission to check your house?'

'Check the house?' said Usha's father, sitting heavily back on the sofa.

Usha said, 'I sent the message, Inspector. But I am free now.

I am sorry to have troubled you. Please accept my apologies.'

'As I said, we still need to check, madam. May we do so? I came as soon as I received the message but if necessary I will get a warrant.'

'All right,' said Usha. 'You can check the house. We don't have anything to hide.'

The inspector nodded and the constables fanned out. Less than five minutes later, they were all back, shaking their heads. Inspector Verma turned to one of them and said, 'Bring the boy.'

The constable went out and came back a few seconds later with Balu. The boy seemed small next to the policeman. He looked around the house with big eyes.

'Do you see the lady who gave you the message?' asked the inspector.

Balu nodded and pointed to Usha. 'There,' he said.

The officer nodded. 'You may go,' he said.

Usha smiled at the boy and said, 'Thank you, Balu. You did a great job. I hope you haven't got into trouble.'

Balu laughed. 'No problem, madam. I got a ride in the police jeep! My friends saw me on the way in and I can tell that they are really jealous.'

Usha said, 'I'll talk to you later, Balu. Go on now.'

The boy ran out of the room.

The inspector turned to Usha and said, 'In your letter, you wrote that your parents were forcing you to marry against your will. What do you say about that?'

'That was a misunderstanding. My father has now agreed to cancel that match,' said Usha. She turned to her father. 'Isn't that true, naanna?' she asked sweetly.

Her father looked at her for several seconds, open-mouthed, without replying.

'Haven't you, naanna?' she said again, her voice like flint.

He glanced at the unsmiling inspector and the grim constables holding iron-banded bamboo lathis and gulped. 'Yes,' he said. 'That match is cancelled. You may go, inspector.'

The inspector sat down on the sofa and said, 'May I have a glass of water?'

'Yes, of course,' said Usha's mother. 'I'm sorry, you caught us by surprise.' She rushed into the kitchen and came back with water for all the police.

'Thank you,' said the inspector and took a sip. 'It's obvious that you have worked as a family and sorted out your issues. That is good. Even though I am a police officer, I don't approve of our force getting involved in domestic issues – some things are best handled within the four walls of a house.'

'That's good,' said Usha's father. 'As you can see, there is nothing for you to do here.'

'Just because I don't approve, it doesn't mean that I won't get involved if I think there is coercion or violence,' Inspector Verma said. He now looked at Usha. 'If the situation changes, let me know any time and I'll be straight back.'

Usha nodded. 'Thanks, Inspector. Sorry for taking up your time. You must be a busy man.'

'Yes, the police are always busy.' He got up and looked at Usha's father. 'Will you see me out, sir?'

Usha's father got up and they walked out. Usha followed a few steps behind. It was obvious that the inspector wanted to have a chat with her father and she wanted to hear what he had to say.

'Whatever you did to solve the problem yourself was best, sir,' said the inspector to Usha's father. 'A senior citizen like you does not want to get involved in police and court matters. It's a lot of hassle and will cost you stress and money.'

'Thank you, Inspector. I appreciate your advice,' said her father, his voice more gruff than usual. 'I am sorry that you had to come out here for nothing.'

'Oh, we are just doing our job. However, the constables will now have to spend some extra time at the station in the evening catching up with their paperwork instead of enjoying it with their families.'

Her father did not say anything for a long moment and Usha caught her breath. She had understood straight away what the inspector was saying.

Finally, her father waved a hand and said, 'Of course, inspector. I am so slow today. What about you? I am sure you've had to take some trouble too.'

The inspector looked through the trees with a faraway expression. 'No, I am only doing my duty, you know. Just for the constables. A couple of hundred rupees each should be sufficient, don't you think? Just some tea-and-snack money.'

Usha's father took out his wallet and counted out ten one-hundred-rupee notes. One of the constables came forward, took the money and saluted her father. The police left and Usha slipped back into the house before her father returned. He did so half a minute later and sat on the sofa.

Usha's grandmother said, 'If I hadn't come when I did and unlocked Usha, you would be grinding lentils at the police station at this very moment.'

Usha's father sat silently with his arms folded across his chest and his head bent. Usha's mother looked ready to burst into tears.

Usha's grandmother continued, 'First, as you agreed in front of the inspector, cancel this match. Tell that Sankar fellow that he doesn't need to come over. Do you understand?'

'You don't—' said her father, looking up.

'Ore . . . Just shut up and listen to me,' said his mother. Usha's eyes widened in shock – she had never heard anybody speak to her father like that before. 'Even as a boy, you always used to act first and think later, and you haven't lost that habit after all these years.'

Usha kissed her grandmother on the cheek. The old lady

turned on her. 'And why are you so happy, little miss? What great task have you done that you are pumping your arms up and down in delight?'

'Er . . .' said Usha, speechless at the sudden attack from somebody she thought was her ally.

'We may not have a choice, but it doesn't mean that we have to be happy about it. No woman in our house has ever had a love marriage. What you are hell-bent on doing does not bring any honour to our family.'

'But nannamma . . . ' said Usha.

The doorbell rang and they all looked at each other.

'Is it the police again?' said Usha's mother, looking like a scared mouse interrupted in its nocturnal travels in the kitchen by a bright light. Usha's father got up heavily and walked to the door in the hall. His footsteps sounded loud on the marble floor.

Usha heard her father open the door and ask, 'Who are you?'

'Is Usha all right?' asked another male voice and Usha jumped up.

'Oh no . . .' she said in panic and rushed to the front door. Rehman had come over. She almost shouldered her father aside and said in a voice that was almost a hiss, 'What are you doing here?'

Rehman jerked his head back slightly. 'I was worried,' he said. 'I called and you didn't answer. I left several messages for you. Then I called your office and they said you had left your job. I didn't know what was going on. I finally managed to get your address and I've come straight here.'

'Oh, Rehman,' said Usha, touched at his concern. 'I am all right. There's nothing to worry about. I was going to call you today.'

Usha's father butted in angrily. 'You,' he said. 'You are the man who is spoiling my daughter.'

'You'd better come inside,' said Usha, pulling Rehman into the house by his hand. 'There is no point discussing family matters where anybody walking past on the road can hear.'

They all walked in. Usha's father sat on the settee next to her mother. Standing next to Rehman in front of her parents and her grandmother, Usha announced, 'Everybody, this is Rehman. Rehman, this is my mother, my father and that's my naan-namma, my father's mother.'

'Namaste,' said Rehman, nodding to everybody in the room.

They all stared at him curiously and Usha tried to see Rehman through their eyes. He was tall and good-looking with high cheeks, a long nose and bright eyes. But Usha knew that that's not what they were seeing. Instead, they were probably looking at his thin beard, his rough cotton ethnic shirt and his trousers fraying at the heels. He was darker than he should be, from the time he spent out in the sun.

'Sit down, Rehman,' she said and pointed to the sofa opposite her grandmother's. He sat down gingerly on the edge.

'What happened? Why have you left your job?' he asked her.

'Never mind that. How dare you come here?' said her father and tried to get up. Usha's mother put a hand on his arm and stopped him.

'So,' said Usha's grandmother. 'You want to marry my grand-daughter?'

'Yes, madam. I wish to marry Usha,' he replied in a soft voice.

Usha could sense her father barely controlling his temper, just from the way his feet tapped on the floor, and she didn't look at him directly.

'What do you do?' her grandmother asked.

'I am a civil engineer, madam.'

'Civil engineer, pah! You look like a mason to me. Are you sure you did not hide your trowel and plumb line in the bushes outside before ringing the bell?' said her father.

Rehman looked at Usha's father but said nothing. Usha was glad to see that Rehman was keeping his cool and not reacting to her father's comments. Her grandmother raised her hand and frowned at her son. 'Usha's father is a little upset but I can see where he is coming from. Most engineers I know dress in smart clothes and drive jeeps or cars. How come you are dressed like a worker?'

'Stop it, all of you,' said Usha, before Rehman could reply. 'Rehman works on social projects. He is not interested in money.' She turned to her grandmother. 'I wrote to you in the letter – Rehman is the man who started the campaign in Royyapalem against the land seizures.'

Her grandmother nodded and said, 'That's very good, young man. I met many freedom fighters when I was a teenager and they were like you. They could have been successful lawyers or industrialists but they gave it all up and followed Gandhi and Nehru in the struggle against the British. But do you know what happened to most of them?'

'What, madam?' Rehman said.

'Once we got freedom, they were pushed back into obscurity, surviving on meagre pensions. They had to run from pillar to post, mounting an even bigger struggle than against the British to secure those small payments. Those who rose to the top and were in a position to change our nation were the politicians who could command vote banks by caste, money and thuggery.'

'That's a very cynical view, naannamma,' said Usha. 'Nehru was not corrupt, nor Patel nor Azad. Lots of good people held power after Independence.'

'You are still young,' said her grandmother. 'When you get to my age, what you now call cynicism, you will begin to call realism. Yes, Nehru and a few others stayed good but most of the others . . .' She shook her head. 'Mera Bharat Mahaan – my India is great; Saare jahaan se accha Hindustan hamara – Our Hindustan is the best in the world . . . Songs and slogans . . . In reality all around is corruption, intolerance and poverty.'

'Madam, that is unnecessarily pessimistic. We still have a

number of problems but things have improved a lot in the last few years,' said Rehman.

'Enough of these political debates,' said Usha's father. 'I want this marriage stopped and this . . . this interloper . . . thrown out.'

'Has anybody asked your opinion?' asked Usha's grandmother, rather rudely. 'Your daughter is an adult and can make her own choice. We can only guide her, not force her.'

'Hear, hear!' said Usha, clapping her hands.

'The reason I brought up the political discussion is simple – in this life, idealism is not enough. We need some worldliness too,' the old lady said. 'Our Usha has grown up in comfort and wealth. She has never experienced want or difficulty. How then can we give her away to somebody who cannot look after her in the manner that she is accustomed to?' She looked at Rehman with her eyebrows raised.

Rehman said, 'Yes, madam. I understand.'

'You were a bachelor until now and you did as you pleased. And that's OK, that's good. But marriage means responsibility. How will you look after my granddaughter?'

'I—' began Rehman.

Usha interrupted him. 'I don't need anybody to look after me. I have my own career. I earn enough money.'

Her grandmother shushed her and turned to Rehman. 'She will get pregnant and may have to stop working. You cannot rely on a woman's income. And even if you could, do you really want to live on your wife's earnings?'

Usha tried to speak again and her grandmother raised a hand to stop her.

'What are you going to do about it?' she asked Rehman. 'I am not saying that you have to give up all the social work you are doing, but you need to balance that with earning enough money to support a family.'

Rehman nodded. 'I understand,' he said.

'You can marry Usha. But there are some conditions. I want you to change to and stay in a well-paying job.' Usha's grandmother looked at him sharply and continued, 'Is it true that you live with your parents?'

Rehman nodded and said, 'At the moment, yes.'

'That won't do. You need to have your own flat in a nice area. And you should own a car. We will wait a reasonable length of time while you arrange all this and show that you can consistently earn money. Come to us again when you satisfy these conditions and we will place Usha's hand in yours with our blessings. Do you agree?'

Rehman looked at Usha but she just bit her lower lip and didn't say anything. Rehman looked at the ceiling for several seconds and then said, 'What you are asking is reasonable. I will work on it and come to you again.'

Usha smiled at him and came over to sit next to him. Her mother stifled a quick sob and dabbed her eyes with the edge of her sari. Her father shook his head like a penned bullock that is being provoked by a man wearing a red shirt.

Her grandmother said to Rehman, 'Have you told anybody about your engagement with Usha?'

'Only my cousin.'

'Please keep it that way,' said the old lady. 'This is for both of you. I know that young people nowadays seem to take it very lightly, but a woman's reputation is extremely important. I don't want anybody talking loosely about Usha and casting aspersions on our house. Until you come to us formally again, neither of you will tell anybody else about this engagement. In fact, you shouldn't meet again until that time.'

'That's ridiculous, naannamma. We won't tell anybody else, but you are going too far by asking us not to meet at all.'

Her grandmother sighed. 'All right,' she said. 'But I expect you both to be discreet. I don't want you to meet too often and I would expect you to act like two friends, not as a couple.'

Usha nodded and said, 'Fair enough.'

Usha's grandmother turned to Rehman and said, 'You look like an honourable man. I want you to promise me that there will be no physical relationship between you and Usha until you get married.'

Rehman blushed and looked at the ground. Usha's cheeks reddened and she said, 'Naannamma . . .'

Her grandmother ignored her and stared at Rehman with unblinking eyes. After a few moments, Rehman looked up and said, 'Of course, madam.'

'Promise me. Swear on your god . . . Allah.'

Rehman looked at her steadily and said, 'I swear by Allah, the all-seeing, all-knowing.'

Rehman left soon after and Usha and her family sat down for lunch. They had barely started eating when the doorbell rang again. Usha's father got up angrily from the table and threw his napkin on the floor. 'Is this house a temple that people just keep ringing the bell?' he said, looking disgusted.

The ladies listened as Usha's father opened the door and spoke to the visitor.

'I am sorry, Sankar. We have decided not to go ahead with the marriage.'

'Do you think you can decide and un-decide and I'll just accept it quietly? Do I look as if I am wearing bangles? You promised me gold, money and land. I am friends with important people and I know how to enforce my rights.'

'What rights?' said her father, his voice rising to match the other man's. 'She is my daughter and I will decide whom she marries. We just had a discussion, that's all – there were no promises involved.'

Usha was tempted to go to the front door and tell Sankar where he could stick his important friends, but she controlled herself. Sankar would not be so easily shaken off. She didn't want to admit it to herself, but she was scared of Sankar. She shied away from that thought and muttered, 'Naanna has brought this problem on himself – let him solve it on his own.'

'What did you say?' said her grandmother.

'Nothing, naannamma,' she said, smiling. 'Here, take some more potato curry.'

CHAPTER THIRTEEN

One evening two months later, Rehman was waiting at Ramakrishna Beach. Now that winter had gone and the days were heating up – the temperature was touching the mid-thirties daily – the beach in the middle of town was buzzing with people. College students, newly married couples, entire clans from grandmothers to babes-in-arms, groups of nervous, shrieking tourists from the interior who had never seen the sea before, peanut pedlars, balloon blowers, seashell sellers, a rusty hand-powered merry-go-round and even a couple of nags offering kids a ride on the sand – all made for a busy scene. Rehman sat on the low beach wall, taking it all in and listening to the sound of the surf pounding the shore.

His work with the housing charity had wound down and he had started a job with a big builder in the city. It is not real work, he thought to himself, just going round the offices of the planning department and the urban development authorities, trying to get their signatures. Actually, his job was even worse than that. It was almost meaningless. Initial plans showing the set-asides on all sides of the plot and the height of the building, labour safety certificates, electricity and water connection permits, fire safety certificates and many more documents are required when constructing a commercial building. Unfortunately, the people in the various agencies who issue these permits invariably demanded bribes to do their work. When challenged, they said, 'You will make so much money once this building is completed; don't be greedy and deny us our cut.'

What was worse was that the certificates were ends in themselves. Once the plan was approved, developers routinely overbuilt on the land or put in an additional floor; once the electricity connection permit was obtained, a transformer was either not used or one of a lower power capacity was substituted. As for fire safety, Rehman despaired. In the past, the kind of projects he worked on meant that he was spared the ordeal of dealing with all these demands, but now . . .

He shook his head. He had been working with the builder for just under a month now and he had already had to stop himself at least twice from chucking it in. His boss was very harsh with the workers and didn't treat them properly. He had very little respect either for the law or for the building regulations, seeing them all as challenges to overcome rather than as guidelines for a peaceful society. Only the thought of Usha and her grandmother's challenge had stayed his hand and kept him in the job. He knew why he was going against his principles and turning a blind eye to corruption and illegality. Love. Love and a happy life with a fantastic woman. Was it selfish to want them?

Somebody tapped him on the right shoulder. He looked behind him but nobody was there. A tap on the left shoulder followed and he quickly turned around to see Usha giggling. He dusted the place next to him and she sat down on her jeans, flipping the bottom of her kameez out of the way.

'Oh, what a big frown you had there,' she said.

'It's good to see you. You are looking great.'

Usha smiled. 'It's been a long time, hasn't it?' Almost a fortnight had passed since they had last met, though they often spoke on the phone. She shaded her eyes with her hand and started scanning the heavens.

'What are you doing?' asked Rehman, looking at the clear blue sky himself.

'I am looking for clouds,' she said.

'Why?'

'I believe you've complimented me on my looks. It's so unusual that I am checking for signs of rain.'

Rehman laughed and Usha joined him. They were still deeply in love and the restrictions placed on them by Usha's family had done nothing to diminish their feelings for each other. 'Has your grandmother gone back to her village?'

'Yes, last night. We asked her to stay for a few more weeks but she had already made her arrangements. The family joke is that her travel plans are more fixed than those of the Queen of England.'

Rehman smiled and said, 'She is one scary lady.'

'You actually came out of meeting her all right. My cousin was once discovered going to a cinema with friends before some important exams. By the time she finished with him and his friends, they were all crying.'

They stared at the colourful bazaar of people on the beach for several minutes, enjoying the salty, cool breeze off the sea.

'How's the job?' asked Usha.

Rehman sighed. 'Painful . . . boring . . .'

'Don't look so glum, darling,' said Usha.

'Sorry, I am being such a grouch. Do you know what happened today?'

'What?'

'This morning, I went to the Municipal Commissioner's office and the clerk couldn't say when the approval would be ready. I told him that we had followed all the rules and the signature should be a formality but he just kept humming and hawing. Finally I left and told Mr Bhargav.'

Usha nodded. Mr Bhargav was Rehman's employer – a real-estate developer and an old friend of Usha's father, though Rehman had only found this out later.

Rehman continued, 'Mr Bhargav sent his nephew after lunch and, guess what, he came back within the hour with the papers. It seems that some people are more persuasive than others.'

Usha shrugged. 'Yes, and a bundle of notes is even more convincing,' she said.

'True, true.' They were both silent for a moment. 'How's your job?'

'Going well,' she said.

Usha had got back her old job at the TV station by arguing that, as she had never submitted a resignation letter, she should never have been struck off the rolls in the first place.

Usha stood up. 'Let's go along the water,' she said.

They walked at the edge of the shoreline, very close to each other, but not actually touching except for the occasional brush of the backs of their hands, soft as a feathery kiss. 'Do you think the waves ever get tired of going up and down the beach?' said Usha.

'An ancient Arab poet once described the sea as a lover and the city as its beloved. He said that the sea rushes up to meet its darling and then falls back when it sees its love's guardians.'

'I guess he was saying that true love never wearies,' said Usha, and Rehman laughed.

'Don't laugh, you brute. What is it with men?'

They continued walking. 'Can you come next week to Vasu's village?' he asked after a moment.

'No,' she said. 'I have to do a special report.'

'Now who's being unromantic?' said Rehman.

'Is it really true what you told me about the wedding that the villagers are planning? I've never heard anything more absurd!'

'Apparently so. That's why Pari is coming as well. It isn't normal for a . . . woman . . . like her to be able to participate in all the wedding ceremonies, so she doesn't want to miss it.'

They walked along the beach until the crowds thinned away,

before sitting on the sand to watch the ceaseless ebb and flow of the sea. Her feet burrowed in the warm sand like a pair of frolicking rabbits. Rehman found the fawn-coloured grains of sand on her golden skin and pink toes an incredibly erotic sight. He wanted to hug his fiancée and bind her to his own body but he could not forget the promise he had made to her grandmother. Rehman sighed. Life was difficult – at work and here as well.

On Sunday, a couple of days later, Aruna fielded phone call after phone call. An advertisement for the younger son of a rich goldsmith had appeared that morning in *Today*, and both she and Mr Ali were busy answering the many people who called in response.

'Yes, sir,' she said on the phone. 'The boy is getting his own shop. The elder son will take over the father's shop but a new shop is being built near Dwaraka Nagar for the younger son.' She listened for a bit longer, put the phone down and wrote the details on a sheet of paper.

Mr Ali was dealing with a couple who had come with a photograph of their daughter in response to the ad. He saw them out and mopped his brow. 'I didn't know there were so many goldsmiths in this town,' he said.

'And I think every single one of them has called this morning.' The phone rang again and Aruna picked it up. 'Mr Ali's marriage bureau.'

By eleven-thirty, the phone calls died away and Mr Ali went into the house, saying that he needed a snack. Mrs Ali came out with a glass of lemonade for Aruna and sat down in her usual chair by the gate. Aruna took the glass with thanks and drank a deep gulp.

'I was so thirsty,' she said.

'I am not surprised,' said Mrs Ali. 'You've been on the phone continuously. Were the calls for the goldsmith's son?'

'Yes, madam,' said Aruna. She took another sip and stretched her neck to remove a kink.

'I thought that would be popular,' said Mrs Ali. 'How are things at home?'

Aruna shook her head. 'Not so good. I just cannot seem to do anything right. I don't mind hearing complaints from everybody else but even my husband finds fault with my actions and that's painful.'

'Things will get better,' said Mrs Ali. 'You know in your heart that you are not doing anything wrong. Just hang in there.'

Aruna nodded. 'You are right. It's got to the stage where I've started doubting myself. I keep thinking that maybe I do resent my sister-in-law in my heart and that's why things are like this. But I know that's not true. I genuinely bear no ill will towards her. I want the best for Mani and her son. I just have to convince everybody else around me about it.'

Aruna had finished the drink and Mrs Ali stood up and took the glass from her. 'I am sure it will be fine. Stay strong and don't despair.'

Aruna started filing away the morning's letters. She looked at the clock on the wall before remembering that she wore a watch. She wasn't fully used to it yet. Another hour before lunch, she thought. The gate opened and a man walked in with long hair combed over from the side to cover his bald crown. Aruna said, 'Namaste, Mr Reddy.'

Mr Ali came out and nodded to him. Aruna could see that Mr Ali did not recognise the visitor. She took out Mr Reddy's file from the wardrobe that acted as their filing cabinet and handed it to Mr Ali. He quickly skimmed through the file and looked up.

'Ah, Mr Reddy!' he said, smiling. He asked Aruna for the photo album and flipped to the photo of a young man standing in front of the tall, wrought-iron gates of a power plant, framed by gnarled ganneru trees with white flowers in bloom. 'The last time you came here, we spoke to this young man's father and you were very happy with the match. Has everything been finalised?' he said.

Mr Reddy shook his head. 'I wish it was,' he said. 'He looked fine until I found out that he has been to a private college for his engineering.'

'So?' asked Mr Ali. 'I don't understand.'

'Don't you know what that means? People only go to private engineering colleges if they cannot get seats in government universities. He is obviously not as good at his studies as my own two children. I cannot countenance such a match.'

'But, Mr Reddy, the young man has a good job, he is good-looking and his family is local. If everything else is suitable, what does it matter how he wrote an entrance exam when he was eighteen years old?'

'No, Mr Ali. I didn't come here to talk about a match I've already rejected. I came to find out if you had a new list.'

Mr Ali turned to Aruna, raised his eyebrows and shook his head almost imperceptibly. 'Please give Mr Reddy the new Kapu list,' he said.

Aruna took out the list and gave it to Mr Reddy, who looked through it immediately. 'This one,' he said, taking out a pen from his shirt pocket and circling an address. 'Do you have any more details?'

Aruna looked at the entry halfway down the list, circled in blue, and took out the appropriate file. She had a quick look at the file and handed it to Mr Ali. 'I haven't seen these people. Did you meet them or was it a postal application?' she said to her boss.

Mr Ali glanced at the file and said, 'I remember them.' He turned to Mr Reddy and said, 'They joined less than a month ago. The boy is a lawyer in Hyderabad. It's a very good family, sir. The father's a simple man who owned a video cassette shop and the mother's a housewife, but their children . . .' Mr Ali shook his head in amazement. 'Three boys and two girls, and each of them is highly educated and well settled – two doctors, two engineers and this boy, the youngest, a BA, LLB, a lawyer.'

Mr Reddy looked impressed. 'Do you have the boy's photo?' he asked.

'No,' said Mr Ali. 'But I've seen him when he came here with his parents and he is a pleasant chap.'

'Thanks,' said Mr Reddy, standing up to leave. 'The family sounds very promising. I'll follow it up.'

'What a strange man,' said Aruna after a few minutes, when they were alone. 'He had a good match and rejected it because of the boy's college.'

Mr Ali ran his hand through his hair. 'Some people are like that – always searching for something better, never satisfied. Makes you wonder if they ever get a good night's sleep. They must toss and turn, dreaming about a softer mattress or a plumper pillow.'

Aruna laughed. 'You know the saying, sir: each man's obsession is his joy.'

Rehman and Pari got down from the three-wheeled auto-rickshaw and went into a busy restaurant. Rehman ordered a plate of idlis, steamed lentil and rice cakes, with sambhar and coconut chutney. Pari declined but ordered a coffee when Rehman insisted. When the waiter went away, she said, 'Why are we here? We had breakfast less than two hours ago. We should have gone straight to the bus station.'

Rehman looked around the café and said, 'How poor are they that have not patience! What wound did ever heal but by degrees?'

Pari waved her hand in front of her face and frowned. 'Don't quote Iago at me when I am asking you a question,' she said.

Rehman laughed. 'Nobody can doubt your knowledge, at least. Did you know that since you've come to Vizag, I've shaken the dust off my old Complete Works of Shakespeare and started reading it again?'

'Rehman!' said Pari. 'Will you tell me or not?'

The waiter came back with the idlis, coffee, a pair of glasses and a jug of water. Rehman ignored the look of impatience on his companion's face and poured the hot sambhar over the steaming idlis until they were completely covered. He then took a spoon and dug it into the soft food, took a leisurely bite and chomped it thoroughly before looking up into her face. 'Aren't you having your coffee?' he asked.

She bent her head and he put his hands up to shoulder height in mock-surrender, saying, 'OK, OK, I give up. Usha wanted to meet us before we went to the village, so we are waiting for her.'

'What?' said Pari, in a high-pitched squeak. Her hand brushed through her hair and she looked at him. 'Why didn't you tell me before?'

Rehman shrugged. 'What's the matter?' he said. 'It's just Usha. I know you two haven't met before but I've told each of you about the other.'

Pari took a deep breath. 'You are such a buddhoo . . .'

'Hi,' said a female voice next to them.

Rehman pushed his chair back and stood up.

'Hello Usha,' he said. Pari stood up as well and he introduced the two young women to each other. They smiled in greeting. Usha was wearing a casual-looking, but expensive, dark-green soft silk top over a churidar, tight silk trousers, in a paler blue. A riff of small white lace flowers ran in two lines down the front of her top. Pari had dropped her mourning monochrome and wore an orange-coloured sari. She also had on her mother's antique silver jewellery.

'Why were you calling my fiancé a fool?' said Usha. 'I am not saying that he isn't, but—'

Pari's cheeks coloured red. 'You heard that . . . Sorry, but my devar, brother-in-law, is a simple-minded fellow.'

'That's why he needs an intelligent girl to guide his life.'

The waiter came over and Rehman was glad of the distraction. He didn't like the way the conversation was going. 'Are you sure you cannot come with us?' Rehman said to Usha.

'Unfortunately, no. My controller's just confirmed the interview with the Superintendent of Police for the special report,' Usha said.

'Do you want tea?' said Rehman.

She shook her head and simply watched while the other two finished their food and drink.

'Well, have fun,' said Usha finally when Rehman pushed his plate away from him. 'Are you guys really going by bus?'

'Yes,' said Rehman. 'We'll go to the RTC complex from here.' RTC was the government-run Road Transport Corporation.

'You don't have to. Our driver will drop you off in the car. He cannot stay the weekend, though. Naanna needs the car in the evening.'

'That's not necessary. He'd have had to drive for a couple of hours and then come back again straight away. It's a waste of petrol and his time.' Apart from the reasons he had given, Rehman really didn't want to spend a couple of hours under the beady eyes of Usha's driver, Narsi.

'Naanna can afford the fuel,' Usha said. 'And as for the driver, we have to pay him whether he is driving or simply sitting outside our house, waiting to take one of us out.'

Rehman gave in. When they came out of the café, Usha took them round the corner into a side street. They walked up to her car and found it locked. Usha looked around in irritation as a young man in grey cotton shirt and trousers came running up to them.

'Sorry, madam. I was just talking to the stall-owner over there,' he said, pointing to a push-cart selling home-made cool drinks.

Rehman didn't recognise the driver. 'What happened to Narsi?' he said.

Usha shrugged. 'I got rid of the wife-beating slime ball. He was the one who carried tales about us to my parents.'

'Oh!' said Rehman. 'I thought he had been with your family for a long time.'

'More than ten years. After his words had no effect on me, he sent his wife to plead his case. Can you believe that?' said Usha. 'I gave her five hundred rupees and told her to leave him.'

The driver took their bags from Rehman and put them in the boot. They got into the car.

'I'll get out at my office and then Srikanth will drop you off,' said Usha. Then, to Rehman, 'Don't look at me like that. Sometimes in life you have to ignore your emotions and make hard-headed decisions.'

Less than two hours later, they were travelling down a narrow lane between mud-walled huts and a two-storey pukka building. Vasu came running from inside one of the huts and hugged Rehman.

'I knew as soon as I heard the car sound that it was you,' he shouted. The boy turned to his companion and said, 'Namaste, Ush—' He looked into Pari's face and stopped suddenly. He gripped Rehman's hand and said, 'But you are not . . .'

Pari laughed and said, 'No, I am not. My name is Pari Aunty.'

'How many aunties do you have?' Vasu said, looking up at Rehman.

'Don't worry about it,' said Rehman, tousling the boy's hair. He turned to Vasu's grandfather, who had just walked out of the hut, and said, 'Namaste, Naidu gaaru.'

After the introductions, the driver lifted out their bags, refused an offer of drink and got back into the car. He would have to reverse fifty yards in the lane before he could turn around for the return journey. Rehman was suddenly glad that Usha had not come with them. He could not imagine her being able to spend the night on a floor of dried and polished cow-dung in a thatched hut.

As if Mr Naidu had read his thoughts, he pointed to the two-storey house next door and said, 'I've arranged for the lady to sleep in my cousin's house. You've met his daughter-in-law, haven't you?'

'Sitakka, the one with six fingers on both hands and legs,' said Vasu, with his hand cupped around his mouth as if he was telling a secret, but in a boy's voice that carried.

Rehman laughed and nodded.

'They've come over as well and your sister-in-law can sleep with the ladies,' said Mr Naidu. 'It's also the bride's house.'

They left their shoes by the door and got out of the sun, bending at the waist to pass under the low eaves. The inside of the house was one large room, dark and cool, with few decorations other than a framed photo of Vasu's parents and pictures of various Hindu gods hanging on one wall. The floor was grey-green in colour and polished to a sheen, while the roof was high and thatched with palm leaves between beams of roughly hewn, fibrous palm-tree trunks.

'You must excuse the condition of my house,' said Mr Naidu to Pari, pointing at the many dusty cobwebs between the beams and the leaves, above head height. 'As you can see, no woman has lived here for many years and there is only so much I can do.'

Prosperity is said to stay away from a house with cobwebs in it. A woman who lets cobwebs into in her house is considered a slattern and one who brings destitution to the family.

Pari said, 'I don't mind. If you want, I can help you spring-clean the house while I am here.'

'No, I cannot let you do that. You are a guest in our house and you have come here to enjoy yourself,' said Mr Naidu firmly.

He led them out of the back door into a fenced compound with a well, a drumstick tree and an outhouse for the toilet. A large stone in a cemented corner was clearly used for washing clothes. Mr Naidu pointed out the well and said, 'My son, Vasu's father, got it dug with his first salary. Before that, we had to go to my cousin's house for our water.'

Pari nodded in understanding. The little tour over, they washed their legs by the well, then returned to the house and sat on a mat unrolled on the floor. An earthen pot in a cradle hung by a thin rope from the rafters. A line of ants was walking down one side of the rope and up the diametrically opposite side.

'Is that sugar in there?' asked Pari, pointing at the pot.

Vasu shook his head. 'Those are curds. We just cannot keep the ants away. The rope trick worked for a few weeks and then somehow the ants found it.'

Pari laughed. 'When I was in the village, we used to put our dairy in small pots in the middle of a large pan filled with water.'

'Good idea,' said Mr Naidu. 'I've seen it done for sweets. We don't actually mind it very much. Not many come down the rope, and Vasu and I don't care about scraping a few ants off when we eat. They are God's creatures and need to live too.'

'I bet you don't say that about weeds in your field,' said Rehman, laughing.

Mr Naidu grimaced and rubbed his dark-brown hand over his white stubble. 'The company sent a scientist last week, as per their contract. He advised us how much fertiliser and herbicide to apply.'

'Was his advice useful? You've been farming since you were Vasu's age and you probably know a lot more than a townie like the scientist.'

'You mustn't mock educated people like that,' said Mr Naidu. 'It's true that most of what he said is common knowledge among farmers but he did help me out with one thing.'

'What's that?'

'Do you remember the north-east corner of the field where my yield is always less than in the rest?'

'You mentioned that when I was here for the harvest. The plants did seem shorter and more sparse there.'

Vasu, probably bored with the conversation, dragged Pari away, out of the hut.

'I asked the man about it, and he took soil samples and conducted some tests. He had a big box with many coloured liquids in his jeep. He mixed the soil and one of the liquids in a long glass tube with a round bottom.' Mr Naidu looked at Rehman with a frown on his face.

Rehman nodded. 'I understand. Go on.'

'The man said that the soil in that part of the field was acidic and he advised me to mix ash in that area of the land. So you see, there are things that I didn't know even though I've been farming for so many years.'

'I have been reading up about the cotton seeds you are using. Some people don't like them and want to ban them.'

'What's not to like?' said Mr Naidu, the lines on his forehead deepening. 'If they help farmers like me to get a better yield using less pesticide, then that can only be good, can't it?'

'Bt Cotton seeds are more expensive than normal cotton seeds but you don't mind paying extra because you have to use less pesticide,' said Rehman.

Mr Naidu nodded his agreement.

'But in the Punjab, in north India, they found that after two or three years of using these seeds, mealybugs started attacking the crop.'

'Don't be silly, Rehman. Mealybugs don't attack cotton. Bollworms are the problem.'

'Exactly,' said Rehman. 'And how do you get rid of bollworms normally?'

'By applying pesticide, of course.'

'Well, with Bt Cotton, you don't have to apply pesticide to control bollworm, so what happens to all the other pests?' Rehman said.

'I see,' said Mr Naidu, slowly. 'But that means we still have to apply pesticide, in which case we might as well use normal seeds.'

'That's in a few years,' said Rehman and laughed. 'You should be all right until the bugs discover your field. But there is a bigger objection to genetically modified crops. Most crops, though not cotton, are modified to be resistant to herbicides, so you can spray fields with herbicide and kill the weeds but still leave the crop untouched.'

'That makes sense,' said Mr Naidu. 'Weeding is a big cost.'

'They are worried that the genes that give the crops their resistance to herbicide might transfer over to weeds in the wild by pollen carried on the wind or by bees.'

Mr Naidu cracked his knuckles with a loud pop, looking at the ground. He appeared deep in thought. After a moment, he said, 'That would be bad. Those weeds would spread like fire through a row of thatched huts and if herbicides don't kill them, then there would be no way of controlling them.'

'That's what these people fear,' said Rehman.

Mr Naidu shook his head. 'I don't believe it. The companies that sell these seeds are run by intelligent, educated men. If a simple man like me can see what kind of problems can arise, these men must surely appreciate it even more. Clever people will not sell something that can cause a disaster. I mean, they just wouldn't do that, would they?'

CHAPTER FOURTEEN

The next day dawned bright. As usual in Mr Naidu's household, they were up with the first light and made their ablutions with the cold well water. Pari joined them soon after from next door with a packet of pulihora, spicy tamarind rice, for breakfast.

'We made it just now,' she said. 'It was fun being in a household with so many women.' She turned to Rehman. 'Especially because no one knew that I was a widow and treated me differently,' she said in Urdu so Mr Naidu and Vasu would not understand.

Pari helped Vasu with his studies while Rehman helped Mr Naidu dig a hole to plant a young mango tree. Mr Naidu folded his sarong-like lungi in half to knee-length and swung the sharp end of a heavy iron bar into the hard ground. The older man's face creased with the strain and his arm muscles stood out in cords under the dark, sinewy skin. Despite the relative coolness of the early morning, drops of sweat soon covered his forehead. As soon as Mr Naidu stopped breaking up the ground, Rehman moved the soil to one side with a small shovel.

'How long does it take for a mango tree to start fruiting?' asked Rehman.

Mr Naidu wiped his forehead with a small towel that was

always on his shoulder. 'A tree like this that's grown from seed? About fifteen or twenty years.'

'That long?' said Rehman.

Mr Naidu laughed. 'You are wondering what an old man like me is doing, planting a tree that will not produce any fruit until after I am gone, aren't you?'

'No, no!'

Mr Naidu said, 'I am aware that I won't taste these fruit. But Vasu will eat them; and his children after him.'

They resumed digging and soon had a hole about three feet deep and over a foot wide. Mr Naidu part-filled it with composted cow dung mixed with straw, and Rehman lowered in the plant. Mr Naidu firmed the soil around the young tree with his dusty bare feet, hard from years of tramping in the fields. Rehman fetched a pail of water from the well and poured it around the sapling.

Mr Naidu said, 'We should leave something behind when we leave this earth and for a farmer like me, a tree is the easiest way of doing that.'

Sitakka and a couple of other young women came over an hour later. Pari left with them to get ready and *make* the bride. Rehman and Vasu came out of the hut to watch the women walk away, their long braids swinging and their silver anklets tinkling in the dust. One of the girls said something that Rehman couldn't catch but he could hear all of them laughing.

'Why do girls giggle so much?' asked Vasu.

Rehman scratched his head. 'You tell me when you find out,' he said.

A couple of hours later, the men got ready and left for the bridal house next door. Pari came out of a room and said to Rehman, 'Do you want to see the bride?'

He nodded and she led him inside. Pari looks really fetching in a pink sari, he thought. I wonder if she will go back to her sober clothes when we leave the village.

They passed innumerable women, from young girls to old dowagers and Pari seemed to know them all. 'That's Sitakka's mother,' she said, pointing to a middle-aged woman. Rehman looked discreetly but could not make out whether she had six fingers on her hands. They were soon in a room near the back of the house.

'There's the bride,' said Pari, with a flourish of her hands. 'Her name is Tara.'

Rehman looked at the small figure in the middle of the room, the red sari almost seeming to drown her. She had a wizened face and appeared frightened as she peered nervously around. She looked ready to jump out of the window. Rehman noticed an iron shackle round her ankle. He almost objected but stopped himself – the poor girl was in no condition to give her consent and she wouldn't be wearing the shackle for long. She would be set free once the wedding ceremony was over.

Tara's mother came up to them and said, 'It won't be the same without her in the house, you know.'

Rehman said, 'You are doing a virtuous thing. Marrying off an orphan is good deed.' After a moment he added, 'Even if she is not willing.'

Tara's mother bobbed her head and turned to Pari. 'These young girls want to make themselves up like film stars. Please help them. You are a city girl – you will know how to paint lips.'

The two women left and Rehman made his way back to Vasu and Mr Naidu.

'How's the bride?' asked Vasu.

'Beautiful . . . and nervous,' said Rehman and laughed.

By this time, several people from all over the village had started converging on the house and the menfolk spilled out into the street. There were several people from the city among the villagers. This wedding was an event and nobody wanted to miss it. A tonsured Brahmin priest in a white loincloth, his chest bare except for a white thread, carried a rolled-up bunch of

banana leaves in his hand. He started preparing a hearth with
bricks in the yard next to the house.

Among the farmers in the crowd, the talk was mostly about
the next harvest and everybody was hopeful that the yield would
be good. Mr Naidu was the only one in the group who had
planted cotton. The other farmers asked him how it was doing.

'It's two months since I sowed the seeds and buds have started
appearing on the plants,' said Mr Naidu.

The sound of a band playing music was heard in the distance
and all conversation about crops and harvests stopped.

'The bridegroom is coming,' said fifty voices.

Soon, a procession appeared around the corner. Men and
women in bright clothes and all sporting great smiles walked
behind the musicians. Unlike in other weddings, the groom was
neither on a horse nor in a car, but sitting on a wooden platform, decorated with red tinsel, that was carried on some of the
men's shoulders. He sat hunched and peered suspiciously at the
sea of people below him. As the procession passed under a
gooseberry tree, the bridegroom reached out a thin arm and
plucked a bunch of the light-green fruit. He put one piece in his
mouth and must have found it too sour, because he spat it out in
disgust on the bald head of the man in front of him. The man
put his hand on his pate and jerked it away when he touched the
wet mass.

The groom's platform wobbled as the bald man stopped but
the others continued walking. The bridegroom plucked
another gooseberry from the bunch and threw it into the
crowd. The small round fruit hit a woman's blouse and she
screamed, jumping round and trying to reach behind her back.
The couple walking behind the woman bumped into her and
stumbled.

The procession dissolved into chaos like ink drops dispersing
in water as the groom started pelting the crowd indiscrimi-
nately with the hard, marble-like fruit. A boy dodging one of

the missiles ran into a dignified-looking man on the edge of the procession and the man's dhoti unravelled. The man clutched the sarong-like garment, trying to prevent his underwear from showing. The long cloth caught under his feet and he stumbled straight into a vat of cow-dung slurry by the side of the road. Screams and curses filled the air.

The band, oblivious to what was happening behind them, continued marching to their beat until they stopped in front of the bride's house. It was only then that they noticed the people pointing and looked round. They ran back to the procession and regrouped.

Mr Naidu said, 'We had better get the poor man cleaned up.' He and another farmer ran forward to the dignitary – covered in smelly green liquid and semi-blinded – and gingerly led him away.

The rest of the party sorted itself out and the band struck up a fresh, jaunty tune:

Aha, it's my wedding; oho, today I shall marry,
The world's laughing for you and I will not tarry,
Oh, what fun to be husband and wife; hurry, hurry.
Aha, it's my wedding; oho, today I shall marry.

The procession made its way forward, stopping only when an old woman with a big, round, red bindi stepped out in front of them. She held a coconut in her hands and smashed it with great force on a stone on the road. The hard shell burst open and the liquid inside spilled out. She threw the two halves away and took out a currency note from a knot in her sari.

The bridegroom was lowered to the ground and held in his father's arms.

Holding the money, the woman circled her arms round the bridegroom three times, then gave the note to a beggar. Women ululated and somebody blew into a conch. Some boys

shook rattles. The noise unnerved the groom and he looked
ready to bolt. He scratched the arm of the man holding him,
raising angry red welts on the brown skin, but the man did not
let go.

'Somebody get the bride,' he shouted.

The bride and groom were quickly brought face to face and
they peered at each other. Suddenly, the bridegroom reached out
and smacked Tara on the nose. She squealed and pulled his hair.
Half the crowd was in despair and the other half bent double in
laughter. People tried to separate the furious couple but were
powerless in the face of their passion.

Pari finally stepped forward with two bananas, holding one in
each hand. The bride and groom stopped fighting and looked at
the fruit.

'Go on, you can have them if you stop fighting,' said Pari. The
couple let go of one another and grabbed the yellow fruit. Tara
fastidiously peeled the skin off before eating. The groom sank his
teeth into the banana, skin and all.

'What monkeys!' said Vasu.

Mr Naidu looked down at the boy. 'Of course they are.
Monkeys don't become humans just because you bring them up
among people.'

Rehman looked at the two Hanuman langur monkeys, eating
the bananas, and had to agree. They were about two feet tall, the
male slightly larger than the female. Grey hair covered their entire
bodies except for their black faces. They looked remarkably like
children, except for the wise looks from their clear eyes.

The crowd moved into the yard next to the house where the
Brahmin priest was waiting for them and Rehman heard several
people talking about the bride and groom.

'Forget your toy and look around,' a mother was telling her
five-year-old son. 'You may never see something like this again –
two monkeys getting married like humans.'

A man he didn't know grinned at Rehman and Rehman

smiled back. 'Have you ever seen a spectacle like this?' said the man, who looked educated and in a professional job.

'No,' said Rehman shaking his head.

'Me neither. Though I have heard of another case of two monkeys being married many years ago. That was near the temple town of Puri, I think.' They shuffled forwards with the crowd and the man continued, 'Mind you, it's a good deed to free captive animals, it will earn you good karma. And if you are going to do that, why not make a hungama, an event, out of it and have some fun too?'

Rehman nodded. 'You are right. Like mixing business with pleasure.'

The man threw his head back and laughed. 'I like that – mixing business with pleasure.'

A giant marquee had been constructed in the yard with long pine trunks and thatched coconut leaves. Pari and Tara's 'mother' joined them. Tara's mother asked Rehman, 'Are you enjoying yourself?'

Rehman nodded.

'Do you know how Tara came into our family?' she asked.

'No,' said Pari.

'About five years ago, we were worried about my eldest son and his wife. At that time, they had been married for a couple of years but they still did not have kids. So we went to the Tirupati temple to ask for the Lord's boon. We went up the Seven Hills in the early morning, queued up and saw the deity. We were then coming back to the bottom and our bus broke down midway. When the bus couldn't be repaired immediately, we started walking downhill to the town. After an hour or so, we were hot and so we rested by the side of the road. We saw a tribe of langurs peacefully grazing and grooming themselves in the distance among the rocks and shrubs. Did you know that there are lots of monkeys on the mountains of Tirupati?' she said, looking quizzically at him.

Rehman nodded and asked her to continue. It was common knowledge that bands of monkeys lived on the slopes and the temple summit of Tirupati.

'Suddenly, they started running towards us. We didn't know what was happening at first, but then we noticed that they were being pursued by another troop of monkeys. One of the members of the first group was slower than the others and fell behind. The leading pursuer caught up with her and we saw why she had been slow. A small baby monkey was clutching on to her front with its arms and legs. The mother monkey turned around and whimpered. She must have been scared, poor thing. The pursuer tried to pull the baby away but that seemed to give the mother a sudden boost; she bared her teeth and screamed loudly before jumping straight for a rock near us. Unfortunately she missed and fell to the ground, landing awkwardly. The pursuers quickly closed on the mother and baby, but my husband picked up a stone lying on the ground and threw it at them. He shouted loudly, flapped his arms and rushed at them like a noisy crow. All the monkeys ran away, except the fallen mother and its baby. When we reached her, we found that the mother was still alive but she couldn't move. I think her back was broken. She still clutched her baby tightly and tried to scare us off. The poor little baby was so small – if its mother died, there was no way it was going to survive.' Tara's mother looked up at the stage where the fire was just being lit and turned back to Rehman and Pari. 'I understood immediately the test that the Lord of the Seven Hills was posing. Was I ready to bring a baby into my house?'

Pari smiled at the woman. 'What happened then?'

'I kneeled down by the mother monkey and told her that I was a mother too. I'll look after your baby as if she is mine, I told her. She must have understood what I said because she loosened her hold on the baby. As soon as I cuddled the baby in my arms, the mother monkey closed its eyes for ever. We brought the baby with us, fed her from a bottle and slowly built her up.'

Sitakka and another woman walked by, leading a little boy of about four, and the older woman called them over.

'This is my first son's wife. And this little fellow,' she said, patting the boy on the top of his head, 'was born less than a year after Tara came into our house. I had read the Lord's intentions correctly. And today, I have to do my last duty for her and then her mother's soul will be at peace.'

All the usual rituals were followed for Tara's wedding as they would be for a normal human wedding. A curtain separated the bride and groom; a prayer was said to the elephant-headed god Ganesha for the success of the rituals; the bridegroom's feet were washed by the bride's 'parents'; the band played music that reached a crescendo at the appointed auspicious moment, and the curtain was whipped away, to reveal the bride and groom peering at each other from hooded eyes. All the correct mantras in Sanskrit were spoken by the priest – at a breakneck speed more suited to pop songs than to sacred hymns. The bridegroom and bride were picked up by their respective 'parents' and taken round the sacred fire seven times. All the guests showered rice on the couple as confetti. Two yellow threads were hung around the bride's neck, by the bride's 'father', instead of by the groom. A photographer shot lots of pictures. The main ceremony of the marriage was complete.

The newly married monkeys were then stripped of their clothes – leading to a lot of ribald comments among the rustic crowd. They were then carried through the village, all the guests following, until they reached the river where trees grew thick along the banks. The monkeys were unshackled and placed on a low, overhanging branch. The bridegroom gave the people one startled look and scuttled up the trunk like a proper monkey until he was hidden in the leaves. He then started chattering, saying something in simian language. Tara just sat there on the branch, alternately looking at the people and up into the branches at her new mate.

'Go on,' said somebody in the crowd. 'Your husband's calling you.'

Tara's mother gave a sob, tears trickling down her cheeks. Tara quickly jumped off the tree and hopped into her mother's arms.

'Oh, my darling daughter,' wailed the woman. 'My heart's breaking but you have to go. When I had only sons, I boasted that I was lucky because I would never know the pain of saying goodbye to a daughter on her wedding day.' She hugged the monkey and nuzzled her tiny face. 'The Lord was watching from his abode in Vaikuntha and he took note of my boasting and gave me a daughter. He knew that just like the pain of childbirth, this pain of farewell too is not a curse but a boon.' She fell silent for a moment and silently wept. 'Go, dear,' she said, wiping away her tears with the back of her hand. 'It's time for you to leave your parents' house. Go, so that when I meet your birth mother in heaven, I can look her in the eye and tell her that I fulfilled my promise.'

The monkey in the tree dropped to a slightly lower branch so he was visible and said something loudly again. Tara mewled, before jumping down to the ground. She quickly crossed the ground on all fours and scaled the tree with consummate ease, as if she had been doing it all her life.

The people were quiet, except for Tara's mother who started wailing even more loudly. Sitakka and Pari held her arms and supported her. Other women told her not to cry, though without much success, as their eyes too were streaming with tears.

Tara shuffled forward on the branch and sat next to her mate. The male langur held out a paw and opened his fist. A shiny red fruit flashed in the sun as Tara popped it into her mouth. A dozen human females went 'Aaah' on the ground below. Tara leaned forward and started searching through the he-monkey's hair for lice. His fur shivered as he was groomed by his bride.

Several minutes later, they stood up on their little legs simultaneously and launched themselves into the upper branches. The
newlyweds' chatter slowly became fainter as they moved away
through the trees.

CHAPTER FIFTEEN

On Monday morning, Aruna got up quietly from her sleeping husband's side, took a shower (hot, as usual), said her prayers and took a cup of tea on a saucer to Ramanujam. Now that winter was past, the tea would remain hot for a long time and he would need to cool it down by pouring it into the saucer before sipping the tea.

She was surprised to see him awake and sitting at the table, working.

'You are up already? Your dad was asking for you. He said he had to meet an official about the electricity connection to the Beach Road villa and he wanted you to come with him,' she said, placing the cup and saucer on the desk.

'Hmm,' grunted Ramanujam.

Aruna pulled up the chair next to him and sat down. She looked at him openly as he wrote half a page, then scrunched up the paper and threw it into the dustbin. The bin was already half full of papers. Some had missed the bin and littered the area round it. His forehead creased as he sat still, staring at the fresh sheet before him. He was still trying to draft his paper on brain tumours.

Relations between them had been pretty chilly since she had found their nephew, Sanjay, fiddling with the papers and pens on this desk and told him not to come into the room. Ramanujam's sister had automatically assumed that Aruna didn't want her son to come in because it was *her* room.

I don't care what Mani thinks, thought Aruna. But why blame my sister-in-law when my husband also thinks like that?

Aruna had a number of chores in the house but she didn't feel like doing any of them. She looked carefully at Ramanujam's face, his eyebrows knitting together as he frowned in concentration. He hadn't shaved yet and she knew from experience that the stubble on his cheeks was as rough as the teeth of a coconut scraper. She hadn't felt his cheeks on her face or anywhere else on her body for days and she missed it like a junkie craving her fix. She almost raised her hands to feel his chin but stopped herself, digging her nails painfully into her palm.

What can I do to show him that I was not being mean to his nephew? I do like him, though I think he is spoiled. It's not the boy's fault though, she thought. He's so young – it's up to the people round him to show what's right and what's wrong.

She remembered what Mani had told her – that when she had her own children, she would change. I am sure I will not treat my own children any differently. I will love them, but I will also be fair and strict, she thought.

Aruna glanced at the paper and just made out the words tumour and blood supply before Ramanujam crumpled up the sheet and threw it at the bin. It missed and fell on the floor.

'Can I help you?' said Aruna. 'If you need to talk . . .'

He jerked his head up and said loudly, 'Don't interfere in things you don't understand.'

She rocked back in her chair. 'Why are you so angry? I am just trying to help.'

'Did you insult amma and Mani's mother-in-law?' he asked.

'What are you talking about?' said Aruna, thrown by the change of topic. 'Why would I insult them?'

'That's what I want to know. Mani told me weeks ago and I've been trying to ignore it but I cannot.'

Aruna tried to think back. What had Mani told her husband? Weeks ago ... Suddenly Aruna remembered. It had been another Monday, about three in the afternoon. Ramanujam was at work and his father was taking a siesta. Aruna had just finished hanging up her ironed clothes and come into the living room.

'Let's go to Mani's house,' said her mother-in-law.

'Why?' said Aruna, looking in surprise at Mani, who was sitting on the other sofa.

Mani shrugged and her mother said, 'I just want to discuss something with her mother-in-law. Get ready and we'll leave.'

'OK,' said Aruna and went back to her room. She dressed in a purple sari with darker stripes and came back to find her mother-in-law had changed as well. They woke up their driver, Peter, who was sleeping in a chair under the mango tree in the garden and left. Mani stayed home.

They soon reached Mani's house and her mother-in-law greeted them. The two older ladies desultorily discussed various matters. Aruna couldn't figure out what was so important about any of these topics that they couldn't have been covered over the phone or left till later. After about half an hour, once snacks had been eaten and cups of tea drunk, Mani's mother-in-law got up and said, 'Let's go.'

Aruna's mother-in-law got up immediately and nodded. Aruna was confused. 'Where are we going?' she asked.

'You'll know soon enough,' said Mani's mother-in-law and the three ladies squeezed into the rear seat of the car behind Peter.

When they were on the main road and Aruna saw the board on the first floor of the building, she turned to her mother-in-law and said, 'Oh no, we aren't.'

Her mother-in-law didn't say anything. She just gripped Aruna's arm tightly as they went up the narrow stairs to the gynaecology clinic. The doctor, who looked like a middle-aged matron, was wearing a simple cotton sari and had a big, red, round bindi on her forehead. She welcomed them and sat behind a small table while Aruna and the two older ladies crowded on three chairs on the other side of the table. It was hot in the room and the fan rattled noisily but created little breeze. The room felt even more cramped because almost half of it was curtained off with thick drapes that went from wall to wall.

'Right,' the doctor said, 'let's take some details. What's your age?'

Aruna did not want to admit before the two mothers-in-law that she was on the pill so she just went along with the questions. After going through her personal history, the doctor checked Aruna's height and weight. The doctor then turned to her mother-in-law.

'She has been married for less than a year, so it is not unusual that she is not yet pregnant. Your daughter-in-law is quite young as well so I wouldn't worry too much just yet. But let me carry out some more checks, so you can be reassured.'

She turned on a switch and lights came on behind the curtains. She asked Aruna to go behind the curtains for a physical examination. It was even more stuffy in the screened part of the room and the heat from the lamps did not help. By the time Aruna and the doctor came out, Aruna was feeling hot and extremely bothered. The slight breeze from the fan did not help her much to cool down.

'Physically there is nothing wrong,' said the doctor to the two older ladies. 'Your daughter-in-law is healthy. She has a nice hip-bone structure, so once she is pregnant, the delivery should be problem-free.' She turned to Aruna. 'Do you and your husband love each other? Do you have a good physical relationship?'

Aruna jumped up. 'I am not answering questions like that in front of—'

'Sit down, girl,' said Mani's mother-in-law. 'We are all married women here and know the facts of life.'

Aruna turned towards her. 'You keep out of this. Don't interfere.' She faced her mother-in-law. 'Have some patience. Why
do you automatically assume that there is a problem? Don't the
shastras tell us that our deepest thoughts – good or bad – come
true? So think the best.'

Aruna pushed her chair back and rushed down the stairs.

'I can see from the look on your face that you have remembered,' said Ramanujam.

Aruna shook her head and came back to the present. She was
sitting in the room with her husband and scrunched-up paper
round them on the floor. 'I didn't really insult them. I was just
standing up to them,' she said.

'Did you or did you not say that you didn't want Mani's
mother-in-law interfering in your life?'

Why didn't Ram understand that the experience at the
gynaecologist had been among the most excruciating in her life?
She was really disappointed that her husband was more concerned with what the others thought than what she had gone
through.

He continued, 'How could you say something like that?
Have you no understanding of the power she has over my
sister's happiness? Do you think my mother and father have
never been provoked by her? If they can swallow their pride
and keep their tongues to themselves, what kind of aristocratic
family do you come from that you had to answer back to
Mani's mother-in-law? Go away, I don't want to see you in
front of me right now.'

He waved his hand as if to shoo her away like an irritating fly
and knocked his hand against the cup of tea. The hot liquid
spilled across the table and into Aruna's lap.

'Oww!' screamed Aruna in shock and pain as the tea seeped
through her clothes and scalded her stomach and thighs. She
jumped up, pushing back the chair, which fell with a crash on
the hard floor.

'What happened?' said her mother-in-law from outside. 'Are you all right?'

'I am—' began Aruna and ended by clutching her stomach and groaning, 'ayyo . . .'

Her mother-in-law pushed open the door and came in.

'Oh! The tea's been spilled. Quick, come into the bathroom, let's splash some cold water on you before you get a scar.' She dragged Aruna towards the en-suite. 'Shantamma,' she shouted out. 'Come and clean this spillage.'

At the door, Aruna turned to look at Ramanujam. He had pushed back his chair and stood up. He looked shocked at what happened, raised his hand towards the women and said something. But Aruna's mother-in-law had already turned on the tap and the water descended in a rush towards the marble floor, drowning out his words. Aruna thought she lip-read an apology.

A couple of hours later, Aruna was sitting in the living room with her mother-in-law, shelling peas.

'These are lovely, aren't they?' said the older woman. 'So fresh and plump.'

Aruna felt a seed between her thumb and forefinger in surprise. She had been mechanically popping the fat green skins and swiping the peas into a bowl without paying any attention to the vegetables. Her mother-in-law said, 'Kaka got them very early from the farmers' market this morning.'

Aruna nodded listlessly. Even though her husband had apologised for the accident, she could not forget his earlier words, '*Go away, I don't want to see you in front of me right now.*'

Her sister-in-law, Mani, sat on a chair with a pillow behind her lower back, reading a magazine. She refused to sit on the sofa, saying that she was finding it difficult to get up afterwards. Mani sniffed loudly and Aruna looked up at her.

'I am not having an affair,' she read in English on the cover of the magazine. There was a photograph of a young actress in shorts and a skimpy top that showed a lot of midriff and cleav-age.

'Why hasn't Ramanujam gone to the hospital yet?' said Aruna's mother-in-law.

Aruna wasn't sure so she said nothing. She didn't want to go to her room and face her husband again. Her stomach and thighs were still sore but the depression she felt wasn't solely from the physical pain. She had been a bit strong with Mani's mother-in-law but she thought Ramanujam shouldn't have minded so much. After all, he was quite a private character too. And he must know how insulting the implication that she was infertile must be to her. But he just didn't seem to care. He was more worried about the possible implications to his precious sister. She didn't see why it should affect Mani anyway. She was well estab-lished there; her husband loved her, she had a son and another child on the way.

They heard steps outside and her sister Vani peeped in through the door. Aruna's face broke into a smile.

'Come in, Vani. What brings you here?'

Vani took off her shoes and walked in barefoot. She said her namastes to Aruna's mother-in-law and sister-in-law, then sat on the sofa next to Aruna. 'I went to your office before I remem-bered that it was Monday and your day off,' she said.

Aruna's mother-in-law picked up the bowl containing the peas and the shallow pan with the skins, and stood up. 'Do you want a glass of water?' she asked the guest.

'No, aunty. I am all right,' said Vani.

'I am going to the neighbour's house for an hour or so,' Aruna's mother-in-law said and walked away towards the kitchen.

'How are amma and naanna?' said Aruna. They didn't have a phone and she got news about them only when she visited them or her sister came over.

Vani shrugged. 'The usual. Naanna's being crotchety as he

sometimes gets and amma, well, amma's just carrying on as normal.'

Aruna laughed. She missed the simple life in her parents' house sometimes. 'How's college?'

'All right,' said Vani. 'Can we go into your room?'

Behind them, Mani sniffed loudly. Aruna stiffened. She still felt sensitive about Mani's accusation about *her* room. Besides, Ramanujam was there. 'No,' she said. 'Let's talk here.'

Vani looked at her oddly for a moment and shrugged. They talked about a movie that Vani had seen a couple of weeks ago. A few minutes later, Vani twitched her nose like a little rabbit. 'What's that smell?' she said.

Aruna didn't notice anything. She looked at Vani quizzically.

'It's like amrutanjan, you know – eucalyptus balm.'

'Oh!' said Aruna. 'That's nothing. Hot tea spilled on my stomach this morning and I applied it to cool it down.'

Vani went quiet for several moments. 'Are you all right?' she said, finally.

Aruna laughed brightly. 'Why wouldn't I be? Just some hot tea. It wasn't boiling or anything. Anyway, what did you want? Why are you here?'

Vani was silent for a few seconds and then she said, 'I need two thousand rupees urgently.'

'That much?' said Aruna, looking up in surprise. 'Why?'

'Actually . . .' said Vani and suddenly broke down. Aruna's eyes widened in shock and she turned and hugged her sister.

'It's all right, baby. Tell me what happened.' She was really worried now. What had Vani done?

'I was working in the computer room at college when a few other students came in and started horsing around, throwing a cricket ball at one another and playing catch. I told them to cut it out but they wouldn't stop. I turned back to my work so I didn't see exactly what happened, but suddenly there was a loud crash. I looked up to see one of the guys on the floor half under a table with his arm raised, clutching the red ball. Several key-boards, mice and screens had fallen off the table round him. He was all tangled up in cables and there was glass everywhere and . . .'

Vani shuddered. Her tears stopped and she wiped them away with a small handkerchief.

'Several lecturers and other staff members rushed over and we were marched to the headmaster's office. I was asked to pay a fine and told that until I paid it, they would not apply for a hall-ticket for the board exam. The last date for the exam application is coming up and that's why I need the money now.'

Aruna frowned. 'How can they expect you to pay when it is not your fault? Did you not tell them that it was nothing to do with you?'

'Yes, I told them. They said that the actual loss was more than fifteen thousand rupees and they are charging the others a lot more. But because I was the one who signed out the key to the computer room, I am being held responsible and getting fined too.'

'That's ridiculous,' said Aruna.

'I know, akka. I've already talked many times to the lecturers and even went to the headmaster a couple of times but they are adamant. I have to get this sorted out by tomorrow, otherwise I won't be able to apply for the exam in time.'

'They probably know that,' said Aruna. 'This is just blackmail.'

'I know. I am sorry,' said Vani. Her face fell and she looked small.

Aruna said, 'Anyway, let's pay the fine now and get your application out of the way. We can then fight later.'

'Thanks, akka,' said Vani, squeezing her right hand in both her hands. 'I knew I could count on you.'

Aruna took a deep breath and thought for a moment. 'I don't have that much money on me right now . . .'

'Oh, what shall we do?' said Vani, wringing her hands.

Aruna compressed her lips into a thin line and closed her eyes. She had almost a thousand rupees. Where could she get another thousand? She felt Vani get up from the sofa and heard her say, 'Namaste, baava.'

She opened her eyes to see that Ramanujam had come in. He was smiling at her sister. She didn't want to ask him for money now, but she didn't have a choice. She stood up and said, 'Do you have a thousand rupees? Vani needs the money urgently.'

'Why—' he started saying.

'I'll tell you why,' said a voice behind them and they all turned around. Mani had been sitting so quietly that Aruna had forgotten all about her sister-in-law. 'The two sisters have concocted a sob-story to loot us. It's not enough that Aruna has more silk and gold than she ever had in her life. She has to keep funnelling more money to her family at regular intervals.'

Ramanujam raised his hands and said, 'Mani, don't talk like that.'

Mani said, 'Don't stop me, Ramu. You are too innocent. You might understand how the brain works, but you don't understand how the minds of these kinds of desperate people operate. They are like those long worms that attach themselves to people's legs and slowly bleed them dry. The only way to detach them is to burn them out.'

Aruna was aghast at Mani's outburst. She had gone far beyond anything she had said before.

Vani started blubbing. 'I'm sorry. I'm sorry,' she said, like an LP record stuck in a groove.

Aruna said to her husband, 'What kind of talk is this? Any money I've ever given my family has always been from my own earnings. I have not even bought anything for myself with your money when you were not with me. Isn't that true?'

'That's right . . .' said Ramanujam.

'Then tell your sister to apologise. What she said is intolerable.'

'Apologise, me?' said Mani. 'Why you . . . Ahh!' she screamed, clutching the sides of her bulging stomach. She sat down heavily in the chair behind her, knuckles white and face screwed up in pain.

Ramanujam rushed over to her. 'Are you all right?' he said.

His sister nodded, slowly. Her eyes were tightly shut and two tears trickled down her cheeks. Mani opened her eyes after some time and smiled at him. 'I am OK. Just a momentary weakness.'

'Thank God,' said Ramanujam and sat down on the chair next to her.

'What are you standing there for?' Mani said to Vani. 'Your little plot hasn't worked. Off you go.'

Vani turned to Aruna. 'I'm sorry, akka.' She started walking towards the front door.

Aruna said, 'Stop, Vani. You needed help and came to your sister. What's wrong with that?' She turned to her husband. 'Are we going to help Vani or not?'

'No,' said Mani loudly before Ramanujam could reply. Ramanujam's mouth opened wide, his face turning from his sister to his wife, like a weather vane caught in a squall coming off the Bay of Bengal.

After several moments of this deadlock, Aruna snapped. 'Fine, if you can't help my sister, I'll find some other way of doing it. And if there is so little respect for my word in this house, then I might as well leave.'

'Akka,' said Vani, her hand at her mouth. 'Don't. Not for my sake, please.'

Aruna's slender frame stood straight as a reed, her fists clenched at her side. 'This is not just about you, Vani. I've had enough. I don't want to live where I'm not respected.' She turned, went to her room and started putting a few saris and other clothes in a bag.

She heard Vani pleading with Ramanujam in the other room. 'Please stop her, baava. I don't need any money but please stop her.'

She heard Mani say, 'Stop it, silly girl. Your sister's not going

anywhere. She's just grandstanding. There is no way that girls
like you from poor families will ever leave a wealthy house like
ours once they get their foot in.'

Aruna stiffened when she heard her sister-in-law. Did that
woman think that she was so enamoured of wealth that she
would lie in a corner and take whatever rubbish they dished out?
She would show her.

In a few minutes, she was ready. Heaving the full bag off the
bed, she took it into the living room. She put the bag on the
floor and went to the alcove in the corner where the family
deity's idol stood. She put her hands together and bowed deeply,
the ever-lit lamp casting a flickering glow on her face. She came
back to her bag and looked coldly at Ramanujam and Mani.

Vani said, 'Please don't do this, akka. I beg you.'

Ramanujam raised his hand but his sister said, 'Let her run.
She is just acting. Where will she go?'

'Tell your parents that I apologise for leaving,' Aruna said,
pleased with how steady her voice sounded. 'I am glad that they
aren't here to see this sorry drama.' She picked up the bag, holding Vani's hand, she walked out of the door. She remembered an
old saying that a woman should leave her home only twice – the
first time to go to her husband's house and the second time to go
to the graveyard.

Peter, their driver, was dusting the car with an old yellow
cloth and came limping over when he saw them. He held his
hand out for the bag and said, 'Where are you going, chinnamma? Let me take the car out.'

'No, Peter. We don't need the car. Just call an auto-rickshaw.'

'It's no problem, chinnamma. Sir told me that he doesn't need
the car today.'

Aruna shook her head. Peter took her bag and walked out of
the gate with them to call a three-wheeler. As they stood outside, Aruna looked back at the house. She knew it so well that it
was hard to imagine that she had seen it for the first time less

than a year ago. A shadow fell on the house as a dark cloud slowly blotted out the sun. She turned to see Vani looking at her.

'What is it?' Aruna said.

'Please go back, akka. It's not too late. You are making me feel guilty now.'

'It's nothing to do with you, Vani, so don't feel responsible. I've made up my mind and that's that.'

She turned her face resolutely forward. The first drops of an unseasonal rain started falling, stirring up the earth and releasing the smell of home as Peter came back with the auto-rickshaw.

Rehman was standing under the eaves of a shop, watching the heavy rain falling on the street. There were many other men and a few women standing shoulder to shoulder with him – the rain had caught them all unawares and they had all scrambled to the nearest shelter. The fat drops of water splattered on the cement at their feet, wetting their shoes and the lower part of their clothes. Except for buses and cars, the roads were empty. Pedestrians and two-wheel drivers had disappeared in the sudden storm.

Five minutes later a car stopped in front of the shop and a tinted window rolled down. Usha waved and beckoned to him. Rehman stepped out into the shower and walked over, hunching his shoulders against the rain.

'What has he got that I haven't?' called out the young man who had been standing next to Rehman. 'Give me a ride and I will show you that I can do better than him.'

'Maybe,' Usha shouted above the noise of the rain and the traffic in the street. 'Let's talk when your moustache is fully grown.'

The young man blushed and Usha laughed.

As Rehman got into the car, rain poured off him into a puddle on the mat. 'Sorry about that,' he said. 'And thanks for picking me up.'

'I'm glad to be of service,' she said, smiling at him. 'Getting wet in the rain is romantic only in the movies. What will you do about your two-wheeler?'

Rehman shrugged. 'I'll come back to it when the rain stops.'

At the Jagadamba junction, the car stopped at a traffic light and Usha turned to him. 'What are you wearing?' she said.

Rehman looked down at himself. He had on a striped black and red T-shirt and jeans. His hair was neatly groomed and he was clean shaven. Instead of his usual sandals, his feet were shod in grey trainers.

'You wanted me to get rid of my ethnic clothes,' he said.

Usha shook her head.

Rehman folded his arms across his chest. 'You don't like it, do you?'

Usha said, 'No, nothing like that. You are looking smart, as I knew you would.'

'But you don't like it,' said Rehman.

'It's just different, that's all. I have to get used to it.'

'I did it for you,' said Rehman.

Usha reached out and touched his chin, smiling. 'I know,' she said. 'I love you. What did your parents say?'

'My father didn't notice but my mother was very happy. She cracked her knuckles to avert the evil eye and said that I looked smart enough to start attracting girls. Luckily Pari was there and she changed the topic.'

Usha drove the car past Ramakrishna beach where they normally met. It was deserted in the rain except for the old woman who sold corn cobs huddling under an opened-up waterproof cement sack; Rehman hoped that the little charcoal brazier that she used to roast the cobs was keeping her warm. The sea was a steel grey and the waves looked higher and somehow more dangerous as they crashed on to the sand. As Rehman watched, the dark clouds were thrown into relief as a long jagged line of lightning whipped across the sky, seemingly splitting it in half.

'Wow!' said Rehman. It was rare to see lightning strike over the open sea without being obstructed from view by buildings or hills. It was several seconds before the thunder rolled over them in waves. 'It's been a long time since I've seen a storm like this,' he said.

Usha nodded. 'We got a fax from the meteorology department at the TV studio. They say this is a major cyclone and they've asked all fishermen out at sea to go ashore immediately to the nearest landfall.'

'We are lucky in Vizag that the Dolphin's Nose protects us from the worst of the weather.'

The protective arm of that mountain jutted out into the sea behind them, creating one of Asia's largest natural harbours.

Usha parked the car at the Park Hotel and they ran into the lobby, laughing as the rain inundated them in the short distance from the car park. The sudden breeze in the air-conditioned restaurant chilled them and they shivered in their wet clothes. They sat by the big glass windows overlooking the wet lawn and a waiter came over.

'Two hot teas, samosas and a plate of onion pakori,' said Usha. The waiter nodded and she added, 'Quickly, we need to warm up.'

Rehman's shoulders shuddered in an extravagant quiver. Usha put her hand on his, looking into his eyes. Her hand was cool, but warmed up very quickly. 'Tell me about the monkey wedding,' she said. 'It sounds like such a funny story.'

'It was a pretty serious affair, especially for the bride's mother,' said Rehman. 'She took it hard. And they spent a bit of money – they followed all the rituals and fed several hundred guests.'

'What did Pari think of it?'

The waiter came over with tea and samosas. 'The pakori is coming, madam.'

Usha bit into the hot samosa and took a sip of the steaming tea. In the background was a tinkle of china and silver, and the low hum of conversation, while the view outside was misty with raindrops playing a vigorous drumbeat on the windows.

Rehman was shocked, and delighted, when Usha's foot touched his leg under the table. Her eyes were hooded and Rehman's senses were suddenly heightened. He was intensely aware of her gently curving eyelashes, the flare of her nose and the sinuous coil of a loose strand of hair on her forehead. She slanted her head to one side and he saw how one of her long earrings rested against her skin while the other was suspended in mid-air. As she took a sip the muscles in her neck moved like the haunches of a deer poised to take a leap. Her foot followed the contour of his leg up to his knee and down again.

'Is there anything more romantic than eating hot snacks indoors while it is raining outside?' asked Usha.

'Yes,' said Rehman, smiling. 'Eating hot snacks by ourselves in our own home rather in a public place.'

Usha blushed, her smile lit up the room for Rehman and her soft laughter was like a sweet Urdu love poem.

'I can't stop myself much longer, Rehman,' she said. 'Hurry up and fulfil my naannamma's conditions quickly.'

The mention of Usha's formidable grandmother was like a dose of astringent medicine and Rehman rocked back a little. He nodded in response. He couldn't wait much longer, either. His passion was a monsoon-fed river in spate, held back with great difficulty. Something had to change soon or he would be swept away and everything in the river's path would be destroyed.

CHAPTER SIXTEEN

Aruna woke up with a sudden jolt and, just for a moment, wondered where she was. The bedsheet felt rough and the arm across her chest did not have the comfortable weight of Ramanujam's. Her husband definitely did not wear bangles, like the ones digging into her chest. The crack that crazed across the ceiling and down the wall reminded her that she was at her parents' place.

She realised that the fan had stopped turning; the power must have cut off. She removed Vani's hand and turned on her side but Aruna couldn't go back to sleep – her mind was too busy.

It had been three days since she had come here. Have I done the right thing? What will I do next? Is he thinking about me? Is he even missing me? What am I doing here? Have I done the right thing?

Her thoughts went round and round like a blinkered buffalo turning an oil mill. Stop it, she told herself.

The next hour passed slowly until her mother got up to collect the water from the tap before the flow stopped. Aruna joined her, putting empty vessels under the tap to collect fresh water while her mother washed the previous night's dishes with the old. The water soon stopped running and they moved on to other chores.

'When does the water come in your mother-in-law's house?' asked her mother.

Aruna thought for a moment and said, 'I don't know. The servants collect it and we also have a well.'

Her mother smiled at her. 'I am glad you still think of it as your house,' she said.

Aruna flushed and did not answer. She pretended to be too busy rubbing the heavy pestle on the stone mortar to make a paste of coriander leaves for the chutney.

'How long will you stay here? You've made your point, now go back to your husband,' she said.

'Is this not my house? Why are you driving me away?' said Aruna. She looked up, pushing back a loose strand of hair. The air was very humid and sweat glistened on her forehead.

'Nobody is *driving* you away. But people talk when a wife leaves her husband's house. Padma from three doors away was asking if you were pregnant. She looked so satisfied with herself when I said you were not pregnant, you would not believe.'

'You don't need friends like that,' said Aruna. 'Cut her off.'

'Who will I stop talking to?' said her mother. 'Everybody was envious that you married into such a wealthy family that had a house with a garden, a car and servants. Naturally they will feel a bit of joy that your life is not a bed of roses. Everybody will feel it; some will be better at hiding it than others. All couples go through problems – how will marriages last if the partners just up and leave instead of sticking it out? You still haven't told me exactly why you left. Has your husband been beating you?'

'No,' said Aruna. 'Of course not.'

'Then why? Whatever the tiff was about, you've made your point. Go back now.'

'Don't force me. If you don't want me here, just say so and I'll go somewhere else, anywhere.'

Her mother did not reply but started muttering to herself. Aruna ignored her and tested the coriander paste between her forefinger and thumb. Deciding that it had reached the right consistency, she scooped it out into a bowl and washed the mortar and pestle. She brought her hand to her nose and breathed in the fresh smell of the coriander. Her mother took the bowl and took it to the hob to sauté it. Aruna heard her talking under her breath.

'I thought she was the sensible one in the family but what did I know? Silly girl.'

'What did you say?' asked Aruna.

'Nothing. Rouse Vani. Otherwise she will only start stirring when the sun is halfway up the horizon, as if she is Lady Curzon.'

An hour later, they had finished their breakfast and Aruna decided to go for a bath. Despite her mother's protests that it was not winter, she heated a vessel of water and mixed it with cold water in a bucket. She closed the bathroom door and looked around in the resulting gloom. It was a tiny room, perhaps four feet by five feet, with an old, tall, plastic bin in a corner that held their soiled linen. A pipe stuck out of the wall; the builder of the house had very optimistically put it in, but no water had ever flowed out of it. The brass tap at the end of the pipe must have been removed a long time ago and sold for scrap. The door was a tin sheet over a wooden frame. Two feet of the sheet near the floor had rusted away and a previous tenant had nailed up a plywood plank to cover the hole. The bottom of the wooden frame had been eaten away by the water like the fingers on a leper's hands. The walls had not been painted in years. Aruna sighed and thought about her airy, marble-tiled bathroom with its wonderful hot shower.

She reached into the bucket and took out the mug. Its handle was broken and the sharp edge almost cut her finger. 'Oww!' she said and examined her hand carefully in the dim light to see if it bled. How expensive were mugs? Time to get a new one, she muttered with a frown, pouring water over herself.

She didn't feel like lingering and quickly finished her bath. As she dried herself and started putting on her clothes, she heard a male voice outside the living room saying, 'I didn't realise it was already the month of Aashaadam.'

'Aashaada Maasam is still two months away,' said her father.

'That's what I thought, but since you are the scholar, I thought maybe I was mistaken.'

Aruna pulled the drawstring of her salwar tight round her waist and tied it with a shoelace knot, listening to the conversation in the other room. She recognised the voice of one of their neighbours talking to her father.

'It's just that I noticed your daughter has come home, so I thought, Mr Somayajulu is a pundit, a man who knows our traditions and customs. He won't suffer his daughter coming home without a reason and, as she is not pregnant, it must be that month in which all newly married women leave their in-laws' houses and come back to their parents.'

Aruna pulled the kameez over her head and missed what her father said in reply. She squeezed her eyes shut. Her actions were affecting the people she loved most. She untied her hair and shook it loose. When she heard the man leave, she opened the bathroom door and went out. The sky suddenly burst open and heavy rain started falling as if somebody up there had opened a spigot. Water splashed off the ground and on to her legs. Aruna yelped at how suddenly it had gone from dry to pouring and she closed the back door. She hoped the interfering neighbour had got soaked.

Aruna took advantage of a break in the rain and made her way to Mr Ali's house. She was really annoyed – trying to avoid a dog on the way, she had stepped into a puddle and at the same time a passing motorcycle had splashed her. She dabbed ineffectually at the brown mud stains on her dress with her handkerchief. She had hoped to wear the dress again but she would have to wash it now. She hadn't taken that many clothes with her when she left her husband's house and it was difficult to wash and get clothes dry with the constant rain.

She gave up on the stains and turned to her work. She needed to prepare the list of Christian bridegrooms – at least she could type it on the PC now, rather than on that old mechanical typewriter. She switched on the computer and started typing the list. Soon Mr Ali joined her and went through the morning post.

About half an hour later, a thin, middle-aged woman rang the bell and came in. 'Is this the marriage bureau?' she asked. She talked in clipped tones and walked with bird-like movements.

Aruna looked up and nodded. 'Please take a seat,' she said.

The woman was very fair, almost pale, with grey hair, and she wore an old-fashioned, light-cream chiffon sari. Dark, squarish glasses sat on the bridge of a prominent nose. Her handbag was of fine leather but looked faded from years of use. Aruna thought she looked like a dowager, except that she was still wearing the black-bead necklace that signified a married Muslim woman.

'How can we help you?' said Mr Ali.

'My son's wedding is in exactly four weeks,' she said.

'Thank you for coming and telling us,' said Mr Ali. 'Not everybody does, you know. However, I don't believe I've seen you before. Please give us your membership number and we can look up your details.'

'I am not a member of your marriage bureau,' said the lady.

'I see,' said Mr Ali and glanced at Aruna. She met his eyes and shook her head slightly. It was clear that he was as mystified as herself. Mr Ali turned back to the woman and said, 'How can we help you?'

'I want you to help me find a bride for my son,' she said.

'Find a bride . . .' said Mr Ali. 'But didn't you just say that his wedding is in a month's time?'

'Maybe the lady has another son,' said Aruna.

'No,' said the lady. 'I have fixed my son's marriage date and booked the wedding hall. I've arranged for the cook, the priest and the videographer. I just need to find the bride.'

'Did . . . Has a prior engagement . . . ahh . . . broken down?' said Mr Ali. Aruna smiled at how delicately her boss was asking the question. She quickly suppressed the smile when she realised that the lady might take offence. A broken engagement was no laughing matter even on the boy's side. On the girl's side, of course, it would be a disaster.

'No,' said the lady. 'There was no engagement.' Aruna and Mr Ali were speechless and, after a moment, the lady continued, 'Both my husband and I are from noble families.'

She looked at them with a flash in her eyes and they both nodded – that was not difficult to believe at all.

'My husband is a much older man than me and very weak. I have to make all the arrangements myself.' She looked at the wall. 'When we were young and strong, we had retainers to do our bidding but now that we don't have the strength, we have to run around ourselves.'

She shrugged and looked back at them. Her voice became stronger again.

'People tell me that my son has a good job in Mumbai and I did not expect any trouble finding a bride for him, so I went ahead and made all the arrangements. Everybody knows the date and if the wedding doesn't take place on the day, then my nose will be cut off – my family's pride will be ground into the dust.'

'I see,' said Mr Ali. 'What about your son? Does he know the date too?'

'Of course he knows,' said the lady, looking at him over the top of her glasses like a schoolteacher. 'How can he apply for leave otherwise?'

Aruna almost grinned. The lady was the first person, apart from Madam, who spoke to Sir like that.

'Why don't you complete one of our forms?' said Mr Ali.

'I don't fill out forms,' said the lady. 'Let me tell you what I want.'

Mr Ali looked at Aruna and shrugged. He took out a form and a pen. 'Yes, lady,' he said. 'Let's start with your name . . .'

Ten minutes later, they had all the details. 'It all seems straightforward. Your son is a vice-president in a multinational company, earning a very good salary, and your family is second to none,' said Mr Ali, putting the cap on his pen.

'I have answered all your questions but I haven't told you the most important condition yet.'

'What is it?' said Mr Ali, unscrewing the cap again.

'Society is not what it used to be,' said the lady. 'People like us have to manage with one or two servants instead of fifteen or twenty as before. My son sells soap.'

'Your son is a top executive, madam,' said Mr Ali.

'Whatever,' she said. 'He is still selling soap to ordinary people. If my father or my husband's father had seen this day, they wouldn't have believed it. Anyway, what I am saying is that families like ours have lost a lot over the years. What we haven't lost is our pride and our pride is in our noses.'

So is your snot, thought Aruna, who was feeling uncharitable because of her own problems. She didn't say it aloud.

'Noses, madam?' said Mr Ali.

'All our family members, for as long back as we have records, have had prominent noses.' The lady touched her beak-like proboscis, almost stroking it. 'I want to make sure that continues. The girl I find should have a long nose too. Otherwise my grandchildren might be stub-nosed and that would be unbearable. Do you have any long-nosed girls on your books?'

Mr Ali shrugged. 'Unfortunately, we don't record that information,' he said. 'So while we can search for girls of less than
twenty-eight years of age or those studying economics, we
cannot ask the computer to give us a list of girls with three-inch-
long noses.'

Just then, the door opened and Pari came in. 'Salaam, chaacha,'
she said gaily and walked through came the house, her ponytail
swinging behind her.

The lady stared after the young woman. 'Who is that?' she
asked.

'That's my niece,' said Mr Ali, shading the relationship a bit.

'Does she have any royal blood in her? She has a fantastic
nose.'

Mr Ali laughed. 'I doubt it very much. She was adopted from
a poor couple who had six other children and couldn't afford to
feed them all. Her father was a manual labourer.'

Aruna looked at Mr Ali in surprise. She hadn't known that.

'There must be some noble blood in her ancestry. You cannot
hide that sort of thing. She didn't appear to be married. Do you
think I can talk to her parents?'

'Her parents are dead,' said Mr Ali. 'And she is a widow.'

'Oh!' said the lady. 'That's a shame.'

Mr Ali turned to Aruna. 'Take out the all photographs we
have for Muslim brides. That's the only way the lady will find
girls with long noses.'

Rehman rode his motorcycle down a plank laid across the
muddy slope and parked the bike under cover. Three unfinished
floors had been built on pillars, all in grey concrete. It would be
another two floors taller by the time construction finished.

Rehman got out of his wet raincoat and handed it to a wiry
man in his fifties. It had been pouring for five days now and the
entrance to the construction site was a quagmire.

'Soori, is everything OK?' Rehman asked. He was enjoying

his job much more now that the actual construction had started.

'Yes, sir. We had a delivery of sand earlier today. The lorry driver said that we may not get another load for a few days.'

'I was expecting that because of the rains,' said Rehman. 'That's why I ordered it even though we don't need the sand for almost a week. Where is it?'

'I got them to put it in the back where the water won't get into it,' said Soori.

'That's very good. Has the maestri, the foreman, come in?'

Soori hung Rehman's coat on a nail that had been driven into a nearby pillar. His wife, a thin, dark woman with a silver nose ring and a tattooed band round her upper arms, brought him a steaming glass of tea. Rehman took the steel tumbler with a grateful smile and took a sip.

Soori, the watchman, lived on site with his wife in a small shack that had been thrown together with palm leaves and opened-up cement sacks, plus other bits and pieces of construction materials. His sons were also watchmen in nearby construction sites and they all lived a peripatetic life, moving to a new building once each was completed.

Rehman had sorted out the paperwork necessary to send Soori's three grandchildren to a local government school and since then Soori and his wife were devoted to him. Rehman was discovering just how much help it was to have a man he trusted on location twenty-four hours a day. Soori and his wife had lived on building sites for over twenty-five years and even though they had never been to school, they had a vast fund of knowledge about the practice, if not the theory, of civil engineering.

Rehman finished the tea and handed it back to Soori's wife, saying to her, 'We don't need to water anything today because the air is moist, so take another worker with you and move the bricks up to the second floor. We'll start building the walls there tomorrow.'

She nodded and left. She earned extra money by working on the site and providing lunches and teas to the workers. He turned to Soori and said, 'Let's meet the maestri.'

The foreman was on the second floor with a gang of workers. Retail, they say, is detail, but this is even truer for construction. A hundred things must happen simultaneously. Rehman was soon busy making sure that the plumber did not interfere with the electrician and that they both finished their piece of work before the plasterers; that there was enough iron for the wire-benders and sufficient cement for the brickies; and while it was easy to remember that carpenters needed wood, he also had to make sure they had screws, dowels and glue.

A couple of hours later, he was pointing out to the maestri that one of his workers was not laying the wall straight when Soori came running up.

'The owner has come,' he said.

Rehman asked the foreman to continue and went with Soori down to the ground floor. A short, sleek-looking man, in a white cotton shirt and dark trousers and black, stout platform shoes, was sitting on a folding metal chair, waiting for him. His nephew, a young man in his twenties, stood behind him, holding a tattered, sorry-looking bag that no thief would pay any attention to. Rehman knew that it contained chequebooks and tens of thousands of rupees in cash.

'Good morning, Mr Bhargav,' said Rehman to the older man and nodded to his nephew.

Mr Bhargav was not actually the owner of the site. The land once belonged to an old man who had lived on the plot all his life, along with his four sons and their families, in a small house with a big garden all round it. When he died, his four sons had inherited the land but could not decide what to do. Because of the lie of the land, it could not be divided into four similar-sized parts of equal value, and none of the brothers had enough money to buy out the others. With their father gone, relations had soured between the siblings until they were barely talking to each other. Their wives were even more antagonistic to one another.

Mr Bhargav had come across one of the brothers, who had told him about the land and their situation. He struck a deal with all four that he would demolish the old house and put up the new building at his own cost, and they would get a share of the profits after the building was finally sold. The brothers could have retained a bigger portion of the final building if they nego-tiated as one entity, but Mr Bhargav had sealed the deal by putting them up in flats in different parts of the city.

The builder, in a rare moment of candour, had once told Rehman, 'If the brothers won't even talk to each other, how can they complain that I am short-changing them?'

Soori brought another chair and Rehman sat down.

'Has the new plastering maestri come yet?' said Mr Bhargav.

'No, sir,' said Rehman. 'I've split the existing team into two, so the work is proceeding on both sides of the building but obviously it has slowed down.' Rehman looked at his watch. 'Oh! I didn't realise it was already eleven. He should have been here well before now.'

'Hmm,' said Mr Bhargav. 'I got a call from the sand supplier. He said he delivered a load today: I thought we had enough for another week?'

Rehman nodded. 'It becomes difficult to dig sand out of the ground when it is raining like this. So, I decided to keep some in stock.'

'Good idea,' said Mr Bhargav. He turned to his nephew. 'See, that's the kind of thing you need to learn. Anybody can shout at the workers and make them run around, but you need to keep thinking ahead to make sure that the work doesn't stop.' Mr Bhargav turned back to Rehman. 'Keep up the good work. It is very important because we are running out of time.'

The agreement with the owners specified that the building should be complete in eighteen months, or there would be penalties to pay, but the work had not started on time because of various delays and now there were less than six months left until the deadline. Rehman was sure that the brothers would not come together and enforce the contract but Mr Bhargav kept reminding him of the time limit every time they met.

A man in his late twenties, wearing a rough shirt and trousers, walked on to the construction site. His fingers were grey with cement and he held a brick trowel and a plumb line.

'Namaste, saar,' he said to them.

'What time did you say you would come? And what time is it now?' said Mr Bhargav.

'Sorry, saar. My little one had diarrhoea because of all these rains. My wife was really worried so I had to take him to the doctor.'

'I don't care,' said Mr Bhargav. 'We don't need you. I hate unreliable people. Get out of here.'

'That's not fair, saar. I had a good reason.' He looked at Rehman who averted his gaze, embarrassed and unable to meet the worker's eyes.

'What are you looking at the engineer for?' said Mr Bhargav. 'Everybody here works for me. I am telling you that I don't have time for unreliable people. Go.'

'I am really sorry, sir. But the young one is not well and I really need the job. The medicines are so expensive and I won't get another job straight away in these rains. Please show some mercy. I will come on time in future.'

'Nothing doing,' said Mr Bhargav.

'Please, sir, I beg you . . .'

Mr Bhargav just stared the man down until he turned and left, his head hanging and feet dragging. Once the plastering foreman left, Mr Bhargav stood up in his platform shoes and patted Rehman on the shoulder before he got up from his chair.

'Right, keep it up.'

He turned and walked out, his short legs moving quickly.

His nephew followed behind, taking deliberately short steps to keep behind Mr Bhargav.

Rehman stared after them. I should have stood up for the worker, he thought to himself. But that wouldn't have helped when Mr Bhargav was so adamant. When had that stopped him before? He was thinking like his father now, weighing up the odds of success before acting.

Two days later, the rains stopped and the sun came out. The sky was a cloudless blue and the air particularly clear, as if it had been scrubbed in the showers. As always, the sun's rays seemed very strong after the rain. Rehman's shoulders prickled in the heat even though it was only just past nine in the morning. He was on the top floor of the construction site, and the whole area in front of him was full of vertical, nine-foot-tall pine logs supporting a ceiling of rough wooden planks. The watchman and general factotum, Soori, set up a home-made bamboo ladder, wedging it against the boundary wall, and they both climbed up on to the ceiling. They were high above the ground with a great view over the town.

Rehman looked around with interest. Ten or fifteen years ago, the houses below him would have been covered with red roof tiles, but now . . . He shook his head. There was nothing less suitable for the hot south Indian weather than rectangular boxes topped by concrete slabs. Solid grey cement clad around iron bars is a combination ideally designed to capture the sun's heat and transmit it downwards into the rooms below, which is not what one wants when the outside temperature is forty degrees in the shade.

'I think we can tell the iron-bending brothers to get their team over to start binding the rods for the slab,' said Soori, shading his eyes and looking into the sky.

'Do you think the rain has really stopped?' said Rehman.

Soori nodded, but Rehman took out his mobile phone to call

Usha. After the usual greetings, he asked her, 'What does the meteorology department say about the weather?'

Usha laughed. 'I've heard that some men call their fiancées just to have a chat. Let me check their fax.' The phone went silent for a little while and then Usha's voice came back. 'The weather front has moved on and it will remain sunny now.'

Rehman said his goodbyes, promising to call again later in the evening, and hung up. He turned to Soori and said, 'OK, let's call the iron-benders.'

Rehman calculated swiftly – it would take three days to prepare the iron framework, so they could start pouring the concrete in four days. Give it one more day just to be on the safe side. He'd better arrange the gang of workers, the concrete mixer, cement and pebble-sized stones. He already had sand, but it was better to get some more. He'd have to tell Mr Bhargav to arrange the cash for all the material and for the extra workers on the day.

Pouring the concrete for the slabs was probably the biggest single task in a construction like this and there was little margin for error. The work would start early and carry on as late into the night as necessary. The entire concrete had to be poured in one continuous operation, otherwise the parts would never join seamlessly and the roof would always be prone to leaks and weaknesses. The two men climbed down the ladder and Rehman got busy arranging everything.

Three days later, everything was going well. The iron framework was almost ready and everything was organised for the slab two days hence. He stepped off the ladder and came down the stairs to the ground floor. A big empty plastic sack lay across the stairs. Picking it up, he called out to one of the women working nearby, watering a newly made brick wall.

'Put this away,' he said. 'Make sure there are no obstructions on or near the stairs. They will cause accidents.'

'All right, babu.' She nodded, taking a stubby, hand-rolled cigar out of her mouth. She probably couldn't afford cigarettes.

Just as he reached the ground floor, his mobile phone rang. He didn't recognise the caller's number. 'Hello.'

'Thank God I got hold of you. I've been trying to get your number all morning.' It was a woman's voice, speaking very fast in Telugu.

Rehman jerked the phone away from his ear and looked at the number on the front for a moment. He put it back to his ear and replied in the same language, 'Excuse me, madam. Who are you and what is this regarding?'

'Oh! Sorry. I am Sita. You picked up Vasu at my place a few months back.'

Rehman remembered the newly married, six-fingered woman who came from the same village as Vasu and Mr Naidu. He had also seen her after the monkey wedding, supporting her mother-in-law with Pari. 'Sitakka! I remember now. What can I do for you?'

He was surprised to hear from her.

'Something terrible has happened. Mr Naidu is in hospital. My mother-in-law said that he has taken poison.'

'What? I don't believe it. What about Vasu? Where is he?'

'The boy is fine, apparently. He is in the village.'

'Which hospital is Mr Naidu in? How unwell is he?'

'Very serious – he still hasn't recovered consciousness. He is at the NTR hospital in town. We are on the way to the village now. Can you come over as well?'

Rehman thought rapidly. 'Of course,' he said. 'He is such a careful man. How can he make a mistake like this? Anyway, that's for later. I'll go straight to the hospital first before coming to the village. Please make sure Vasu is all right. I am worried about him.'

He put the phone down. Mr Bhargav was walking over quite rapidly for a man with such short legs. His much taller nephew walked several steps behind him, carrying the usual tattered bag.

'Thank goodness you are here, Mr Bhargav. My . . . er . . . uncle is seriously unwell and in hospital. I need to go straight away.'

'Of course, of course. Will you be back in the afternoon?' said Mr Bhargav.

'No, sir. He is in a village outside the city. I'll be at least two days.'

'Oh, that's bad timing. There are a hundred things to be done for the slab work.'

'I am sorry, sir. But I have to do this.'

'All right. Two days maximum, though. You have to be here for the pouring of the concrete.'

Rehman nodded. 'Thanks, sir.'

Mr Bhargav held up two fingers. 'Remember, I hate unreliable people,' he said.

Rehman turned and went to his two-wheeler, calling to Soori. When the watchman came over, Rehman spent a few minutes giving him instructions about what needed to be done in the next couple of days. Finally, he was free to leave.

He drove quickly to his parents' house. His father and his assistant were busy with a client and his mother was in the kitchen. He called both of them into the living room and told them what had happened. He stuffed a pair of trousers and a couple of shirts into his old cotton bag along with a toothbrush. His mother rushed into the kitchen and returned in a couple of minutes with a plastic packet.

'There's rice, dhal and a cabbage curry in there. I've put in a plastic spoon as well.'

'I am not hungry, ammi. This is not the time to be thinking about food.'

'Don't be silly. You will be hungry soon. Eat this on the way in the bus and you won't need to waste time once you get there.'

Rehman slung his bag over his shoulder and took the food packet from his mother. Less than a minute later they were hailing an auto-rickshaw.

Rehman got in, telling the driver to hurry to the RTC bus stand.

On the way, he called Usha and told her what had happened. She said, 'I am coming to the bus stand. I'll be there in ten minutes, wait for me.'

'I don't want to delay, Usha. I'll meet you when I come back.'

'I am leaving now. I will be there almost at the same time as you. Just look out for me.'

'All right,' he said. 'Come to the ticket counter.'

As soon as the auto-rickshaw reached the bus stand, he rushed over to buy his ticket. The queue wasn't too long. There was an Express Volvo bus to his destination in fifteen minutes. He looked at his watch impatiently and scanned the crowds. He would give Usha another five minutes. He didn't want to miss the bus.

She came just as he was about to give up. He gave her a fleeting smile and started moving towards the buses. She followed with rapid steps, almost running. Her high heels click-clacked on the hard floor and many people turned to stare at the unusual sight of a glamorous lady running for a bus. As they reached the bus, he turned to say a hurried goodbye. She had a grim look on her face.

'Take care, Rehman. I have a bad feeling about this.'

He nodded. She quickly rummaged in her bag and took out a bundle of hundred-rupee notes.

'That's ten thousand rupees,' she said. In answer to the question in his eyes she said, 'It's from my emergency stash. After what happened when I told my parents about our engagement, I always keep some money with me.'

Rehman wasn't happy about taking money from Usha but he could see that she wouldn't give in easily and he didn't have time to argue with her now. The bus was likely to leave any moment now.

'Thanks. But I don't need so much money.'

'Keep it, just in case. Hospitals are an expensive business.'

CHAPTER SEVENTEEN

Rehman jumped off a rickshaw and ran into the hospital. He had forced himself to eat on the bus and spent the hour and a half journey wondering how the accident had happened and what would happen to Vasu now.

He went up to reception and was pointed to the second floor. Climbing the stairs, he noticed several men from Mr Naidu's village, sitting on benches along the walls. Mr Naidu's cousin and neighbour stood up when he saw Rehman and took him by the hand into the ward.

There were several beds cordoned off by curtains and Mr Naidu was lying on the bed nearest to the door. His eyes were closed and he was hooked up to an intravenous drip. His face looked shrunken and his white hair contrasted with his dark, tanned skin. Mr Naidu's forehead was deeply lined and his breathing appeared regular. It was easy to believe that the old man was just sleeping.

They quietly stepped out of the room. Rehman was led towards the nurses' station at the other end of the corridor.

'You speak to them,' said Mr Naidu's cousin. 'They don't tell us much.' Rehman nodded. Mr Naidu's cousin added in a whisper, 'Speak in English, they will be more forthcoming.'

'Excuse me,' said Rehman in English when they reached the end of the corridor.

A doctor sitting with the nurses immediately jumped up. 'Yes, what can I do for you?'

'Mr Naidu, the patient in the first bed in the ward, what can you tell me about his condition?' said Rehman, still in English.

The doctor came out and they moved into the corridor.

'A large quantity of pesticide was ingested by the patient. We pumped out his stomach as soon as he was brought here and put him on a saline-solution drip, but the poison had been in the patient's body for several hours so it has affected various organs. The prognosis is very poor.'

'But how can such an accident happen? Wouldn't Mr Naidu have noticed the taste and smell of the pesticide?' said Rehman.

'It was no accident,' said the doctor. 'The villagers brought the container with them. The old man drank the pesticide straight from its bottle.'

'What?' said Rehman. 'Why would he do that?'

The other man shrugged. 'I am sure I couldn't tell you why he took the poison. I am only a doctor, not a mind-reader.'

Rehman blindly sat down on one of the chairs by the wall. After some time, he looked up at the doctor and said, 'What now?'

The doctor looked at him for a moment and said, 'We can do nothing but wait. But to be honest, I don't hold out much hope. There's been too much damage. In fact, I am surprised that he is still hanging on. I can only attribute it to him being a tough, old farmer. People like you and I would have given up a long time ago.'

Rehman thanked the doctor and went to join the rest of Mr Naidu's relatives. Time passed slowly in silence and eventually some of the men left to go back to the village.

Late in the afternoon, Mr Naidu's cousin turned to Rehman. 'What shall we do?' he said.

'I was wondering the same thing,' said Rehman. 'I want to check up on Vasu. It must be such a shock to the poor boy.'

'Humph!' said the other man, and Rehman was surprised at his lack of sympathy for the orphan.

The door to the ward opened and they both looked up to see a nurse beckoning to them. They hurried over and she said in a whisper, 'The patient has woken up and wants to speak to somebody. You must not be loud or you will disturb the other patients.'

They nodded and went in quickly. Mr Naidu's eyes were open and he was looking straight up at the ceiling. Rehman sat on a stool next to the bed and held the old man's free hand. Mr Naidu turned his head slowly towards Rehman and tightened his fingers round Rehman's.

'I knew you would come,' he said in a hoarse voice.

Rehman said, 'Why? Why did you do this?'

Tears trickled down the old man's craggy cheeks like a slow stream through the forest of his stubble. 'A farmer without land is like a bull that has been castrated. He is good for hard labour but nothing else. I did not want to live such a life.'

'Without land? What are you talking about?' said Rehman. He looked across the bed but could see that Mr Naidu's cousin was just as surprised.

'Make sure that my grandson is taken care of after I'm gone,' said Mr Naidu.

Rehman's eyes filled. 'Don't say that, Mr Naidu. You have woken up when the doctor said there was no hope. You will soon be treading the mud of your fields once more.'

'No,' said Mr Naidu. 'That will never happen again. I failed the trust of my ancestors who tilled our land for hundreds of years and passed it from generation to generation. I have to now go and face them all and I wonder how I'll respond to their unanswerable questions. I don't want to die in this strange place. Take me back to my own house.'

'We won't do that until you get better and then you can walk out of here on your own two feet.'

The doctor came in and Mr Naidu turned to him. 'Tell me honestly. Is there really any chance that I will get better?'

The doctor was still for a long minute, then shook his head.

Mr Naidu said, 'Thank you, doctor. I don't want to stay here any more. I want to die in my own house.' The doctor left the room. Mr Naidu closed his eyes and would not respond further.

Rehman and Mr Naidu's cousin left the ward and went to see the doctor. 'What do you say, doctor?' asked Rehman.

The doctor shrugged his shoulders. 'If he leaves the hospital, he will die soon. We can keep him alive here for a longer time, but it will cost money and it is unlikely that he would ever leave that bed anyway. It is up to you. If you want to take him away, I will write a prescription for painkillers in case he becomes uncomfortable. Go to the accountant and sort out the bill if that's what you want to do.'

Rehman looked at Mr Naidu's cousin and said, 'What do *you* think we should do? Keep him here or take him away?'

The older man looked weary. 'I've known him since we were both boys,' he said. 'So naughty, he was – always getting into trouble. But he was our naannamma's favourite and she made sure that he did not get punished. She used to say that he was her only grandson who physically resembled her husband – our grandfather.' A smile came over his face. 'I remember the time when we sneaked into the sugarcane field on the other side of the river. That farmer and our family were bitter rivals over the piece of land by the temple.'

Rehman realised that sugarcane still grew beyond the river and the temple still stood on the way to the fields. It would be so interesting to talk to Mr Naidu and find out what had changed in the village since he was a boy and what had remained the same and what had not, thought Rehman. Cities changed but villages were more unvarying.

Mr Naidu's cousin continued, 'The farmer and his sons chased us and caught us when I sprained my ankle and we both tripped over. We were roped to a tree on the edge of the field and the farmer made dire threats saying that we would be tied there for ever until we starved to death. Nobody knew where we were and I started crying. I don't know how my cousin did it, but after an hour his hands were free from the rope and then he untied me. By that time my foot was swollen and I couldn't walk. He carried me all the way home.'

Rehman nodded, silent.

Mr Naidu's cousin's eyes shed their faraway look as he said, 'It's my turn to take him home now.'

They went to the accountant's office. A plump, middle-aged woman ahead of them was telling the man behind the counter that she had only one thousand rupees with her.

'How many times should I tell you?' said the accountant rather rudely. 'That is not enough. We need at least three thousand rupees before the operation can start. Don't waste my time and yours by standing here arguing with me.'

'Please, babu,' said the woman. 'The doctor said that if the operation doesn't start soon, my husband will die.'

The man sighed. 'You are wearing gold bangles. There is a man outside who takes gold as security and gives loans. Get the money and we can save your husband's life.'

She turned away, blundering into Rehman and Mr Naidu's cousin.

'Sorry,' she said, her eyes wild and hair flying in all directions.

Rehman stared after her, shaking his head in sympathy as she rushed out.

Mr Naidu's cousin took out a receipt and handed it to the accountant. The man fished out a file and flipped through the contents, punching several numbers on a calculator. He finally wrote a number on a piece of paper and pushed it towards them. Rehman's eyes widened when he saw the cost. He took out the

bundle of hundred-rupee notes that Usha had given him and
paid the bill, thanking his fiancée in his heart. The accountant
wrote another receipt and passed it through the hole in the
grille to Rehman.

'You go upstairs and talk to the doctor,' said Mr Naidu's
cousin. 'I will bring the cart round.'

Ten minutes later, a sleeping Mr Naidu was laid flat on
straw in the open cart, with Rehman next to him. Mr
Naidu's cousin sat in the front, driving the bullocks. They
had left the town behind and were making their plodding
way between fields when Rehman saw Mr Naidu opening his
eyes. The old man beckoned him closer and Rehman bent
over him.

'Make sure that Vasu is looked after,' he said in a croaking
whisper. Rehman nodded and put a finger to his lips, asking him
to be silent, but Mr Naidu shook his head. 'I tried to kill Vasu
too,' he said and Rehman's head went still, his eyes wide. 'But I
couldn't do it, so I sent him away.' Tears rolled from his eyes. 'I
failed in death, just as I failed in life.'

He didn't talk any more and seemed to go back to sleep.
Rehman sighed and sat back, resting against the side of the cart
as it slowly made its way. Occasionally lorries went past in both
directions, their brash horns overpowering the gentle tinkle of
the cow bells. They were passing a small hamlet now and smoke
from several cook-fires rose into the sky.

As they neared their village, Rehman looked at the sleeping
man. There was something different about him and Rehman
quickly put a hand on his chest. Mr Naidu was dead, just outside
the village, only a few minutes short of home.

Rehman never remembered how that night passed. Early the
next day, all the people from Mr Naidu's caste came together and
soon strict ritual took over. Vasu's head was shaved, while Mr
Naidu's body was prepared and carried to the cemetery on a

ghat by the riverbank. The same Brahmin priest who had solem-
nised the monkey wedding now presided over the funeral
ceremony.

Mr Naidu's body was laid on a flat pile of logs that was then
topped off with more wood until only his face was visible. Vasu
was given a filled pot with a hole made in it. He was told to go
round the pyre with it – a thin stream of water encircling the
pyre. The priest chanted Sanskrit mantras for the departed soul's
welfare as Vasu was given a long, flaming torch. The boy looked
pale and determined as he carried it to the pyre and lit it. The
flames soon caught, greedily consuming the oil-soaked wood
and the dead man's body.

In the absence of any immediate family women, the day had
been a relatively sedate affair with no excess lamentations. Even
Vasu had been very silent and grim. While the men were at the
funeral, the caste-women had prepared a vegetarian lunch for
the priest and all the mourners.

Everybody soon dispersed and only Rehman and Vasu
were left with Mr Naidu's cousin's family. Mr Naidu's cousin
signalled to his daughter-in-law and Sitakka took the boy
away.

'What are we going to do about Vasu?' he said to Rehman.

'I don't know,' said Rehman. 'I've been wondering the same
thing. Obviously, he cannot stay by himself in the cottage. Can
he stay in your house?'

'No,' said the cousin. 'My wife and I are too old to look after
children now.'

Rehman looked at him, surprised. Their older son and
daughter-in-law lived with them and they had a young grandson.

'Where else then?' said Rehman. 'You are the closest relatives.
If not you, then some other Naidu family. It is best if he is
looked after by one household, but if not, he could divide his
time, I suppose.'

Mr Naidu's cousin sighed and was silent for a long time. 'For the sake of my cousin, I am willing to overlook everything and take Vasu into my house, but my wife and sons are adamant. They don't want him here.'

'But why?' said Rehman.

'We discussed it yesterday before you came,' said the older man. 'We know that it is our duty to look after Vasu. If we drive the boy out, people all round will spit on the Naidus in the village. But even so, nobody wants to take the risk.' He peered into Rehman's face, looking for support. 'I can see that you don't understand. Vasu has the evil eye on him. Whoever looks after him winds up dead.'

'That is silly,' said Rehman. 'He is a young boy who's suffered a misfortune early in his life.' His voice rose, and towards the end, he was almost shouting.

'Nevertheless, that is what we believe,' said Mr Naidu's cousin, in a soft voice. 'Look at the evidence – his father dies in an accident, then his mother kills herself and now his grandfather. At what point do we say that he is causing these events rather than having these dreadful things caused to him?'

Rehman stood up and loudly said, 'How—'

The older man quickly raised his hands. 'Please sit down. I don't mean that Vasu is personally doing anything. But some people are just born at the wrong time, under a malevolent conjunction of planets, and misfortune stalks them all their lives. If they till a field, the rains will fail that year; if they need to cross a river, they'll find it in spate; their wife might be barren or, if not, then their sons turn out uxorious and ungrateful. It is the opposite with some other people, born under a lucky star. Their fathers live long to guide them wisely; they buy a barren field and strike water underneath, their wives are loving and their sons many and respectful. So, as an educated man, you tell me: which category does Vasu belong to?'

'Whatever has happened until now doesn't have to blight the boy's future. If he is given a loving home, he can still grow up to fulfil his grandfather's dreams,' said Rehman.

'That's not going to happen in this village,' said Mr Naidu's cousin. Everybody here is afraid that if they take in Vasu, they will die and their own families will be ruined.'

'In that case, I'll take him to town with me. He can live in my house,' said Rehman. He thought for a moment. 'It's probably for the best. Both his father and grandfather wanted him to be educated properly and that will be easier in the city.'

'Think carefully before making such a decision,' said Mr Naidu's cousin. 'Ill-fortune can strike in a city as easily as in a village. On top of that, you are not a married man – who will give their daughter to you if they know that you are already looking after a boy?'

Usha's face swam briefly before Rehman's eyes. What would she say? He pushed the thought firmly back. 'You are not leaving me much choice. I need to go back to work so I'll leave tomorrow and take Vasu with me.'

The old man nodded. 'You are a brave and good man. For your sake, I hope that what I said is not true and that your life will be prosperous and long.'

They were both silent for a moment. Rehman heard the chirp of a cricket and the sound of a dog barking. He could see the heads of people over the wall as they passed by. It was difficult to believe that Mr Naidu was no more while the world just carried on as if it didn't care about the death of a good man whose only wish had been to break free of the conditions in which he was born.

Rehman said to the older man, 'Please find out what happened to your cousin. Why did he take such a drastic step? I have to get back to my work, otherwise I would have stayed to investigate.'

Mr Naidu's cousin nodded. 'I will try. But when a man's time comes, he doesn't have a choice.'

★

As expected, once Rehman was back in town, he became very busy. There had been the concrete pouring for the slab immediately on his return and after that something or other kept going wrong on a daily basis. Seven days had gone by since Rehman and Vasu had come back to Vizag and every single one had been hectic. He had met Usha briefly a couple of days ago and filled her in on what had happened. She had gone very silent when he had told her that he had brought Vasu to live with him. He had been reluctant to push it any further, relying on time to bring the matter out in the open.

Today had been a long day too and it was almost eight in the evening when he drove home from work. He began thinking about Vasu's schooling. He knew from his experience with the watchman Soori's grandchildren that schools insisted on birth certificates and a parent's signature before enrolling children. How was he going to get them? He would have to go to the village and see if he could locate any certificates. It was just so difficult to find the time to do that. His work was taking over his life.

That led his thoughts on to Mr Naidu's death. Rehman still found it difficult to believe that the old man had gone. He could see before him Mr Naidu's dark face with its white teeth, his grey stubble, and his thin, sinewy arms and legs and he expected a call from him at any moment. Rehman had still been unable to figure out why the farmer had taken such a drastic step. The cotton contract that Mr Naidu had signed must have something to do with it, thought Rehman. But what? Was his work really so important that a dear friend had died and he couldn't investigate?

The marriage bureau was closed and the verandah in front of the house was dark. He walked through it into the living room. His mother was sitting on the settee, with Pari on the floor in front of her, applying a compress.

'What's happening? Are you OK?' he asked his mother. He

smiled at Pari and said, 'Hello, stranger. Long time, no see.'

His mother got up, wincing as she straightened her knees. 'My arthritis was acting up, so Pari is applying warm salt. Go and wash your hands and legs. I'll serve dinner.'

Rehman looked into the bedroom and saw Vasu sleeping, sprawled all over the bed. He went outside and ran the tap in the backyard to wash himself. He could hear sizzling in the kitchen as his mother heated up something on the gas hob. The aroma of spices wafted through the door, making his stomach rumble. He hadn't eaten anything since a hastily grabbed lunch many hours ago. Soon he and Pari were seated at the dining table with rice, fried fish, soya bean curry and chaar – a thin, spicy, tamarind dish – in front of them.

'I've already had dinner,' said Pari. 'But I can't resist a little bit of chaachi's cooking.'

'Go on, eat,' said Mrs Ali. 'You can fatten up a bit. I don't understand this modern fashion of girls being thin, as though they were famine-struck peasants.'

'Where is abba?' asked Rehman, not seeing his father.

'He has gone out with his retired friends. One of them has come back from visiting his son in America and they are all having a get-together,' said his mother. She opened the fridge, sending a cool blast of air over Rehman's back and legs. She closed the door and put a stainless-steel bowl of home-made yoghurt on the dining table. She handed a yellow envelope with a printed stamp to Rehman and said, 'This came for you today.'

Rehman held it in his left hand – he was eating with his right hand – and looked at the cover. He couldn't figure out who had sent him the letter. His name and address were written in Telugu and he didn't recognise the handwriting. There was no sender's address and the postmark across the stamp was smudged so he couldn't make it out. He tried to tear it open with one hand but his mother took it away from him.

'Eat first. You can read it later.'

They finished their dinner. Pari and Mrs Ali cleared the table while Rehman washed his hands, dried them and impatiently tore open the envelope. The letter was written in Telugu, just like the address.

'My dear Rehman,' it began and Rehman's eyes moved to the bottom to see who had written it. The letter was signed off, 'Bangaru Naidu'. It was sent by Mr Naidu! Rehman quickly looked at the date – the day before he had taken the poison. Mr Naidu was illiterate, thought Rehman. How did he write the letter? The handwriting was very neat with regular-sized letters. Mr Naidu must have used a professional letter writer. Rehman started reading the letter quickly:

You have always been a great friend and, for the last few years, I've thought of you as no less than a son. I have asked for this letter to be held back a few days so that by the time you read this, the initial shock would have passed.

I have lived my life as my ancestors have lived for hundreds of years before me. When my son was born, I decided that his life would be different. My wife never understood why the life of our parents and grandparents was not good enough for our descendants. She thought there was nothing wrong in living from harvest to harvest, always looking into the pitiless sky for a sign of clouds. I could never explain to her why I felt that there must be a different way of living with more security and once she died, I never had to. My son justified the faith I reposed in him and became an engineer. The day he got the well dug in our backyard was the proudest moment of my life. He married a lovely girl, though not from our caste, and soon Vasu came along. My son and then my daughter-in-law passed away one after the other and these shocks almost laid me low. But I recovered. After all, as a farmer, I am used to reversals – monsoons that fail, rivers that breach their banks, pests that devour plants and even rare hailstorms that strip away crops – these have all been a normal part of my life. And I had young Vasu to look after.

I wanted my grandson to follow in my son's footsteps. However, I realised that my strength is not what it used to be. Each season I find myself taking longer to plough the field and prepare it for sowing. You know all this information, but please forgive an old man's rambling because I feel that I have to justify my decision to you. Vasu and I are going away on a journey and this will be our last communication with you.

Rehman looked up from the letter, confused. Then he remembered what Mr Naidu had said in the cart as they were going back to the village: I have failed in death. At the time he was dictating this letter, Mr Naidu was fully intending to take his grandson's life too. Rehman tried to imagine the poor man's last minutes as he called Vasu over to drink the poison, but failing to administer it. He shook his head with pity and read on.

Why am I going away? The rains have washed off the crops. The field is waterlogged and the cotton plants are dead. This has happened to me several times before and each time I've tied the panchi round my waist tighter and went hungry until the next season. The difference this time is the contract with the company. I know you warned me against it, but I was too anxious to secure my grandson's future to pay much heed to your words. The company's representative visited me a couple of days ago. He said that according to the contract, I owed them payment for the seeds, fertiliser, herbicide and the time of their professor who visited and gave me advice. I told him that the crop was no more but he said that had nothing to do with the company. I had to pay, either as part of the crop, or in cash by the original harvest date. I said that I didn't have any other money and he said that I could always sell my land.

A farmer without land is no better than a beast of burden and I refuse to be that. So goodbye, my friend. Wish Vasu and me the best of luck on our journey.

CHAPTER EIGHTEEN

Aruna was at work, answering the day's post. The cotton Punjabi dress she was wearing needed a heavy hand with the iron to smooth out all the wrinkles and she hadn't been able to do that so it was looking crumpled. Mr Ali had gone to the bank with a couple of cheques that had come in from out-station clients.

Around eleven, Mrs Ali came out of the house, went into the front yard and adjusted the angle of the solar rice cooker so that it faced the sun properly. She came back and sat in one of the chairs on the verandah with a pen and paper, saying, 'It's good under the fan. The kitchen is boiling.'

Aruna nodded. The rains were a fading memory and the heat had taken a grip. A car honked continuously as it went past and Mrs Ali look out, annoyed. The street wasn't particularly busy and there was no reason to make such a racket. Mrs Ali started writing.

'Are you still practising your English writing, madam?' asked Aruna.

Mrs Ali looked up from the paper and said, 'Yes. I am not doing it very regularly now, but whenever I see something interesting, I read it and try to write it in my own words.'

Aruna smiled and went back to writing addresses on postcards. Soon the only sound was the scratch of pens on paper.

'How do you spell fertiliser?' said Mrs Ali after a little while.

'F–e–r–t–i–l–i–s–e–r.'

'Thank you,' said Mrs Ali, going back to her paper. After some time, she put the cap on the pen and flexed her fingers. 'How come you are walking to work nowadays rather than coming in the car?' she asked.

Aruna looked up quickly and bent her head again. 'Erm . . . No reason, madam. Did you pass on the letter to your son?' A few days ago, she had almost opened a yellow envelope that had come in the post before noticing that it was addressed to Rehman.

'Yes,' said Mrs Ali. 'And don't change the topic.'

'Change the topic, madam?' Aruna said. Why was her voice suddenly squeaky?

Mrs Ali sighed. 'What has happened?' she said. 'If you tell me that it is none of my business, then I'll go back inside.'

Aruna closed her eyes. 'I would not be so rude as to say something like that, madam. It's nothing. I am just staying at my parents' place for a little while, that's all.'

'Oh,' said Mrs Ali. 'Is your father all right?'

'My father, madam? Yes, he is well. Why do you say that?'

'Why else would you leave your husband and go to your father's house?'

Aruna went back to her writing and Mrs Ali fell silent. All was quiet except for the noise of the fan and the traffic outside.

After a few moments, Mrs Ali said, 'When are you going back? This weekend, next month or next year?'

Aruna threw down her pen, looked into Mrs Ali's steady eyes and burst into tears. At that moment, an old woman came up to the gate carrying a basket on her head and shouted, 'Do you want to buy roasted peanuts, lady?'

Mrs Ali waved the old woman away brusquely and went to Aruna. 'Let's talk inside,' she said and led an unresisting Aruna into the living room. Mrs Ali switched on the fan and they sat side by side on the sofa. 'Right,' she said. 'Now tell me what this is all about.'

Aruna wiped her eyes with the edge of the long dupatta that covered her chest and went over her shoulders. 'That's exactly the problem,' she said. 'I cannot explain exactly what has gone wrong.'

'Did you have a fight with Ramanujam?' said Mrs Ali.

'Yes . . . No . . . I don't know,' said Aruna. She stared with great interest at the pattern on the granite floor and twisted the strings of her dupatta round and round her fingers.

'Hmm . . .' said Mrs Ali, scratching her head. 'Don't explain. Just tell me what happened on the day you left the house.'

'Well, things have been a bit cold for a while and I think it is because my sister-in-law complained to Ramanujam that I had been rude to her mother-in-law. But it all came to a head when Vani came to our house and said that she needed some money urgently. My sister-in-law heard her and started shouting at Vani.'

'What did Ramanujam do?' said Mrs Ali.

'He didn't do anything. That's exactly the point. He didn't support me. And this is not the only time. He always believes the worst about me. Whatever accusations his sister hurls at me, he takes them as if they are mantras from the holy Vedas.'

'Why don't you just ignore it and go back home?' said Mrs Ali.

'How can I do that, madam? I won't go back unless he comes and takes me.'

'It's your house, Aruna. You don't need anybody's invitation to go home. How are you going to resolve these differences if you hide your face away?'

Aruna shook her head. 'Sorry, madam. I cannot go back in defeat.'

'Nobody is talking about victory or defeat,' said Mrs Ali. 'There is a Brahmin family in the second-floor flat there.' Mrs Ali pointed out of the window at the building next to their house. 'The husband is a clerk in the university. Do you know them?'

Aruna said, 'No, madam. I don't believe I do.' Although she was a Brahmin, her community was a large one and she didn't know every member. She was also puzzled by Madam's change of topic.

'They know you,' said Mrs Ali. 'The lady came over yesterday and was asking about you.'

'Yesterday was my day off. I wasn't in,' said Aruna.

'That's what I told her. But she didn't come to talk to you. She actually came over for gossip. She said that you had been thrown out of your house by your husband and your in-laws.'

'What?' said Aruna, aghast. 'I left on my own – nobody threw me out.'

'I asked her how she knew,' said Mrs Ali. 'She said that Ramanujam's maternal cousin's sister-in-law was her husband's sister. She said they had been considering giving her sister's hand in marriage to Ramanujam but now she was really glad that the match had not been proposed. She said that your in-laws had always been dead against your marriage because your parents are poor and because of that they have been ill-treating you.' Mrs Ali looked at Aruna and continued, 'She leaned forward on this very sofa and told me: they look like such respectable people. Who would have thought that they are capable of hurting their daughter-in-law?'

Aruna's eyes widened in shock.

Mrs Ali went on, 'She said that they made you work in the kitchen every day and even burned you a few times. She said that they finally lost their patience and one day when your whole family came to visit, Ramanujam beat you and threw you all out of the house.'

'I don't believe it,' said Aruna. 'They've taken isolated incidents and twisted them . . . But none of it is true. My in-laws were initially opposed to our wedding – which rich family wouldn't be? But there is nobody more kind to me than them. And while I am angry with my husband for not supporting me, how dare they talk about him behind my back? He is the best husband any woman could wish for. They are all jealous. I feel like going to her flat and telling her to stop talking nonsense about me and my family.'

'Who else will you silence, Aruna?' said Mrs Ali. 'When a husband and wife split up, people talk – that's only natural. And what this woman was saying wasn't too bad. Who knows what others are saying about your character or your husband's morality and the reasons for your break-up?'

Aruna's hands flew to her mouth in horror. 'Do people really think like that?' she said.

Mrs Ali shrugged. 'What do you care about others? You've made your decision. Let them say what they want.'

'But I do care,' said Aruna. 'I wish there was some way to stop them all from gossiping about me and my family.'

'There is,' said Mrs Ali.

'How?'

'Simple,' said Mrs Ali. 'Go back home.'

'But—'

'This is bigger than your hurt feelings, Aruna. Your family's reputation is at stake. Whatever issues you have are not going to be resolved by running away from them. Go home and fight for your rights. Solve your problems from within.'

'Oh, look what's come crawling back,' said Mani to her brother Ramanujam. This was exactly what Aruna had dreaded. It was the evening of her conversation with Mrs Ali and Aruna had taken an auto-rickshaw back to her husband's house from work. In the past, Aruna would have kept silent and slunk past her sister-in-law to her room, preferring to avoid a confrontation.

'Nobody here is creeping around,' said Aruna, throwing her head up, making an escaped lock of hair bounce. 'I went of my own accord and have come back on my own. This is my house even more than it is yours. Just because I have been silent so far, don't think I cannot talk. Give me respect and you will get respect back.'

Mani's jaw dropped. She looked at Ramanujam. Aruna discreetly squeezed her hands into fists to stop them from trembling.

Ramanujam said, 'That's true — it's her house and she has every right to be here.'

Before Mani could reply, they heard a crash and a boy's scream. Aruna and Ramanujam rushed to their room, where the sound had come from. Mani followed much more slowly, her hand pressing against her stomach. Mani's son, Sanjay, was standing by the table. All around his feet were broken pieces of glass; blue ink had splashed across the papers on the table and spread out in random patterns on the milky-white marble floor. They all stood frozen for a moment until Mani came into the room.

'Amma,' cried Sanjay and started to move towards her.

'Stop!' shouted Aruna. 'You'll cut your feet.' They were all barefoot. She moved forward, stepping carefully around the ink and the glass, and lifted up the surprisingly heavy boy. She came back and handed him to his mother.

'What have you done?' said Ramanujam to the boy, trying to blot the ink with a handkerchief. 'All my papers . . . I won't have time to prepare another draft.'

Aruna waved to Mani to take her son away. Once they left, she closed the door and leaned against it. 'It's OK. Take a day off from work. I can help you. We can do it.'

Ramanujam looked at her strangely. 'You are amazing,' he said, finally. 'I love you.'

Her head shot up and she stared into his eyes; a smile came to her lips. Each took a step towards the other and they were in each other's arms. Ramanujam hugged her tightly and bent his head to nuzzle her cheek and ear. His rough chin abraded her soft skin; his musky aftershave invaded her nostrils. Oh, how she had missed him.

'You are never going to leave me again,' he said in a whisper, his lips moving against the lobe of her ear.

She jerked her head back and looked into his eyes, the smile on her face replaced by a frown. He put a long finger against her lips before a word came out of them.

'It's my fault, I should have given you a chance to explain. I found out why you spoke like that to Mani's mother-in-law. I didn't know that they had taken you to see a gynaecologist. I thought she had said something during a routine social visit and you had responded to that. I think Mani's mother-in-law deserved it. In fact, if I had been there, I would have been even stronger. I have also told my mother that what she did was wrong.'

'Oh!' said Aruna. 'I didn't know that you knew nothing about the doctor's visit. I didn't tell you because I was embarrassed about it but I thought you . . . Anyway, that's why I couldn't understand why you were being so angry.'

They held each other for a few more minutes while Ramanujam nibbled her ears. Then he said, 'And I shouldn't have let Mani's tongue run away like the Rajdhani Express speeding to Delhi, especially with your sister. But Mani had pre-eclampsia when she was pregnant with Sanjay and we are all worried that she might develop it again. So . . .'

'What is pre-eclampsia?'

'High blood pressure during pregnancy. It is very dangerous for the mother and baby. That's why we are just going along with whatever she's saying. We don't want to give her any cause for tension.'

'Why didn't you tell me about her problem? I would have made sure that I didn't provoke her in any way either.'

Ramanujam sighed. 'She almost lost Sanjay and she didn't want anybody to know.'

Aruna freed herself from his arms. 'That's wrong. It doesn't matter what anybody says, you have to tell me these things. We cannot have any secrets between us. If you had told me to keep it hush-hush, I would have. Look at what problems were conjured up because we both kept things from each other.'

'You are right, of course. I am sorry. I should have trusted you. And you should have told me about the visit to the gynaecologist before I went charging off like a bull that had seen a red rag.'

'You are right – we were both wrong,' she said with a small laugh.

His hands slipped around her slim waist again and she reached up to circle his neck. She didn't know how many minutes they stayed like that, but at some point he looked meaningfully at the bed. She laughed lightly and pecked him quickly on the cheek before disentangling herself from him.

'Let me get the mop,' she said.

It has been a long time since all five chairs were in use, thought Rehman, as he looked across the dining table. The table was usually set against a wall and only three sides and four chairs were in use. Today, he and Vasu had pulled the table forward. It meant that they could not open the fridge but his mother had taken out everything she needed and Vasu had taken out the bottles of cold water. It was Sunday and there was meat on the table; Pari had come over to help his mother prepare the meal. Vasu, as the youngest and thinnest, sat in the chair against the wall while everyone else sat on the other three sides.

Vasu was still not going to school because it had been difficult to organise all the certificates needed, but Mrs Ali had arranged with Aruna for her father to teach him. Aruna's father, a retired teacher, taught the boy Telugu and maths for two or three hours a day. Rehman had asked Aruna whether

her father would accept any fees. Aruna had shaken her head.

'Oh, no. He will not take any money. To be honest, I should be paying you. It's doing him a world of good to teach again. He is looking a lot healthier and more interested in the world than he has been for a long time. Both my mother and sister also say that he is less grumpy and easier to get along with nowadays.'

Pari served herself a second helping and got a bone. 'Do you want to suck the marrow?' she asked Vasu.

Vasu nodded, his eyes shining. His body was filling out, but meat was still a rare treat for him. Pari placed the bone on his plate. Vasu gnawed off the meat clinging to the outer bone, then put the end of the bone in his mouth like a straw and sucked it. His cheeks went concave and his eyes bulged but the marrow did not come out.

Pari laughed and said, 'Bang the end on the plate.' The stainless-steel plate rang like a damped bell as he hit it with the bone.

After several strikes, Vasu shouted, 'It's coming out.' He sucked again with renewed strength as the marrow slipped into his mouth.

After lunch had been cleared up, they all went into the living room. Pari joined them with glasses of buttermilk on a tray. The adults started sipping but Vasu polished off his drink in a moment, wiped away the white moustache it left on his lips with the back of his hand and ran off to the front yard to climb the guava tree. Mrs Ali turned to Rehman.

'Why are you so glum, son?' she said. 'I've been noticing it for several days now. Is it work? I know you are working long hours.'

'It's not that,' said Rehman. 'I don't know what to do about Vasu.'

'You mean about his school? These things take time. I am sure you will able to sort it out soon.'

'It's not so easy,' said Rehman. 'The schools are asking for a birth certificate and they want the signature of the father or mother.'

'I have been thinking about it for some time now,' said his mother. 'I think you should adopt Vasu.'

'What?' said Rehman.

His father lowered the paper and looked at her seriously. 'What are you saying?' he said to his wife. 'He is a bachelor. Who will marry him if he is lumbered with a son?'

Mrs Ali said, 'The adoption is only a legal nicety. The fact that there isn't anything on paper doesn't change . . .'

Rehman tuned his parents out. Vasu was Lalitha's son. He had promised her father that he would look after the boy. So why was he so reluctant to do what his mother was saying? His father was telling the truth, though, wasn't he? Would Usha marry him if he adopted Vasu? Even if she was willing to overlook it, what would her family say? They were already unhappy about the match, so adopting Vasu would only pour kerosene on the fire. What should he do?

'Can I say something?' said Pari, after the silence had stretched for almost a minute. They all turned to face her. 'After my husband died, I had many regrets. With time, I am making my compromises with them and, thanks to you all, I have started to live a little again. But the one gaping hole that I thought I could never fill is being childless. The feeling that, while I am a woman, I will never be a mother is very sad.'

'What are you saying, Pari?' said Mrs Ali.

'If Vasu wants me, I would like to adopt him,' she said.

Rehman was thunderstruck. 'Are you sure?' he said. 'It's a big responsibility.'

Pari nodded mutely.

Rehman looked at his parents but they were dumb too. 'What about your work?' he said.

'He will be at school most of the time while I am at work. I will make some arrangements – I can book an auto-rickshaw to pick him up and drop him off.'

'Yes,' said Mrs Ali. 'The auto can drop him off here. We don't mind looking after him for a few hours a day. That would be great.'

Mr Ali nodded. 'Yes,' he said.

Rehman stood up and went outside. He came back with the boy, sat him down on the sofa and kneeled on the floor in front of him. Vasu's legs barely reached the ground and he swung them like pendulums.

'This is very important, Vasu, so listen carefully. Pari Aunty wants to adopt you. Would you like to live with her?'

The boy frowned and ceased moving his legs. 'Will I still see you?' he asked.

'Of course,' said Rehman. 'You will spend at least a couple of hours here every day and we will meet whenever I am home. I will come to your place too and I will take you to the beach, to play games, everything.'

Vasu nodded slowly. 'If Pari Aunty adopts me, will I have to call her amma?'

Rehman glanced over at Pari and turned back to Vasu. 'You will have to,' he said.

The boy thought for a few seconds, then jumped up and rushed over to Pari. 'Yes,' he said, throwing himself on to her. 'I would love to have you as my mother.'

Pari hugged him back tightly and swung him round, his legs flying in mid-air. They all started laughing, but Pari was crying too.

On Monday, Aruna's day off, she got up as usual in the morning, said her prayers and switched on devotional music in the early-morning Suprabhaatam Raaga. Her father-in-law left early to talk to a builder who wanted to show him a new site. Ramanujam had already gone to the hospital for half an hour before Sanjay came down for breakfast on his own.

'Where is your mother?' asked Aruna's mother-in-law.

'She doesn't want to come out of the room. She says her tummy is hurting. I am hungry,' he said.

Aruna and her mother-in-law looked at each other for a split second before they both broke into a run.

'I am hungry,' said the boy's piping voice.

'Ka-aka-a-a,' shouted Aruna, without breaking her step. 'Serve breakfast for babu.'

They found Mani lying in bed with her knees bent and her feet flat on the mattress. She had her hands on her stomach and she was groaning. Her forehead was beaded in sweat, even though the air-conditioner was on full blast and the room felt chilly.

'Are you OK?' said her mother, sitting on the mattress. 'Has the labour started?'

'I don't think so,' said Mani. 'It doesn't feel like the last time. It must be gastric trouble.' After a moment, she groaned as another spasm gripped her. 'Ohh, ohh!'

'Get a soda,' the older lady said to Aruna.

As Aruna turned to go, Mani gave a scream that ended in a sigh of relief. Mani's mother jumped up.

'It's wet,' she said. 'Her waters have broken. Oh! What do we do? Mani's father has taken Peter and the car and gone to see the builder, and Ramanujam's at the hospital. Quick, call them back.'

Aruna called Ramanujam but a nurse answered his mobile phone and said that he had already started scrubbing up for an operation and could not come for a few hours. Her father-in-law did not answer his phone, so Aruna left a message asking him to come home immediately. She was able to contact Mani's husband but he had visited them all day on Sunday and then left for an overnight out-station visit. He said that it would take him three or four hours to get back to town.

'Oh, what are we going to do without the men and the vehicles?' said Aruna's mother-in-law.

Hearing this, Mani began wailing. Aruna said to her mother-in-law, 'You are not helping Mani. Calm down, please. It is OK, we'll get her to the hospital. We've already arranged everything, remember?'

Her mother-in-law put her hands over her chest and said to Mani, 'I told him not to go today, but who can talk to your father when he gets a thought in his head?'

Aruna practically pushed her mother-in-law out of the room, saying, 'I'll look after Mani. You go and make sure that Sanjay is eating his breakfast. If he comes here, he will get upset too.'

She closed the door in her mother-in-law's face and turned to Mani.

'Relax, now. Nothing's wrong. Your labour has started and your waters have broken. Everything is normal – just a few days earlier than expected, that's all. We'll get you to the hospital in the next twenty minutes.' She mopped Mani's brow with the dry end of the bedsheet. 'Stand up and get into your maternity dress before your next contraction starts. Come on.'

Soon Mani was dressed in a loose-fitting kaftan. She then had to sit down abruptly on the edge of the bed when another spasm took hold of her. After the contraction had passed, Aruna said, 'Just stay here. Let me make some arrangements and get you to hospital.'

Mani nodded weakly and Aruna left the room, thinking hard. She could get an auto-rickshaw but she doubted whether Mani had ever travelled in one in normal circumstances, let alone when she was in labour. She had a sudden thought and dialled 108 to call an ambulance. A room in a private hospital had already been booked for the delivery. She went through Ramanujam's papers, found the number and alerted them that the labour had begun and that they were coming over.

Aruna and her mother-in-law served themselves a quick but hearty breakfast, not knowing when they would be able to eat again. The ambulance, its siren wailing, came before they finished. Hurriedly they washed their hands and helped Mani into the white van. Mani's contractions were now coming every few minutes and she moaned every time the ambulance jolted on ruts in the road. Aruna and her mother-in-law each held one of her arms.

The orderlies at the hospital put Mani on a stretcher and wheeled her into a shared ward with four other moaning women. The room was hot in spite of the big industrial fans that blasted air and noise in equal measure. This made Mani livid and she called for the director of the hospital. A fat woman with thin hair and a nervous tic rushed over and stood before them, bowing obsequiously.

Mani shouted, 'What is the meaning of this? Don't you know who I am? How dare you put me in this common ward? And it is not even air-conditioned.'

The woman rubbed her hands together as if washing them. 'Of course we know who you are, madam. But this is the best we can do at short notice, madam.'

Mani said, 'Then I want to get out of here.' She turned to her mother. 'Take me out of this dump to a proper hospital.'

Aruna turned to the woman. 'We have already put down a deposit for a private air-conditioned room. This is not good, is it?'

'I am sorry, madam. We will of course refund the difference between the room you booked and the price of this room, madam. But all our private rooms are busy at the moment, madam. We were not expecting you for a few more days, madam.'

Aruna said, 'As soon as one becomes free, can you make sure we are at the top of the list to move into one?'

'Of course, madam. That's not a problem, madam.'

'Make sure you do that. And have you called the doctor?'

'Yes, madam. We have the lady's doctor on site, madam. As soon as she finishes her current examination, she will come up straight away, madam.'

Mani said, 'I don't care. I want . . . Oh! Oh!' A contraction had seized her and she sank back. The administrator rushed out of the room.

Aruna mopped Mani's brow and said, 'Don't worry about anything. Your doctor's coming over soon. Just concentrate on the baby.'

The labour lasted more than four hours but Mani would not let either of them leave her side.

'I hate my husband,' she screamed as the contractions became more frequent. 'I wish I had never set my eyes on the bastard . . .'

Mani's mother talked soothingly to her. Finally, the doctor said, 'Yes, just one last push. I can see the head.'

Aruna's fingers were almost crushed by Mani's superhuman strength and she could see her mother-in-law wincing on the other side.

'Ahhhh . . .' Mani gave a scream that went for several seconds and then she collapsed like a punctured balloon.

A wail filled the room and the doctor slipped the baby out in a red, liquid mess. 'You are lucky,' the doctor said, lifting the infant. 'You have a boy.' Mani's body went limp; Aruna disentangled her fingers and massaged them.

'Congrats,' she said to Mani and her mother-in-law.

'He is healthy. Everything is fine,' said the doctor, as a nurse brought a bowl of warm water to clean the baby.

'I'll go out,' said Aruna and her mother-in-law nodded. She emerged from the ward to find her father-in-law, Ramanujam, Mani's husband and his father sitting waiting there as men were obviously not allowed in the labour room. They all stood up when they saw Aruna.

'How—' said Mani's husband.

'Good news!' Aruna said, a wide smile breaking out on her face. 'You have another son. Mother and baby are both fine.'

Mani's father and husband collapsed into their chairs. 'Thank God.'

Ramanujam came and stood next to her, almost touching her side. She looked up into his face and their smiles were only partly because of the good news.

The fat woman came up to Aruna and said, 'Congratulations on the birth of a boy, madam. The private room has been vacated, madam. When we've cleaned it up, we'll move your sister-in-law there, madam.'

Aruna's mother-in-law came out of the delivery room, sank into a hard chair next to them and closed her eyes. Her forehead was bathed in sweat and the weary lines on her face made her look aged. After a few minutes, she sat up straighter and looked at Aruna.

'I am really happy that you were around but at the same time I am sorry that you had to watch that.'

Aruna nodded and said, 'I didn't mind.'

Her mother-in-law shook her head. 'No, you don't understand. Women who have not yet had babies should not be present at a birth.'

'What kind of superstition is that, amma?' said Ramanujam, butting into the conversation.

Aruna looked at her husband and thanked him silently with her eyes for his support.

Her mother-in-law gave a snort. 'I am not talking about myths. What I am saying is mostly for your benefit,' she said to Ramanujam. 'If a woman who is not yet a mother sees the whole process of childbirth, she might get scared and stop sleeping with her husband.'

Ramanujam opened and closed his mouth like a goldfish, goggling at his mother. Aruna blushed deeply and could look neither at her husband nor at her mother-in-law.

Several hours later, Mani had been moved over to the private room, the air-conditioner was working, there were flowers in the vase, and the baby had taken his first feed and was sleeping in his grandmother's arms.

'Thank you, Aruna,' said Mani. 'I couldn't have done without you today. I am glad you are my sister-in-law.'

CHAPTER NINETEEN

Rehman left the motorcycle in the shade of the trees on the opposite side of the road and crossed over to his parents' house. Mrs Ali was in the front yard, sweeping away fallen guava leaves.

'How did the vaccination go?' she said. Rehman had taken Pari and Vasu to the doctor for his immunisations.

'It went well. He was very brave – didn't cry at all. I've left him with Aruna's father, so he doesn't miss his lessons.'

Rehman went onto the verandah to find Aruna and his father in front of the computer. A client with a bald patch barely covered by a comb-over was sitting on the sofa, waiting for them.

He was about to go through to the living room when his father called to him. 'Rehman, do you know how to select matches where the bridegroom is Kapu but not Toorpu Kapu?'

Rehman went over and Mr Ali moved to sit next to the client, telling Aruna, 'Note what he is doing so we can do it ourselves next time.'

Aruna smiled at Rehman and stood up so he could sit in front of the computer. While Rehman was searching for the right menu option, his father started speaking to the client.

'Mr Reddy, you rejected the electrical engineer who had such a good job because he studied in a private college and now you tell me that the lawyer from Hyderabad is no good too.

What is wrong with him? Did he study in a private college too?'

'Oh no, sir,' said Mr Reddy. 'He went to a good college but he got only a second-class degree. Sudha has a first-class pass and my son is studying at Princeton. You tell me, how can I agree to such a match?'

'No, no,' said Mr Ali, looking very serious. 'Of course you cannot agree to marry your daughter off to such a man.'

Rehman looked at his father in surprise. He then glanced at Aruna and she grinned at him.

'Tell me, sir,' continued Mr Ali, still serious. 'Do you really, really want to marry off your daughter?'

The man jutted his chin out. 'What do you mean?' he asked aggressively.

'I am just trying to understand,' said Mr Ali, holding out both his hands, palm outwards in a placatory manner. 'You are a widower with no one to look after you. It must be such a comfort to have a daughter to cook and clean for you in the house. It is natural to try to delay saying farewell to such a daughter.'

The man stood up and his eyes bulged. 'How dare you say such a thing? Is this your business – to take money from people and then insult them? I am merely looking for the perfect match for my Sudha.'

'Sit down, Mr Reddy,' said Mr Ali. His voice was suddenly stern. 'I am just telling it like I see it. You said that before you came to us, you had already spent six months looking for a groom for your daughter but found nobody suitable. We've given you a long list of which two matches look very good. I know that not every match that looks right works out in the end but you seem to be rejecting boys on very specious grounds. So I was wondering whether you are going through the motions but, in your heart of hearts, you really don't want to marry off your daughter.'

Mr Reddy slowly sat down. 'I assure you, sir, that I am very serious. I really want my daughter to marry and live a happy life. I am not the kind of man who will destroy my daughter's happiness for my own selfish reasons. I just want to make sure that the match is perfect.'

Mr Ali smiled at the man and said, 'I am really glad to hear that you have your daughter's best interests at heart. But, sir, think about what you said. There is no such thing as a perfect match. There are only somewhat good and somewhat bad matches. A couple are like two pebbles that are next to each other on a beach. They will have rough edges and rub each other the wrong way initially. But as they spend time together and the waves pound them, the edges rub off and they will seem made for each other.'

Rehman stopped working on the computer and looked at his father with new respect. Mr Reddy promised to think about it and left soon after.

Rehman fiddled with the software for some more time and then said, 'Sorry, abba, you probably have to write a macro to do something like that. I can get Venkatesh to come and show you.'

'I don't even understand what that means,' said Mr Ali. 'It sounds too complicated. We'll just do it the old-fashioned way.'

Rehman smiled at Aruna, then followed his father outside. His mother was buying custard apples from a thin, dark, young woman by the gate. Both women were bent over a round wicker basket. Mrs Ali was making sure that the green, knobbly fruit were the right level of squishiness before transferring them to a steel bowl. They watched silently for a little while and Mr Ali said, 'How much for the custard apples?'

'Thirty rupees a dozen,' said the woman who was selling them.

'They are so plump and just ripe. Why are you selling them so cheap?' Mr Ali quipped.

The woman giggled and Mrs Ali glared at her husband. 'Be

silent,' she said in Urdu, so the fruit seller wouldn't understand. 'I bargained hard with her and I don't need your jokes to spoil it.'

The woman left soon after and Mrs Ali went back inside, leaving father and son alone.

'Where is your bike?' asked Mr Ali.

'There,' said Rehman, pointing across the street.

Scooters and cycles went past on the road. A broken-down white Ambassador car was being pushed by three men and two grinning boys. A man went past on a motorcycle with one hand on the handlebar and the other holding a mobile phone to his ear. He swerved past the trundling white car and accelerated away, not stopping his important conversation.

'What an idiot,' said Mr Ali, going out on to the road and looking back at the house.

Rehman joined him.

The sign hanging on the wall now seemed part of the fabric of the house. 'Ali's Marriage Bureau for Rich People' it proclaimed in big red letters on a blue background. Underneath, in smaller letters, it said, 'Prop: Mr Hyder Ali, Govt Clerk (retired)' and 'Ph: 236678'. The red of the letters and the blue backdrop were faded from exposure to the sun. The corners where the sign was screwed into the wall were brown and corroded and a couple of long streaks of thin, reddish-brown rust ran down the wall from behind the frame.

'It seems so long ago that I started the marriage bureau but really it is little more than a year,' said Mr Ali. 'All I wanted was some time-pass so I didn't trouble your mother too much, but it has done fantastically well.'

A bus went rumbling past just behind them, but apart from a backward glance, they didn't stir.

'We have helped so many clients,' continued Mr Ali, who seemed to be in a reminiscent mood. 'And Aruna has been an absolute godsend. I don't think we could have done this without her.'

Rehman nodded. 'Yes, you were very lucky to get her.'

'It was not just luck,' said his father. 'It was your mother who stopped Aruna when she was walking down this very road and offered her the job. I suppose we changed her life too by finding her a husband. Did you know that he was a client of ours and that's how they met?'

'Yes, I know,' said Rehman.

'In those days, I didn't even want to talk to you very much because we invariably fought about everything. I think that the fact that we are standing here calmly means that I am a wiser man than I was then. Mind you, I like the fact that you have taken up a steady job and that's probably the reason I am so much more at peace with you,' said his father.

Rehman felt uncomfortable. To change the topic, he said, 'Why did you call it the Marriage Bureau for Rich People? We never talked about it and I never understood the name.'

Mr Ali laughed. 'I don't remember now whether it was your mother or your uncle Azhar who suggested it. We were all discussing it one day after I had decided to open this business and I said that at my age I didn't want to deal with every two-bit person who walked off the street. That's when this idea came – to restrict it to wealthy people so as to keep the riff-raff away.'

Rehman nodded. It made sense in a way. The open discussion of how well-off the families were, and how much dowry was going to be paid, had always left him uneasy. Not only was it illegal but he also believed that the dowry system was a social evil that needed to be curbed. A year ago he would have brought it up and had an argument with his father, about how he was not only condoning but actually encouraging an appalling practice. Now he kept silent, because he knew he couldn't convince his father to change and his father couldn't single-handedly transform age-old customs either. He supposed this restraint was wisdom too.

Mrs Ali called out from the verandah, 'Will you two men just

stand there admiring your own house as if it was the Taj Mahal
or will you come in and eat something?'

They looked at each other, smiled, and walked back into the
house as one.

'That one over there,' said Aruna, pointing.

The waiter nodded and led Aruna and her husband to a table
between two shrubs that had a bit more privacy than the others.
Ramanujam had suggested going to a restaurant after his sister
had come home from the hospital with the baby. They had
invited the others but they had all declined.

'This is a nice place,' said Ramanujam, looking around at the
large yard. 'How did you find out about it?'

'It's beautiful here, isn't it?' she said.

They could hear the twittering of birds that went about their
business before another day came to a close and the sound of the
surf was in the background. Tables were dotted among shrubs
and trees bearing yellow and orange flowers. A few lights had just
been turned on even though they were not yet strictly necessary
for illumination.

'I heard Madam's son talking about it to Pari, the widow-girl
from the village. And thanks for the idea of going out for dinner.
It's been a long day and this is really relaxing.'

'Anything for my lovely wife,' he said.

'Shhh . . . Somebody might hear.'

Ramanujam looked up into the trees and pointed to a mynah
sitting on one of the branches. 'That bird over there, it's listening,' he said.

Aruna laughed. It had been a while since they had gone out
on their own. They sat down and Ramanujam held her hand on
the table. His hand felt warm – his fingers were so long; he could
have been a musician if he wasn't a surgeon, she thought. The
waiter came over and she jerked her hand away from her husband's. They ordered food and Aruna relaxed again once the

waiter was gone. She looked around and saw a young woman sitting two tables away. She pointed her out to Ramanujam, the shrubs giving them the privacy to stare.

'Talk about coincidences. She's the journalist who interviewed Madam and her son about those farmers' protests.'

'Who—' began Ramanujam loudly, before recognising her and lowering his voice. 'I remember seeing her on TV.'

'I wonder who she is waiting for? I am sure she is not married,' said Aruna, talking just above a whisper. 'Her father came to us recently to find a groom for her. I was really surprised that they needed to use a marriage bureau for such an eligible girl.'

'Gossip!' said Ramanujam.

Aruna laughed. 'You know something else? Sir and Madam's son, Rehman, was very happy to see her details. I could never figure out why.'

At that point the waiter came back with drinks and they moved on to other topics – the paper he had sent off for the neurological conference; one of the marriage bureau's clients who refused an otherwise perfect match because the bride's father was a lawyer; Vani; Mani's sons, and others besides.

'Look,' said Ramanujam pointing through the shrubs. A man had walked over to join Usha at her table.

Aruna was scandalised. 'Why, that's . . . Madam's son, Rehman. I wonder whether his mother knows that he is meeting the journalist? Then why was he so delighted when her father was arranging for her marriage?' She shook her head in bewilderment. 'She's a Hindu as well . . . Oh, my God . . .'

Ramanujam shrugged. 'Maybe they are just meeting to discuss his next interview.'

Aruna glanced at him with a look as if he were a dunce. Her husband started to speak but Aruna put a finger to her lips. If they stayed silent, they could hear what was being said at the other table.

Usha smiled at Rehman, leaned forward and patted his hand. 'You are looking so good. How's your job?'

Aruna glanced significantly at Ramanujam. 'I wish I hadn't seen this now,' she whispered. 'What do I tell Madam?'

Ramanujam shrugged. 'Why do you have to tell her anything?'

At the other table, the conversation continued. 'The brick-work is more than half done and we'll be starting to wire the first two floors soon.'

The waiter came over and they ordered fresh-lime sodas.

'Tell me about your work. Did you manage to get the inter-view with the District Collector?' Rehman said.

'I did. He didn't want to meet me because it must have been pretty embarrassing to admit that his office had done nothing even though almost a hundred people had fallen ill, but I just camped outside his office until he had no choice.'

Rehman smiled at her and said, 'Poor man – to come up against you. Was it really the water supply that was at fault?'

'Oh yes. The reservoir had gone dry and then partly filled up in the rains, and they think that caused the supply to be con-taminated.'

The breeze increased suddenly and brought with it the subtle fragrance of jasmine. A stalk of small dried leaves swayed and fell from the hedging tree that towered over Usha and Rehman on to the table between them. Usha picked it up and absently started twisting it. The waiter came over to their table with the glasses. After he left, Usha raised her glass and pursed her lips round the blue plastic straw; the cloudy liquid rose and her throat moved. Rehman stared at her intensely.

'What are you looking at?' Usha said, putting the glass down and raising an index finger to her nose. 'Have I got something here?'

'No,' said Rehman shaking his head. 'I was just looking at you and thinking . . . that straw is so lucky . . . to be in such close contact with a beauty like you.'

Usha blushed. Then suddenly her eyes clouded over and she looked inexplicably sad. 'Do you still think about Mr Naidu's death?' she asked.

'Yes,' said Rehman. 'Ever since I received his letter, I can't help wondering about the circumstances of his passing. Farming is a chancy business – anything can go wrong over such a long growing season. And most Indian farmers don't have much spare cash lying around; they live from harvest to harvest. So how can the company draw up a contract where they pile all the risk on the cultivator? It may not be illegal but it's surely immoral, especially when you consider that a lot of farmers are illiterate and don't understand what they are agreeing to.'

'You've told me that before as well,' said Usha. 'But what can be done? It is a contract between two independent parties, after all. Do you think contract farming should be banned?'

'These contracts have come to India only in the last few years and I don't think banning them again is the answer. Farmers do benefit from modern technology and new techniques. You are right; the two parties to the contract are independent. But they are unequal. We have to equalise the playing field somehow.' Rehman leaned forward while talking and, towards the end, he was poking the table with a finger.

Usha drew him out, like the journalist that she was. 'So how do you propose that should be done?'

'The one strength that farmers have and companies don't is that there are many of them and they each have a vote – more, if you consider their families. Also, even the non-farming public is generally sympathetic to people on the land. After all, as Lal Bahadur Shastry, the second Prime Minister of India, said: "Hail Soldier, Hail Farmer."'

Usha smiled slowly at him. 'Go on,' she said softly. Something in her tone checked Rehman for an instant but then his passion drove him on.

'We have to make use of that respect – most politicians will jump through hoops to avoid antagonising farmers. That's how we won in the Royyapalem land campaign. Once we got the public interested, the government backtracked.'

Usha had covered the campaign, which was how they first met.

'That was an easy issue to publicise. You had a whole village being thrown off their lands so a multinational company could build on it. This is very different.'

'You are right,' said Rehman. 'But Mr Naidu cannot be the only man who has killed himself.'

'He is not,' said Usha. 'I've been looking into it. More than ten thousand farmers commit suicide each year in India and our state is one of the worst affected. But most of the suicides are not related to contract farming. Farmers have many problems – lack of credit, lack of irrigation, too little rain, too much rain, arbitrary changes in government policies . . .'

'That's true,' said Rehman, taking a deep draught from the glass. 'But contract farming is still at a very nascent stage in our country. Beginnings are such sensitive times – we can make the most difference now. If we let it go unchecked, it will make the situation worse in the coming years. We have to make sure that standard contracts are used that share risk and divide profit equitably between the parties – that the inevitable loss of the occasional harvest does not result in destitution and loss of ancestral holdings.'

'How, darling?' said Usha.

Her endearment did not go unnoticed by Rehman. Her right hand was lying on the table. He took it and held it in both hands. Her skin was silky and he almost brought her hand to his lips. After a moment, Usha extricated her hand and folded her arms in front of her. Tiny coloured lights strung on the trees came on. It had grown dark while they were talking. A shiver went through her.

'Are you cold?' he asked.

She shook her head and asked him to carry on.

Rehman took a deep breath. 'Where were we?' he said, before remembering. 'Yes, harvests fail every few years but that should not mean that farmers lose everything. For that contracts need to be drawn up by an independent body that balances everybody's rights and the companies should be forced to use only those contracts. The first step is to investigate some of these suicides and find other instances where farmers have taken their lives because of a contract with a company. Once we've collected a number of cases, we can then go to the media, to officials and to the elected leaders. I am sure something can be done. There is no doubt.'

Usha remained still, her back straight.

Rehman went silent. His throat was dry and he took a sip from the glass. The juice had finished and all that was left was water from the melted ice cubes.

'But I can't do it right now. It will be pretty much a full-time job to go to the villages and talk to people, here and possibly in Hyderabad, the state capital, to gather momentum.'

Usha nodded.

'This is all academic,' said Rehman, shrugging. 'I've given up all that. My target is simple. Stick to my job, save some money and buy a flat and a car.'

Usha put her hand on his and squeezed it gently. 'I love you,' she said simply and they both fell silent for a while. Then she said, 'What happens afterwards?'

Rehman was puzzled. 'What afterwards?'

'You stay in your job, earn money, buy a car and move into a nice flat. Then we get married. After that? You will have to pay the mortgage every month, you know. And buy petrol for the car. And school fees when we have children. And . . .' she trailed off.

Rehman stared at her, his eyes open wide. 'I haven't thought about it that far,' he said.

'It's like joining the queue of pilgrims at Simhachalam temple when they reveal the face of the idol, Rehman. Once you get stuck in that crush, you can't turn back. You have to keep moving with the rest of the crowd.'

'What can I do?' said Rehman. 'I love you.'

Usha squeezed his hand again. 'I know that, darling. And I love you too. But what makes you unique, and what I love more than anything else about you, is that you are a free spirit. Your heart dictates what is right and you follow its direction like a sailor following a compass. You don't think about career, money or a nine-to-five job; about savings accounts or mutual funds. At least, you didn't. I cannot take that away from you.'

'You are not taking it, Usha. I am giving it up, freely, so I can live with you, enjoy life with you. That's why I will now have to start taking an interest in all those things.'

Usha gave the twig in her hand a final tug and threw the fragments away. 'How long can you live a normal life like everybody else, Rehman? Eventually, you will become frustrated by not being able to follow the dictates of your heart. I don't know if it will take six months or six years, but one day you will. And what will happen that day when you wake up and realise what you've given up to be with me? Will you stop loving me? Will you go so far as to be angry with me and despise me?' She jerked her hand away and folded her arms in front of her again. 'I couldn't bear that, Rehman.'

Rehman murmured an indistinct denial. 'That will never happen.'

'No,' said Usha, more strongly. 'I think we should stop this now. Rehman, I am breaking off the engagement.' Her voice broke into a sob, but she continued to look at him.

Rehman rocked back in his chair and closed his eyes. The image of her grim expression did not fade. He felt as if a khanjar had been driven into his chest, the sharp dagger piercing his heart.

'No . . .' he heard himself say. The sound of blood rushing in his ears was louder than the crash of the surf on the beach. 'No . . .' he repeated.

He opened his eyes after what felt like hours and he was surprised to see that she hadn't moved an inch, and was looking at him with the same stern expression.

'Yes, Rehman. It has to be this way. Goodbye.' She stood up and almost staggered.

'Don't do this, Usha,' said Rehman. He hadn't felt this close to crying since he was ten years old and their cat had disappeared. 'Don't destroy our love.'

She walked over to him and gently stroked his cheek with her fingers. 'I am not destroying it, darling. I am preserving it.'

She walked briskly away while Rehman just sat there like a soldier who has been too close to a shell burst.

'Oh, my God, this is awful,' said Aruna, her hand covering her mouth. 'Did you hear that?'

Ramanujam nodded, frowning.

At the other table, Rehman got up blindly and started walking down the path. The waiter carrying a tray with glasses on it came running up to him and said, 'Sir, the bill.'

Rehman continued walking forwards like a bull that doesn't change direction even when its keeper shouts at it. The waiter reached out and tapped him with his left hand. Rehman turned and flung the waiter's hand away, knocking the tray down. The glasses fell on the red dusty ground, all without damage, except one that hit a stone and shattered into a hundred pieces. Rehman moved on doggedly. The waiter stared at Rehman's back and gave a roar.

'Thief,' he shouted. 'I'll call the police.' He tackled Rehman like a kabbadi player and knocked him to the ground. Rehman hit the waiter on the jaw. The waiter grabbed Rehman's hair and pounded his head into the dust.

CHAPTER TWENTY

Usha never remembered how she got back home. Thinking back about it later, she was surprised that she had hit nobody with her car. Only the sheer unpredictability of traffic on Indian roads, and the consequent cautious self-preserving nature of every person using them, must have saved them from her automaton-like driving.

When she reached home, she walked in and found her grandmother sitting in the front room, watching a devotional programme on television. Her parents were nowhere to be seen. She sat down stiffly next to the old lady, her back not touching the sofa. Her grandmother must have sensed something, because she turned to her and said, 'What is it, my dear?'

Usha burst into tears. Her grandmother switched off the TV and hugged her. 'It's OK. Tell me what the problem is and we'll solve it.'

It was several minutes before Usha freed herself from her grandmother's clasp and sat back, wiping away her tears with the edge of the old lady's soft cotton sari.

'You planned this all along, didn't you?' Usha said.

'Planned what, dear?'

'I broke off the engagement.'

'Ahh!' said her grandmother. 'Why did you break it off?'

'Why do you think?' said Usha bitterly. 'You and your conditions – steady job, nice flat, car . . .'

'Has the young man given up, then?'

Usha shook her head. 'I said *I* broke it off. Rehman was suppressing his heart and doing exactly as you asked him. If he had continued like that, our love would have been dust.'

'I didn't plan it, dear. I just hoped that something like this would happen. Either your young man would give up the struggle and prove himself unworthy of you, or he would persevere and you would realise that you could not hold him in such thrall. Whatever happened, I would win.'

'Why?' cried Usha. 'Why did you do it?'

'The marriage really was unsuitable, Usha. How could you think of marrying somebody outside our caste and a Muslim too? Your father was right to say that our family's reputation would have poured down the gutter. But he was wrong in how he tried to convince you. You are a girl after my own heart and I knew that you could never be thwarted from your course by threats. I realised that the whole family would be ruined if your father continued his reckless way. But I also knew that you were a sensible girl. You would never marry a man who could not look after you. And that's why I did what I did.'

'I thought I could trust you, naannamma. That is why I paid the boy for those marbles and sent the letter to you when I was trapped in my room. How could I have been so mistaken?' said Usha.

'It depends upon what you mean by trust, dear. I just gave you a chance not to be swept away by emotion and make a mistake, that's all. I prefer to think that I discharged my responsibility as a family elder properly. It's a pity because your young man is actually very good. I can see why you fell in love with him – idealistic, handsome, responsible. But I am sure that in time you will also come to look on this affair as a rainy season's dream, sweet but short-lived and doomed from the start.'

Usha shook her head. She wanted to hate her grandmother but she couldn't. She was honest enough to recognise the truth of the older woman's words. 'Where are amma and naanna?' she asked finally.

'They've gone to see a first-show movie. Your mother said that the dinner is on the dining table and asked you to eat when you came home.'

Half an hour ago, the very thought of food would have made her sick, but now her stomach rumbled like an empty cavern.

'OK, let me wash,' she said. At the door she turned to her grandmother. 'You tell my parents that I've broken up with Rehman. And tell them not to mention it again. I don't want to talk about it. And tell them not to go looking for another husband for me. I will never marry and I don't want to go through those arguments again.'

'Don't say never, Usha. That's too melodramatic. I will give you one year to mourn your love and, after that, we'll find somebody who's suitable for you. Don't worry, as long as I am alive, nobody will force you to marry against your wishes.'

Usha returned to her grandmother and hugged her, wondering how such a thin, frail frame could hold such a strong spirit. 'In that case, I hope you live for a long, long time. But I am sure I'll never find a man as good as Rehman – not in a year, not in a lifetime.'

Aruna and Ramanujam ran up to the fighting men. Aruna was surprised to see Rehman so angry – he was usually so calm and even-tempered. Ramanujam pulled the waiter away. Rehman got up slowly but before he was fully standing, the waiter made a wild kick that connected to Rehman's groin. He groaned, clutched his privates and staggered backwards, half bent. Aruna raised her hands in horror and moved towards her boss's son. He looked at her like a wild dervish, then turned and half ran, half stumbled down the path, towards the beach.

Ramanujam almost pulled the waiter off his feet. 'Who do you think that man was? How dare you hit him?'

The waiter's anger left him and he suddenly looked small. Ramanujam let go of him in disgust and the waiter collapsed to the ground. 'I am sorry,' he said. By this time, two other waiters and a cook came out and pulled their colleague to his feet again.

'Let's go,' said Aruna. 'We have to inform his family.'

Ramanujam nodded. 'The sooner the better. Let's go.' They both turned and walked towards their car.

'Sir, madam. Your dinner is about to be served,' said the dishevelled waiter. When they didn't respond, he continued in a small voice, 'The bill . . .'

Ramanujam snorted in anger, took out a couple of hundred-rupee notes and flung them on the ground. 'That's to cover our and the other gentleman's bill,' he said.

Half an hour later, they were back at the restaurant with Pari in tow. On the way from the restaurant, Aruna had decided that she didn't want to tell Mrs Ali what was going on. She knew that Pari lived in a room opposite the Alis' house, so they had gone straight there. Pari had immediately left Vasu in her landlady's care and come with them.

'Where is he?' asked Pari.

'That way,' said Aruna. The trio went down the path and on to the sand. The beach was dark and stretched for miles in both directions, the only light coming from the soft glow of the surf. The pounding of the waves was a continuous roar. Pinpoints of lights tinkled far away and the stars hung low in the moonless sky. Tiny soft-shelled crabs skittered along the sand, diving into small holes as they walked past.

'There he is,' said Ramanujam, pointing to a seated figure.

'Let me go on my own,' said Pari. 'I'll call you if I need you.'

Husband and wife nodded, and Pari walked alone towards Rehman. Crossing the sand with her shoes on was difficult, so she kicked them off, continuing barefoot, even though she felt squeamish about the crabs.

As she approached him, she saw that Rehman had taken off his shirt and was bare-chested. A wave rushed up the slope, reaching Pari's knees and more than halfway up the seated Rehman's chest. Pari stood still while the water swirled round her legs and then receded. She dropped to her knees next to Rehman and touched his bare shoulder.

'Let's go home, Rehman,' she said.

He turned to her, taking his fixed stare off the horizon. 'She left me,' he said, his voice hollow.

'I heard,' said Pari softly.

He laughed wildly, a dry sound. Another wave engulfed them and Pari gasped even though the water was warm. She tightened her grip on Rehman's surprisingly muscled shoulder as the undertow tried to sweep her away.

'Do you know why she dumped me?' he asked.

Pari shook her head, trying to look puzzled. It seemed a good idea to keep him talking.

'She didn't understand that you don't have to take one big step. You can do it in small stages, each one not very painful . . .' said Rehman.

'What steps?' said Pari, genuinely mystified.

'First, you change the clothes you wear – it's a bit uncomfortable, but doesn't really signify anything, does it?'

He looked at her and she nodded.

He continued, 'You give up your promise to an old man and abandon his grandson.'

'You didn't abandon the boy,' said Pari. 'He lives with me and you will still spend a lot of time with him.'

'He is Lalitha's son and I gave him up like so much unused furniture that was getting in the way.' Rehman's gaze went back to the horizon.

Pari looked at him sharply. A line from *King Lear* came to her mind: Alack, the night comes on, and the bleak winds do sorely ruffle; for many miles about there's scarce a bush.

Rehman continued, 'Once I discarded Lalitha's son, it wasn't any trouble at all to give up any ideas of fighting for other people and just look out for my own self.'

He stood up and walked deeper into the sea and Pari followed him, half afraid of his fey mood. Rehman stretched up to his full height and opened his arms wide to the uncaring sea. Pari glanced over to where Aruna and her husband were standing. They were almost indistinct against the trees but it looked as if they were huddled in each other's arms.

'Free!' shouted Rehman. 'I am free! Do you hear me? I renounced Lalitha, gave away her son and then abandoned her father's cause. Compared to that, you are nothing.'

He held his pose for a few seconds more, then dropped his arms, turning away from the water. 'Come on,' he said. 'I have work to do.'

Pari trotted behind him, trying to keep up with his long strides. 'Rehman . . .' she said, once they were above the water-line. The cold she felt was not entirely due to her wet clothes and the strong breeze.

He turned and stood stiff as a policeman's lathi. 'Yes?' he said.

She reached out and cupped his chin in her hands. His eyes were tiny mirrors that glittered like cold ice. 'Rehman, trust me in this. I speak from experience. You don't have to be strong – it's OK to let go.'

'Let go?' he said.

'Yes,' she said, her hands falling to her sides. 'Weep for what you have lost.'

Rehman stared at her with an unseeing gaze for a long moment, then sank to the ground as if his knees had turned to sand; his head dropped to his chest and he started crying.

EPILOGUE

After an undefined passage of time, a young pair who were not a couple were sitting on a mountain top. From their perch, they could see the beach of that dreadful night's events and the same tireless sea. The man's cheeks were hollow and his long kurta hung loose on his body as if he had lost a lot of weight very quickly. He had a straggly beard. The woman was fair and her salwar kameez fitted her well. She had a long nose.

'Look at the sea,' muttered the man. 'It never gives up trying to meet its lover.'

'Turn this way,' said the woman, pointing in the other direction, due west. 'Isn't the sunset beautiful?'

The red ball of fire was sinking behind a further mountain, setting aglow the trees along the skyline. The man stared at the glorious sight and appeared unmoved.

The woman continued, 'A nawab's family want to see me.'

The man looked puzzled. 'So?' he said.

'*See* me, you buddhoo,' she said. 'They want me to marry their son. Imagine that – an orphan girl like me marrying into royalty. I will be a princess. Isn't that what happens in a fairy tale?'

The man's look of despondency lifted a bit and he looked at her with more interest. 'Congrats,' he said. 'But is it *your* fairy tale?'

'I don't know,' she said slowly, considering. 'But it will be worth finding out, don't you think?'

He nodded. Gloom settled over him like an old cloak too comfortable to cast away and the conversation sputtered to a halt.

'How long does it take for a broken heart to heal?' he asked after several minutes.

The woman looked into his face and she suddenly appeared wise beyond her years.

'I have some knowledge of these matters,' she said. 'The sadness will always be there. But your heart *will* mend and happiness can find a home in it sooner than you imagine.'

EXTRACTS FROM MRS ALI'S ENGLISH ESSAYS

Extract 1

I haven't written any English for several months. I was writing regularly and then we went to visit Pari's father who was very unwell at that time. You know how it is when there is a break in the routine? Rehman got these papers about cotton and they were very interesting, so I decided to start again.

For me, cotton is a very ordinary plant. It used to grow in my neighbour's backyard when I was a girl. From what I remember, many green pods appear on the branches and slowly become bigger and bigger. Finally, they burst open and white fluffy cotton appears. I used to pull it out and feel the small, hard seeds inside the soft fibres. These seeds are entangled in the long threads and quite difficult to remove. I wonder how they remove all the seeds from all the cotton in the world. It must be a lot of work.

According to Rehman's papers, cotton has been grown and used in India for more than six thousand years. About seven hundred years ago, cotton reached northern Europe where they did not know anything about it except that it came from a plant. Because it looked like wool, they thought that it came from plant-born sheep. They thought that little lambs grew at the ends of the branches of cotton trees. When these lambs became hungry, the branches bent down so they could feed. It is unbelievable what people make up when they don't know the truth. Rehman tells me that in Germany, cotton is still called tree wool!

For a simple plant, cotton had a big impact in world history. When the British first came to India, they used to export beautiful muslin and calico cottons to their own country. Then they destroyed the weaving industry here and raw cotton started to be sent from India to be turned into cloth in a city called Manchester and re-exported back here. Then cotton started to be produced more cheaply in America because they used unpaid slaves, and Indian farmers suffered. When the Americans started fighting among themselves in a civil war, these cotton supplies got cut off and people started buying it from Egypt. The Egyptian government took out loans to grow even more cotton. But then the war in America ended and the Egyptian government went bankrupt and Britain took over Egypt as part of their empire.

We have started using foam mattresses now, but until recently we slept on mattresses stuffed with cotton. After a couple of years, the mattress becomes hard. We then look out for a pedlar who softens mattresses and pillows. He is easy to recognise because he carries a long bow over his shoulder. For a small fee, he attaches his bow to a wall, slits open the mattresses and pillows, and takes out all the cotton. He then twangs (is that the right word?) the string of the bow through the packed cotton until it has become fluffy again. This is hard work and takes him a long time. Cotton dust gets everywhere. If you pay him, he will also replace some of the old cotton with fresh cotton that he carries with him. He then stuffs the soft cotton back into the mattresses and pillows, and stitches them up again. They are much fatter and more comfortable after this.

Cotton crops attract a lot of pests, and farmers have to make heavy use of chemicals to control them. Not only is this bad for the environment, but they have to take loans from moneylenders and banks to pay for this. When the crops fail, they get into a lot of trouble and we hear of many sad stories of farmers killing themselves, like Vasu's grandfather.

Extract 2

The other day Pari made bone soup. It is not a dish that I had ever made. We normally don't have bread, or soup for that matter, but the combination was quite nice. I was busy looking after Vasu so I didn't see how she made it. I asked her later for the method and this is what she told me. This soup will serve four as a starter or two people as a full meal.

½ kg lamb bones (preferably leg) with some meat on them,
    cut into 2-inch-long pieces if possible
2 medium-sized tomatoes, cut into eight pieces each
1 medium-sized onion, diced
2 carrots, diced
salt, to taste
½ teaspoon ginger paste
1 teaspoon garlic paste
1 tablespoon oil
½ inch cinnamon stick
2 cloves

Cover the bones, tomatoes, onion and carrots with 3 cups of water in a large pan. Add the salt, and the ginger and garlic pastes, and boil until the vegetables are very soft.

Remove the bones from the pan and separate the meat. Set the meat aside and discard the bones.

Liquidise the rest of the soup and strain.

Heat the oil in a pan big enough to hold all the liquid, and add the cinnamon stick and cloves. After a few seconds the cloves swell up. Then pour the soup into the oil and add the meat.

Serve hot with bread.

Extract 3

Many people in Vizag are becoming richer, of that there is no doubt. The sheer amount of money that is being thrown around nowadays is astonishing. Shops used to be small with one or two light bulbs at the most, but now they are huge. They have wide fronts and they have bright lights all year round, not just at festival time. Earlier, if a shop was big, colourful and employed lots of salespeople, people used to say that the shopkeeper must be adding the cost of all that show into his products and they would go to a smaller place. Now it is the other way round. People are dazzled by the glamour and don't care about the cost.

Rehman's father tells me that they use different currencies in different countries. I had always known it, I suppose, but it is not something I had ever thought about. I saw this table in a magazine recently.

Currency	Rate in rupees
US dollar	45
Pound sterling	80
Euro	60
Swedish kroner	300

What is surprising is that so many people have so much money to spend when prices of everything are soaring. Tuvvar dhal, the lentils used for making sambhar, cost about sixty rupees a kilo. I remember a time, not that long ago, when it was around twenty rupees. I use sunflower oil for cooking and it costs over one hundred rupees a litre. Others who are not so well-off use groundnut oil, which is about eighty-five rupees. I pay Leela, our servant maid, five hundred rupees each month for cleaning

the house once a day and doing the dishes twice a day. She
works in five other houses, so her monthly earnings are about
two thousand five hundred rupees. Poor people like her hold a
white ration card while middle-class people like us hold a pink
card. The government supplies white-card holders with five
kilos of (poor-quality) rice per family member for two rupees a
kilo. They also get some palm oil for cooking at thirty rupees a
litre.

I think life is actually more difficult for lower-middle-class
people. They earn about ten thousand rupees a month but their
outgoings are bigger. The rent is higher. They have to pay for a
mobile phone, petrol for the scooter, school fees for the kids and
many other expenses. And they do not have a white card, so the
government does not help them as much. And while everybody in a poor family works, only the men tend to work in the
middle classes. This is changing slowly as more women are starting to work. I can see this in the marriage bureau. Earlier the
kind of richer people who come to us for matches used to ask
for girls who would be housewives, while now people are asking
for career girls. Strangely, poorer people still look for a stay-at-
home wife when you would think it should be the other way
round. I suppose it shows that the more money you have, the
even more money you want.

One interesting fact I found out is that many countries of
Europe have decided to give up their own type of money and
have a common currency. I am very surprised at this because I
have only known about countries splitting up. Pakistan separated
from India and my uncle and his family migrated over there. The
rest of our family stayed behind in India. My grandparents were
never the same afterwards. As children, whenever we saw a plane
in the air, Azhar used to shout to my grandmother, 'Look, daadi.
Chaacha is coming to see you.'

My poor grandmother! Losing a child like that, never again
having contact with my uncle, not knowing how he and his

family fared – it was very difficult for her. Did the great men who partitioned the country for their selfish reasons think about ordinary people like my grandmother and how her eyes never stopped searching for her missing son even on her deathbed? It is good that the people of Europe are going in the opposite direction, burying their differences and getting together, rather than finding silly reasons to fight with each other.

Extract 4

Years ago, when you were invited to a wedding, the choice of gift was simple. You just gave money and the amount depended upon how rich you were and how close you were to the people getting married. The usual gift was one hundred and sixteen rupees for close family members or half that, which would be fifty-eight rupees. You could also give twice or four times that amount. I heard about a contractor who gave one thousand one hundred and sixteen rupees for an official's daughter's wedding but no ordinary person could afford that kind of money in those days. Weddings have always been expensive affairs and the gifts helped pay for some of the cost. You had to be careful to keep track of what everyone gave because you had to give back the exact same amount when it was your turn to be invited or it would be a disaster. People would feel insulted and relationships could break down.

I think it all started to go wrong around the time that Rehman was a small boy. It was suddenly considered – what's the word – tactless to give money and people started gifting household items, usually pressure cookers or milk cookers. I remember that when Chote Bhabhi, my youngest sister-in-law, got married, they were given five milk cookers as presents. At least, these gifts were useful, even if you couldn't use all five of them, but then things got worse.

I don't know if they changed because gift and novelty item shops opened, or if the shops came about because of the change.

Regardless of the cause, it suddenly became unfashionable to give useful items. Gifts now have to be useless. So people give photo frames, or plastic and melamine trays, or crockery, and things like that. Because nobody actually uses these items, people just give them as gifts at the next wedding they go to. The items have to be stored as carefully as any precious jewels; after all, it is cheap to pass on as a gift an article that's chipped or scratched.

I think this mania for giving useless items must be something to do with people getting richer and having more money. I went to my servant Leela's daughter's wedding a few years ago and they received money and steel utensils as gifts. I wonder what happens to people's minds as they become wealthier.

You have to be careful to remember what everyone has given you because if you gift them back the same item as they gave you, it would be a disaster. It would be seen as an insult and they may cut you off. Some things never change.

Farahad Zama moved to London in 1990 from Vizag in India, where his novels are set. He is a father of two, and he works for an investment bank.